TIME IN A RED COAT

George Mackay Brown (1921–96) was one of the twentieth century's most distinguished and original writers. His lifelong inspiration and birthplace, Stromness in Orkney, moulded his view of the world, though he studied in Edinburgh at Newbattle Abbey College, where he met Edwin Muir, and later at Moray House College of Education. In 1941 he was diagnosed with pulmonary tuberculosis and lived an increasingly reclusive life in Stromness, but he produced, in spite of his poor health, a regular stream of publications from 1954 onwards. These included *The Storm* (1954), *Loaves and Fishes* (1959), *A Calendar of Love* (1967), *A Time to Keep* (1969), *Greenvoe* (1972), *Hawkfall* (1974), *Time in a Red Coat* (1984) and, notably, the novel *Beside the Ocean of Time* (1994), which was shortlisted for the Booker Prize and won the Saltire Book of the Year.

His work is permeated by the layers of history in Scotland's past, by quirks of human nature and religious belief, and by a fascination with the world beyond the horizons of the known.

He was honoured by the Open University and by the Universities of Dundee and Glasgow. The enduringly successful St Magnus Festival of poetry, prose, music and drama, held annually in Orkney, is his lasting memorial.

D1334863

TITLES BY GEORGE MACKAY BROWN
AVAILABLE FROM POLYGON

NOVELS

Greenvoe
Magnus
Time in a Red Coat
The Golden Bird
Vinland
Beside the Ocean of Time

NON-FICTION

An Orkney Tapestry

AUTOBIOGRAPHY

For the Islands I Sing

GEORGE MACKAY BROWN

Time in a Red Coat

First published in 1984 by Chatto & Windus.
This edition published in Great Britain in 2019 by
Polygon, an imprint of Birlinn Ltd.

Birlinn Ltd
West Newington House
10 Newington Road
Edinburgh EH9 1QS

www.polygonbooks.co.uk

9 8 7 6 5 4 3 2 1

ISBN 978 1 84697 507 3

British Library Cataloguing-in-Publication Data
A catalogue record for this book is available from the British Library

Typeset by Biblichor Ltd, Edinburgh
Printed and bound by Clays Ltd, Elcograf S.p.A.

Contents

To
Margaret Marshall
Neil Scott-Moncrieff
Magnus Brunner
and
Sigrid Weber

The Masque

It is the courtyard of the palace of the great Khan.

A little stage has been set up for a performance of some kind, a crowd of villagers and country folk wait on three sides of the stage. There is mingled laughter and shouts, and sometimes a scuffle. A deep country voice shouts, 'Come on. Hurry. I've got goats to milk . . .' And a girl's voice, 'Yes, butter and cheese to make, I can't wait all day.' And an old man, 'They're never so long as this when it's tax-gathering day.'

The palace and its parterre and fountains and pavilions was the peasants' idea of heaven. On this one day of the year the peasants – beekeepers and fowlers and ploughmen – and the villagers were allowed inside the palace gates to attend the Masque of Peace. Some of them liked the performance and some of them didn't, but it meant that there was a holiday in the kingdom, and at nightfall every tavern in every town and village would be thronged with merry-makers.

The peasants didn't really mean that they had work to go back to that day. That was only a way of speaking. It meant that some were eager to have the Masque over and done with, so that the real rejoicing could begin.

They stamped their feet and laughed and complained all round the little stage. From the huddle of bodies rose a country incense, smells of dung and earth and sweat and corn-dust.

Beyond the palace garden, far away, stretched the mountains with a faint blue bloom of mist on them. Across mountain and mountain marched the Great Wall, sometimes hidden in a fold of valley, sometimes eagle-high. That wall was the boundary of the Empire; beyond it, the barbarians went about their own crude beast-like business, and their wars that seemed never to cease. Sometimes, on a pellucid clear day, the palace could hear a distant confused noise of bronze on stone, bronze on bronze, bronze on skull. Then a little wind would come and blow the disagreeable sound away.

'Bring on the masks and the maskers!' yelled the smith from the village. The smith had a flagon in one hand; he had been at the wine already.

'Bring on the clowns!' – a ragged country chorus.

A sneak-thief, smiling, went among the crowd. A piece of silver would wink for a moment between his fingers, before his pocket gaped for it. And the sneak-thief glided and smiled like an eel, this way and that through the crowd.

'I'll tell you what the delay is,' said the butter-girl to her neighbour. 'There's a baby coming today, in the palace there. It's her time. The princess is going to have a baby.'

'I heard that too,' said the girl from the flax-field. 'They're all too excited in there. They've forgotten about our masque.'

The village butcher cried, 'Forgotten the masque! They can't forget the masque. That's what we're here for, the masque. If there's no masque, I won't answer for what I might do.'

The butcher too had a flagon inside his blouse. He put it to his mouth, his throat worked.

'Nor me either!' said a little hunchbacked man who went about the villages with a box of bees on his shoulder, to cure pains in the joints and bone-marrow with bee stings for a farthing.

And the boys from the sheepfolds yelled in chorus, 'Hurry up with the masque!'

'A birth is more important than a piece of play-acting,' said a man. He smelt of fish. The villagers and the country folk kept well back from him. He was a stranger from the river a hundred miles away. They held back from the queer river smell.

Small boys and girls were making their own impromptu masque among the flower beds, neighing, laughing, prancing, playing at horses and horsemen. There came a yell from the heart of a rose bush. A small girl was dragged out, all tears and rose-prickle scratches.

Very far off, an eagle (a throbbing needle point) rose above the mountains and wheeled north, and soon was a nothingness in the veils of mist.

The man who kept the wine shop in the village said to the man who kept the pie shop, 'We'll be ruined, if they don't start soon.'

The man from the pie shop yelled, 'The people are hungry. It's a holiday!'

One of the shepherds said, 'You're right there, Mr Tengis.'

Mr Tengis said, 'I baked twenty score of pies this morning.'

The butter-girl said, 'Sh-h-h! Something's happening.'

As if the butter-girl had uttered a spell, silence like a dove-wing shadowed the crowd. There was a glug-glug between the butcher's flagon and the butcher's throat; then silence.

Upon the stage, suddenly, stood the Masquer, wearing a coat of a hundred colours. His face was splashed white and purple and gold.

At the first sight of him, the crowd gave a ragged yell of welcome, or derision, or both.

He stood there, the coloured creature, as if he didn't mind what they threw at him, roses or stones or rotten eggs. He stood silent for as long as a butterfly-passage between two tulips. Then he spoke, just like any flunkey or gardener; and this ordinary speech spread a ripple of disappointment through the crowd, for they expected the Masquer to speak like the Masquer – this is, in a high stylised voice, with marked rhythms and assonances, and strange images, and extravagant gestures, producing fire or a fluttering bird from his wide sleeve.

The Masquer said, in a plain voice, 'I'm sorry to have kept you so long. Something important is going to happen in the palace today, in that room up there with the open casement. An announcement will be made in due course. You understand. I could get no help with my make-up, I had to do it all myself.'

'Hurry up, you flower!' yelled the joiner. 'Get on with the act.'

'Yes,' cried the old blind one who painted stones for ornaments to put on door and windowsill, 'I'm as dry as a cork. I should have been drunk an hour ago.'

The Masquer held up his hand. 'I'm sorry to say, furthermore,' said he in his dry matter-of-fact voice, 'that this year I'll be performing the act solo, without musicians or assistants of any kind. The musicians are required to celebrate the birth. I will do my best. It will not be a perfect performance by any means. I crave your indulgence.'

'He craves *what*?' said Mistress Poppyseed the midwife to Mistress Grassblade who worked at the silk-weaver's.

Mr Tengis the pie seller said, 'I'll be ruined.' For his four hundred pies must be growing cold in his bake house.

'Me too,' said the keeper of the wine-shop. (But his wine would keep.)

The children gathered as close as they dared about the foot of the stage.

There came a dull boom, the faintest of reverberations, from the foothills of the mountain; as if the blacksmith had got tired of this poorest of all holidays that anyone in the kingdom could remember. But the blacksmith was still there, red as his forge from flagons.

Then this happened on the stage. The Masquer stood rigid, as if he had gone into a trance. He closed his painted eyes. He opened his mouth. The words that issued were as high as a boy's, when boys are playing in the ravine where the seven echoes are.

I recite, as every Spring, the annals of the empire.

What is there to say?

Tell me, how shall I announce a new thing?

Our country has been at peace for so long, only the Song of Tranquillity is sung.

I sing the plough song, and the vineyard song, and the song of the hunt.

Ever since our ancestors built the Wall, we have known peace. Swords and bugles rust in the museum.

Therefore, praise the Wall.

Beyond the Wall, the barbarian tribes fight among themselves. They fight and stink and utter barbarous breath.

In our villages we know only the beauties and blessings of love.

'Well, it's begun,' said the bee-keeper.

'Not before time,' said Mr Tengis. 'The pies will all be burnt.'

'I never heard his chant so high and tremulous,' said the woman from the silk-looms.

'Beauties of love!' said Mistress Poppyseed. 'I like that. My hero, he upped and left me for a slut from the marshes. Twenty years ago, without so much as a farewell. Well, she's welcome to him. Only, don't let him come crawling back to my house when he's a wreck and she throws him out. Blessings of love, indeed!'

And the men with the flagons passed them from one to the other.

Now the Masquer had opened the chest on the stage, and he fitted puppets on to his hands. One puppet was a young man, the other was a girl. The puppetry began.

At first the silk boy and the silk girl did not look at each other. One looked at clouds, one at a hyacinth in the garden. Then, as if the Masquer were Fate itself, their faces turned to one another. The boy doll could not take his eyes from the other, that only glanced once and away again, but then (Fate had decreed it) returned his look of hunger and hope. The face of a doll does not change, but any fool could see acquiescence and joy in her movement, her dance, her slow circling towards the boy, who stood there incredulous, as though a bird-of-paradise were hovering above his shoulder, ready to furl and fall.

Then from the sleeve of the Masquer – who knows how? – the boy puppet produced a paper rose and held it out to the girl puppet who – needless to say – clasped it to her wooden bosom.

Then they linked arms, the lovers, and what happened then could not be known; for the Masquer turned his back for as long as a bee forages among two lilies, and when he turned round again, behold, his hands were empty: the lovers had fled, like shadows, into the summer.

There was ragged applause all round the stage.

'It's nothing without the musicians,' said the miller to the blacksmith. 'It's wanting the flute and the drum.'

'Love!' said the blacksmith. And spat into the goldfish pool. And took another pull at his wine-bottle.

'That was beautiful!' said the milkmaid to the girl who did the laundry in the village. 'Even without the music, it was lovely.'

'That's the way I want it to happen with me,' said the laundry-girl with the washed-out shell-like hands. 'But not a man so much as looks at me. Not a tramp. Not a beggarman.'

'Count yourself lucky,' said Mistress Poppyseed. 'Thank your lucky stars.'

The Masquer acknowledged such applause as there was: by no means as enthusiastic as in former years.

He lifted up his hands.

Ah, what a doleful face he presented to them now! It looked as if he had wept a moon out. His parti-coloured face hung upon his shoulder. The way he crossed his arms upon his shoulders – it seemed that he gathered all the grief and pain and sorrows of humanity to his heart. Never, never again would a child laugh or a lover sing. And yet his stance of grief was beautiful, most touching, perfection itself. They would not have it otherwise. This gesture he did as well as ever he had done it.

The Masquer spoke: as if his voice echoed in a chamber of shrouds and skulls:

> Here we celebrate the beauty and the terror of death.
> Wasn't a hunter taken from a wild boar's tusk yesterday?
> Last winter, weren't five old breaths quenched like candle flames?
> And a little girl withered, like a flower a worm had entered.

The Masquer took from his box a tall puppet with a spear, dressed in black. The puppet was a young man, he was going into the forest, he wouldn't come back without some trophy, a wild pig or a wolf, across his shoulders. The hunter-puppet flourished his spear, he danced (before the event) his dance of triumph.

Then the Masquer turned his back on the audience for as long as it takes a drop of water to gather and fall from an eave after a shower; and when the hunter-puppet was seen again what a change in his condition! His spear was broken, he staggered, he stumbled, he reeled with pain, and there was a red patch on his hunting coat, half-way down the side, where the wild boar had turned on him and torn him. It was pathetic in the extreme. The puppet sagged, he could no longer stand, he was down on elbows and knees, himself like a stricken animal. A tremor went through him.

And a sigh of sorrow went through the audience; that is, through such of them as were not drunk, or had hearts of stone that nothing could move.

'He should have bidden at home,' said Mistress Poppyseed. Mistress Grassblade agreed: the hunter would have done better to stay in his yard and prune his vines.

The butter-girl and the girl with wasted hands from the wash-tub were both weeping, silently. Their eyes and their fingers glittered. And the fingers of the pickpocket glittered more than ever, though not with tears.

The hunchback with the box of bee-stings said, 'It's well done. Every man should die at the height of his strength. If only you could see some of the poor old things in the mountains that I bring my bees to, sticks and rags that suffer! Better for them if they'd died young in the river or on the mountains.'

'Shut up, you toad!' yelled the blacksmith to the bee-man. 'The masque's only half done.'

'Yes,' said Mr Tengis, 'the hunter is on the point of death. Show some respect.'

They were not, however, permitted to see the actual death of the hunter. For once more the Masquer turned his back on them, lingered, and came full circle. And then the people could see that a great change had come about. The puppet was horizontal, and instead of the one red rag at his side he was a tumult of red rags, the scarlet tatters covered him from face to feet. Then the audience understood that the unlucky hunter had

had a decent funeral pyre prepared for him, and soon the flames would leave nothing but a few cinders.

'That's what comes to us all,' said Mistress Poppyseed.

'Yes, sooner or later,' said Mistress Grassblade.

The village butcher had caught the sneak-thief at his pocket. He held the sneak-thief like a daddy-long-legs caught in syrup. 'That's as good a fire as ever I saw,' said the butcher to one of the boys from the sheepfold. 'Look in your pockets. See if you have as much money as you came with . . .' Then the butcher turned the thief upside down and a shower of silver and bronze glittered and rang on the stones of the garden.

It is possible the shepherds and the village men would have beaten the sneak-thief black and blue, were it not that the Masquer, having put the cremated hunter back in the box, was composing hands and clothing for the performance of the Masque of Birth.

So the men contented themselves with binding the sneak-thief's arms, and gagging him with leaves. 'You're for the magistrate before this day's out,' said the butcher. 'You're for the magistrate and the turnkey.'

Mumbles came from the sneak-thief.

'Be quiet,' thundered Mistress Poppyseed. 'The best is to come. Something you brutes of men know nothing about.'

'Nor ever will,' said Mistress Grassblade. 'I'm sorry to say, and I'm glad to say, they never will, men. Birth is for women alone, alas. And hooray.'

Most grave, most stately, the Masquer. He held up a palm. White peace flowed from it over all the people; even the drunks forgot their flagons for the moment, so pure was the gesture.

Then an unprecedented thing happened. A boy had entered the Palace garden from the direction of the mountains, and was running towards the crowd and the stage. He was in such a desperate hurry that he began to tear his way through the crowd, going like an otter through a torrent, gasping, holding up his hand urgently, butting with his little round head, till girls screamed and villagers kicked the intruder, especially the village tailor whose flagon had been almost knocked from his hand, in a scatter of bright drops and runnels. And still the boy bored his way through, and stood between Mistress Poppyseed and Mistress Grassblade, and gasped out, 'There's a noise in the mountains. A shifting of stones.'

And he would have fallen from sheer exhaustion had not Mistress Poppyseed held him up by the scruff of the neck.

The Masquer was seriously displeased. It had never been known for the three-fold masque to be interrupted in such a gross way, and by a boy too who was half-dead with running – who would have been much better building snowmen in the mountains. (He had the look of a mountain boy about him.)

The Masquer shook off the remnant of his trance. He glared at the boy. 'Isn't your father the royal fowler?' he asked.

The boy could only nod.

'Go back to him. How dare you interrupt the Song of Peace? You will be in trouble for this.'

Mistress Poppyseed shook the boy so vigorously that she shook words out of him. 'My father says there's a sound of iron on stone. *Run as fast as you can to the Palace. Tell them.*'

'Iron on stone!' cried the Masquer. 'What kind of a message is that?'

'Barbarians,' said the boy, trembling. 'There's a breach in the Wall.'

The fisherman from the river, that everyone avoided because of his fish smell, had been the first to leave the garden. The ears of fishermen are delicate as shells: perhaps he had been the first to hear the sound of iron on stone, brimming over some fold in the hills where the Wall had been breached.

In ones and twos they left the garden. For now, indeed, everyone could hear it, the song of iron on stone, very faint still, like a bell whose clapper is bound thick with leaves, but goes on giving out muffled reverberations.

Now they were leaving the garden in groups, some through one gate, some through another. They drifted, they hastened, towards the village and to their farms and vines and beehives on the plain. Even the drunk men knew that something was amiss; they staggered, holding each other up, towards the gate that led to the village. The vintner had hastened on before, either to tap the first barrel of the day, or to put up his shutters against the barbarians (who knows? – it had happened long ago, far away, and more than once).

Even Mistress Poppyseed and Mistress Grassblade had gone, their hearty faces grey with shock, their crooked fingers up at their mouths.

Nobody was left in the royal garden but the Masquer whose performance had been maimed for the first and only time. He stood on the stage with his fist at his head, a ruined man. And among the flower-pots writhed the pick-pocket like a snake who had been tied in a knot. And the boy sat with his head on his knees, utterly exhausted.

Far away, like the muffled jangling of a dozen bells, came the music of iron on stone, and a different noise: torn masonry.

A peacock strolled through the garden and looked at the three useless bread-less people in it; then turned and strolled disdainfully away.

Then this was heard from the open casement on the second floor of the Palace: a thin cry of pain. And another. Then, after a longer pause, another longer cry.

Only the boy looked up and listened. What had screamed, the peacock or the princess?

The boy got to his feet. He had promised his father he would return as soon as he had delivered the message. He knew a way back to the mountain hut, through any mounted barbarian outriders or scouts. His feet would crash through the snow, at last, after dark, to the lamp in the window of the royal fowler.

Mistress Poppyseed was back! As if in answer to the cries in the Palace, Mistress Poppyseed had hastened back from the distracted village. As she hurried between the trees and the goldfish pond, she rolled her sleeves up over her mighty forearms. She stirred the slumped Masquer with her foot, contemptuously. 'Out of my way, you play-actor.' Then she called up to the room with the open casement, 'All right. Hold on, I'm coming!'

She went in at a side door of the Palace, for even the keepers of the doors had fled at the terrible tidings: *The Wall is breached!*

Still nearer it drew, an ordered confusion of horsemen: stones scattered, streams silvered and muddied, the nests of wild birds broken. There was a flash now and then between the sinking sun and hidden swords. Now the roots of the great trees took the distant pulsation of hooves.

A chambermaid left the Palace, her blouse stuffed with mirrors and pictures and bits of linen. She hung in the garden like a butterfly, this way and that, and at last took the road away from the village.

Meantime, from opposite ends of the Palace came a figure in white and a figure in black; they mounted, silently, the stairs to the casement and squatted down, one on each side.

What stirred under the dragon-tree? Three musicians were there, a drummer and a piper and a viol-player. They made little preliminary sounds, like a bat squeaking, or the leap of a frog, or of a hand plashing in a stream.

(Iron on stone, iron on grass, iron in a rushing burn.)

The White Guardian opened his mouth, and as blithe a sound issued as if he was a country boy going to a fair, and could smell the apples and the new bread and the girl-clusters in the square:

'Come, child. Come now into the kind air. Come among leaves, flowers, butterflies. Listen – a flute is playing. It will be very beautiful, the wind through your hands, wind sifting hair. Birds are singing. It is beautiful, the high blue roof of the sky. It is all for you. Come.'

Like an echo from a vault came the voice of the Black Guardian:

'Think this of the air. Every breath of it is a stitch in your shroud. The air will stamp you with wrinkles, it will torment your bones with needles. A hawk hangs in the wind. Take one breath, then be quiet. One breath is enough.'

The three musicians played The Song of Air.

From inside came the hearty voice of Mistress Poppyseed, 'Lie quiet. Take deep breaths. Don't be frightened.'

A stir went through the Masquer, slumped still on his stage, as if he was himself a puppet and the strings had been pulled out of him. A stir and a whisper – 'These things are said at every birth. But every new person goes a different way to The Dark House . . . This is a long labour, full of pain.'

(Iron on rock, iron on thistle, iron on the bank of the river.)

The White Guardian spoke again:

'Come soon. See, I am putting a handful of earth on the doorstep of the King your grandfather's house. The fullness of earth is yours. Corn, honey, oranges, they will be a delight to your mouth. Your flesh will grow tall and strong and lovely with the goodness of earth.'

Then the dirge from the Black Guardian:

'Dust. Shadows. You will labour among dust to fill yourself with dust to lie at last among dust. Never wish to travel, shadow, across that long desert of dust. Turn in soon to the sweet shadows of The Dark House.'

And Mistress Poppyseed inside, while under the tree shaped like a burning dragon against the sunset the three musicians played The Song of Earth: 'Bring hot water. Lazy trollops! Bring towels. Hurry!'

And the Masquer, a stir and a whisper: 'It is the same earth for all, but every man makes his own sign and footprint on the earth . . . This one is very reluctant to be born.'

(Iron on cobbles. Iron on a rosebush. Iron at a well.)

How sweetly it pleaded, the voice of the White Guardian:

'Come. The sun has set a sign on your door. The sun waits to greet you. The sun, even in the dark of the year, is the fire in your hearth. The sun in winter is the candle-light in your niche. There you will stand, reading with joy the ancient poems and tales. The sun is the bread you eat and the wine you drink. But now the sun is new, it is springtime, the sun is a fountain of innocence and delight for you. Come soon.'

The charnel elegiac voice of the Black Guardian:

'A ball of burning dust, the sun. Listen, little one. Listen. Listen. I have heard ancient prophecies concerning that fire in the sky – how, long ago, it sowed dragon seed in the earth. That some day the dragons would rouse themselves. The first dragon is already among us: gold. Men murder for a handful of that yellow dust. Why, beyond our impregnable Wall, do the barbarians throw down each other's walls? For gold, emerald, onyx – for the black power that goes with that trash, that treasure . . . There are worse dragons than gold, worse children of the sun, in the earth laid, waiting. Come out, for the dragons to scorch you to the bone.'

Then they under the tree struck and blew upon their instruments a Song of Fire.

The voice of Mistress Poppyseed was like a trumpet in the birth chamber. 'Bring wine, an old strong flagon! That'll comfort her, poor thing.'

The Masquer stirred and sat up. He murmured, 'The same always. We take a first kiss of the sun, and we break out in grief. Each person has his own salt handful to dredge up out of an ocean of sorrow. I have not known such reluctance to be born.'

(Iron on steps. Iron in the roots of the apple-tree. Iron at the fountain.)

Will it never end, the birth chants? For now again the white word:

'Listen. The song of water. Raindrop – sound of a small bell on a stone. The water drops congregate. They make mirrors and harps. And the mirrors and harps are broken. The torrent falls down the mountain into the lake. The birds of light, swans, drift on blue and green and grey circles. Their shadows are solid carved marble. Men strike the earth in a dry time. There is a gush of brightness – a spring, a fountain! Women come, they fill their jars with the lustre and purity of water. The river – it carries the things that men have grown and made from village to village downstream. At the last village, beside the sea, men carry upstream in exchange the lovely creatures of water, fish. I have said that word, sea. Come quickly, if only to feast your flesh on the sea. Delight your senses with raindrop and well and the endless circling ocean. Come.'

The Black Guardian, then. He held out his hands, a gesture of denial. He stretched his mouth to the shape of a black cloud. He cried: 'Stay. Water is—'

There was a shriek inside the birth chamber. Then, after a silence, one thin lost cry.

Madame Poppyseed's voice was not brazen now. But still it had command of the situation, having experienced it a score of times. She said urgently to the frightened girls, the assistant midwives, all six of them, 'Stop your snivellings. The mother's dead. The bairn's got breath in it. I'd better take the little thing home for a day or two. If she was left here, with you useless things, she'd die too. I'll keep the breath in her. I know a woman who has milk. I'll bring her back in a week or so. Tell His Serene Highness he's got a granddaughter. She might live, with a bit of luck.'

Mistress Poppyseed appeared at the top of the steps carrying a bundle.

She said, 'What's that fire for in the next village? Is it for the birth? Is it for the death?'

The Masquer said, with some dignity and assurance, 'The child has come to us in the sign of water. She will be a water princess.'

The White Guardian took from his blouse an ivory cylinder, carved with a sun and a horse and a bird. He stood. He curtsied to the silence in Mistress Poppyseed's arms. He said, 'I give her the whole world in this flute, songs for a journey.'

The Black Guardian was not to be outdone. From inside his blouse he brought a heavy bag. 'I give her the world too – earth's whole heart's-desire, silver and gold – enough for a very long journey.'

Mistress Poppyseed brushed them and their offerings aside. 'Painted fools,' she said. 'Out of my way.' And with such commonsensical words Mistress Poppyseed took her way, with the swaddled child 'born in the sign of water', to the gate in the garden that leads down to the village, where folk must live and suffer and die without the help of puppets, masks, music, painted rags.

Now the tumults of iron were so loud that it drowned the music of the trio, who nonetheless continued to puff cheeks and strike with fingers or knuckles.

The boy, the fowler's son, is suddenly back in the garden! He has not, after all, been able to break through to the snowline and the falcons folded in the rafters. He spoke but his voice was lost in the on-coming wave of war. He pointed. The gate-house was burning.

The Masquer had recovered his whole dignity now. He picked up flute and money-bag from the top step of the Palace. He whispered urgently into the ear of the boy (for only a whisper in a shell could have been heard in all that terrible music of hooves, crackling torches, stirrups, bridles, foreign shouts). 'Follow that woman – the huge woman with the voice like a trumpet. Mistress Poppyseed. She lives in a little blue hut at the end of the village street. Give her this ivory stick and this bag. Say, "They're for the child." With luck, the soldiers won't trouble a poor place like that.'

Then the Masquer turned gravely to face the barbarians. The boy slipped like a shadow through the gate. The sun was down, he was a shadow, they were all shadows in the garden, even the soldiers who held high the torches were lurid shadows.

The hooves broke the musicians and their music.

The White Guardian and the Black Guardian had gone their ways.

Hooves splashed through the goldfish ponds. Scent of trodden roses was everywhere. Hooves broke the branches. Hooves reared against the first stars.

Then smoke hid everything.

Out of the smoke, the Masquer's voice: like a man tied to a burning stake.

The dove has left this garden. It is now the time of the dragon.

[II]

Farewell, Mistress Poppyseed

At first glance, it could have been an ivory doll sitting erect in the tall chair, a doll swathed in white silk and carefully carved from ivory by a master.

Then the doll gave a yawn, and it was a girl.

No peasant girl, though, tanned and crinkled by the sun, with the marks of the four elements on her hands and face.

Now that she had composed her features again, she looked more like a corpse rigged out and bedizened for a funeral pyre. She looked like a girl who had died after a long illness in a shuttered bed; and now the nurses, having prepared her, had left her to the undertakers and the fire-builders. She looked like a girl alone with the gods, in the brief stillness between pain and the flames.

The girl fluttered her eyelids. She gave an impatient kick; one white shoe came off and made a tiny clatter on the floor.

A large woman came, flustered, from the next room. It was Mistress Poppyseed, with a few more wise wrinkles on her, and a greater girth than before.

But the voice like a bugle, what had happened to Madame Poppyseed's voice? It had dwindled to a conspiratorial whisper, as though for a dozen years she had lived among secrets and spies. There was a bar across the door – across Mistress Poppyseed's door, that in the time of the kingdom had stood open to all the blue winds of heaven, and to every vagrant and gossip that chanced to pass by.

The shuttered house of Mistress Poppyseed was as secret as a morgue or a prison, and had been for some time; on account, there was no doubt about it, of the little doll sprawled awry now in the great chair, that could both yawn and lose her temper, briefly.

'What now?' said Madame Poppyseed, as though there were ears at keyhole and window-latch and chimney. 'Kicked off your silk shoe, have you? Don't lounge like that in the chair – princesses don't lounge, they sit up prim and proper, as if they were carved out of ivory, indeed – yes, as if all that passed before them, people and processions and flowers, were only shadows. You *are* a princess, never forget that, never. I've kept you here like a dove in a cage, and I've nearly lost my wits with the worry of it. Today's your birthday, you're twelve. Time for a twelve-year-old girl to be married. You can't expect to get a prince for a husband – the barbarians have killed all the princes, or else driven them across the sea. They'd have killed you too, that night twelve years ago, if I hadn't saved you. (You're to be grateful to me for that. Some day I'll be a poor old woman, all pains and wheezes, and who's to see to poor old Poppyseed then?) Well, let that be. The human heart is fickle. The gods see to us all, in our ends and our beginnings . . . I've kept you here like a dove in a cage, hidden. Mr Tengis has been to see me, and I have been to see Mr Tengis. We have reached an agreement, we settled things the night before last. You're to be Mr Tengis's wife.'

Dimples came and went on the ivory face. Mistress Poppyseed didn't notice the smile; she was on the full flood now of whispers and secrets; she might indeed have been talking to an ivory doll, or to a girl embalmed for the pyre.

'Mr Tengis's old, I know. All the better. He's rich. Mr Tengis's well in with the military, he owns the whole village now, every stick and stone. Mr Tengis has made a fortune from the barbarians, selling thin wheat and thin sour wine up at the barracks. (They don't know any better, them ignorant murdering Mongols, in their messes.) So, you won't ever have to soil your pretty hands with earth, wind, fire, or water. Not that you've ever had to know what earth, air, water or fire are, common things, things for peasants to struggle with. (Put that shoe back on your foot at once.) No, a lady will still come and rub you with sweet-smelling oils every new moon . . .'

Excitement like fireflies glittered in the girl's eyes, then she closed them again, the better to guard her inner flame, or perhaps maybe to concentrate entirely on Mistress Poppyseed's nuptial homily.

'Now,' went on Mistress Poppyseed as if she had a fog in her throat, 'Mr Tengis is a good man of business, he expects a dowry. You are not entirely poor. There was saved from the Palace, the night you were born, a bag of silver and gold coins – that, and a stick of carved ivory. It looks like a kind of flute, only there's, never been any songs in it. What does a rich girl want with flutes and songs? Mr Tengis keeps trained musicians in his pavilion. You'll have all the music you want. Mr Tengis smiled and smiled when I told him about the bag of imperial gold and silver.'

The girl's eyes fluttered like butterflies. She brought the white glove up to her teeth and bit on the thumb, whether to stifle laughter or boredom or screaming it would be hard to say. Her teeth were like pearls.

'Mr Tengis,' said Mistress Poppyseed, 'doesn't know about your royal descent. Nobody knows about that but you and me. (Don't bite your finger like some peasant slut.) Mr Tengis only knows that you're well-off. He thinks I'm your mother and your father was a rich silk merchant that happened to be passing through, far away and long ago . . . Now, I want you to sit up straight on the cushion and smile prettily. Mr Tengis is on his way. Tonight there's a new moon. Tonight you're to go with Mr Tengis to his house. Mr Tengis's chief clerk has written out the articles of marriage. My dear, I can hardly speak for tears. I'll never see you again. You've been here with me, hidden, since that terrible night twelve years ago, when the Mongols took bronze and fire to the kingdom' . . .

Indeed there was a plangency and a sob or two among Mistress Poppyseed's whispers. As for the girl, she smiled so that not only the dimples showed but all her ivory teeth as well, and her eyes were almonds of delight. Thus a prisoner might look when she hears news of her imminent release.

'Perhaps,' whispered Mistress Poppyseed, when her sorrow had abated a little, 'perhaps I will get a glimpse of you, now and then, over Mr Tengis's high garden wall, between the peacock's tail and the fig-tree. You will have books about battles and knights and lovely ladies to read. Don't look so sorrowful. The good times will come back again. The foreigners rule every-where but we've learnt to get along with them. Their horsemen rode west a year ago and more. That's where the war is now, in India or Tartary. I wonder what's keeping Mr Tengis?'

The girl, sitting white and erect on her cushion, struck the arm of her chair until dust flew: as if a small gust of rage or sorrow or joy had gone through her.

'What's that knock?' said Mistress Poppyseed. 'I thought for a moment it was Mr Tengis at the door. Isn't it marvellous? – Mr Tengis began as a baker of pies and he got on so well that now he owns the whole village . . . Now, you are not to let the sun on your face and hands, ever. Sit always under a parasol, in Mr Tengis's garden. If it rains, in Mr Tengis's garden, go inside at once. Young ladies get wet, then they sneeze, then they cough, then they get roses in their cheeks, then they die of consumption. Never put your fingers among roots and worms – Mr Tengis has gardeners to see to that. Now then, a nice smile. Here's your dowry. Hold the bag of money in one hand and the flute in the other, when Mr Tengis enters. Today your new life begins. I wish Mr Tengis would hurry. I think I'll go out. I'll see if I can see Mr Tengis the merchant coming along the road. There's to be a girl carrying orange blossom, and a boy with a peacock, to celebrate the wedding. Can you hear a scream? Mr Tengis will be nervous, that's why he's late. I'll just go out. Sit still. Smile.'

Mistress Poppyseed flustered out through the door that opened on to the garden.

The girl sat, her face blank as a moon. What did she hear then? She tilted her head. From the mountains, far to the west, the delicate shell of her ear held for a moment a wind-borne confusion of bronze and hooves, muted, fading.

She hesitated on her silk cushion, but only for a moment.

Then, with the bag of money in one hand and the long carved ivory cylinder in the other, she went out through the second door, into the sun and wind, for the first time in her life.

She came back, trembling at her trespass and her presumption. The fire of the sun had hurt her eyes, the wind had blown a strand of black hair across her cheek like a whiplash. She stood in the open door. She whispered, 'Farewell, Mr Tengis. Farewell, Poppyseed. Goodbye, cage.'

Then she said, 'That it should rain! That I should feel a raindrop on the back of my hand.'

She turned. She had gone out among the elements.

How long was the house of Mistress Poppyseed empty of breath? With the guardian and the girl gone, it seemed like a death house that takes no account of the hours, the seasons, the years.

But suddenly the peacock and the flowers were there, in the door that led into the garden in the village, followed by a boy and a girl, their arms overflowing. They stood, burdened, look-ing around the room.

And then was heard Mistress Poppyseed's voice, in all its brazenness, from the garden path. 'Come out, precious. See the sun for the first time. Mr Tengis is at the gate. The clerk with the wedding scroll, too. Poor Mr Tengis, his blushings come and go – I have to laugh.'

The boy said, 'She isn't here.'

Mistress Poppyseed possessed the room. The tall silken chair was empty. Mistress Poppyseed gaped at it like a fish.

A girl, spilling orange petals, ran to the other door.

She said, pointing (so that more petals fell about her feet), 'Look! – over there, on the mountain road, somebody in white!'

And the boy said, 'She's gone into the sunset.'

Mistress Poppyseed had to sit down on the chair for a full minute, gasping, before she could speak.

'Far away. Long ago,' she said. 'Poor Mr Tengis will break his heart. She's taken the dowry, too, by the look of it. She'll be back, frightened, under the first star. I'll break a stick on her back, the gadabout.'

They came on the wind then, a few flute notes.

Mr Tengis, his face wrinkled as a walnut, stood on the threshold, in a yellow coat and blue trousers; and at Mr Tengis's shoulder his secretary, head bowed humbly, the scroll containing the unsigned deed of marriage tied with a white ribbon.

Mistress Poppyseed turned to the bridegroom. 'Mr Tengis,' she said, 'you're still a bachelor. The bird's flown.'

The peacock shrieked in the boy's arms.

III

The Well

In the mountain villages, it had been a summer of unusual drought, so that the stalks of corn had come up short and thin.

Most summers, the stalks grew tall and yearned towards the sun, green and dewy, and larks sung above the fields morning and evening. Then, yearning too ardently, the stalks drooped their overburdened heads, and they had a burnish on them, to signify that they were kin, the benign fire in the sky and the bronze whispering hosts in the village fields below.

And then the peasants, on a given morning, blew the cobwebs from their sickles and went out – themselves children of the sun – to cut and gather.

But this summer the sun had been no benign king; no, he had raged like a tyrant in the sky from April to September, and his fiery breath had burnt and blasted the corn as soon as the first green shoots appeared.

Day after day, week after week, the sun poured his pitiless gold on the peasants' corn patches; and never a grey cloud, a rain-bearer, was seen in the western sky.

The ox, tormented by flies, raised his black horns to the sun and bellowed.

Soon it would be winter, coming right on the heels of that stupefying summer, with no harvest-time between.

No lark sang. A child had found a little heap of bones on the wayside, and three broken eggs.

An old man grumbled, swatting at horse-flies with his woollen bonnet: 'I thought to die in the winter, when most of us old ones go. It's always in winter that the gravedigger has trouble breaking the earth to make us graves. I never thought, no not once, to be shrivelled to death by the sun, like a moth in a lamp. Another week of it, my friends, and I'll be nothing but a handful of dust. Give me a cup of wine. Wind of sunset, blow me away' . . . For always, at sunset, a hot wind got up that year and blew the barren dust of the fields against the thresholds.

The old man shook his fist at the sky-furnace, but did not die. No, his granddaughter brought him a cup of wine. He drank it. And then he died, in that bitter time of no ripeness and earth-gold between summer and winter; when King Harvest ought to have bidden all to his broad table.

There was one blessing in the village; in the village square, a good well of water that never dried up, even in that summer of dust. From deep down, at a root of the mountain, the water kept on singing – it rose in bright circles, and the women came there with their jars; to steep the sweat and dust from the peasants' smocks, and to make beer, and to wash the doorsteps so that a girl could see her face in it, and to rinse their hands and faces before they went on a saint's day or a Sunday into the church with its holy ikons; those same ikons were a consolation to the women all through that summer of the lion.

The local landlord, without saying a word to anybody, had packed seven trunks in early summer; he had stowed them in his fine oak cart, and locked the three doors of the hall; he had set out with his wife and children to the city a hundred miles away. 'It's the war,' the village elder Ilyich had told the peasants and their wives. 'There's some war or other in the east, yellow men on horseback. The great man – he's frightened the war might come this way. What army would want to trample on a poor village like this, eh? This year, especially, when we have nothing.'

But sometimes, on a still hot evening, when the sunset wind had died away, the ears of the children (delicate as shells) could hear, very far off, a sound of iron on stone; and once, on a mountain ridge beyond the eastern bank of the river, very far off, far and faint, two children had seen at sunset a rose of fire where once there had been a distant village, a rose that quickly shed its petals, and put a black hot stink on the wind after nightfall. 'Two little liars,' said their mother. 'They listen to the old men's stories till they swear they see marvels and monsters everywhere.'

The village elder, Ilyich, said, 'War? We have plenty to endure this summer without battles. No, no; there'll be no soldiers here. If the barns were bursting there might be soldiers – I've heard of that – or if the lord hadn't taken his gold mirrors and silver candlesticks away – a few foreign soldiers might be tempted here by the likes of that. They know what they're about, the yellow-faced soldiers. Just go on praying for rain, you women. If it rains for a week there might still be enough bread in winter to keep a mouse or two alive.'

A holy man, passing through, pointed eastward and made gestures, signs of burning and breaking and blood. The villagers realised that the traveller was dumb. But his mime of battle was so vivid that the older women blanched; and the girls danced with excitement in the doors, for to them the word 'soldier' signified excitement and romance. The village elder bade them go indoors.

They gave the 'starets' a cup of sweet water to drink, and let him go. Most men of that kind go at a leisurely pace, as if they move obedient always to the slow pulse of the earth and there is nothing to make them hasten; for death is at the end of every road, whether they run or saunter or dance. This tramp gulped down his water and wiped his mouth on his sleeve, and fairly stumbled out of that village. He turned once at the road-end and held up a finger, as if summoning an angel to come down and keep the village.

Another morning without rain. The sun in the east was a wakening lion.

A thickset woman and her small daughter set out from their cottage to the well in the village square early, to be there before all the gossips and trollops came with their jars and their bell-mouths. She was a secret woman, who kept her own counsels. The little girl had no father, and the woman would name no name. This, to begin with, had only whetted the curiosity of the village women. Was it Vassily the woodman and carpenter? Was it a tramp that had passed through under a winter moon? The more brazen ones went so far as to say it was Ilyich the elder: the child had his very shape of ears and curve of nostrils . . .

The sun, for yet another morning, had risen warm and cloud-less. The brief dawn wind blew the dust everywhere; it brought to the child's ear new noises, iron on stone, the hidden broken rhythms of horses' hooves, multitudinous murmurs from far up-river. The wind brought too – which only the farm animals sensed – smells of blood and charred wood. The horse in the meadow flared its nostrils, its fore-hooves pawed the air, its high shuddering neigh sounded like a trumpet in the clear morning.

The child pulled its mother's sleeve, put a tanned forefinger first to her lips, and then cupped her full hand to her ear.

The mother shook her off.

'Don't hold me back,' she muttered. 'Hurry. I want to get my water before the sluts come.'

(Indeed there was a sound of the village women stirring round their hearths and pots; shaking gently or with vigour their slum-bering ox-headed husbands and sons.)

Hunting: the men would have to hunt for wild pigs and birds quickly, now that winter was about to follow so quickly on the hot barren heels of summer. In a good year, summer came and sat at one end of the long harvest table, and winter sat gaunt and cold at the other end, and the country-folk sat between, and the board was loaded with loaves, apples, nuts, and flagons of white and red wine. Winter and summer saluted each other from opposite ends of the board. That ceremony went on in a good well-balanced year.

Not this year, the sweet and beautiful gathering. No, the table would be strewn – if at all – with a few bones and smears of blood. For it was by no means certain that the village men had kept their early skills of hunting. Ceres had been so boun-teous to the people for so long.

'I hear sounds like war,' said the child. 'From up-river, there, behind the foothills.'

'What does a thing like you know about war or the sounds of war?' said the woman. 'Ilyich, he's told us not once but twenty times that the war's far away, among the Urals some-where. It won't touch us. Why is that horse rampaging about the field there with his eyes rolling? That horse'll come to no good. He'll be chopped up for meat before winter, mark my words. A danger. Look at that hoof of his, like a thunderbolt!'

By this time they were at the well, and the woman was tying the rope round the handle of one of her wooden buckets.

'Here's an angel coming,' said the child.

A young woman was coming up between the fields, in a gown that had lately been white, but now the dusts and flow-er-juices of a hundred miles had stained it. Birds had passed over it. Thorns had torn it here and there.

'Angel!' said the women. 'I'll give you angel. Bring the other bucket here. The only angel that'll be coming to this village soon will be the Angel of Death, and it looks to me *he'll* get a good harvest, at least. You listen to too many stories. The only angels are over there painted on the walls of the church.'

She wound the bucket up with vehemence. Water splurged out.

It was then that the shadow of the stranger fell across the well.

The woman turned and stared at her. The child touched the sleeve that had once been white as lilies.

Water-drops, hundreds of them, showered from the bucket and made little dark circles in the dust.

The young woman couldn't take her eyes from them, or from the blue restless circle of water that lapped the bucket's rim; and slurped over still, but in lesser quantities.

'What's that beautiful stuff?' said the girl, pointing to the stilling water in the bucket, that reflected the blue of the sky, and then (most wonderfully) the face of the child bending over it.

The village woman gathered her brows against the stranger. 'What? This!' she said. 'Are you a simpleton or something? I had to break ice in the well this morning again. It's winter down there already. My hand's blue – look at it.'

The child said, 'It's water.'

The girl looked deep into the shadows of the well. She touched the water bucket and set the surface trembling slightly. Her broken face looked back at her.

'Could I take a little of it in my hand?' said the girl.

The child said, 'She wants to touch the water,' as if that was a thing more of wonderment than foolishness.

The woman tied the rope to the handle of the second bucket.

'What are you?' she said, and began to winch the dry bucket down. 'Are you one of them wandering crazy ones, eh? . . . You, Natasha, get behind me. She might be dangerous.'

The bucket crashed into the water and thin broken ice below; the bucket gave three great gulps.

The child stood between the girl and the mother. 'She just likes water, that's all.'

The dogs at twenty thresholds smelt blood on the wind. They wound their tails into their bellies, they crouched back indoors, their eyes mistrustful.

The horse went round and round the field as though a wolf-pack were at his heels.

The girl took from her shoulder the bamboo pole she was carrying. On one end of it was a leather bag, bulky and weighty; from the other end dangled, long and light as a river-bird, a flute.

'A travelling musician,' said the woman. 'You've come to the wrong place, lass. Unless you want to stay on and play the funeral music. They won't pay you, they have no money. You can sleep in the barn, I suppose, and starve with the rest of us. You'll have to ask old Ilyich. This village is penniless, and like to be worse, deep in debt, up to their eyes in it, if they have to buy bread from the villages further up. They'll bleed us dry. There'll be need for a lot of black music before this coming winter's done.'

And the woman wound the second bucket up into the light, until the slurps and spillings of water made little falling tatters of rainbow. Then, a second later, the well rang a muted carillon, deep down.

'I have money,' said the girl. She loosened the thong on the leather bag. 'If I give you a silver coin,' she said, 'will you let me have a handful of water?'

The woman gazed at the white coin in the girl's fingers, as if a star had fallen.

'A shilling!' she cried, and then clapped her hand to her mouth. Any cry of delight or anguish brought out the village besoms in a flock. She took the white coin, gazed at the gravured head on one side and the dragon on the other, bit the rim with her strong teeth, and stowed it into a pocket of her blouse.

'Well,' she said to her daughter, 'for a shilling she'd better have the water in a cup' . . . There was an iron cup chained to a stanchion at the well. 'Here.'

The water moved again about the iron rim of the cup, in smaller circles. The sky, an unquiet blue, trembled in it. Once the sun flashed out of it. The girl held the iron cup of water as if simply to hold it was sufficient.

She whispered, 'It's more beautiful than the coin. Living silver, with blue flashes. Could I put it to my mouth?'

The child danced. 'It'll freeze your lips together! It's so cold.'

At that moment Ilyich the village elder walked through the village in such a hurry that now and then he stumbled on a stone. His face was as red as wine.

Ilyich's passage through the village brought the gossips and the breakfast-making trulls out in a flock. Never in their experience had Ilyich been in such a hurry before. Excitement crackled through the village, from door to door to door.

Ilyich didn't stop till he came to the well. He was angry, frightened, confused. He looked as if he had drunk two flagons before his breakfast.

'War,' he said. 'It's war.'

He pointed at the stranger. 'Who's this?' he said hoarsely. 'Who's this woman?'

'I don't know,' said the woman. 'She's a flute player. She must be good at it, she's made a pile in the cities, it seems. She's—'

'Shut up,' said Ilyich.

Time in a Red Coat

He turned to the girl whose mouth was shivering and bright with water. 'Who are you?' he demanded. 'What are you wanting here? Speak up.'

'I'm a travelling musician,' said the girl. 'The water woman was right.'

Ilyich was far from satisfied. 'You don't belong hereabouts. Have you got papers? There's a war.'

'No,' said the girl.

Ilyich considered. He stared at the cobbles. He stared at the girl. The village women were a fluster of hens behind him now.

'Musicians,' said Ilyich at last, 'are suspect. Tramps too. They belong nowhere.' Ilyich lowered his voice. He pointed his finger at the girl. 'I think,' he said in a dark whisper, 'you might be a spy.'

'A spy?' said the girl. 'What's that?'

'She's my friend,' said the child, and dabbled two fingers in the water; she put one drop of crystal in her mouth and let another crystal fall and ruin in the dust.

The mother: 'Be quiet, you, when Ilyich is speaking.'

'You're coming with me to the big house,' said Ilyich. 'The seigneur isn't in residence. Never mind that. There's the butler and the gardener. I'll see that they lock you in the cellar, till we find out more about you. Stand over there meantime. Don't try to run away. She's dangerous. You women, watch her.'

The girl said, 'I have to cross the river today.'

The horse stood trembling against one wall, exhausted, in lathers of sweat.

Ilyich almost screamed. 'You can't get across the river. The bridge is down. So I've been informed.'

'The bridge down!' came from the flock of women in every kind of utterance from a whisper to a shriek.

'Burnt!' cried Ilyich. 'The soldiers set it on fire two days ago. The duke's soldiers. That means – make no mistake about this – there are two armies not ten miles from this village. There's been a skirmish already. The duke sent a soldier to my door when it was still dark this morning. It's a matter of utmost urgency.'

Ilyich's song varied between abject fear and self-importance.

The girl said, beginning to move away from Ilyich and the chorus, 'I think I must go now. You've told me where the Dragon is.'

'You'll stay where you are!' cried Ilyich. 'Stand close about her, you women. Don't let her through. I'll attend to her in due course. What does she mean, dragon? Now listen to what I have to tell you. It's orders from the duke's headquarters.'

The village women stood all about the well and Ilyich. Some of them had their pitchers on their heads; some on their shoulders; some between their hands; some at their feet.

A shadow passed swiftly over the village: a raven flying north.

The child put her hand into the hand of the flute-player and dragon-seeker.

'Look, you women,' said Ilyich, and cleared his throat to give room to the urgency and importance of the intelligence the duke's man had entrusted him with. 'The Tartar soldiers – that's who the enemy is, the Tartars – no wonder you're white in the face all of a sudden – the Tartar soldiers are only a day's march away! Now listen carefully. The duke wants you to carry a thousand pitchers of water from this well to the wine cellars up at the hall. Yes, at once. I said, "A thousand pitchers," before sunset. You're to pour them into the large vats. That's my orders. I've never known anything like this in this village before, man or boy, and I'm seventy-two.'

A mingled cry went up from the women, 'A *thousand pitchers*!'

And the weaver's wife, an old dour creature, said, 'What for?'

Ilyich waved his arm in the air. 'What for? Because the duke has sent word. All the wells are to be poisoned.'

The women looked at Ilyich as if he was the village simpleton telling them a dream.

The child tugged the girl's sleeve. She whispered, 'The bridge is burnt, that's true. I saw the smoke a while ago. The ferryman lives down there, in that hut. He'll take you across the river.'

The village women burst into speech – 'A thousand pitchers! who for? A thousand pitchers won't last very long . . . What can we do with poisoned water? . . . Can we make porridge and soup? . . . Can we wash our floors? . . . Can we keep our children clean? . . . Water's meant to be pure and sweet always . . . You old fool' . . .

Ilyich blanched under their indignation.

The girl wasn't in the village square. She was gone like a white shadow in the direction of the blood-stench and the smell of burning.

The child piped up, 'Water's precious all right. My mother, she's just got a shilling for one cupful. Show them the shilling, mother.'

'Be quiet,' whispered the mother.

'It's orders from the duke and the general,' Ilyich said at last. 'That's all I know.'

Tanya the midwife said, 'Men are even stupider in wartime than they are in peace, if that's possible.'

Another woman said, 'There'll be no wells poisoned in this village.' It was said simply and easily, as one might say 'A stone is a stone' or 'Water starts on the top of the mountain and falls to the corn-roots'.

A woman cocked her head.

The cheese-and-butter woman said, 'I hear it too. River music.' The weaver's wife said, 'You might as well pour the poison down our throats now.'

It was seen then that old Ilyich was carrying a stone jar with a seal and tight rounds of wire at the neck.

Ilyich felt himself between the dragon and the deep blue sea. Yet he was more important than he had ever been – the agent not of the absconded landlord but of the duke and also the general. Those hussies were there to carry out those august commands without question.

'What do you know about important things like that? Even you can see how useful our wells would be to the enemy. They've even sent a spy to test the water. The girl with the flute is a spy, of course.'

Ilyich's eye looked round at vacancy.

Suddenly he was furiously angry. He did a kind of broken dance on the dust. 'Where is she? Where's that girl? I thought I told you not to let her through. She's dangerous. I can't keep my mind on *everything*.'

Some of the women smiled at the antics of the old creature. Some of them glared at him still. The midwife seized the stone jar of poison and smashed it against a stone. With gulps and a long gurgle the dust drank it. It left a wet purple stain; then it fumed and set the child coughing.

The horse in the meadow had roused itself again; it began to career round the field faster than ever, with blood-boltered eyes. Inside the houses the twenty dogs whined in their corners. For now the reek of blood and wounds came pungent on the wind, and then the cry of a bugle; and iron on stone, a thousand mingling sounds.

'There,' said the child. 'Look. Listen. She's halfway across the river.'

And the women called, in their twenty voices, 'Farewell, stranger!'

IV

River

It is a worn metaphor, surely, that sees life as a river issuing from high mountain snows, with cataracts and torrents, down to a fertile plain and then, with many windings and turnings, finding its way to the vastness of the sea.

And yet, when it was new-minted, the metaphor must have seemed beautiful and true.

Doesn't life begin with the high snow-bright innocence of childhood; and have great mountain tumults and sonorities in adolescence and young manhood; and afterwards there are the slow fertile turnings of maturity, when the river becomes ever deeper and wider; until at last it empties itself into the bitter immensity of death, the ocean of the end?

And by an extension of the metaphor, the river is not a figure for the life of a single individual, but the life of the whole tribe, the whole nation, the totality of the human race, and indeed of all creation.

More, poets have seen the river as time itself, all legend and history, and tales as yet untold by children's children.

It is endlessly intriguing to think of a snowflake, or a rain-drop, falling from a torn cloud upon a stone. Then there are many snowflakes, a blizzard; great drenches of rain; until, obedient to the laws of gravity, the beaded wetness leaves the stone and becomes a trickle, a rivulet, a little brook or burn tumbling over bare rock, down, ever downwards, and growing always by tributaries and by what new clouds torn by summits give out, their crystal blood. It becomes strong, it creates a channel for itself in the hardest rock, it makes ever more tremendous music – 'the cataracts blow their trumpets from the steep' . . . In the foothills shepherds water their flocks at the bank, women wash their clothes beside a broad tranquil pool where two swans swim and there is the occasional flash of a trout. Woodmen and shepherds build houses beside the murmurous flow; there is a village; there are barterings of fish and wool with other villages cradled high in the mountains, or flatland villages that deal in butter and cheese and wheat. Among those fruitful barterings the minds of men and women broaden, they think, they dance, they make music and ballads and imagine beautiful shapes inside stones and oak-trees.

They mint money.

They march against each other in ragged troops with arrows and knives. They bring torches to thatched roofs in the dark of the moon.

The river flows on, ever deeper and broader. Here and there, it is stained with blood, drops that are soon diffused and lost in its irresistible surge; as are the salt drops from the eyes of widows and children.

Greater villages appear on its banks. A first perilous bridge, a thing of ropes and wattles, is hung from bank to bank across a gorge. A hallowed-out tree trunk is entrusted to the flood with a hero-craftsman in it. Further down-stream, the first ferryman asks a wandering man if he needs a passage to the other shore, and holds out his hand for a small coin to be put in it. They argue for a brief while, half in earnest, half out of a pure joy in words and bargaining.

And then the river turns about rich cornlands, where there are castles and churches, and country folk with sun-dark faces anxiously watching the innumerable barley-heads for the tranquil change from green to bronze; so that there will be food for them and theirs next winter, besides the baron's and the king's shares. They have lived so long beside this turn of the river that it might be said the river flows in their veins.

But no: it is bitter red liquidity that courses through their veins, and issues grey from their eyes; as their great-grandfathers knew, that summer when the baron and the king fell out, and armed horsemen trampled the corn to a yellow mush. They do not know it yet, the simple country folk, but next summer the swords and hooves will be in their fields again.

It would be tedious to follow the river any further, though in the course of this tale – which is like a river too – we will have to go downstream a little. Here we must pause; a girl is in a ferryboat, and the ferryman is sculling the girl across from bank to bank. The girl is dressed in a white gown, that has here and there stains of travel on it, flower and butterfly juices, and even a little thorn tear on an upper sleeve.

How many lonely girls have been ferried across this stretch of the river? No one records such trivial events; there may have been hundreds since the banks were first cleared of virgin forest.

And some have gone for a love-tryst on the other side. And some have taken rings from the drawer of a carved paternal chest, and half-terrified and half-exhilarated have fled from the crime to a place of masks and whispers. And some have been sent with an important letter, to be delivered by hand at a secret door. And one or two have become river-borne for the sheer joy of the brimming and the buoyancy and the music of the waters, and to delight in the skill of the ferryman with his oar. (But few peasant girls would ever think of such luxuries of adventuring. Maybe the village elder's daughter, once or twice in a century.)

A girl in a white gown that is in need of bleaching and stitching is afloat on the river of time. She has a flute; she has a purse of silver and gold thonged to her white waist-band. Occasionally she puts the flute to her mouth and a few notes are scattered and lost among the perpetual murmurations of the river.

Nor is she alone. In a sense – in the poetical way of looking at things, which packs a whole world into a symbol, in order to make simple and joyous and comprehensible the manifold confusions of life – in a sense the young girl in the boat crossing the river is not only all the young women who have crossed the river in time past and who will cross it in time to come. She is all the young women in the world trembling on the verge of love, whose lover perhaps has been dragooned for a soldier; she will follow the war till she finds him, drunk or dead or wounded. She is more, she is all women, all the girl children and the old ones who have added their salt drops to the sweet on-flowing river of life, and who hate war and war-makers with a bitter hatred.

This girl is all women, princess and peasant-lass and fish-wife, who have lived or who will live in time to come (if indeed there is much time left – perhaps the river is nearer the bitter-ness of the end than we think. A few have heard, they say, breakers on rocks, far away, the cry of a seabird).

The ferryman stands in the stern and manipulates his oar with skill and strength in the broken water.

Time passes.

The ferryman turned his head (still wielding his oar with power) and said to the girl, 'The fare's a penny.'

The girl was utterly absorbed in the behaviour of the river, and the boat on the river. The river changed from moment to moment, yet it was always the same. It was dappled with shifting gleams and shadows, for now the sun had gone into a purple-black cloud near the summits of the mountain range. The river was a thousand little swirls and eddies, each with a life of its own, yet parts of the one great irresistible onward flux. Sometimes, where the river-bottom had different depths, there was a commotion on the surface, whorls of water like the ends of bottles, yet alive and vibrant; and a lacework of spume trembled, and shed bits of itself, and changed shape, but was always there, a grey tissue wrought by uneven rocks on the river bed.

The ferryman urged on the boat with fluent rhythmical manipulations of his oar. His body was a part of the river rhythm; his feet were rooted to the bottom-boards but his torso moved in undulant circles. It was as if he had set the river of his veins into a joyous combat with the river itself. And the boat itself was a part of the river, like a young horse matching itself against terrain and wind, with tossings of the head and plunging hooves; but the boat was obedient to the delicate flick of the oar and the oar's urgent tug. It seemed to know its way across the wide river – how cleverly it edged round a large grey rock that reared up in mid-stream; a rock fretted always by little waves whose cold fingers worked lace about the edge of it.

The girl said, 'River. So this is what a river is. The river water is more beautiful than the water in the well.'

The ferryman's torso went in strong undulant circles. This with the rock sticking out of it was a tricky piece of river. The urgent onset divided into two currents, and it behoved him to order the underwater twistings of the oar to suit the new broken rhythm.

The ferryman knew his work so well that he had energy and time to spare for the turning of his head towards his passenger. 'Beautiful!' – he laughed out of his strong chest and throat.

'Beautiful – Tell that to the river folk! The banks burst last November. They lived on the roofs for a week. You never saw such filth. Drowned hens and sheep everywhere. The river is a nuisance. It has always been a nuisance to them. And now the soldiers have burnt the bridge. I'm not complaining. I get my living from the river. Since the bridge was burnt I was never so busy . . . I charge twopence.'

The girl, looking down from the bow of the boat, could see round boulders bedded in the silt of the river-bottom. Once, a swift darting shape glided from boulder to boulder, going up-stream.

Now a fire could be seen on the river bank, miles up. Some large building, a mill or a church, was ablaze.

The ferryman surged and fell about the oar, and his hands were round it in a firm unyielding grasp, as if the singing blade was an extension of his arms.

The bow headed always slightly upstream, to counter the torrents of water falling about it. And like a young horse, it plunged and flung spume on either side of it: a young horse in the mistral.

'Where does it begin?' said the girl.

'What?' said the ferryman, this time not turning his head.

'The river. Where is it born?'

The ferryman nodded his head towards the immense purple cloud that had just then swallowed the sun whole.

'Up there somewhere,' he said. 'A cloud on the mountain tops.'

'And where,' said the girl, 'does it end?'

This time he did turn his head, as if she was some kind of a simpleton or as if she was trying to make a fool of him. He even let the oar rise, it hung in the darkening air, raining back dull drops into the river. In the pause, a cluster of spume drops eddied into the boat and clung grey to the girl's white collar.

'In the sea,' said the ferryman. 'All the rivers run into the sea.'

'The sea must be the most beautiful water of all,' said the girl. 'The harp with many strings.'

Such words as 'beautiful' were never used by the ferryman and the river folk and the peasants. 'Beautiful' was a word in the special vocabulary of the nobles and their scions. Poor lives knew nothing of beauty, except perhaps the icons in the church, and the chanting and the incense. But that Sunday experience was something far beyond a word like beauty to comprehend. There the peasant women gathered in a mysterious omnipotent peace, that gave a kind of rough meaning to their lives, and pierced them to the heart with the mysteries of love and suffering and death.

Nor, to them, was a rose beautiful, or a nightingale's song, or the moon in the river. Only the ladies in the palace considered them to be beautiful, and they had poets to make the beauty linger out for a time in words. For the river folk and the peasants, roses and nightingales and the moon were there, parts of the web of creation like themselves, and so the lives of flowers and birds and winter skies were grained into their own flesh and blood; all created beings belonged to each other.

A fine golden harvest – a basket of sturgeon – meaning full bellies for today and tomorrow and perhaps the day after: perhaps, if they were forced to use the word beauty, they would apply it to those needful things, a tilting of the scales slightly on the side of bounty. Necessity and beauty were one.

Nor was the great wheel of the year beautiful – it might be, if the snow kept the seeds warm and if the sun loaded their barns, and the cider press was busy at summer's end. But, as often as plenitude, the turning seasons brought worm and blight. Poverty was not beautiful if a man had hungry mouths at his board all winter; poverty was seemly only for the wandering holy men who sat in the village square with their palms outstretched, and perhaps responded with a blessing on houses and beasts and fields.

The ladies and the courtiers were so far removed from the deep earth-essences that they even thought of war as a beautiful and goodly thing – and they had poets about them to make the carnage and the crushed corn beautiful for ever with a proper ordering of words and images. If a knight was brought into the courtyard mortally wounded, words like 'heroism' and 'glory' and 'fame' were invoked to cover the ugliness – and beautiful words were carved on his stone tomb.

There was no beauty whatsoever in a conscript soldier who straggled home wanting a leg or an arm. Better that he should have lain with his suppurating stump on the battlefield, and died of wolves and cold stars. For such a one was worse than useless in the labour of agriculture from seedtime to harvest. Sometimes he was tolerated for his stories beside the winter fires; yet he was a perpetual weight round the necks of the community, and though nothing was said it would be thought a good thing if, soon, the elements took him back to themselves for a last mingling.

So, this girl in the white gown with a grey blob of river-spume at the neck, she with her superior words that meant less than nothing, must be one of the great ones. What disgrace was she fleeing from? Was there a hidden lover on the far river-bank? Whatever happened to these great ones, it was beautiful if only it could be looked at with the eye of a bespoke poet.

The ferryman plunged his oar in so deep that the bow of his boat eddied and pointed downstream for a perilous minute, until he had regained his composure; until he and the oar and the boat were once more parts of the river rhythm.

'The sea beautiful!' he shouted above the noise of the waters. 'Tell that to the fishermen! A hurried patch on a boat, between a nor' easter and a westerly. Ask the women at the shore. There they stand with their knives till the tide turns. A cold night watch. There might be a fish or two under the last star. There might be nothing.'

He spat the word 'beautiful' out of his mouth and returned vehemently to his task, as if he were a woman at a milk churn and a hundred cheeses had soon to be paid in rent.

The high-born girl, whoever she was, seemed not to hear him.

She said, as if she were uttering magical words, 'Sea. Fish. Stars.'

Suddenly, the delicate equilibrium of man and river and boat was violently upset. The ferryman stumbled and almost fell out over the stern, and if he had not snatched at it quickly the oar would have slithered into the sea.

'Look out!' he yelled. 'Oh God, I struck it with my oar. There, over there! Push the thing out and away. Hurry!'

What seemed to the girl to be a sodden bundle, heavy as if it held stones or bones, was trailing athwart the bow. She took the boat-hook and thrust it at the bundle; it was solid and hard to push clear of the boat. But she did, at last; almost losing her balance with the effort.

'What is it?' she asked.

'A corpse,' said the ferryman. 'A dead man. A soldier.' He spoke brutally, as if to crush out any element of beauty and chivalry that this high-born one might entertain. 'There's been skirmishing up-river. One of the duke's soldiers, by his uniform.'

And then, as if to cancel beauty for ever, the river corpse turned right round, and a blind bloat purple face, streaming water, looked up at the deepening purple cloud above the river.

'Farewell, soldier,' said the girl, as the currents and eddies bore the dead man downstream.

There she was at it again, trying to cover the ugliness with valediction and epitaph! *Farewell, soldier.* The soldier's ears were stones. The soldier had fared to the sharp edge of a sword, and there all his faring had ended, and now he could fare neither well nor ill.

The ferryman said brutally, 'The rats and the eagles, they'll have him by sunset. Then the crabs. There'll be nothing left of him in the morning – a bone, a few buttons.'

'There'll be his story,' said the girl. She put the ivory flute to her mouth. She turned her face downstream. She sent a few notes on after the dead soldier: to cover his water withering and unwinding.

The girl glimmered there in the bow, in her white dress, under the dark of the purple cloud.

A spasm of terror went through the ferryman. A fragment of a folk legend flashed through him: the ferryman who ferried the souls of the dead across the river to the shore of Hades.

Perhaps the girl was dead, a ghost! For she acted and spoke more strangely than any woman he had ever known, even his old granny who was a witch (or so the love-sick girls said, and the farmers who visited her, coin in hand, to bespeak them good weather for the lambing and the harvest).

The ferryman said, over the idle oar, 'This is none of my business. But where exactly are you going?'

The girl said, 'To the war and the wounds.'

Another legend bit into the ferryman's mind: the women far in the north, near the snowline, who carried the souls of slain heroes from the battlefield. (But they were old hags, they laughed over the dead with dry shrunken mouths, as if it was a joy to them to snip as soon as possible the threads of heroism.) The creature he carried in his boat was as fresh as a milkmaid.

The girl went on, 'I was born in a burning palace. I was taken and hidden away like a butterfly in a box. I came to the Well.

I'm here now, on the River. I must come to the Inn, then the Forest, then the Town, then the Burning Mountain . . . I can't see further than the mountain. Wherever war is, that's my place. It's all written out for me. In the end, there's the Dragon to meet.'

She was probably a crazy one, the ferryman concluded. Beautiful but mad. Such things happened from time to time in houses along the river shore or in the green foothills: but more often in the in-bred families of the great ones. What family would be mourning for a lost crazy girl? – or glad, maybe, that she had broken free out of the web of watchfulness, and freed the watchers and sorrowers at the same time?

The ferryman stole a quick look back at her. She gladdened him too, it was good to be carrying such a passenger from shore to shore; she put a small flame about his heart.

He said, 'This is a bad time for a young woman like you to be travelling. Alone too. Well, it's none of my business. But I wish you well, wherever your journey takes you.'

They were approaching the far shore. Now it was very dark and cold. The sun was under the hill. The purple cloud had grown and grown from a drifting island to a huge sky-covering continent. On the far bank, the girl could see a small firefly-flicker.

The ferryman shouted through the trumpet of his free hand, 'Boy, I told you not to light the lantern. Put it out!'

The boy's voice came frailly across the dark murmurs and cadences of the river, 'It's dark. That purple cloud! I had to take the lantern.'

The rhythm of the ferryman and his oar were easier now. They were out of the main fret and thrust. They had come to a place where the duck could lead her little flotilla of ducklings, and where otters could slip in and out of the translucency.

The ferryman said, 'The fare is threepence.'

Now the firefly in the lantern was a burning bird. The boy's hand, half the boy's face, shone yellow. He was standing among the roots of irises and marigolds, one bare foot in the river.

The ferryman, guiding his boat now to a little wooden jetty, said to the girl, 'He knows no better. A lantern nowadays draws every kind of cut-throat and thief. Where an army goes, there's always stragglers, the murderous fringe.'

The hull of the little boat touched the jetty, and trembled. The ferryman brought the boat alongside.

'Take the lady's hand then,' he said to the boy. 'Help her ashore.'

The small carrier of light said, smiling, 'You're welcome to this side of the river, stranger.'

The girl had wondered at the little spots of coldness that touched her here and there, her neck and her hand. Now she saw the snowflakes drifting idly athwart the lighted candle. She plucked one out of the air.

'What's this?' she said, astonished. 'A white petal. Did it float from a tree?'

'It's a snowflake,' said the boy. 'It's only a snowflake.'

'Oh, the shame!' cried the girl then. 'It's dying in my hand.'

The ferryman was tying up his boat to an iron ring on the jetty.

'There'll be millions of snowflakes before morning,' he said. 'Five pence, please. Did I tell you that before? Well, there's one good thing – the snow chokes the passes. It drifts into the mouths of the guns. There's never fighting in winter. The price of the fare is six pence.'

The girl unthonged the little heavy bag at her waist. 'Ten pence,' said she, 'for all the marvellous things I've seen on the river! That's a fair price.'

'You're welcome to come in my boat anytime,' said the ferryman. 'Thank you for the music.'

'I won't be coming this way again,' said the girl. The bronze coin was a bridge between their fingers long enough to drip with one melting snowflake.

'The inn's that way,' said the boy, pointing into the blackness. (No one had mentioned 'inn' to him, but he seemed to know the next stage in the girl's journey.) 'I hope you get to it before the real blizzard begins.'

The girl disappeared, a white glimmer, beyond the glim of the lantern.

'Farewell, traveller,' the boy shouted after her.

The ferryman shook his head.

The snow fell thicker. It hid the river and the boat, the ferryman and the boy; there was only the ghost of a golden bird.

What sound was that, far on? The ferryman listened. Nothing. There was only the hush of snow falling into time, falling into the bare forest and into the river that was beginning to stiffen already at the margins, waiting for the solid frost and the winter armouring of ice.

It came again, from far on, the stops and steps of music through the hushed dark siftings of snow.

V

The Inn

It is a worn metaphor, too, that sees life as an inn, a hostelry where we stay for a few nights, warming us at the fire with mulled wine, sitting at the broad table with strangers that one will never see again – and yet Fate has drawn this assorted company together, for purposes that we delight to speculate on; or it was simply an accident, a fortuitous coming together, with little or no meaning: a grey congress.

Since Fate, or Chance, brought the group together, let them make the most of it; let them dip their spoons deep into the pheasant pie, let them broach a bottle together, let there be stories, songs, mingled laughter, while the host stands anxiously at the door between kitchen and dining room, rubbing his hands, waiting for the least nod or sign from his guests – another flagon, a wedge of goat cheese; and a girl is busy bringing new logs to the fire – then back with her to the spit in the kitchen where a small pig is roasting over another fire.

Here, in the inn, there is a cross-section of humanity; the pattern is the same yet always changing, an infinite variety of faces appear at the door asking for shelter, then a few days later drift away again, separately; after a brief exchange of silver coins, and a merry questioning smile from the host upon their departure.

A near-infinite variety the landlord has entertained in his inn; yet he has ruled it for so long that, within that variety, he has shrewdly guessed that only a few main types predominate – say, seven, to name a number that is beautiful and mysterious in itself, and seems to be man's favourite among the ten ciphers.

Seven main types, then; and the landlord, bowing and rubbing his hands, can tell almost at once to which category his new-come guest belongs.

Happy in that inn is the time – alas, too infrequent – when representatives of all the seven types sit at his board stuffing themselves with veal and ale, and trading stories, for then it appears to the wise old host that he has all of humanity gathered together under his roof. Yes, even the melancholy man who sits at the end of the long table and speaks to no one, nor ever laughs, but picks at his food as if tomorrow was his execution day, and rises all of a sudden when the pledging and the tales on each side of him are at their merriest, and then goes without a word into the secrecy of his chamber; and the chambermaid follows with a taper to light his candle. Even such a one, in the innkeeper's estimate, contributes to the life of the inn; for the good fare and the joy are the better for that comparison.

All too seldom, as I said, do the seven types come together in the inn and bide their night or two, and go again. The innkeeper has known it; but he does not expect it, nor does he ever complain; for, whoever comes and goes, the silver or gold coins will shine for a moment in his hand before he puts them in the blackness of the oak chest under his bed, double locked there and entered in the ledger.

What the innkeeper dreads is a time when harvests are poor and business bad in the cities and ports. For then there are few travellers on the road, few men of business going between merchant in one town and banking house in another.

He listens eagerly every morning for the clatter of hooves on the courtyard cobbles, or the rattle of wheels; but when business is bad they are heard only rarely on the great roads, one of which goes east and west, one north and south, making a cross only a hundred yards from where the inn stands; for the innkeeper's grandfather, who built the inn, was a shrewd and a prudent man, and knew (in spite of his merry eyes and apple cheeks) exactly the place where travellers would like to eat and sleep, after warming them at the fire.

The present innkeeper has known such bad times, twice or thrice in his lifetime, and he has a constant dread of another economic depression in the kingdom before he dies – a bad year, when only an occasional guest knocks at his door. What is the use of keeping a warm cheerful well-stocked inn for one man, or two at most? No, but there are plenty of beggars and vagabonds and idlers at such a lean time, knocking at the door day and night, whining ones wanting a bone to gnaw at, or the dregs of a bottle of wine – and worse, there are thieves and cut-throats abroad.

Once, in his father's time (before he himself was born) plague had stalked the land like a skeleton with red-splashed cheek-bones! . . .

His father had told how, that festering summer, shuttered inside the inn, he had felt like the last living man in the world; the chambermaids and scullions had flitted about him like ghosts. They had heard feeble cries for help from time to time at the door, scratchings and kickings. His father had forbidden anyone to answer by as much as a whisper, lest one breath of fever burnt them all to the bone. But every evening at sunset the old man had gone out and left loaves and a leg of ham and a flagon in the ditch outside; they were not there in the morning.

That such a thing might come again puts a shudder on our landlord; the dread of it dulls his eyes.

Well, but his good wife Mitzi is a constant joy and comfort to him – let what will happen. This present landlord had never, by nature, been a merry man like his father and his grandfather. True, he had their red round cheeks, but when he was alone a kind of melancholy veiled his eyes. He had had the good fortune to meet and marry his dear good Mitzi when he was still a young man; and Mitzi had been such a beautiful girl that even to think of her now made a catch in his breath. Without Mitzi, even in the normal course – not taking into consideration bad harvests, plague, or war – he might well have sunk to the level of his melancholic guest (the one in seven), and picked at his food, and stolen early to his bed, away from the laughter of fools that was like the crackling of dry thorns under a pot.

But Mitzi too is dead now. Were a bad time ever to come back again, there would be no Mitzi to cheer and comfort him; for Mitzi, whenever he looked at her – even in her days of illness, even when she lay a stark corpse on the shutter – his Mitzi seemed to him to be little changed from the day he had first met her at the Cracow Fair, and bought her (his blushes foretelling the red merry anxious face he was soon to wear always) a silver ring.

And Mitzi had died last spring, and an old man had buried her young under the young green leaves.

And everywhere in the inn the whisper of Mitzi's slippers and Mitzi's mouth followed him, and gladdened him for a second; but when he turned to take her in his arms there was nothing, she was air and light again; what he had heard was a mouse or the sift of ashes in the great fire.

But, for innkeepers, there is a state worse than economic depression, worse even than the burying of a bride under the lyrical trees of April – and that is war.

There had been a war when the innkeeper was a lad and his father kept the hostelry, and that was a time branded in his brain. For a great army from the east had passed like locusts through the inn and left it bare – the well-stocked cupboards empty, the cool cellar below a strewment of broken glass. The paymaster-captain had, after that locust-cloud had passed on to other inns and other corniand villages, reined in his horse in the courtyard. 'I believe,' said he, 'the hussars passed this way and enjoyed your hospitality. You have done a good work for the kingdom. You shall not go unrewarded. Of course, landlord, you understand, so long as the war lasts there is a certain dislocation in the economy. I am giving you this chit, signed by myself. At the end of hostilities – which won't be long now, I assure you – our armies are victorious everywhere – when the war ends (as I said) you may redeem this chit for money, plus interest, at the king's exchequer. And once more, I thank you . . .'

Well, that war had ended, right enough; but it had ended in defeat for the king and the king's armies.

His father had taken the chit to the capital, to the royal exchequer, and put it on the table before the clerks. The clerks had looked from the chit to the old man, and then one of them had burst out laughing; it was followed by a full chorus of mockery. There and then the old man had torn the chit across and across, and gone back to his inn, and slowly replenished his stocks. The inn had not been left entirely bare by the regiment. He had taken care to hide as much provender and wine as he could in the secret underground chamber that the first innkeeper, the grandfather, had the prudence to put into the architect's plan.

But it was a matter that the innkeeper never forgot. He did not wish it to happen again in his lifetime. (Let them fight as much as they liked when he was lying – old crooked bones – beside the honey-smelling bride Mitzi: decay could not touch her.)

A hasty traveller, ten days ago, who came and stayed one night and was on his way again at dawn, breakfastless, had muttered to the innkeeper in the courtyard, after the passing of a silver coin, that he must hurry, he had not a moment to spare, he was the king's messenger. In the cities the bells had rung for war, a week ago. He was on his way to the general with an urgent message from the king.

Then there had been a throng on the roads, families with handbarrows laden with sticks of furniture, grey-faced men, wild-eyed women, children laughing with the excitement of it all – all in flight from the advancing army of the other king-dom beyond the river. A few lingered but had no money to pay for a meal or a bottle of wine. Next day the foreign regi-ment came, and billeted itself on the inn – at least, a dozen officers and their servants did – and like rats they were at once in every corner where there was a smell of food and drink. 'You'll be paid,' said a foreign lieutenant. 'At the end of the war, which will be soon now, you will redeem this chit at the headquarters of the paymaster-general.' He signed his name with a flourish and handed the useless thing to the innkeeper.

'Make sure you have nothing hidden here, when it is asked for – no food, wine, or blankets,' said a particularly vicious officer called Luntzen, 'or you will be shot' . . . And Luntzen aimed an imaginary blunderbuss at the keeper of the house.

It was a dream – surely it was an evil dream. He would wake up and there would be the good guests calling into the kitchen for their breakfast. He would leave the golden bride Mitzi sleeping with her fragrant breath about her; he would go downstairs and harangue the cook and the chamber-maids and the scullions; then he would join his laughter to the seven-fold laughter at the board, while the breakfast (bacon and new-baked bread) was brought in.

It could not be that the beastliness of war would happen twice in his life-time.

But the bad dream went on all summer and autumn.

And he woke, and the inn was cold and empty, with white gleams on the wall from the first whiteness of winter outside.

The inn was empty. The giggling servants had gone away with the soldiers. The war had moved on, taking the last of the wine and the wenches. The inn was white and bare as a bone.

He saw Mitzi's smock and shoes and linen hat draped over a chair beside the dead fire. 'Mitzi,' said he, 'you didn't go, after all . . . No, I'm sorry, of course you're dead, Mitzi. You're lying under the bare tree out there, young for ever. I'm glad you weren't here when the soldiers came. Well, it won't be long now till I come and lie beside you. Not long, Mitzi. Not all that long.'

He was aware of a young voice chanting over by the window seat.

Who on earth could she be? Had Mitzi gone back in time and become a girl again? No, here was Mitzi, warming her at the unlit fire: the clothes with the ghost inside.

Then he remembered. His daughter in the besieged town fifty miles away had sent her little girl to the safety of the inn, on the last carriage that ever left the town. 'Safety of the inn' – the old man could not but snigger when he thought of the locust-cloud that had passed through the inn from May till November, and left a flurry of chits, and stripped the inn of everything.

'Mitzi,' said he to the empty smock, 'it's a wonder we're both still here, after what's happened.'

The child chanted words out of a book. What was the child's name? He had forgotten. Could she by any chance be called Mitzi, after her grandmother? No, there could only be one Mitzi in the world.

He slept. He woke again. There had been more snow. Through the window, six opaque green whorls in an oak frame, an unearthly light was flooding into the inn, as if it was sunk in the sea. He squinnied at the icon on the wall, the Blessed Virgin and the Child. So: an inn too, an inn in midwinter, and in a crib in that inn had begun the true history of man, after the false start in Eden. Yes, with that sleeping infant the world had woken to full knowledge of itself. There, on the Virgin's arm, silent, reposed The Word that was to flood the whole universe with meaning.

Well, the old man thought, smiling, inns are of great importance in history. An inn with its beds and fires and broad table and well-stocked cupboard: in such a place as this had the new time begun, the Light and the Way and the Word. And in that wonderful story too there had been horsemen and soldiers, Herod's bloodthirsty troop. All through the village of Bethlehem they had clattered and shouted, and they had murdered Innocence in its hundred cradles. But when they came to the inn, the inn was empty. The one child had moved south and west, weeping (it was likely) for the slaughtered children who had come into time about the same time as itself; but his Mother comforted him; and Joseph led the donkey, and they came at last to the borderland between pasture and desert; and so went down into Egypt, like the patriarch Jacob and all his children and flocks long before . . .

A wintered inn, with soldiers all around: that was where the great story had its second beginning. There, unheard, except by angels and a few shepherds, the music had had its pure source.

It did not occur to the old man, whose hands were blue with cold, what an equivocal part in the story that other innkeeper had played. He had taken the two strangers into his hostelry, certainly; but he had lodged them, such was the press and tumult of guests that day, in the poorest meanest part of the inn, that was not a room even, but a shed where his ox and his ass tholed the bitterness of winter. 'There,' that innkeeper had said brusquely, 'take it or leave it, many a one's slept comfortably enough in straw. No, no fire – whoever heard of a fire in a cowshed?' . . . But the place was warm enough from the breath of the animals; there they stood in their stall, Betsy the she-ass and Sam the ox, and all the warmth of last summer was in their breath, together with the sweetness of grass and clover . . . Then, by lantern-light, he saw with a start that the girl was with child, and far gone too, so far indeed that the event was imminent; a first low sweet moan was on her lips. The purity of the girl's face touched him, as he held the lantern high – she must be half-dead from the long journey and the burden inside her. More kindly he said, 'Come, you'll be safe enough here. Betsy and Sam – that's them, over there by the wall, ogling us with big eyes – Betsy and Sam eat their hay out of this wooden trough. When the little one comes – and God grant you a safe delivery, lady – just lay him in that trough, the straw's warm enough. I see you've brought some clothes and wrappings to put round him. If anything goes wrong (said he, turning to the grave bearded man whose arm was about the shoulders of the tremulous girl), if anything at all goes wrong, don't hesitate to climb up to the inn and tell me. The truth is, I'm almost swamped these days with country folk, come to Bethlehem about some tax or census or something – that's why I was a bit short with you when you knocked at the door an hour ago. I was half out of my wits with that horde of yokels, wanting beer and pies and hot soup. They'll be gone in a day or

Time in a Red Coat

two, thank God. There isn't a square inch in the inn for another sleeping-bag. I know at least three good midwives in the village, if you think you need one. There, my dear, it'll soon be all over. Then think how happy you'll be with the little new-born one in your arms. I'll send down some bread and wine – now I must go. Don't you hear the shouts and clattering of my hundred guests, up above? They'll be starting to dance soon – it'll go on well after midnight, not a wink of sleep I'll get – there, they've started to tune a harp already.' Thus, perhaps, the Bethlehem innkeeper to the strangers from the north. He had behaved, that hard man, very gently after all, once he had seen their plight by the glim of his lantern.

Our old innkeeper thought all these thoughts, as he looked at the icon on the wall, in the green underseas glow of deepest winter flooding through his six whorled panes.

He smiled to himself, and nodded over into sleep again, for the bitter cold was in his veins, that inclines an old person to sleep (such is the kindness of Nature) rather than to suffer the daggers of frost.

Was there a fire? There was the merest flicker of life in two charred logs, they licked each other with red tongues. Kicked, they emitted a few sparks and fed on each other again, sparingly. The old innkeeper was poor, very poor; but by no means so poor as he imagined. He had a huge stack of logs in the shed outside. The whole inn could have been a cave of warmth. The truth is, he had such terror of the soldiers that he dared not set his hearth fire into a leap and a dance, lest some errant troop of mercenaries saw from outside the flush in his window, and came kicking and yelling at his door.

He jerked awake again.

His granddaughter – whose name he couldn't quite remember – was curled in the window-seat reading a book in the green dazzle:

. . . The prince rode and rode till he came to the palace. It was a palace made all of ice. The princess was locked in the inner-most chamber of ice. Her mouth was ice and her heart was ice. Then the prince knocked three times on the door of the Ice Palace. All was silent for a long long time. Then in the cold corridors and stairs of the palace, candles began to be lit . . .

The old man said to the smock and bonnet on the other side of the hearth: 'Snow. It's snowing hard, Mitzi. Good. Good. Let it snow. Snow keeps the soldiers away. Are you warm, old woman? I can't afford big roarers of fire any more. The soldiers have ruined me, Mitzi. I have a drawerful of chits that'll never be honoured. Never.'

The child looked up from her book. 'Grandma's dead,' she said. 'She died after harvest. She's buried under that tree beside the church. You're talking to a ghost. You're talking to grand-ma's old smock.'

'What?' said the innkeeper. 'Who are you, child? Oh, it's you. Keep away from the window. Soldiers might see you. No, they won't, they won't. There's nobody out in snow like this. Mitzi, my dear, warm your hands.'

(A cat would have been cold at such a fire.)

The child said, 'Grandma's hands are cold as roots. She's dead. That fire's too small to warm a moth.'

'No smoke!' said the innkeeper sternly. 'If the soldiers see smoke, they'll come.'

At that moment the child heard music, a few scattered flute-notes. The innkeeper heard nothing. His ears were two ruined shells, so much time and noise and inn-bustle had flowed through them in sixty years.

The child pressed her face to a clear corner of a pane. 'There's somebody out there,' she said. 'Listen, a bird. A white lost bird.'

The old man said irritably, 'I told you, keep away from the window.'

The child gave a cry like a little bell – 'It's the snow princess!'

'Nobody can be out on a day like this, child,' said the innkeeper. 'Snow princess – you read too many silly stories, that's what.'

A low knock at the door made the old man start as if a pistol had been fired.

'*Don't answer,*' he whispered harshly . . . 'I thought we might get some peace in winter. Sh – h – h!' . . .

The knock came again, hardly louder than the thud of a robin.

The child got up from the window seat and unbarred the door. 'Come in,' she said. Then she turned to her grandfather. 'It *is* her, grandfather.'

The girl in a white mask came in. She was soaked through, her gown clung to her, hung from her, a grey heavy down-dragged dampness. She leaned against the door post; when she breathed her ghost was on her lips. She had white eyelashes. Her hand, that she supported herself with at the doorpost, was like a gauntlet of thin ice.

The child smiled at her. The innkeeper looked at her in terror.

At last she spoke, a silver whisper. 'Please, a bed for the night.'

'Sorry,' said the old man. 'No room. Isn't that right, Mitzi?'

'No, it isn't,' said the child. 'There's a dozen empty rooms. You can stay.'

The mask slid from the girl's face in pure quick drops.

'Lady, whoever you are,' said the old man, 'it's like the child says. The inn's empty. In more ways than one. We're eating blackbirds and roots. The soldiers have taken everything. So you see, it won't do you much good, staying at this inn. Will it, Mitzi?' He said to the child, 'Let her go back into her fairytale.'

'She can sit at the fire,' said the child.

The old man, turning, saw the Nativity icon on the wall. The first innkeeper, hidden, was whispering to him across a waste of white winters, fire-splashed.

'You'd better come over to the fire, then,' he said. 'I'll put a log on. You can talk to Mitzi. Can you afford to stay here? The charge is one rouble per night with breakfast.'

The girl unthonged shiveringly the bag at her waist, and put a coin on the table, a silver piece.

The inn-keeper squinnied at it. 'That's a piece of ice,' he muttered. He touched it, he held it up in the green air. 'No it isn't.' He bit on it. 'It's money right enough, a crown piece. Where did a wandering musician get money like that from, eh?'

The girl said, 'A cup of hot water, please.'

The old inn-keeper smelt the money. 'Water's a farthing a cup,' he said. 'The well's frozen. Go out with the pot, child. Fill the pot with snow. She has money. She can pay.'

The child took a pitcher from a shelf. 'Water's free,' she said. 'Snow belongs to everybody.'

And out she went, the pitcher between her hands, into the dense weave of snowflakes, slowly and softly criss-crossing and falling.

'What town were you in last, eh?' said the innkeeper. 'Was there any news of the war? Is it true the king was killed in that last battle? Terrible times. Bandits and cut-throats everywhere. What takes you to a place like this in winter, eh?'

The girl said wearily, 'To kill the Dragon.'

The old man was startled out of greed and terror. 'What's that?' he cried. 'Dragon? Am I hearing right? Mitzi, did this young person say something about a dragon? I could have sworn – Mitzi, you talk to her. Where's that child gone now?

Surely I need a little peace, after all I've been through. No, I *am* sleeping. I'm sleeping and I'm dreaming all this. When I wake up you'll be gone. You and that child too. Then there'll be just me and Mitzi in the churchyard, side by side. That'll be a good thing. I'll turn over now and go to sleep again.'

The child kicked the door open. She entered, balancing the pitcher on her shoulder. Handful by handful she emptied the snow into the black pot that hung over the fire, that merely whispered and had two tongues, a yellow one and a red one. The child kicked the logs. A big flame leapt out. The fire sang in the chimney. She drove the black poker into the thickest log. The child was surprisingly strong. The log cried, it purred, it bled flames.

The child said, 'I saw soldiers among the trees just now. I must go and get another log from the yard.'

The old innkeeper covered his eyes. 'Bar the door!' he whispered to the shivering girl. 'The bar, there it is at your elbow. Child, if you're telling more lies ... Don't speak. Say nothing. How many soldiers? – Three. Maybe they won't see the inn. The inn's nothing but a lump in the snow.'

'Princess,' said the child to the girl, 'you're sitting in a pool of water. You must put on dry clothes. Here, put on grandmother's. She's dead. She won't be needing them ... Oh, that's beautiful – you look like a swan that's come out of a mirror! Put on the smock now, now the bonnet. If the soldiers come, bend over the fire. Look old and wicked.'

The hearth was really alive now, it was a bundle of flames, it sang, it chorussed, it sent waves of warmth into every corner of the inn.

The girl hung over the fire as if she would take it in her arms; but her flesh still gave out blue tremblings.

There was a thunder of fists on the door!

The innkeeper whispered, 'We're closed for the winter.'

A voice shouted, Open up! Major Luntzen is outside.'

The innkeeper whispered between hinges and doorpost, so that not even a mouse could have heard him, 'I've nothing for you.'

A precise cold voice said, through the hush of the snow and the flame-song, 'Knock the door in, corporal.'

The timbers of the door thudded and trembled from boots and butts.

The innkeeper cried, 'Don't. Please. Mitzi's not well today. I'll draw the bar.'

There entered three white figures from the fairytale, who stood, shook snow from capes and overcoats and breeches, thudded blocks of snow from boots, knuckled snow out of eyes, flung arms round chests again and again to get the blood flowing, blew into bunched blue fingers.

The three wicked snowmen were three soldiers.

Major Luntzen cast his cold blue eyes here and there. His face was like a hatchet.

'Yes,' he said. 'This is the inn. Good. I recognise it. Been here before. More dismal than I remember. Good place this, once. Last summer, good. Landlord.'

'I'm sorry, sir,' said the inn-keeper.

'A meal,' said Major Luntzen. 'I want a meal. Broth. A side of sturgeon. Steak. Bottle of Bull's Blood, your best. For the soldiers, plate of sandwiches, jar of beer.'

Three strayed travellers from the feast of war, three dogs, come to gnaw at a bone.

'There's nothing, sir. Nothing,' said the innkeeper.

'Nothing?' said Luntzen. He had an important little moustache on his upper lip. His speech was bright and sharp as pieces of broken glass. War, for Major Luntzen, was something between a holiday and the stern service of a god. When the great red mills of war turned, only soldiers counted, only the wounds and valour that are the fine essence of man. Whatever else fell between the stones was no concern of his: of course they would be broken, and the atoms of grain inside them would nourish the war, and their chaff stoke war's fires. The soldiers and the service of the god were all. This was Major Luntzen's considered creed. And yet at best he had seen a skirmish at a bridge; he had been at the burning of a shepherd's hut at night so that the column across the river might know the signal; he had examined the official papers of a hundred frightened women. The major was still an acolyte of war. It was hard to say how he might comport himself when the red scythes were in the harvest and the thunder of the great stones began. That would be the hour of his proving. Meantime the armies were held in the enchantment of winter. A soldier must laugh and quaff while he can. Who could tell what next April would bring, when the seeds began to shoot, and the acolyte must show whether or not he was worthy to be a good server at the altar of Mars?

'Sir,' said the innkeeper, wringing his hands as in the good times of old, 'soldiers of your regiment were billeted here all summer. They cleaned out everything. The cupboards, the cellar – empty. Nothing. They left a chit, to be redeemed, with interest, after the war.'

'Hard times,' said Major Luntzen. 'War. Everyone must do his bit. I need a bed.'

'The major needs a bit of warmth and comfort,' said the corporal, and winked at the private.

'The rooms are cold and damp,' said the old man, quavering. 'Like the inside of icebergs. The soldiers took all the blankets away.'

'I won't be sleeping in the bed,' said Major Luntzen. 'Soldier's reward. Where are the wenches you have in the kitchen, eh?'

'The girls,' said the innkeeper, 'went away with the soldiers in October, sir. More fun in the barracks than here in this poor inn. That's what the sluts said – the sluts!'

'Landlord,' said Major Luntzen in a low considered voice, 'is that so, no wenches? I'm beginning to think I've had a wasted journey. In the snow, too. Dark, no moon, drifts – might have trouble finding the way back. I'm seriously displeased with this inn, landlord. It's cold. I remember Peg and Lou from last summer.'

The corporal said, 'When the major's upset, that generally means trouble.'

'There's no females here,' said the innkeeper, 'but Mitzi my old woman. She's eighty-six. Dry as a bone. To me she's the fairest of April flowers. And this child. She's not right in the head. She's only seven. I forget her name.'

Major Luntzen looked from the girl dressed in the clothes of the old hostess dead and buried, to the child, and back again. 'Tell the old one to turn her head,' said he.

'I must warn you,' said the innkeeper, 'Mitzi has the evil eye, as far as soldiers are concerned.'

The corporal said, 'The major doesn't give orders twice.'

'Mitzi,' said the old man, 'turn round. Look at the kind of soldiers they have nowadays.'

The girl turned her head and looked at the three soldiers for as long as a butterfly takes to hang between two flowers. Major Luntzen rubbed his eyes; the millions of tons of snow he had laboured through to reach the inn that day had deadened his optic nerve – that a withered crone should look like a most lovely girl! The soldiers gaped – they were too common to have delusions – this lissom creature was well worth their snow trek – only, of course, she was for the major, not for the likes of them.

The landlord looked at a flower eighty-six Aprils old. She was young for ever, his Mitzi.

Major Luntzen rubbed his eyes. It was a snow transfiguration: purity and coldness had wiped away the reticulations of time.

Meantime the girl had turned back, and given her hands and face to the hearth-fire once more.

Major Luntzen said bitterly, 'She must have been pretty once. Congratulations, landlord.'

'They're not making girls like Mitzi nowadays,' said the old man. 'Oh no.'

'She's the snow princess,' said the child. The child was back in the window seat with her book of pictures and words. In her book the soldiers were tall handsome heroes with silver scars on their cheeks, stigmata of honour, not at all like the lingering trash who had just come to the inn.

Major Luntzen was examining closely the nails of his long white fingers, a sign always that he was turning events over in his mind, and would presently come to a decision.

The soldiers looked at him expectantly. What was he waiting for? Why didn't he drag the lovely creature out by the hair of her head, and throw her down, and earn a hero's reward?

'Landlord,' said the major at last, 'you know Major Luntzen. Everybody knows Major Luntzen. Major Luntzen doesn't like to be thwarted. Landlord, I must tell you something – Major Luntzen has had a bad day. That's why Major Luntzen has come here, through all that snow and darkness: to get some joy. Corporal.'

'Sir,' said the corporal, snapping his heels together and standing his full city height; then a salute.

'Take a log out of the fire and stick it in the thatch,' said Major Luntzen, as if he was asking a lieutenant at the mess table to pass the port.

'Yes, sir,' said the corporal. He jerked his head at the private and said, 'You heard what the major said!'

The private went over to the hearth, stole a quick look at the beautiful girl in old wife's garb, and plucked a half consumed log, smoking and flaming, out of the fire. He staggered with his burning brand and thrust it into the thatch, just where rooftree and rafter met.

Major Luntzen rose to his feet. 'Major Luntzen,' said he, 'always leaves a sign of his coming and going.'

'Beg to report, sir,' said the corporal, 'the fire is in the thatch.'

A hundred little yellow worms and moths twisted and eddied in the thatch. There were curls of grey smoke.

'Time to be going,' said the major. 'The fire will light us back to the barracks. Major Luntzen bids you goodnight, landlord. I will not be coming this way again.'

Major Luntzen saluted. He turned. He went out into the night; and the corporal and the private followed him.

Now a rafter began to crackle and smoke and spit sparks.

The old innkeeper stood there, helpless. It was all a dream still, images of beauty and horror tumbled one on the other.

Suddenly he awoke. His inn was on fire. 'Get out!' he cried. 'Oh Mitzi, go through the door quick before it burns too. Go out, child. There's nothing left. There's nothing we can do.'

He wept. He wrung his hands. He took hold of Mitzi's smock by the sleeve.

'The end,' he wailed. 'This is the end.'

But the girl and the child were standing nearer the sources of time, where one drinks hope and delight.

There was a ladder lying lengthwise against one wall. The girl propped it against the burning roof-beam. She beat at the flames with her bare hands. Sparks flew about her like golden bees.

'No, no, Mitzi,' cried the innkeeper. 'It's too late. You'll hurt yourself. Come away.'

The child took the pitcher of melted snow from the hearth-stone and handed it up to the girl. The girl threw it, like a thousand opals and emeralds, against the rafter, into the smoking crepitating thatch.

'Leave it, Mitzi!' cried the innkeeper.

The child ran out into the night with the empty pitcher and came back with it lipping snow; and the girl dashed that jewellery down the throat of the fire. The fire gasped. It choked. It hissed. It was at last (after a third pitcher of snow) only wet black straw and a dying wisp of smoke.

The old man was out under the stars; for now the immense snow cloud had moved westward, taking with it death and enchantment.

The child danced. She danced on the threshold. She chanted, 'Grand-da, the fire's out! Come back. The snow princess, she put the fire out.'

The old man came back, sober and star-pierced. He looked at the girl, astonished. 'A stranger,' he said. 'Who are you? What are you wearing Mitzi's clothes for? What a mess, water and soot! I'm glad Mitzi isn't here to see this. Mitzi always kept a clean hostelry. Rest in peace, Mitzi. Sleep under the snow.'

The girl on the ladder was quenching last sparks with finger and thumb. (She would have two blisters there in the morning.)

'Will I go out for another pot of snow?' said the child.

'It's freezing hard as nails,' said the innkeeper. 'There'll be nobody here till spring. You'd better stay, stranger. I've saved a bottle or two of good red wine. I've got half a pig and half a cow salted and buried. We'll live. You can stay, stranger.'

The girl said, 'Thank you.'

'I can't keep you for nothing, understand that,' said the innkeeper. 'You'll have to light fires, and bake and brew. You could play your flute sometimes. I feel young again when I hear music.'

'I'll do that,' said the girl.

The child came back for the fourth time with a snow-filled pitcher. She set it down on the hearth-stone; there was no need for more fire-fighting. They would mix the snow-water with red wine, and heat it in a pot, all three; and drink the mulled wine beside the fire; and go to bed, all three, ruddy and heavy-eyed.

'There's two dozen blackbirds in the net,' cried the child. 'We can have a blackbird pie tomorrow. You too, princess. It's begun to snow again. Snow and stars. What a beautiful world, outside.'

'Good,' said the innkeeper. 'I hope he dies in the drifts, Major Luntzen. Trash! – do you know what he used to be before the war? A pen-pusher in an office.'

The child was curled up in the window seat, trying to read her book by the firelight. But the first poppies of sleep were falling on her eyelids and fingers, petal by petal.

'It's time she was in her bed,' said the innkeeper. 'I'll light a candle for her. Then I'll get another log or two for the fire. I expect you have a lot of things to tell me, stranger. Well, I'm very glad you came. Mitzi would like you to be here – I know she would.'

And out he toddled, for candle, flint, steel, and the cut kindling that is the kindly friend to bewintered man.

The child was curled in a snow dream in the corner of the window seat.

The girl put her flute to her mouth, to earn her supper.

[VI]

Forest

Time is a dark wood, in which men and animals and birds and worms live and have their being: the creatures with immediacy and innocence, the men and women questioning all that they experience, leaf and branch and trunk, birdsong, the animals' circuits of hunger and renewal and death. Men feel themselves to be kin to the branches that blossom and wither, and to the animals that have their hour of brutishness and beauty and then die. But men question: 'What are we here for? What or where is a meaning? What are they, birth and love and death?'

There is no certain answer. The dark wood: another worn metaphor. But when it was new-minted by that austere poet in Florence, the woodland paths led three ways – to the gate of abandonment, to the gate of purifying fire, to the paradise of saints and angels. But the dark forest itself, that is all we know for sure: in the middle way, many men are troubled by the paradoxes and manifold cruelties of existence. Little enough light filters through the thick woven branches above; his seeking foot squelches into a sudden bog, he puts his questing hand into a nest of thorns.

He will leave his skeleton at last, a long articulation, under a tree, somewhere. He must share the fate of the leaves and pigeons and squirrels. And then the spirit, freed, will hasten like light or a shadow to one or other of the three gates.

He sleeps, under a tree, in the middle way, in a void of hopelessness. The leaves fall on him and cover him up; a few stars brighten his sleep, but at midnight they are sharp as nails, and his dreams are strange and broken. The man wakes. The winter is over and done! A few last crumbs of snow linger among the roots. He is alive still! And the sap that rises like a fountain has studded bough and branch with tight buds. The forest is awake again – it is spring. The sap of joy rises through the man as surely as through oak and birch – his branching veins bud and sing. He is not dead yet – his time has not come – he has a year or two of life left, to prepare his soul for its journey to the door of saints.

The birds sing too, as if the gods had given them new throats. And the animals, clothed in beauty, move through the forest; though the end of their goings is death, often in the redness of tooth and claw. Even the squirrel that nibbles nuts nourishes itself with death for death.

A nightingale falters into pure patterned fragments of song. There will be a time for the soul, and its candles and orisons: at the time of the falling of the first leaf. Not yet.

Meantime, the forest is a place of joy and peace. If we listen, we can hear from some neighbouring glade a boy calling to his dove. 'Come, I have a ribbon to tie on your leg! Come, I have a fine cage to put you in. Why are you hiding from me?'

Voices of innocence and delight. Voice of boy, voices of black-bird and thrush. And there, very far off, but coming closer, flute-notes, a scattering. A musician is on a forest path, somewhere, with a pastoral.

No: something is wrong in the forest today.

And here, now –

The girl coming into the clearing with her flute saw five red trees in the forest. The sun glistened, a morning prism, into her eyes.

They stood, five red trees. No, *men* – they moved. Five ordinary men, foresters or fowlers bound for some forest task or other. No, they are uniformed like soldiers; they drift here and there, come together like a red clot (whispering) and drift apart again. And now that we see the five more clearly, there is terror on one face, and recklessness on another, and a mask of apathy, and one of malice, and one of outrage and betrayal.

She turned, she lost herself in the multitudinous green shadows. Standing there in a tight group, facing inwards, arguing, they hadn't seen her.

They do not even walk, the five redcoats; they slink like dogs that have fled from some hard master, and are after the throats of squirrels and any carrion that might be lying about, to gorge themselves, and perhaps sleep then and forget for a while a horror behind and a worse horror to come.

Soft as animals they go, but with no grace or purpose in their going. A bough snaps. One of the deserters shrieks and blanches and covers his mouth.

'It was a dry stick that broke,' said the reckless one, and he laughed (but softly) as if their situation was a great secret joke.

Nearby – who can say how near or far, for the great trunks and branches and leaves magnify sound sometimes, and sometimes diminish it – a boy was summoning his dove, still . . . 'Come to me, come . . . Where are you hiding? . . . Why have you flown away? . . . Nothing here to harm you . . . I have a red ribbon for you . . . I'll clip your wings – I will . . .'

The five soldiers, off-scourings of a continuous campaign, stand silent and uncertain; they drift about each other; they linger, listening. One puts his finger to his lips.

Further off than the boy's cajoling of the dove, the notes come, they sift through the greenery, now loud, now soft, a few flute-scatterings. A song of peace – what those deserters dread to hear is the swart music of fife and drum, the mighty crashings of a search party through the undergrowth, closing in on them, drawing the cordon tight about them.

'I think,' said the first deserter, the merry reckless one, 'this is the place. Right here. We'll go no further. They'll never find us here.'

'We're not deserters, us,' said the second one. 'It was the army left us behind.'

Three of them laughed, but quietly; as if laughter too full-throated might trouble a column on the march, miles away, on the other side of a green hill: going urgently on, with measured clash, to relieve the besieged town. (But the laughter of one of them was a hollowness, more like a gasp.) One of them did not laugh at all.

'There's no better place to hide than a forest,' said the third deserter. 'We'll do well enough here till the war's over.'

'Look how thick the branches are,' said the fourth. 'They'll be thicker than ever, the leaves, in high summer.'

Boy – bird cry. Further off, the flute music, but now it seemed to come from another direction altogether; as if the forest had moved about them, about its own business of burgeoning, while they lingered and laid their lawless plans.

'They'll find us all right,' said the fifth deserter. 'They'll hang us from five trees.'

It must be said that this deserter-in-the-greenwood kept himself apart from the other four: as if, in a way, he had nothing to do with them; yet he dared not leave them and go, for a city youth like him could not know what danger lurked in the wood: some danger worse, perhaps, than his four companions.

The four deserters let on not to have heard the disturber of their peace; but the one whose face changed colour at every green shadow-dapple and fern-snap looked as grey and haggard as if the tree he stood under was indeed his gallows.

The boy summoned the hidden dove – 'This way. Come' – sweet and pure, but the dove kept silence in the green whispering clusters, content to be lost.

The laughter-loving one said, 'I've had my eye on this place ever since the war moved hereabouts. I live in that village between the forest and the hill. I know this place all right. "If they press-gang you," I said to myself, "run away, hide in the black heart of the forest."'

The one who kept his distance from the other four said angrily, 'The city's starving! Our own people. We were on our way to lift the siege. We do wrong to be here, surely.'

The four had had enough of this prophet of doom. They turned bitter faces on him; three bitter faces and one haunted one.

Flute song, behind them now. But in their panic and uncertainty they turned about each other, took a few steps and came back again, mixing and melling. They had lost all sense of direction.

The third deserter, the vicious one, said quietly to the reluctant deserter, 'You're a danger to us all with that kind of talk. Look – you got them all confused.'

(Perhaps there would have to be a throat-wound in the night.)

'Who is he, anyway?' said the fourth deserter. 'We don't know him. He wasn't in the plot we hatched in the hut after lights-out. How does he come to be here?'

'I don't want to be here,' said he who kept himself at a certain distance from the four. 'I woke up in my blanket. The column had marched off. It isn't my fault. I'd drunk too much in the mess the night before.'

At that the jovial one began to laugh. He threw back his head and yelled with mirth, as if it was the greatest joke since the world began. Two laughed also, but with less conviction. Even the frightened one gave a wan smile.

And when the peals of laughter died down at last, there was no dove-call, no flute music; only a fading sinister echo among hidden distant trees – hollow mockery.

The merry deserter wiped tears from his eyes. He pointed an unsteady finger at the red-coated youth who was a deserter on account of a hangover. 'Tell that to the tribunal,' he said. 'If we hang, mister, you hang too.'

A little sweat came on the coward's upper lip. The threatened one moved away a step or two from the other four. The face of the rogue was red with mirth, still.

'We'll lack for nothing here,' he said. 'I know this place. I know every tree in this greenwood. I know every leaf. We'll have a good time here, while the heroes are getting their legs shot off, yes, and the sabres are flashing and clashing at them. Everything we need is here. Rabbits and pigeons. Wood for fires. We can make a hut of wattles. We could have bee-hives. We could live here till we're old men.'

The hidden boy urged, 'Come down. I'm holding out my hand. See, bread, twenty broken pieces. White bread, cherries.'

'Who's that chanting?' said the gloomy one.

'The forester's boy,' said the laughing one. 'I know him. I've spoken to him. He'll bring us news now and then. I spoke to him and I gave him a penny.'

And at that moment a grey dove flew from the tree where it had furled and folded, lost in foliage, straight into the clearing. At sight of the five red coats it veered off again, wings whirring. It was the cowardly deserter that reached for it, more out of a nervous spasm than any skill, and twisted its neck, and laid it twitching on the ground.

'There's our supper,' said he, and looked with satisfaction at the heap of feathers; and looked for approval round the four faces; and looked suddenly appalled, as if he had foreshadowed his own death.

'Good for you, Bertie boy,' said the chief of the small band of outlaws. 'Only, it happens to be the boy's dove. At least, I think it is. And if it is, we'd better get out of the forest as fast as we can, because the boy isn't going to like us any more. We have to depend on that boy to help us. He's our life-line.'

'How can you tell one pigeon from another?' said the gloomy one. 'There's a thousand pigeons here if there's one. He can get another pigeon for his cage.'

The chief, the laughing one, shook his head.

They heard singing: first flute music, then a song, then more flute notes. It was a high cold treble, as if a winter voice was abroad under the branches. Was the boy singing? No: the notes were deeper and colder. They listened. A breath of winter moved under the spring branches.

The voice rose and fell, moving from tree to tree. Now a great oak smothered it; now it came rinsed through lattices of virgin leaves.

> 'In winter
> The world was white
> A white weave
> Wolf and crow and thorn in a white
> stillness.
>
> *The sword*
> *Went red through all.'*

Silence then.

'What about money? What about girls?' said the gloomy deserter.

'We must get rid of our uniforms,' said the coward who had killed the dove.

The red-faced one, the leader, said, 'No trouble. We'll visit the farms after dark. I know this countryside – this is my home ground. I know where the villas are, all the rich houses. It won't be the first house I've broken into, believe me.'

Then, through a bird silence, the five heard a whisper in the undergrowth, a fusillade of twigs snapping: now here, now there.

They froze with terror. Four of them went into a huddle. The fifth stood apart, vigilant, waiting.

The chief flung the terrified three from him. His face could be red with anger as well as with laughter. 'Don't be fools!' he chided. 'It's somebody by himself. A deer. Some gypsy. The boy.'

The fifth apart one said, 'Whatever it is, it's very light of foot.'

It was the singer. Her feet approached, with moss-whispers and twig-snappings. Now her voice came clear, unhindered by trunks and nests and foliage.

> 'In spring
> The world is green,
> A green web.
> Bird and leaf and boy in the green
> tremblings.
> *The sword*
> *Goes red through all.*'

The voice of the dove-seeker was closer too. 'Come back,' he called. 'You've gone the wrong way, lady! Help me find the dove. You promised.' The boy: hidden, watching, warning.

The girl came into the forest clearing again. She had wandered round in a circle. Her eyes widened when she saw the five soldiers. She made as if to step back, lose herself once more in the great green palace. Then she turned to face them. The deserters said nothing. They stood rooted like the trees themselves, all five faces turned on her: mask of lust, mask of fear, mask of mockery, mask of uncaring, mask of concern and pity. Five rooted trees, red, putting out five varieties of foliage and berry. Not a breath or a whisper from any of them. Three fingers stretched out to her.

'I'm sorry to disturb you,' said the girl. 'Are you the foresters? You have a good place to work in . . . Oh, no – you're soldiers, I see that now – the sun dazzled me . . . Your faces, how grey they are! What's the matter? You don't need to be frightened of *me*. The war won't touch you in a green place like this . . . Why don't you speak?'

The five red trees uprooted themselves, one after another. They came and stood around her, not too close.

'I'll go,' said the girl. 'I see I'm not welcome.'

Three stood closer about her.

Her fingers trembled as one hand wavered towards the money-bag at her waist.

The reluctant deserter took a larger step than the others; so that it was not a pure circle that girdled the girl: the one seemed to stand between her and the four.

The girl took out a coin: silver.

'If I give you this,' she said, 'will you let me go through? I have to be at the city with the guns pointed at it.'

Eight eyes were on the purse; six shifted to the lissom leaf-dappled body. Two honest eyes looked for a possible gate to open, to let innocence through.

The girl whispered, 'There's a dove lost. I'm helping that boy to find it. Will you help us find the dove, please?'

The first deserter said, 'The purse first.' And he put his hand on the wrist from which the purse depended; his knuckles were white.

The hand of the second deserter was at the collar of her coat, tugging it, testing it.

The girl said, 'You're hurting me. My wrist. Oh, please! You're tearing my coat!'

The hand-hold on the girl's wrist tightened till the money bag fell with a clank to the ground. There was a tearing of fabric, a fragile white collar-bone showed.

The jovial deserter laughed, 'Off with it, man! Gag her. We can't have yells.'

'I think,' said the fourth deserter, 'we'll lay her down there, among the roots.'

The girl struggled against eight hands. The money bag, kicked, clanked. She held tight to her flute. A shoulder shone to the sun. The girl covered her throat. Her hair was twisted into a rope and wrenched; her hands were pinioned behind her: she staggered forward like a young doe to the axe.

They were so worked up, they were making a botch of everything. There were too many hands, one pair of hands urgent against the six frantic half-mad hands; another pair of paralysed hands; so that they fumbled and clawed the air and fell away, with a few blood-drops and bits of fabric.

'You'll kill her!' cried the reluctant deserter. 'No.'

The girl broke through the ring. She turned; she ran to a little grove of six trees. She stood there, her flute at her mouth. A stir of morning rustled the tender leaves of the grove, whispered through the spread arms of the girl, her slack fingers, and they too were branches and leaves, and her body was a thin rooted trunk; there was a fresh scar in the bark where, before, had been a quick tearing of fabric.

The deserters fell against each other, a disordered grappling and twisting. But their prize, the first marvellous loot of their freedom, was no longer there, trapped in the raging centre.

Where was she? Where had she fled to? They flung their eyes everywhere.

There, right enough, was the heavy purse. There, under a green whispering tree, lay the ivory flute.

They ventured, three of them, a little way into the forest, along a track. She could not have gone far. She had been so terrified her flight would be like the frantic flutterings of a broken-winged bird.

But one of the deserters, the frightened one, stood between the treasure and the twitching dove: either to guard the hoard or if they were a long time getting back with the girl, to make off with it himself in the opposite direction.

The reluctant deserter lingered at the edge of the clearing, keeping his eye on the three, keeping his eye on the grey-faced guardian of the gold.

The girl was the seventh tree in a grove of six trees.

The lost neck-wrung dove: it twitched, it stirred in the dust. It opened its wings, closed them, opened them again. It opened emerald eyes to the sun. It flew and whirred up brokenly into a branch of the girl-tree.

'That bird was dead,' said he who walked around the money-bag, between loyalty and greed and terror. 'I'm sure I killed it.'

'We couldn't make a good job of killing a pigeon,' said the reluctant deserter. 'And here we were going to live happy for fifty years. But the colonel, he'll make a good job of us, never fear. No flying away once the rope's round your neck and they kick away the ladder.'

The three girl-hunters had come back, empty-handed. They heard the words of the man who was one with them and yet was apart from them. Could such a one be trusted? The greed and lust in them had changed to rage. It was this reluctant deserter who had ruined everything. The girl would have been theirs if he had not come between them and her. This one, his words had served only to put a doom on them. Well, then, now that the hussy was out of their power, it might not be a bad thing to despatch the traitor in their midst. He was strong, but there were four of them – or three, not counting the coward.

There would be a grave in the forest before sunset.

'No good,' said the reluctant deserter. 'Everything fails. We're finished.'

'*You're* finished, man,' said the jovial leader of the gang.

At that, there was an almighty crashing and multitudinous crackings in the forest, broken branches everywhere, a frenzy of thuddings and thrustings in all directions; a converging.

And the boy's voice, 'Soldiers! A search party. They're everywhere. They have ropes and guns! Good – I'm glad. This way, sergeant. They've just killed a girl.'

The deserters scattered in all directions. They were up and away with such speed, every man for himself, that they even forgot the money-bag. They made, orb-eyed, for the thickest greenery. Even the innocent deserter, he who had lain in his sleeping-bag too long and had not heard the summons of drum and fife, even he was swallowed up in dense green shadows; for not even an innocent young man wants a shameful rope-death.

The girl was a tree; the turtle crooned, half-throated, on a branch of her.

There was more snapping and cracking, but small random sylvan sounds, one pair of feet, not the dense surgings of a search-party.

The boy that we have heard and not seen was suddenly there, looking in all directions, shading his quick dark eyes against the sun, quicksilvering glances here, there, everywhere.

In the grove of seven trees one of the trees turned into a girl with a torn coat and a ragged red wound between throat and shoulder.

'There you are,' said the boy. 'I told you, I kept telling you, it's dangerous in the forest in spring. It's been doubly dangerous since that gang of soldiers came a week ago. Well, I think they've caught my dove. They've eaten it. It's in their bellies.'

'It's here, in my hand,' said the girl. And she put the grey furled bird into the wild hands of the boy; and he laughed, holding the hoarse-throated pigeon to his wet face.

Far off, five distracted forest-goings, broken twigs, agitation of birds and squirrels and adders.

'This is my green house, the forest,' said the boy. 'Who wants rats in his green house? That's what they were, five ravenous rats. There's no search party. I can play on this forest like a harp.'

'I'm going to leave you too,' said the girl.

'Not yet,' said the boy. 'Listen. This forest is a green palace. Let's pretend. You'll be the princess. Stay for a month. The cowards won't come back. There'll be just you and me and the dove. And a few squirrels. And there's a cat at my father's door. He's the forester.'

'I'll stay,' said the girl. 'I'll stitch my coat. I'll finish my song. Then I must go.'

The boy was wrong. One of the cowards was suddenly there, he who had indulged too much in the grape and the poppies of sleep, and had not heard the summoning fife.

The forest boy came between the reluctant deserter and the girl. 'The search party,' he whispered. 'They're here. They're eating their pies, just now, over there. Then they'll have you.'

The deserter said, 'I'm sorry, girl. I didn't want to harm you.'

'They'll hang you high, mister,' said the boy.

'Where are they?' said the deserter. 'Where's the search party? Tell me. I want to give myself up.'

The forest held its breath. Then a blackbird sang.

The girl said, 'There are no searchers. Only the boy and myself. We were looking for a lost bird.'

'Listen to that blackbird!' shouted the boy. 'Just listen!'

'Sweet green lies in the air,' said the girl.

'If I hurry,' said the deserter, and cradled the dove in his hands. 'I mightn't be missed. I *might* get to the city and the siege. I've always been a good soldier up to now. They know that. They haven't a black mark against me in their book. I'll explain everything. But I must hurry.'

'Go anywhere you like,' said the girl. 'Save the city. Knock the city down. Yes, go. The war's waiting for you. Be a hero. Go on to the fires. See how many you can kill.'

The young soldier gave her a hurt look; he set down the dove beside the money bag and the flute. His strong red back was soon lost in multitudinous green shadows, that flowed and whispered and eddied over him like sea-depths.

'Stay with me,' said the boy. 'Stay as long as you like. This bird, it loves you.' (The bird had flown on to her finger.)

The girl said, 'I have to be where the Dragon is.'

The blackbird sang and sang. His throat swelled with rapturous intimation of roses and honeycombs and harvest stooks.

> Summer!
> Blue and yellow
> Are caught in the shuttle.
> They're cast from the loom of the sun,
> cornstalk and fish.
> *The sword*
> *Unfolds, a rose.*

Where did it come from, the verse? bird or girl? The girl had picked up her flute but she wasn't playing it.

The dove had flown back to the forest. And the boy was after it, helter-skelter, scolding, coaxing.

There was a drum-beat at the forest's edge.

VII

The Smithy

Early summer, in a fair region of farms large and small, with here and there a little market village, and fields green with the first shoots of corn.

A region of gentle hills, well-watered by streams and springs.

The wind comes warm in early summer, and sets the hills murmuring, with the different whispers of pasture and tilth.

Here, in such a landscape, is the very heart of peace and plenitude. Pastoral slopes, a shepherd boy under the tree with his pipe; the milking-girl crossing the field from the cows to churn and cheese-press, a wooden bucket of milk in each hand (white heavy brimming circles) and the beasts languid and herb-smelling after the sweet burdens have been drawn from their udders; they lie about the field, white cows and dappled cows, gently shifting their jaws on the cud.

The farmer stands at the end of his steading. He licks his finger and holds it above his head. Will the wind blow soon from the west, bringing rain from the distant Atlantic? There has been no shower of rain for a full week, and the earth is dry, dust puffs from his feet as he walks back to his open door; inside his good tobacco pipe is waiting to be filled and lit, and his mug to be filled to brimming with cider. That the rain should come tonight, when all the household is asleep, when all the farms and villages are wrapped in the warm darkness of early summer! . . . Upstairs, in the loft, his children are teasing each other and telling stories in their beds. Little do they care whether it rains or shines, life is so full of laughter and joy for them, with (it's true) an occasional tempest of rage or tears . . . The goodwife of the farm throws another log on the fire; it will be cold once the sun goes down. A very ancient voice creaks from the corner, 'Rain? It will come to rain, and that before long. I feel the ache of the rain in every joint of me.' Old wisdom out of the cluster of gathering shadows.

And the horses: in such a favoured place they should be going like the wind through the meadows, heads high and manes flung, hooves drumming on the hard ground. Until, from a group of young men, a youth leaps down from the stone wall that encloses the herd of young horses, and with another two leaps seizes the rampant mane and is on the horse's back, shouting and waving high his free hand. The young men applaud his skill and daring. Only the horse is outraged; his eyes orb and flash, he flings his head down like a wave and up again like the crest of a wind-spurred wave – and he is off, now thundering round the meadow twice as fast as the other beasts, but whether in joy or rage who shall say? He stalls, stops, flings up his rear hooves till the rider is almost flung – almost, but not quite, for the mane is wound in both his tight fists, and he rides out the tempest. The horse stops, quivering. The young men shout and applaud. But it is to a girl at the far end of the meadow that the young horse-conqueror raises his hand. And she looks away. Round and round still go the milder horses, all but he who must concur soon in the ancient bond between man and horse – some day, at harvest perhaps, he will be willing to serve, he will bring the sheaves into the barn. He is not broken, not yet; there will be one or two mad plungings and rearings before he is broken. But broken: that is not the word to use. This recent meadow-tempest was but a ritual horse and man have to pass through to reach their peace. The young man pats the trembling animal; but when, dismounted, he turns again to wave to the girl, she is not there, she is gone.

Who the girl was, the boy could not tell; she was too far away, her features were not familiar. A gypsy, possibly; there had been a glimmer of rags about her elbow . . .

The young men drop down from the wall, one after the other. They and the champion among them – the breaker of horses, the hailer of wandering girls – all set out on the road to the village, to the ale house. They will sit at the table of the young men till lamp-lighting time, while the old men sit apart at their own tables, uttering now and again things out of the past – the far lovelier girls that had been in those days, the harvests so bounteous the barns were full to bursting, the crow-killing cataract-stilling snows of yesteryear. Tugging at their little sparse beards, sucking clay pipes and spitting. One, with a wooden leg, speaks of the campaign, the general, the last battle of the war, the great iron ball that struck him on the knee.

'Liars!' laugh the young men at their table, their faces flushed with beer and sunset. The innkeeper's daughter comes among them with a tray of foaming mugs; to her they make protestations, appeals, finger-kissings, mock grief at her heartlessness; she comes and goes again disdainfully, as though they were tramps, and ill-favoured ones at that. (*Yokels! – who do they think they are?*)

Ah, happy rich countryside, where such things happen with a sure and sweet monotony, year after circling year. Only six weeks ago lambs were being born in the last blizzard of winter. Six weeks on, and the scythe-men will be spitting on their hands, and sharpening their curving blades on a stone, and making first steps, swinging and circling and flaming into the first broken gold of harvest.

So the life of this blessed countryside goes on, year after year, childhood to grey hairs. (There was that one half-forgotten war, that merely brushed the region, and left a pinleg behind.)

But this good night of early summer, in the inn-yard, with the songs, and pipe-smoke and the blowing of ale-froth: a young man here and there at the inn-yard tables, in a thoughtful moment, does not know if it will ever return to them. Who can say where they might be this night next year? Life is uncertain, that is about the only wisdom they have learnt as yet. The tomb-stone with its carved skull and hour-glass and spade waits for all men born, sooner or later. Meantime, for this one certain night, the flowing ale-cups, the songs, the amorous dallying with the innkeeper's daughter and the three barmaids, two blond and braided, one with the torrent of blown black hair that she has to keep pushing away from her lovely face.

Over the hill to the east the full moon rises. For a minute there is no sound in the inn-yard, not even from the two old men who remember the burning of the witch ninety years ago. The moon enchantment has taken hold of them all.

An owl hoots from the belfry. A young man – the handsome tamer of horses – feels a cold kiss on the back of his hand. Rain? – the gentle first clustering of the dew, rather. (But dew is not enough: the rain-wind from the hidden ocean hundreds of miles to the west must blow soon. It will rain – of course it will rain. But even that boy, the horseman, remembers the summer of no rain, and how the corn rose barely six inches above the scorched glebe, and the streams and the wells shrank, and the roan horse died at the hot rock; bitter the winter that followed that year of drought; hungry and thin and fever-ridden, so that only the strongest survived. To the field round the church they brought in the first frosts many an old man, many a withered child.)

The moon, the splendid full-globed summer moon, has risen clear of the hill now.

'I know the colour of that moon,' says an old farmer. 'It's a rain moon. There'll be rain before morning, buckets of it.'

'More ale!' cry the young men, and ring coins on the table top. 'Bring six more mugs of ale! Oh, you sweetheart with the honey-coloured hair, why don't you hurry up with the ale! We mightn't be here next year.'

It is she of the black blown hair who comes to the table of the young men to collect their empty mugs, dimples at her elbows and cheeks, dodging like an African butterfly their delicate finger-beckonings and their dove-cooings and one brazen hip-girdling.

And then into the inn-yard rides a stranger, a soldier in black uniform with cocked hat, sword, and black leather gleaming boots. He dismounts lithely from his mare, whose hooves still make a scattered cloppering on the cobbles.

'You,' he says to the landlord's daughter, 'get the innkeeper. I need to see him at once. It is a matter of urgency. What's that? – He's setting up a new barrel of ale. Never mind that. I'll see him now. I'll go in. I'll speak to him at his fire!'

The three barmaids – two blond and one dark as Egypt – stand looking at him, their hands up at their half-open mouths. Never have they beheld a man so handsome and so richly accoutred. The full moon that night put magic into every sight and sound.

'You,' says the soldier to the young man who had shown his horse-prowess earlier in the day, 'see to this horse of mine. Put him in the stable. See he gets the best of fodder.'

The soldier, stooping, enters the inn.

The door of the inn has a horse-shoe nailed to the centre of it: sign of peace and good-fortune.

But, when the young man goes to take the rein, the war horse rears from him in such a surge of rage that the boy is flung his length on the cobbles.

'Oh yes,' says the old man with the pin-leg. 'It looks like it. That time's come again. Rain or shine or snow – it's all the same to soldiers. It looks like the emperor's making a requisition.'

It was high summer, a month later, when the girl returned that way with her musical instrument and her money bag.

At a turn in the road, seeing again the deep well-watered valley with its farms and churches and little market villages here and there, it seemed still a rich fair region, at peace under the ripening sun.

At peace? It was too much at peace. For nothing moved: there were neither sheep nor cows nor people to be seen. Perhaps all the living had hidden themselves away in the shade for an afternoon siesta. The tall green corn would go on growing; even at night, under the stars, it grew, drenched and flattened a little by heavy night rains; but in the first sun of morning, nourished and refreshed again, it rustled and yearned through fifty more suns towards the consummation of harvest.

The girl saw promising crops in every wide green field; but the corn folk themselves were not to be seen, nor the shepherds nor cow-herds nor horsemen nor children either. Not a dog barked, near or far. Not a cock saluted the afternoon.

A single hawk paced round the sun, and paused over a sheep-fold, high hung, watching. It came and stood black against the door of the sun, aloof, lingering; it paused upon an imminent earth plummet.

It was then the girl saw that the church in the nearest village had a broken roof, and a wisp of grey smoke drifted on the butterfly tremblings of the wind. Bees and butterflies, and the hawk hung high: these were the only living creatures to be seen.

What careless altar boy had knocked over a candle?

The sight of the hawk and the fire put urgency and eagerness into the girl's going. She was not in search of country idylls.

The wind, as she turned on the turning road, brought the blue maggot-flies about her in a cloud. Then a pungent penetrating stench, like from a shambles or a primitive fire-feast where guts are roasted and eaten.

A sheep in a field: heap of bones and dirty wool.

The village was shuttered and barred. Did eyes peer at her through chinks? – She had a vivid sense of eyes watching.

The church was entirely burnt out. It gave out heat into the warm summer wind like a bakehouse; and a scorched timber, fallen among statues and candlesticks, smouldered still.

She stood for a long time inside the church. The bell had fallen through the belfry and lay beside the font, which had a finger-depth of smoky water in it. She touched the bell; her finger stung and recoiled from the heat of it.

She was on the right road after all; having thought for a week that she had lost the spore of the Dragon. The soldiers had been this way, cavalry and musketeers and gunners, only the day before yesterday. The flags and the fifes and drums had passed through, in marching order, and the standards; and the army had eaten up the countryside in its onset. The soldiers had been billeted a night or two in the barns. They had roasted oxen and swine in the open fields: bones and burnt stones lay here and there.

The inn was not shuttered; it was empty and open. The girl stood in the door; there were breached barrels, wrenched cupboards, broken bottles. The door with the horseshoe on it hung from one hinge. But the kind host and his servants and all his country customers old and young had gone on the summer wind. Where?

The soldiers had feasted themselves heartily in the inn: the officers. The common infantrymen and gunners had been allowed free range and licence in the farms around.

Turning from the door of the inn, the girl saw that the inn-yard was not deserted after all. The landscape had one figure, an old man who sat at a wooden table with his wooden leg splayed out on a chair. Was he asleep? Was he dead? The girl, going closer, saw that he was in a drunken stupor. A half-empty wine flagon stood on the round table. This one old man, out of all the village, had come through the storm. It had passed him by, unscathed. It left him sprawled there with a flagon of good red wine. It had given him the oblivion of grapes.

But surely, once the Dragon had passed through, on its way to the siege twenty miles away, the villagers would have returned to their houses, to salvage and to salve and to patch . . .

It had been an onset so terrible that the villagers were still hiding in the hills. What could they know? – It was more than likely that another division, more columns and hooves and drums, would pass through. Some cities took a long time, a winter of eating rats and moss and spiders, to surrender. It was more than likely that another army would come to lend support and new strength to the besiegers . . . Between times, it might be just possible for them, in early August, to quickly cut the wheat fields. Therefore a shepherd waited and watched from a coign in the hills, under the morning and the evening star, to let them know how it went with the farms and the fields.

And then the girl, leaving the village, walked between more wide fields, and she saw that no harvest would be reaped there that summer. The hawk-neighboured sun was pouring out his benisons in vain. For the road had been too narrow for so many columns; the cavalry had gone by way of the cornfields, and in their clamorous going the horses, thousands of them, had beaten the midsummer corn to a vast green pulp. Everywhere she looked, near and far, the people's winter bread was one vast mush and tramplage, crushed sodden greenery, except for a cornstalk here and there that nodded and danced still in the buttercup-gentle and maggot-humming wind, and made a lonely bread sign under the sun.

Well, the field mice would do well out of the wreckage, once the single green stalk in every thousand had drooped its head with the crowned heaviness of gold.

Stench of guts and scorching everywhere now: the blackened remnants of field fires where the beasts had been turned and roasted, raining back their rich fat into the flames. Who shall blame the soldiers? – their bellies were hollow often enough – their ribs might be showing by the time the great city twenty miles on had opened its gates to them.

Even the farm horses had been butchered and eaten. Had wolves come down from the mountains at night? Not even the hawk and his hundred fellow circlers could have picked so clean the skeletons of the horses in the meadow. One skull was beautiful beyond all the others; it had belonged, the girl supposed, to a young burnished stallion, a wind drinker, a proud hoof-whirler. While the girl watched, a butterfly emerged from the horse's skull and drifted out and off.

The girl turned a corner. There, in a ditch, touching the petals of a marigold, a child sat. The child did not lift her head as the girl approached; she was intent on the flower, she inspected with great concentration each separate petal. The girl came nearer. The child put the flower to her chin, an inch under it, and the yellow shadow lit the little cleft between underlip and throat. She turned the flower round, till the bead of dew among the petals set a tiny prism wavering on her chin. Then she looked up at the wayfarer. 'Tell me,' she said, 'do I like butter?'

'Whether you like butter,' said the girl, 'and I see you do like it, thick on bread as the bread itself, you won't be eating butter, no nor bread either, for a many a day. The soldiers have seen to your butter and bread.'

'Oh, them!' cried the child. 'I never saw anything so exciting as that army marching through. I thought it would never end. The horses and the drums! And the flags fluttering in the wind! The whole valley, it shook with the beautiful marching that went on and on. Why did she gather me up in her arms, my mother, and run and run with me into the hills? I was so wild with her I yelled, yes I did, and I scratched her face. And I saw that all the stupid red-faced farmers and their wives were making for the hills too, driving a sheep or a cow. And old Mada had her white hen under her shawl. My father was in front of us, he had a box on his shoulder and he was driving our two pigs up the hillside. You see that little farm over there, that's my father's farm. He had twelve pigs but he only took two with him. The noise of the trumpets and the marching got fainter. I fell asleep on my mother's shoulder. It was all like a beautiful dream. This morning, when the men were all whispering together in the cave up there, and the women were gathering sticks to make a fire, well, I ran back home when they weren't looking, and here I am. This flower is a very truthful flower. I like butter well enough.'

'Go back to the cave,' said the girl. 'There'll be more soldiers coming.'

'I hope so,' said the child, and threw the marigold into the ditch. 'Oh, if more soldiers come, I'll sit here and watch them passing, mile after mile of soldiers and trumpets and horses! Where are you going? I don't know you. You don't belong to this valley, nor the next valley either.'

'I'm going to kill the Dragon,' said the girl.

'A dragon!' cried the child. 'The world's a fine place, right enough – dragons and soldiers. They're all in my picture book. Can I come with you?'

'No,' said the girl. 'No, you can't come. But it does my heart good to see you sitting here among the fields. Stay among the fields for ever. This is the happiest place, believe me.'

'Goodbye, princess,' said the child. 'I'll go back now. My mother, she'll be wondering about me. She'll give me a wallop when I get back. But I'll go all the same. Goodbye' . . .

The girl passed on through the scorched and broken land. She came to the crest of the road and saw, below her, a little hamlet, and from that church too smoke drifted and spun and teased itself out on the summer wind. More than smoke, a small flame shook out from a broken window of the church. The torches had been thrust into this church more recently; the day before, perhaps; the fire was not yet out.

Then a frightful sound beat about her head, a great clangour and outcry of metal on metal, as if the bell of the ruined church had come to life of itself, and was making a mad irregular music. Peal and clang and metallic stammer – the girl's flesh winced from the terrible din!

Another fire, on the outskirts of the hamlet, a blown roaring red caged beast of a fire! It was from this place that the insane clangour was coming. She recognised it, of course, it was a blacksmith's yard.

And there stood the creator of all that din, between forge and anvil, the blacksmith, rooted and strenuous: a little stout man with his face sweat-bedewed. It was no easy matter, living between the fire in the sky and the forge-fire. Often he had to set down his hammer and take his hairy forearm to his silvered brow. Then he addressed himself once more to his task.

You might have thought the sudden appearance of a girl in his yard would give him pause for a second or two. If a butterfly had floated in, even that (you might think) would be a small refreshment to his fire-red eyes and his iron-brimming ear. He seemed not to be aware of her presence, there was so much to be done, and so urgently.

Then there was a splashing and a clattering at a corner of the smithy, and into the yard came a tall gaunt woman bowed slightly under a two-bucket yoke of water, that splurged out a dollop with every step she took.

She saw the girl all right. She set down the two buckets and stared at the girl, unwelcoming.

And the black music went on and on, as a glowing lump of iron was hammered into a roughly spherical shape on the anvil.

The iron spheres were everywhere: about the size of a child's head. They were strewn all about the anvil, they were piled in a rough pyramid in a corner of the yard. But such spheres as no good tradesmen would, out of self-respect, have put the seal of his approval on. They were lopsided, some of them, or ragged, or rocky; artefacts as strange and ugly as had ever issued from forge and anvil. What would any villager, or farmer, or lord, be wanting with those ugly things?

The blacksmith's wife could not be done staring at the girl. What trollop was this, come to tempt her husband maybe?

But the blacksmith was good and faithful. He was paying not the least attention to the slut. Instead he put down his hammer and moved into the shade where a wine-jar was standing. He lifted the jar, he tilted his head, and his powerful throat worked strenuously on the cool lessening ellipse of wine.

In the silence between two pieces of black music, the black-smith's wife decided that the girl was no discarded soldiers' slut, though she was dirty enough in all conscience, in a gown that once at time's beginning might have been white but was now more like old ivory and old snow. Was that, at the shoulder, a splash of old blood? Coarse farm wine, more like.

Yes, she must be a farmer's daughter, or servant; and if so she must come from one of the more distant farms, one that the wheel of war had not gone over – and that would explain too why the girl's face was strange to the long gaunt cold-eyed one.

The smith came back, his arms laden with rust and iron screechings. He stuffed old scraps of iron into his forge and blew up the fire with his bellows till it was as white as a star, and sang like a crazy star; and he withdrew the burning rubbish of metal from its heart and laid it on his anvil; and down came his hammer like the clang of a bell in a drunken belfry, and a thousand little red bees flew up and away from the assault of cold metal on red-hot metal.

It was between bouts of clanging of the immense black bell that the blacksmith's wife spoke to the girl.

'What do you want, eh? . . . What farm, eh? . . . Your father's plough, eh – is that what you've come about? . . . The plough'll have to wait till the war's over. Heinz here, he has more important things to do – war work. He gets well paid, more than ever the farmers pay for their ploughs and horse-shoes, I can tell you that . . . What's that you say? – I can't hear for the din. What's he making, what is Heinz making? Aha, you never saw things like that before, eh. You and your country innocence . . . Cannon-balls. That's what Heinz is making . . . Stop a minute, Heinz, till I speak. The man hears nothing, he's that possessed with his work . . . Well, never mind. The ordnance officer was here on Friday. "Stop all other work," said he. "Stop everything. The city walls are strong," he said. "The general is running short of cannon-balls. I hear you're a good blacksmith," said he. "Heavy iron cannon balls, fifty pounders. Make as many as you can. A florin for every cannon ball you turn out," said he. "The prince will see that you are personally honoured for the making of cannon balls when the war's over. Blacksmith, you will have a silver star pinned to your breast by the prince."

'So that's what Heinz is at. He's hardly slept since Friday . . . Look at that heap of cannon balls there in the corner of the yard . . . Did you ever see anything so fearful? What stone walls would ever stand up to cannon balls like them? . . .

'What's that you say? Speak louder. Heinz, stop that row for half-a-minute. "What is it all about?" – is that what you said? Fat Luther and the fat Pope, they're not getting on with each other, that's what it's all about as far as I can gather . . . What do we know, eh, about important affairs like that? . . .

'Come back when the city surrenders. And may that be many a long day . . . Heinz and me, we'll have horses and a carriage, yes and servants, by the time fat Luther and the Pope give each other the kiss of peace . . .

'We'll be a bit deaf, maybe, with the din. But we'll be rich . . .

'Heinz, he hardly eats or sleeps. Just a jug of wine and a leek now and then, then it's back with him to his black work . . . I'm feared he'll kill himself . . . We haven't been paid a penny yet – just notes signed by the ordnance colonel – to be redeemed once the city's taken and the war's over . . .'

The blacksmith had beaten the mass of iron into a shape roughly resembling a sphere. He took the thing in his tongs and plunged it into a bucket of cold water. It hissed like a snake, it gave off little whorls and shreds of steam. Then he tossed the squint cannon ball among the strewment of other crazy cannon balls in the yard. They bore a rough and ready resemblance to each other, no more.

The mountain dwarves would not have used them for their game of bowls.

The blacksmith went, grunting and sweating, to a rusty little hill of scrap, and threw another armful into the forge's glower. He drove the bellows up and down. The fire in the forge roared like a little dragon.

Perhaps the blacksmith was dumb. Perhaps he was keeping his breath for his immense labour. He pointed to his wife, he pointed to the empty wine jar. He gave her a swart look. She was to replenish the jar at once.

Then he noticed the girl. He put his fat fingers to his mouth and blew her a kiss. He gave her a sooty wink.

The gaunt wife who was soon to be a lady hoisted the jar on to her shoulder.

'Tell your dad,' she said to the girl, 'there'll be a time for horse-shoes. When the war's over, eh?'

The fire beat and sang like the white-hot heart of a star.

'If I was you, girl, whoever you are, I would go back to the hidden farm quick as I could . . . I wouldn't go that way, if I was you. That's where the guns and the soldiers are. That's the road to the siege and the city.'

The blacksmith aimed a powerful kick at his wife. She talked too much. He was thirsty. The fire in the sky was killing him. The wife departed for another jar of wine.

The girl was out and away on the road.

As she went, she smelt a tiny singeing. A live coal had jumped out of the forge and clung like a bee to a fringe of her gown. She let it burn itself out.

'Heinz,' said the bearer of water and wine, 'I looked in the drawer just now, when I was in getting the wine. Do you know how many ordnance chits we have now? – ten . . . That's good, eh? That's fifty crowns if it's a penny' . . .

Her words were lost in another powerful assault of metal upon metal. The black song was never-ending, it seemed. But even that music had to have its pauses. In a brief blessed spell of silence in the yard, it came to them on the wind, growing fainter: the flute song.

VIII

The Taken Town

The city had fallen. The wall of the city had been breached a month before and the soldiers of the besieging army had poured in like ants into a wounded gazelle.

Many of the troops guarding the city had been wounded in the course of the six-month siege, which had spanned a harvest and a seed-time, and most of them had died of their wounds, for the city physicians had long run out of salves and herbs and proper bandagings. Many of the soldiers had eaten rats and insects before they had grown hollow-cheeked and died. Many more had been taken prisoner and led away to quarry or factory, long lines of them linked by ropes, urged on by bayonets. Many, of course, had been blown to pieces by the besieging cannon. A few of the younger soldiers – hardly more than boys – had gone mad and had had to be shot by their own comrades so that total hysteria and despair might not engulf all the defenders. A few who were there against their will, country boys mostly, the conscripted sons of shepherds and beekeepers, ploughmen and foresters, had slipped out of the city and through the files of the besiegers by night, and turned their faces homeward; for in the country one gets to know the subtle ways of hunter and hunted. Some of these deserters were caught, of course. If they were caught by the defenders, they were summarily shot. If they were caught in the net of the besiegers, they were taken to be spies and either shot or hanged after a brief cold interrogation.

If the soldiers had to eat rats and insects to keep up their strength, what did the citizens eat, those who had no fighting to endure, and only waited? (It's true, sometimes a cannon ball lifted over the city wall and smashed a house front or the façade of a shop, and then the citizens could be seen briefly in their beds or in their baths; a housewife with a half-raised broom; a poet writing words at a table through all the tumult and ruining; a child with a doll.) Somehow or other most of the citizens managed to avoid death by starvation. No one was exactly big-bellied or apple-cheeked after the first snow of winter. A few old ones withered and died, but even at the best they could only have expected to live a year or two more. A few children got big-bellied (but not from gluttony) and stick-limbed before they died; but then the wise ones said they were well quit of the world and its woes. 'Better to draw but a few breaths under the sun, then turn into the kindly House of Darkness' . . .

Somehow or other they endured that terrible winter. In a certain quarter of the city, so secret that only a few trusted ones knew about it, there lived behind locked doors certain men. These men had sacks of flour in their attics, mounds of apples and potatoes, delicate structures of eggs, bunches of rabbits hanging by their hind legs from nails at the wall, even boxes of fish (that stank a little, it's true) and barrels of red wine and white wine.

A citizen, seeing his hungry children and his wife with no fire in her, would put a silver candlestick under his coat, a family heirloom, something handed down from his great-great-grand-father perhaps; and he would go out under the first shadows and stars, and speak to a certain little furtive man who was often to be seen under the marble Statue of

Peace in the municipal gardens. The citizen would give the candlestick to this hardly-more-than-shadow. The shadow would whisper and slip away into the deeper shadows. And would return, maybe an hour later and maybe a day later, with a little linen bag containing (it might be) an egg, and a paper screw of sugar, and a half a loaf and a half-bottle of wine. Then the citizen would hurry home before curfew time: to be found wandering the street after that bell had struck meant at the very least arrest and a night in the guardhouse – at worst, depending on the interrogating lieutenant, a rendezvous at dawn with a line of raised muskets.

The shifty little man whose permanent station was by the statue of Pax in the municipal garden – he was the busiest man in the city at that evil time, apart from the half-dozen physicians and the half-dozen masons who had been rounded up to repair minor cannon breaches in the wall, a hazardous trade.

So the richer houses of the city were gradually despoiled of their paintings, tapestries, jewellery, gold and silver articles; so that the people in the richer houses could live for another day, or another week.

But the multitudinous poor of the city, who had no heirlooms and no box of gold buried in the garden: how did they contrive to live? Nine out of ten of them managed, somehow; they clung with determination to life, to the basest kind of existence, 'by their fingernails' as the saying goes. They could not, they did not, trouble the doors of the black marketeers, they didn't have the secret channel of communication, for a start. For the poor of the city, the little shadowy man under the statue (whose arms were full of sheaves and grapes, and who had a marble dove on her shoulder): to the poor this creature was almost as permanent and meaningless as the statue itself. He was one of the city 'characters' – he smiled, and came and went – they never gave him a thought.

But the poor must have scratched nourishment from *somewhere*. The poor have their own secrets, their own devices. The road between burgesses and black marketeer was barred to them. But it was as if they came closer somehow to the very roots of life, and drew hard invisible nourishment from it. Ancestral images quickened them, ten thousand harvests were in their thin blood, a hundred plagues and famines and wars had toughened their flesh. At the end of every evil time, after bitterest anguish and suffering, their country ancestors had opened hollow eyes and seen the golden cornstalk. That image, renewing itself year by year across dynasties and conquests and civilizations, was more potent by far than the vacuous white statue in the municipal garden. The shadow of the cornstalk fell across their days, even in winter, even in this time of war and disease and hunger.

The poor endured: even though it seemed they had only the dew and the wind to nourish them.

Some of the sons of the city labourers and sweepers took to crime, as always happens in such circumstances. They operated in gangs, by night; not a few magistrates and merchants had their valuables spirited away before they could bring them to the shadowy statue-haunter . . . Some of the young thieves were caught and despatched according to law before they entered upon even worse ways. What could those young thieves do with the ormolu clocks and the little exquisitely-painted miniatures in golden lockets? – I think they took them because the whole city was in flux, social structures were breaking down, excitements hitherto forbidden were in the air – was not one civilized nation battering at the gates of a neighbouring principality? Chaos was squandering the world's goods and gear everywhere, indiscriminately, and they would be fools not to gather up the pieces.

The secret food stores of the rich those gangs could not get near, for they (the half-mouldering loaves and the stinking turnips) were hidden away, and double-locked, far more securely than the jewels.

Those young laughing criminals of the city: in the last month of the siege they had to be very careful, because the military commandant issued a proclamation that all young able-bodied citizens of the male sex were to be put into uniform and given short sharp instruction on how to throw down enemy ladders set against the city wall, and hot burning tar, and great stones. (There were, now, not sufficient muskets for the new recruits.) When the time came, they would have to go with their teeth and nails at the throats of the invaders.

The very poor went on existing under the sign of the corn-stalk.

Now the first signs of plague were in the city. In a certain tall tenement in the lower city a tradesman – he was a cartwright – began to shiver, then he sneezed uncontrollably, then the 'roses' of disease came here and there upon his body. His wife nursed him, but he died on the third day. Then an old man (he had been a teacher of music in the conservatoire) cried out one night in the same tenement, so loud that a dog woke and a soldier on the street below beat a warning on the door with his musket butt; and when the cartwright's wife, the stains of sorrow still on her face, went in to him, his body too had become a garden of deadly roses. Then a child three stairs below . . .

Dogs and cats – now that I think of it, that winter there was hardly a dog or a cat to be seen in that city which, like most cities, had its tumults of cats and dogs. I think the poor must have devoured the dogs and the cats, and afterwards the rats that went in rivers and torrents through the ghettos and sewers.

I have read that, in the last week or so of the siege, the black marketeers had little bunches of rats hanging in their stores instead of rabbits; and the bread had become very black and very precious indeed. (One carved ivory cameo, one potato.)

Then, too, the street where the plague tenement was became a raging rose-garden. The roses ran in a riot through the neighbouring alleys and wynds, vennels and closes.

The first snow fell. The great guns were brought up a hundred yards from the city wall. The guns spoke. The wall was breached. The general in command of the city garrison ordered a white flag to be run up at the tallest battlement. A trumpet was blown from the headquarters of the besieging general. It was answered by a trumpet from the city wall. The defeated general appeared at the breach, in his full uniform, a figure of great heroism and splendour. He carried a ceremonial sword across his hands. He was cautiously let down by three of his staff, so as not to soil his ceremonial dress. He was courteously received outside the city wall by three staff-officers of the enemy. He was conducted to the headquarters tent. There stood the victorious general. The defeated general approached; he saluted and bowed; he proffered his sword, which was accepted and at once given back to him. The necks of the two generals crossed, twice, this way then that.

A paper was brought out and set, with inkwell and quills, on a small table. Two chairs were brought. The grey general signed. The blue general signed. Then the blue general, magnanimous in victory, put his arm about the shoulder of the grey general and led him into his tent, no doubt to pour wine down their throats – that is, upon the wound that had, so unfortunately, had to be given and taken for half a year. It was a symbolical libation.

Then the defeated army – what remained of it – marched out as brave and honourable prisoners-of-war.

An hour later the advance troops of the blue general entered the city.

It was deserted. Every citizen had vanished; seemingly they had locked themselves in their houses.

In the lower part of the city a whole street was burning; this was the area where the plague had first broken out.

The troops marched in, with flags and trumpets: an incessant afternoon-long pulse of marching feet.

At five o'clock in the afternoon the victorious general entered on his grey horse.

Ah, there were some townspeople, at last! A little group of them – the mayor, the city medical officer, the city engineer, the city banker, the chancellor of the university – stood in a frail little line outside the great door of the City Hall, on the highest step.

The general turned his horse.

The mayor, wearing his chain of office, slowly descended the twelve steps. He said, in a clear calm voice, 'On behalf of the citizens, I the mayor surrender the city.'

The general smiled. He raised his hand in a courteous salute.

But where were the citizens, rich and poor? Surely they must have known the reputation of this general for clemency and mercy. In other towns he had taken – this was well known all over Europe – the first thing he had done was to order in from the countryside round about cart loads of wheat, vegetables, pork and mutton, wine: which was available to all the citizenry, of course at a price. (The days of every black marketeer were soon over once this general breached the walls.) After this siege, alas, the countryside was as broken and drained as the city.

Surely the city square should have been full of citizens, all the same, to observe such a historic event.

The ranked army of occupation threw ten thousand eyes around, looking for inns, wine shops, places of pleasure. Everywhere the shutters were up.

One only blackbird hopped between the mayor and the general; and flew away.

Night in the city, a month later. Erect at the city wall, black against the stars, stood twenty sentries of the occupying army, at a score of separate battlements.

It was a night of such intense frost, you might have heard the stars snapping silver fingers.

What stirred on the street, or under the street, of the city? If anything stirred, the sentries, facing outwards over a ruined countryside, did not hear it. It was a thing more silent than the finger-snapping stars.

A square of street lifted, a trapdoor of cobbles so cunningly designed that a walker on the street would not have guessed the hollowness beneath.

From the cellar a shadow rose with a noose in its hand. It went, crouched and silent, towards the nearest sentry. Within seconds the sentry was dead; the shadow from the cellar caught the falling corpse by the shoulders, caught the musket that would have made an outrageous clatter in that silence, and let the soldier down gently – very gently – the way a sleeping child is lowered.

The murdered soldier's passing had been so soft that his fellow-sentries were unaware of it. But one battlement of a score was unattended.

The shadow, without the noose now, went back the way it had come; and the cunningly-made trapdoor closed upon its going.

The light of dawn kindled coldly in the east. One by one the stars waned. Startlingly, a blaze of sound, a bugle brazened from the battlements!

Then from every commandeered house in the city the soldiers poured out, with shining faces and immaculate uniforms and gleaming leather (for they had had little to do during the time of occupation but spruce and preen themselves, and with commendable precision they now sought their ranks and appropriate columns in the city square, the standard flying, the drums throbbing and growling, the cavalry trotting up from the stables on the edge of the city and forming a snorting clattering open square on each side of the serried columns of infantry, artillery-men, sappers and pioneers. Such plumes of smoke from the tossing nostrils of the grey horses and the chestnut horses and the black horses and the dappled horses! – such pride, as if each knew he bore upon his back the elite of all that great army.

Now the winter sun was clear of the city wall; the point of a bayonet glittered.

Round the corner of the City Hall came the colonel-in-chief and his subordinate officers, on horseback. A sergeant barked like a fox in the clear morning air; like a crashing wave the foot-soldiers presented arms.

The general, having taken the city, had not remained in it above two days. He had ridden on to other consultations, other duties. The war was by no means over. There would be two or three battles between now and the peace treaty with its seals and signatures; its ten thousand crosses, its innumerable crutches and eye-patches.

The colonel who had been left to rule the city was a capable and efficient officer; as will presently appear.

The sergeant barked. The ranked soldiers stood at ease. The hooves clopped and clobbered the cobbles.

The sun shone now unquietly from the bridles, and flashed from the idle bayonets, and glittered on the single star on the chest of the colonel's blue tunic.

The colonel, having cleared his throat, spoke: 'Soldiers, I have to tell you, today we leave this city that we captured a month ago. That is a victory written upon the scroll of martial history. It is a thing you will tell to your grandchildren, at the fire on a winter night, in the long age of peace that is to come once this war is over.

'Meantime, there is nothing left for us to do here. This city has strategic importance no longer. The war has moved far away from here, into the north-west. There the armies are gathering for the next battle. Our general is already there, he has set up his headquarters. He has issued a new mobilization order.

'To that field, wherever it is, you will take your valour and your resolution now.'

A low murmur went through the ranks – a mingling, it could be, of protest, anticipation, fear, excitement.

At this moment the roving eye of the colonel fell upon the dead sentry at the battlement. The colonel bent down along his horse's neck. 'Sergeant,' he said, pointing, 'is that soldier asleep, or drunk?'

'Sir,' said the sergeant, 'I have ascertained that he was murdered on sentry duty last night.'

The colonel sat erect in his saddle, he drooped his cheek on his spread fingers for a full minute. He frowned. He nodded. He cleared his throat again.

'Soldiers,' he said, 'before we leave this city, I will give you a spectacle.'

He turned towards a young officer immediately to the right of him. 'Lieutenant,' he said, 'Order 12B is to be carried out immediately.'

'Yes, sir,' said the lieutenant, who sat on his horse there as immaculate and gleaming as a soldier carved out of wood and new lacquered in glossy blue. His voice too seemed unreal, like the voice of a ventriloquist's doll. (Such a one, it was plain, would go far in the service.)

'Sergeant,' came the wooden voice, 'select eight musketeers. Order three drummers to the station indicated in Order 12B.'

It was obvious that such a contingency as this – a sentry murdered at his post, the last of many – had been discussed and planned for and rehearsed in some detail. At once, having saluted the colonel, the lieutenant and a dozen soldiers broke rank and proceeded, the young lieutenant clip-clopping on his horse along-side, to a fine stone house on the other side of the square – it was the kind of house a merchant might have lived in, or some minor nobleman from the provinces might have kept for a city residence in winter. Except that one tower had been demolished by a cannon ball early in the siege, it stood there whole and handsome.

The lieutenant took a key from his pocket; he unlocked the door and went inside. The dozen soldiers waited on the square, four on one side of the great door, four on the other, four in front of it.

And now the ranks buzzed like a beehive. Order 12B – what, in the bureaucratic jargon of the army, was Order 12B? Life in that army, apart from the crashing boredom and an occasional feast of blood, was a meaningless reticulation of such orders, signals, and secrets understood only by the commissioned officers and, sometimes, sergeants; the troopers, gunners, sappers, and pioneers had simply to submit without question or demur to the whims or iron-fast wisdom of those in authority.

A sentry had been strangled, eh? Another one? Well, it might have been one or other of themselves. They still breathed and felt the winter kiss of the sun. Today they were to march away to a distant battle. Meantime, the colonel had promised them a spectacle; some kind of farewell to the city, it must be. Well, it was better than nothing. But a better spectacle would be a hundred barrels of free beer, and a score of long tables heaped with cheese and pork and pieces of chicken.

It might turn out to be an extravaganza of fireworks.

A girl was suddenly there at the end of a long broken street that gave on to the city square where the ranked infantry stood and shuffled, and the horses pranced and tossed their heads, and the colonel sat smiling in his saddle.

More than a few of the soldiers saw the girl at the end of the broken street. They nodded, they winked, they fluttered their free hands; one of them whistled.

Was this the promised spectacle? The girl was young and of a surpassing loveliness, though her white dress had seen better days. The rags and stains and rents seemed, if anything, to enhance the beauty of the wearer.

They had not seen a single decent girl for a whole month. No: the town had been drained of girls. A few trollops, it's true, always followed the army, hags and harridans that made the gorge rise.

The rare creature at the end of the broken street, she was not for the likes of them, who might be dead in a month or a year. Nothing below the rank of major had a hope of tasting such a morsel.

For a few seconds this girl was the focus of the city square. Many of the soldiers were sure they recognised her from a past campaign. To many she seemed the image of some girl they had admired or even been in love with, long ago, a thousand miles away, in some mountain village – or a marvellous figure that entered their dreams sometimes, so beautiful and good that they awoke resentful of the grey light of morning.

No, of course not: this solitary gleam was not the promised spectacle. The promised spectacle had something to do with the fact that eight of their number – eight musketeers – had been drawn up in a line twelve paces from a drab wall which looked as if it might once have been a pawn-shop wall, so shabby and peeled it stood. Midway between the line of musketeers and the wall stood three drummers, their drum-sticks at the ready between their fingers, angled, crossed; their little drums slung slantwise at their hips. The drummers faced the serried murmurous ranks.

The girl stood at the end of a broken street. The girl too carried a musical instrument. The girl edged round the corner of the city bank till she was actually in the square, clinging to the wall like a moth.

Meantime, from the stylish house on the far side of the square emerged the wooden lacquered lieutenant, followed by the mayor and the other leading citizens who had consid-ered it their duty to remain in the city in the time of its agony, while a hundred or so of their equals had stolen away one by one with what was left of their silver plates and their women and title deeds and jewels. Now the faithful ones were being led out of their fairly comfortable place of confinement, blinking, into the first light of morning: the mayor, the city engineer, the city physician, the city banker, the chancellor of the university. Elderly decent men, it was obvious that they had not had too bad a time of it. The mayor stood smiling in the light, at the brave array drawn up in files and columns in the square.

Then even the dullest of the troopers began to realize what it meant: the spectacle.

It was a matter that neither distressed them nor gladdened them. They had all glutted themselves with death in all its shapes on this battlefield and that, they had brushed death so close with their own sleeves, death had seemed more than once to be beckoning to them and then at the last moment had turned to a comrade or an enemy and put the spell of wounds and stillness and putrefaction on him instead; the sure know-ledge of the imminent death by musket-balls of five old venerable men meant little or nothing to them.

Some spectacle! If a dozen fires had been lit and a dozen oxen lashed to the spits for a farewell feast, that would have been a spectacle worth talking about.

Meantime the five silver-haired citizens seemed to be thinking that here they were, free at last; and that they had been brought out so that the colonel and officers, on behalf of the whole army of occupation, could take a ceremonial farewell.

Silver nods, smiles, in the morning sun. The lieutenant invited them, with wooden courtesy, to approach the officer-in-command, the colonel.

They walked, the little group, the twenty paces to the steps of the City Chamber, where the colonel waited on his pawing chestnut.

'Five nice old men,' thought this soldier and that in the ranked ten thousand, 'poor old bastards. They don't seem to know what's coming to them. Well, I suppose they've had their time – nothing for them to make a song and dance about – I might be a corpse myself before the end of the month. Still, when the muskets are silent again, may their souls have a peaceful passage. May their good angel be there to take them by the hand, the bright guardian they never saw with the eyes of flesh. And you too, *my* good angel, see that you're there when my time comes – no desertion, mind, stick close at my shoulder, comrade – I might need you tomorrow or the next day. Oh, poor old men, they should be let die in their beds. Nothing I, or anybody, can do about it. It's Order 12B. Anyway, I mean you no harm, old men. Go in peace.'

Thus a soldier here and there in the watching ranks, in silent compassion. But most of the heads had a brutish uncaring ox-thrust. Kill them and be done with it. At once. We want to be out of this damned place. Under the horizon are battles, women, loot.

The girl held the flute in a delicate intricacy of fingers. More wounds were about to be put on the web of music that held creation together. How could such rents be mended with one small ivory flute?

'Mr Mayor,' said the colonel, after clearing his throat.

'Colonel,' said the mayor cheerfully: before nightfall he would be master in his own city again, out of the ruins of which, come April and seedtime, new life would rise. Much work for masons and joiners and locksmiths.

'Be so good,' said the colonel, 'as to stand against that wall over there – the half-broken one. The lieutenant here, he will tell you where to stand, he will position you. The other gentlemen will be so good as to go and stand against the wall, two on each side of his worship. If it's not too much trouble. Good. I hope you kissed your good ladies before you left. Please give as little trouble as possible. The lieutenant is about to cover your eyes with napkins.'

The university chancellor seemed the first to be aware of the meaning of this strange ceremony. As the lieutenant approached him with the handkerchief, he said firmly, 'Not mine – I want to drink the sun to the last drop.'

The city physician was bewildered. 'I'm the city medical officer,' he said fussily. 'Blindfold, what nonsense is this! This is the day I consult.' . . . And then, with a slight whimper, 'I'm not very well myself.' . . . Nevertheless, the blindfold was put on him.

'This cures everything, doctor,' said the colonel on horseback. 'Tie their hands.'

The city engineer began to bluster. Very red in the face suddenly, he shouted, 'I want to make an official protest.'

The kerchief was knotted behind his head: hidden, then, the outraged eyes.

'Your protest is noted,' said the colonel. 'I'll see it's forwarded to the general.'

Far away, through the furthest gate of the city, the baggage carts began to roll and rumble. The exodus was beginning.

The colonel addressed the condemned men in clear icy words: 'Mr Mayor and citizens, a month ago our general accepted the surrender of the garrison of this city. The city was placed under military rule. You five were entrusted with the maintenance of civil peace, by our general. A week later, our general had to depart to headquarters, about the furtherance of the campaign. The general delegated his authority to me as colonel-in-command. Since then, six of my soldiers have been murdered. At the bridge, in the river, in the public park. Poison, rope, knife, battery. Six honourable soldiers.'

The mayor said, from his blind world, 'Some of the citizens are very brave. I don't know who they are' . . . Then he shouted, 'I salute you, hidden ones!'

'You city fathers,' said the colonel, 'were kept under house arrest. You were supplied with every comfort that is possible in wartime. You were allowed to move freely about the city, except at night, when you had to sign in at your comfortable sleeping quarters, at curfew time. Nor were your wives or lady friends denied you. It was an eminently generous arrangement, I think you'll agree.

'I had the honour to call on you after the sixth murder last weekend. I said, "Another murder, Mr Mayor, and I will render an account." I have to tell you, a brave sentry was killed on duty in the darkness of last night. I now therefore render the account.

'Sergeant.'

'Firing squad, level muskets,' barked the sergeant.

'You and your men, sir,' said the mayor, and was lost for words. He went on, 'Once we had a plague of rats in this city . . . You have desecrated a beautiful place. You have gnawed the statues and the libraries, the looms and the music, girls and gardens. Our hidden citizens were quite right to set traps.'

'Sergeant, proceed,' said the colonel. The sergeant had hesitated. It was unusual for the utterance of something that sounded like poetry on the near side of the fires of death.

The chancellor of the university said, wonderingly, 'There's a girl at the end of the street . . . I'm glad they didn't bandage my eyes. Goodbye, girl!'

The muskets had been levelled for a good minute now. The sergeant raised his sword. The three drums rattled, a ragged tattoo. The sergeant's sword flashed downwards. There was a line of flame and smoke and thunder. This way and that the city fathers fell, with breached chests.

In the brief silence, a thin clear thread of flute-song.

For the next hour the business of an army of occupation leaving a ruined city was under way.

Far away, diminishing, the baggage carts: stuffed with food and fodder, booty and bandagings, water-barrels and wine for the officers, whatever was needful for the victualling of an army on the march to a new battle.

The sergeants and the corporals knew their duties. Their mouths issued commands with the precision of robots. Column by column, the army turned and marched away from the city square. The stones of the city shook with the immense rhythm of the march. Column by column the army left the square. It took more than an hour for the rear-guards, the pioneers, to march out, somewhat less smartly than the gunners and the infantry.

There followed the cavalry, the splendid greys and chestnuts and bays and their brave riders, pennants fluttering, with leather agleam and bridles making small sweet vagrant tintinnabulations.

The colonel's hand was at the brim of his helmet all the while, in a long paralyzing salute.

The city beat from end to end like a great gong, rising to full power and resonance, then slowly diminishing as the army left the cobbles and flagstones for the dusty road and the grey frosted fields beyond.

Last left the colonel-in-chief and his staff. The colonel's saluting arm hung limp from the shoulder. The officers rode, some before and some after. Beyond the gate, a carriage was waiting for the colonel.

They were not quite the last. Behind rode, on asses and mules, a disordered troop of soldiers, blue-jowled and gorilla-browed, their bayonets up and out and at all angles. (Who knew what devilries the citizens planned in their hidden nests? It would be quite in keeping with their behaviour to fall on the last troops out of the city and score wounds on their backs.)

The last ruffian soldier clipper-cloppered out of the city square.

From the elegant house that had held, until their sudden end, the chief citizens, a frantic screaming broke out; then an old cold voice said, 'Silence,' and the ladies' anguish petered out in a few sobs.

The square was empty. Not even the girl with the flute was to be seen.

It must have been towards noon that the trapdoor, so cunningly contrived in the street, was pushed open cautiously, inch by inch. A head appeared, a face as pale as a mushroom looked here and there. Then a man hauled himself on to the street. Other faces like mushrooms rose into the light. If the cellar people spoke to each other, it was in whispers. Mostly they did not look at each other; as if they didn't trust even themselves. One by one, silently, the sewer folk dispersed in search of their houses and shops.

Yet these were the roots. In them, huddled underground all winter, the strength of the city had lain sunk and coiled.

Now pale, distrustful, with their resurrection the sap began to stir again.

One citizen strolled over and looked down at the bodies of the city fathers at the wall. He laughed, spat, went his lonely way.

Hands pushed a boy out of the cellar. The boy's face was as white as chalk. He covered his eyes, briefly, from the blade of the winter sun. Then he looked with utter amazement at the change that war had wrought in the city.

A girl he had never seen before was standing in front of him; she gathered him safe on to the pavement; he was uncertain on his legs.

'Hello,' he said. 'I don't know you. Do you think the soldiers have gone? Where did you hide all through the siege?'

'I've come in from the country,' said the girl.

More and more citizens with paper-thin hands were climbing out of other cellars have and there in the city square – whispers – white looks – silent dispersings.

The boy said, 'Did you see my mother anywhere? Everybody knows my mother – she's called Anna. She has red cheeks and thick arms. She laughs a lot.'

'No,' said the girl. 'I've seen nobody like that. I saw a few silent women in streets further back.'

'Or my father,' said the boy. 'Did you see him? He's a printer. His shop's a ruin. I went to see it one night in the dark. Paper everywhere in the workshop – manuscripts, army forms, posters.'

'I saw a poem blowing in the wind,' said the girl. 'The paper was all scorched.'

'It started last autumn,' said the boy. 'Will I tell you? The leaves fell. Soldiers came to protect us – our allies, supposed to be. We went down into the cellars. We took bread and blankets and wine down to our cellar. The good soldiers, the allies, they were eating up everything. Then the siege started. We heard nothing day after day but the noise of guns and a house falling here and there above us. It got cold in the cellar at night. There was only a candle or two. Then the water drops turned to icicles in the ceiling.'

'That's the way it goes,' said the girl.

'An old man died in the cellar,' said the boy. 'I'd never seen a dead man before. We ate rats. We ate beetles, we ate candle-wax. Two children died. They wouldn't let me see them. I don't know what they did with the bodies. Then the guns stopped. I wanted to run out into the square! My mother said, "This silence is worse than the guns. *Stay*."'

'Yes,' said the girl, 'silence can be the worst lie of all.'

'Next morning,' said the boy, 'the foreign soldiers came. First a trumpet. Then the tramp-tramp-tramp of their marching. Then we heard them running everywhere, the foreign feet, just like rats over a dead ox in a slaughterhouse. Then the fires – we could hear the crackling of flames for three nights. We were cold and blue as fish down below. A man counted on his fingers, he said three months had passed. Then this morning the cellar beat like a drum. The soldiers were marching away. It got silent as a grave down in the cellar. My mother said, "All the soldiers are gone now, ours and theirs. I know" (said she) "where a sack of flour is. I hid meal and wine bottles after harvest . . ." She went out. I haven't seen her since.'

'Women go out,' said the girl. 'They don't come back. That's the way it is, in a war.'

'Have you seen any of my friends?' said the boy, 'Tomas or Phyllis or Rachel?'

'I've seen no children for a long time,' said the girl. 'Only you.'

'I'm glad they didn't find you,' said the boy.

'We'll look for a little shop somewhere,' said the girl. 'We'll buy pies and oranges. I have money. Listen.'

'There are no shops,' said the boy. 'I came up out of the cellar once or twice, when the moon was dark. I think I went along every street almost. The shops are bare. Money's no good in a town like this.'

'Come with me,' said the girl. 'I'll take you to a safe place somewhere.'

Far off now, the beat and throb of the foreign army diminished.

'There's a good place near the sea,' said the girl. 'Far away. We'll be safe there.'

The boy considered the proposal, while he studied each of his blue finger-nails in turn. The sea. Ships. Whales. (He had heard of such wonders.)

Then he shook his head. 'No, this is my town,' he said. 'I'll wait. Maybe Tomas or Robert will come out of a cellar somewhere. They're my friends. We know how to steal eggs and apples.'

'Goodbye, boy,' said the girl.

She turned. She left the boy and the city square and the stiff wounds of the city fathers where winter flies were beginning already to gather and gorge. She went out through the scorched labyrinth. Following the victorious army, she passed through a scorched city gate.

The boy shouted, 'Tomas! Liza! Where are you hiding? Don't you hear the music? It's peace. Come out.'

More mushroom faces appeared at a stone trapdoor.

They tilted their heads. They listened. They drank the flute-troubled wind.

[IX]

A New Field

You might have sworn it was impossible that anyone could have dreamt of taking a spade to such a stony place.

Yet here they were, a young man and a young woman, digging with spades in a waste of stones.

It was no rhythmic digging, I assure you, such as gives joy and urgency to hard toil. Their spades struck raggedly, and some-times jarred like out-of-tune bells as this metal blade or that struck a hidden stone.

A waste of stones – more than half their time was spent not digging at all but lifting and pulling and dredging stones out of the earth.

Whenever one or other of the delvers found what they considered to be a good stone, it was added to a growing heap; ragged misshapen stones were thrown into the adjacent acre of marsh-land.

Hard back-breaking toil. And yet the young pair sang as they worked, striking their spades into the earth, and bending every now and then to separate good stones from bad stones.

> Shift a stone
>   Sink the spade
> Turn the earth

> Break granite
> > Blacken the spade
> Slice a clod

> Gather good stones
> > Brighten the steel
> Open the clay.

A strange thing was, though they sang together the same work-song, the words were from different languages.

We must understand this at once, in reading this chapter. The two earth-toilers had been, until fairly recently, strangers to each other. They came from different nations and different cultures. Tillage was certainly not their everyday trade. It was quite likely – such was the rage and confusion of the times – that their two nations were embattled. But this young man and this young woman who didn't understand each other's language were here together, working in this near impossible place.

In fact a third character, a girl, appears, and they all communicate with each other. The girl, who has come from who knows where, is in fact already here, she is standing at the edge of the little marsh into which the 'bad stones' are thrown. But the marsh is beautiful in its own way with marigolds and cotton-flowers.

Their communication, it would seem, must be impossibly complicated, because the girl speaks yet another language; so there ought to be a triangle of incomprehension and bafflement.

But it did not turn out that way. Understanding flowed from one to the other, without hindrance. Perhaps language, which seems to be among man's greatest gifts, is really a source of discord, confusion, and death. Perhaps in the end, in that good age when the lion shall lie down with the lamb, there will be no need of speech. Men and beasts, birds and fish and plants, will converse with each other in a pure silence beyond utterance; the body's gestures, like a dance, will say everything.

We who deal in words cannot believe that, of course. Language is one of the greatest and most marvellous of gifts, though it separates us in a way from the rest of creation. But it is a perilous gift all the same, for the utterances of Homer and Shakespeare – not to speak of prophet and psalmist – can be twisted by worthless men into all manner of lies and bad contrivance. We who deal in words must strive to keep language pure and wholesome; and it is hard work, as hard almost as digging a stony field with a blunt spade. There is the constant temptation to write the facile fictions and poems that the public demand in order to pass an idle hour; and for that pulp the public will pay, and often richly. But once a field has been dug and seeded and harvested, the rare true writer considers yet another acre, stony and un-promising, that ought (he thinks) to be opened to the sun and rain and wind . . .

A far wandering this from the three people we have set in this unlikely place, two toiling and singing the same song in different languages; the third whose feet are bright beside marsh marigolds: the girl.

They speak, a confusion of languages; and by the chapter's end they communicate in a pure wordless flow, with little gestures of the hand and the head, and smilings, and frownings, and silences.

But I beg you to understand my difficulty, as a writer. I have to make them converse with each other, as if they shared one language, like medieval scholars going with their Latin through all the babels of Europe.

The girl in the soiled coat said, 'Hard work. Your field's full of stones.'

The young man straightened himself and looked at her. Another foreigner – a girl in a dirty coat! It seemed as if all the peoples of Europe were trekking from place to place, into ever-deepening squalor and incomprehension. His brow was silvered with sweat.

'We're making a new field,' he said in his own language. 'It's hard work – that's true.' And his bright blade flashed in the sun, striking.

The young woman bent and plucked up a ragged stone and sent it with a splash into the marsh.

'We're going to sow cabbages,' she said in her language. (And the young man, and the girl, knew precisely what she meant, by a certain intonation that is perhaps basic to all languages from the Arctic to the equator; by a little moulding gesture of the hand, signifying fruitfulness.)

'Yes,' said the young man, 'we'll make a hut out of the good stones over there. A little house with a tree and a well outside.'

'We're tired of being moved here and there by soldiers,' said the woman. 'For me, this is the fourth year of it. I was a seamstress in the city – oh, long ago, before the siege.'

'As for me,' said the young man, 'I was a scrivener in Leipzig. Far away. The office I work in, it was burnt. The old advocate I worked for, he was lost in the flames.'

The young woman smiled. 'We came by two different roads to the same place.'

'That's a fact,' said the young man. 'We woke up under a wall one morning. We didn't know we'd been sleeping under the same stars, three yards or so from each other. We looked at each other. The sun was rising. We greeted each other. But we were speaking different languages.'

'And we still do,' said the seamstress from the city, 'though we're trying to learn words from each other. But it isn't easy. His language is like a coil of barbed wire, but I love the way he speaks it. And I don't know why I'm saying all this to you, because it's obvious you speak another language still. And yet, from the way you nod and smile, you seem to understand what I'm saying.'

The scrivener said, 'She speaks too much, like all women. But I can't have enough of her words, that's the truth . . . Well, but the way women go on, you lose the thread of your story. Let me see. Where was I? Yes, we woke up under that wall, with the sunrise in our eyes. We didn't know where we were. We hadn't a word in common. We got to our feet. We walked on together. About one thing we agreed right away. We must find a place so poor the soldiers wouldn't bother us.'

'So here we are,' said the seamstress. 'Here we are and here we mean to stay.'

'Yes,' said the scrivener, 'at least till the cabbages come up.'

'All the world's on the move,' said the seamstress. 'Where are you going, stranger?'

'To the battle,' said the girl. 'I must go to the battle.' She frowned. She pointed with her fingers at blue distant mountains.

'To the battle!' cried the young man, and thrust his spade so violently into the clay that it clanged against a stone; and the stone whined and whined like a cracked bell. 'Everybody else is running away from battles. Look at them, over there! Folk trudging from place to place, with chairs and clocks and cages. Not one of them knows where he's going.'

'No more of that for us,' said the young woman whose fingers had been more used to needles-and-thread than to the tearing up of stones. Splash! – another stone went into the marsh, the stone that had been struck and loosened by the young man whose fingers were more used to pens and blotting-paper than stones.

'We came to this good barren place yesterday,' he said. 'And here we're going to bide.'

The trio, the three instruments of their voices, mingled for the last time and rounded out into a good silence.

From now on it was mime and gesture, a slow dance of hand and head and torso. (Yet a storyteller must overcome such a difficulty in the only way he knows, by articulation of signs. These will have to serve. It is an agreeable difficulty. They spoke, and yet they did not speak.)

'Going to the battle, are you?' said the seamstress, wonder-ingly. 'The whole of Europe's a bedlam. This acre – it's going to be a little green kingdom of peace at the heart of it.'

'We're young,' said the scrivener. 'We're strong. We'll be king and queen in this little green kingdom. Tomorrow I'm going to drain that field.' He pointed at the acre of bog cotton and marigolds.

'We don't know at the moment,' said the seamstress, 'where we'll get the cabbage seed. But we will.'

'We will,' said the scrivener. 'We'll water the field and we'll dung it. We'll pick the caterpillars off the green curls.'

There was silence for a few seconds. The young man angled his thin ledger-writing shoulders to the earth and turned three spadefuls over. The young woman seemed lost in a brief dream of spinning-wheels, a cradle, pots of cabbage broth.

A shadow passed across her face. 'The only thing is,' she said, 'once the crop begins to green, some horseman with a scroll is sure to come.'

'Nothing surer,' said the scrivener, straightening himself. Would his frail spine last out the digging of the field, the building of the house? 'This is what he'll say: "Trespassers. Thieves. This land belongs to the lord Pedro in the castle up there."'

'I think we're in Spain, but I'm not quite sure,' said the seam-stress. 'We crossed mountains, I know that. Yes, this factor of Don Pedro, he'll say, "Now you've begun you might as well finish. Only – half the cabbages belong to the lord Pedro, remember that. I'll be calling for the rent twice a year, in May and November . . ."'

'I've thought about it,' said the scrivener, 'and we'd be better off begging. But a family likes to live in one settled place.'

The girl said, listening, looking everywhere, '*Where is it?*'

'What?' said the seamstress. 'Are you expecting to find something here, apart from us with the blistered hands?'

'The child,' said the girl. 'There's always a child. In every winter place, a child. In every broken and burnt place. They come, they drift round me like spring butterflies. I don't know why that should be. It happens.'

The young woman was suddenly shy and proud. She stroked, gently, her slightly-rounded belly with her hand. 'He's inside me, stranger,' she said. 'He's too small and hidden to welcome you yet. He'll dig the field after us. Then his son after him.'

The man said, hard and practical, 'There's too much talk! Women! The field must be dug.'

They set about the stony field again with their spades, open-ing the clay, striking a stone sometimes, carrying a good stone to the heap of stones that would be their house, sending an ill-shapen stone into the marsh with a splash, so that a clump of marigolds trembled for a moment.

It seemed they deliberately turned their backs on this root-less girl, the better to dig the place that was not yet quite a field, before sunset. How their office- and garret-nurtured bodies would sleep that night, in the lee of the good stone hoard, under the first spring stars!

The girl, now that they were ignoring her, unthonged the bag of money at her waist and put a white coin under a stone; and then, after a pause, a yellow coin under another stone.

'This is for the cabbage seed,' she whispered. 'This other is for an apple tree beside the house, for the child to play in.'

Then, from the mountains beyond, could be heard a prolonged rumble, as if the mountain dwarves were setting out with their carts to mine and to smithy. Another cart! – it lumbered distantly across a precipitous mountain track.

'Thunder,' said the young woman, pausing, spade uplifted, listening.

'Not thunder – guns,' said the scrivener, without pausing in his work; for, if he did, those two women would fall to idle chattering again, about babies and cabbage broth. 'They've been shifting guns up the mountain for days. There's going to be a big battle up there, among the mountains.' And he struck the earth with the sharp glittering edge of his spade, as if to cancel with one stroke all wars for all time.

The girl's face was turned to the trolls' business, the muted rumbling, the brazen stammers, that issued from some fold of the blue distant range.

How to describe the look on her face? It is beyond the power of a storyteller like me to describe that mingling of fear and expectancy. A painter like Goya might have caught that look with his pad and pencil, as the girl looked and listened to the battle hatching far away: holding her flute at a delicate tilt.

'I must go now. Goodbye,' she said to the urgent backs and arms.

They did not notice that the girl had gone until, as if possessed by one rhythm, they straightened themselves, putting their left hands to the small of the back, and looking around. Who knew what bandit or factor might come on them suddenly, and stick a notice of protection or of rent on the gateway of their little green kingdom?

And there the girl was, far away, on the crest of the road, going on towards the mountain and the growing rumble in the throat of the mountains.

The young man called after her, 'Come back in the autumn, stranger. We'll have a roof up. We'll have a fire and a cradle.'

'A pot of cabbage soup too,' said the mother-to-be.

The girl heard them; she heard their two languages that she did not understand. She turned. She waved her free hand back to them.

And then the girl was gone, under the ridge.

'I think,' said the man, 'she was a travelling musician, that girl. She had a flute in her belt. An ivory flute.'

'Listen,' said the young woman.

The young man listened. He heard silence. He shook his head. Silence only, except, of course for the dwarves assembling murderously in the mountain passes, for the staking of claims and the 'proper distribution' of gold and silver, which is the root of all wars. It would be a thunderous assembly, up among the mountains. (Helen of Troy was no fleeting loveliness and lissomness; she was a statue of solid gold in a niche of Priam's palace, that filled the hearts of foreign men with a fiercer kind of lust.)

And then – this sometimes happens – a brief silence supervened, as if the iron flower of war was folded for a minute. Through the silence came the frail flute-music, a hardly-heard scattering of notes.

'It's the sound of corn growing,' said the seamstress. 'Listen.'

Again, the flute-music, fading. It was the sound of corn growing, and of cabbages and apples and hidden children.

They smiled at each other. The young woman looked at her scarred hands. She would have to see to it that her fingers did not lose their suppleness and cunning; there would be things to sew at the end of summer, though where the linen and needles would come from she did not yet know.

But first the digging of the field. 'Dig,' said the scrivener, but the word was lost in a clangour from the mountains, iron on stone, as if a black distant bell was being struck, again and again.

'Dig!' said the scrivener. 'That's the word for it: *dig*. You really must learn my language, and fast, so that we can have a good row with each other next winter, and know what insults we're flinging. *Dig*: that is the correct word for what we're doing, for what we must do, year after year till we die.'

'*Dig*,' said the young woman, 'that's the right word for it, that's the one and only word used where I came from. Dig.'

But the sounds the lovers made were utterly different. That they were monosyllables was the only similarity – one basic urgent fruitful syllable: on it rests the whole of civilization – music, philosophy, law.

They stood for a while close together. They made their different sounds for 'dig', a sweet strife that did not last long, and did not end in insults or blows. No, they leant towards each other, there in the broken stony earth, with their spades in their right hands trailing, and they kissed each other.

After the kiss, the young woman said 'dig' in the young man's language.

But she had her revenge. She stroked the small curve of her body and she said 'child'.

The young man said, smiling, 'child', in the way that it was said among her people. In the way that it was said where he came from it was equally beautiful; *more* beautiful, in his opinion. But he touched her body gently and said 'child' as she had said it; but with such a comical ordering of vowel-and-consonant that she had to smile. She kissed him again.

A thread of sound between two breezes: the strange girl and her music, was it? That was a fragment of the language that knows no frontiers, neither race nor colour nor creed – the language of the stars in their courses – the sweet discourse that brought even the animals round the feet of Orpheus, and birds and plants and stones.

The two new peasants stood listening till it was heard no more. They looked at each other. They saw rears in each other's eyes.

'This won't do!' cried the young man. 'All this silly talk in two languages! That beggar girl and her bit of a tune. What we are here for is to dig and plant cabbages and build a hut.'

And, in a kind of rage, he drove his blade into the earth, which rang like a dissonant bell. A stab of pain shot up his arm to the shoulder, a sheer flash! He cried out in agony.

'Look,' said the new young peasant woman. The stone he had struck had shifted somewhat. Something glittered in the sun, a round gold sovereign!

The new young peasant bent down. He lifted the treasure carefully with his fingers, and kissed it, and put it into his pocket.

Kiss gold! – gold was what all the gathering din in the mountains was about, gold and cupidity and sovereignty. Evil seeds of the sun: to put one's mouth to that!

No: but this was good wholesome lawful gold, that is used in the commerce of open simple people, without any thought of amassing it in brass-bound chests or banks or royal treasuries; they know it is only to buy the daily bread with.

The blade trembled still, from its encounter with the stone, and the small wind-sweetening bell-sound was so different from the evil iron clang and the pandemonium of bells in the blue mountain-range beyond. For the spade in the half-dug acre was the little bell of peace.

'Dig,' said the peasant.

They dug raggedly, without rhythm.

After a time they joined their voices in the work chorus: the same tune, two languages.

Knock on earth
A door will open
Inside, a sweet green curl.

Later that day, the young peasant woman turned over a stone with a silver crown under it.

'This for the apple-tree,' she said.

After a mild disputation, he said that he would call it 'apple-tree', after the manner of her people to say it.

[X]

The Mountain Village

On the lower slopes of the mountain was a little village; it was held in the lap of the mountain, you might think: a nursling, a ward.

It was like any village in any part of the world, almost; with its church, its wine-shop, its smithy – also the little group of houses where the tradesmen and their families lived, weaver, joiner, tailor, cobbler – and the scattered houses of the foresters and the shepherds.

This bore all the marks of a mountain village. Higher up was a great dark forest, with clearings towards the west for the charcoal burners and falconers and a few lead-miners. Further down, on the gentler slopes, roamed flocks of sheep and goats and the herdsmen.

It was an isolated community; the people in the city across the river might curl their lips a little, speaking of it and the yokels who inhabited it and could hardly be understood, so thick their dialect was, so shy and crude their ways whenever – which was rarely – they had to cross the river and come into the city to transact some business: sell eggs and cheese and mutton, perhaps, or see the moneylender about a little advance (at exorbitant interest), or visit a son or a daughter who was in service there, perhaps, or labouring in a factory.

Mostly the villagers kept to themselves. They traded or rather bartered with each other; all the families were united in some way by kinship close or removed, so that there was a complicated social network, which only a few very old women understood with any thoroughness; for the cousins of every degree and the siblings reached back for generations, beyond the haphazard records kept in the church, and were half lost in legends at last. It was not a totally harmonious web, by any means. Families had feuded, had accused each other before the visiting magistrate; the young men of the squabbling law-en-meshed families gave each other bloody noses in the wine-shop courtyard on a Saturday night, sometimes. That bitterness might have gone on, in some cases, for fifty years or more, until some village Romeo and Juliet healed the breach . . . And the foresters fell out about the ownership of an oak, sometimes; and sometimes a shepherd would steal two or three lambs from another shepherd, before there had been time to put the identifying clips in the lambs' ears, and then there might be another lawsuit or another fight outside the wine-shop. But the law was costly, and fist fights could end with knives; so usually the village elder, a man trusted by most of the villagers, stepped in and sorted out the difficulty at an early stage. They trusted him more than the visiting magistrate from the city, who had been known to have young men sent to prison for behaving in the way of young men always and everywhere. The thought of prison blanched the cheeks of the villagers: to lie for a month, maybe, in dampness and darkness, they who breathed the same air as hawks and wolves!

The village priest was an elderly man who, apart from his religious duties, kept very much to himself. The bishop had sent him to this lonely isolated place five years before, and whether justifiably or not he considered himself to be an exile. 'I am an old man, you can see that,' he would say to a parish-ioner after a wedding or a baptism or a funeral. 'I'm too old to get to know you all. Besides, I don't want to pry into your affairs. Nor do I want to sit at any of your fires or tables – I do for myself – I am quite happy with my books and my microscope. So don't bother to ask me for supper, any of you. It would embarrass you and it would be a misery to me. We'll go our own ways, eh? Good. That's settled, then. Of course I expect you all here, at Mass, every Sunday morning, and on feast days too. Here we'll all meet together, in God's house. Of course, also, you know that I'm available whenever there is a great event in one of the families – a new baby, or a marriage, or a death. Send for me then, by all means – don't delay; I'll be there like a dove to a ship's rigging in a storm. Is that clearly understood? Good, now we know just where we stand. I will have one more drop of that very good apple-brandy, then I must go in and see to Snowdrop the cat . . .'

The villagers would see, night after night, the lamp in the presbytery window, and an old white head, spectacled, bent upon the open halves of a book, or peering down a microscope at some rare herb he had discovered in the forest or beside the burn. That was his hobby, botany: the villagers smiled to each other behind their hands, thinking that was a queer way to spend good time; but then, apart from his daily Mass, the old man had very little to do.

'A fight,' he would say, 'a forester and a shepherd fighting last night? Is that so? I thought I heard some shouting last night, right enough, before I went to bed. Well, well, what of it? Young men are always fighting with each other about something, a girl or who stands the next round of drinks – they always have done and they always will do, if you ask me. Gets rid of a lot of excess energy. They're usually good friends afterwards. What, they're vowing to do each other in? Is that a fact? Send for the elder. Old Andrew, he'll sort things out for them, he knows them better than they know themselves – he knows every tincture of blood in them. See old Andrew, before it comes to knives. We don't want that little game-cock of a magistrate in the village, do we? Therefore see Andrew. If there's one thing I hate, it's reading the burial rite over a young strong man with a knife-mark in him! . . .'

Two miles from the village, right down where the wheat-fields begin, there stood a little turreted towered castle, where the feudal lord of the district resided. I should say rather, where he nominally resided, for the young baron who had inherited the domain from his bachelor great-uncle three years previously, was hardly ever in residence. He had hardly been installed, the young lord, in the bare draughty labyrinth, than he decided that it was his prime duty to go on 'the grand tour', to acquaint himself with some of the great cities of Europe: Rome, Paris, London, Vienna. He owed it, he said, not only to himself but to his tenants and bondman: what use would a gawky youth new out of the university be to them? They needed a man who had had first-hand experience of the stylish world and its manners and customs. Only a man who had knowledge of what was best and most cultured in the modern world, could see his little domain in relation to the whole totality of things. From that experience would flow justice, enlightenment, kindness, and understanding.

The young lord had ridden off in his carriage one fine autumn morning, and that was the last that had been seen of him. In what great city of Europe he was gathering up knowledge and understanding, for the ultimate good of his shepherds and foresters and husbandmen, no one knew; and it seemed that no one cared greatly, either.

On a slope above the fruitful bend of the river, bowered among little hills and plantations, stood the little medieval keep, which had been added to and altered from time to time, as fashion dictated, by the young man's ancestors. A household of twenty servants – stable-boys, skivvies, gardeners, a butler, an ostler, a cook – kept the heart of the house beating. Girls saw to it that the young lord's room was kept clean and fired; who knew at what hour of what day he might not return, as suddenly as he had gone away?

After the second winter, the butler and some of the boy servants were sometimes to be seen drunk in the middle of the day. The wine cellar was being broached, bit by bit.

The girl servants would, under the first star, open a little side door to a furtive shadow, and there would be an hour of giggles in an alcove of the long corridor. Three summers ago, the gaunt housekeeper would never have allowed that.

In the rose-garden, in the third summer, weeds grew taller than roses, and the smooth lawns sprouted with dock and hogweed and thistle.

This was a state of affairs that had not been known in the great-uncle's days, when the household, set in motion by the butler at six o'clock every morning, moved like clockwork to the last drawing of curtains, covering of fires and locking of doors.

And things were getting worse.

Some said, 'The young baron, he'll never come back. He hated this place from the moment he set foot in it. Why should he come back? He can draw money in any banking house in Europe. We knew, right away – that young dandy will never bury himself in the country.'

'Wild oats,' said some of the neighbouring gentry. 'He's sowing his wild oats. What young Louis said was true, a man is the better for experiencing all that life offers – especially a man who can afford it, like him. He'll come back all right, he'll grow old and wise and quiet among his hills and forests' . . . That was the opinion of those round about who might be invited for supper to the castle once or twice in the course of a year; for they were not of the same social standing as he who lived in the castle, being at best gentlemen farmers, but of course altogether superior to the dung-and-dirt twenty-acre farmers, and to the dull inbred villagers above, to whom nothing exciting ever happened, or could conceivably happen.

Some thought their young baron had been caught up in the great war that was shifting here and there across Europe. Young men love the pomp and circumstance of war: that is well known. But not all of them see the pomp and glory and circumstance through to the end . . . This might happen, that he had died, mutilated beyond recognition on a battlefield, and so would never come home. And the castle of twelve honourable generations would wither on its foundations, for there was no heir: unless, from some corner or other of Europe a fifth or a sixth cousin appeared at last, accompanied by a sleazy attorney who bore a parchment with a family tree on it, and a red ribbon and seal.

Up in the village, they did not know anything about the state of affairs down in the castle; perhaps old Andrew had heard a rumour or two.

The rent-man, however, did not fail to appear twice in the year for the estate's due of wool, wood, honey, and salted game birds.

And the vintner, the man who kept the village wine-shop, he knew. He knew everything there was to be known. The vintner drove his cart into the city wine-stores once a month, and returned with a barrel of red wine and a barrel of white wine; also a cluster of flagons near a feast day. He kept his eyes and ears open in the city. He was no fool, the vintner.

The vintner was quite excited one Friday afternoon when he returned to the village with the barrels of wine in his cart. The vintner was very strong. He lifted the barrels, grunting, and set them on his wooden porch. Then with a stick and his hand he whirled them and twirled them inside the open door of his shop, and brought them to rest behind the counter with sudden thumps.

He came back at once to the cart and took an armful of flagons, a dozen at least, into the shop and behind the counter; and came out and went in again, flagon-encumbered; and yet again . . . Something between thirty-six and fifty flagons – the like had never been known before in the village. What was going to happen? Forester and shepherd looked at each other. There was no feast-day in the calendar for weeks to come. The village women were perplexed (pleasantly so) to get large orders that same day from the vintner: turkeys, honeycombs, eggs, goat-cheeses (the biggest ones). Also would the village ladies hold themselves in readiness to bake considerable quantities of bread? Also buckets of home-brewed, beer. The vintner gave the village women to understand that they would be paid in cash with the utmost promptitude, on the nail. Let the good ladies see to it.

That evening the vintner casually remarked to the drinking villagers that he had heard rumours in the city that morning – an army of the Emperor was encamped twenty miles down river, beyond the medieval city walls. Let them look through their windows after sunset: they would see a hundred camp-fires twinkling through the gloam, a sight to make the pulses race. Rumour had it that the Emperor himself was leading the army. The Emperor, in fact, was installed in the château of the absent seigneur. He, the vintner, intended to look out his father's telescope from the beetles and cobwebs of the attic: through the telescope he might even see the Emperor with his little pot-belly and right hand stuck inside his waist-coat, the greatest soldier and the greatest man on the earth . . .

The villagers sipped red wine and shifted on their benches.

But there was more, said the vintner. Let them dig the wax out of their ears. Another army, of mixed Prussians and Poles and English, mercenaries and riff-raff from all over Europe, was marching on the city from the south-west. He had seen with his own eyes the advance troops of this army in the city that same day, horsemen and foot-soldiers, to the no small consternation of the citizens.

What, he would like to know, did that mean, a city with an army outside it, encamped, beginning to filter in, and another army marching on it with all haste?

The villagers shook their heads.

'It means, pig-heads,' said the vintner, 'that there will be a battle somewhere in the vicinity of the city. And that soon. And that soon. In the next day or two.'

Abel the weaver remarked that that might well be true. The animals and the birds had been behaving very strangely in the last week, going by ways and tracks they had never gone before. And, sure enough, he, Abel the weaver, had seen a cluster of fires far to the west of the city these two nights past. Very good. Very exciting. But Abel the weaver didn't see how it affected the mountain people. Let the fools fight till they had all murdered one another – the village would continue in its usual way, cradle to grave, a leisurely shuttling.

'The Emperor,' said Erik the charcoal-burner, 'what's he? An upstart. He has a lot to answer for, that Emperor, the deaths of tens of thousands of fine young men. May the Emperor not get out of the shambles alive.'

The vintner polished his pewter pots with a rag. A grey smiling ghost looked back at him.

'There's a stranger in the village,' said Samuel the shepherd. 'A girl. Who is she?'

Nobody paid any attention to Samuel. He saw many strange things in the course of a year, especially after he had been look-ing deep and long into his tankard.

Simon came in: the fowler. He was out of breath, he was red in the face – a most unusual thing for Simon; he was mild as a bird on the wrist. He put his head down on the counter. 'A measure of red wine – a double measure. Quick.'

He had lost his hawk – that must be it. Simon's hawk had flown into the forest and not come out again. Now he would have to find and train a new hawk – no easy matter.

Simon gulped down his wine as though it was from the world's last barrel.

'Now, now, Simon,' said the vintner, 'take it easy. I want no puking in here, no fighting. Sip your wine like an honest man, slowly.'

'More,' said Simon, and he glared at the vintner, and he set down his tankard on the counter with a little clang.

'If I was you,' said Simon the fowler, turning to the half-dozen tipplers in the shop, 'I would get out of here fast. Leastwise, I'd get the women to some place in the forest, safe. And the young ones, too – get them out. And get as much stuff out of your houses as you can carry. No, I know I'm talking nonsense – the men must stay. We must hang on and see what way the dice will fall. But the shutters, put them up on all your windows. And lock the doors. Bar them first, then lock them.'

'Don't drink so fast, Simon,' said Abel the weaver. 'No good getting upset about a hawk. He might come back tomorrow.'

'That girl,' said the shepherd, Samuel. 'Does anybody know where she's living?'

'A hawk?' said Simon, his words slurring a little. 'Fill her up, landlord. What hawk? Whose hawk? My hawk's safe in the rafters. Hawks, is it? (I said *red* wine, not white, you scoundrel – you've been watering it too – I know – you can't fool me.) Hawks. There's hundreds of hawks, no, thousands, tens of thousands on the far side of the mountain! Hawks, war-men. The first of them are in the fields above the village now, beyond the forest, just under the snowline. I was up there this morning, I saw them. They're pitching tents like mushrooms.

Thousands of others are working their way round the mountain. They're coming as quiet as hawks, right enough, high hoverers. The tents, hundreds of them, are going up, between here and the summit. Listen.'

It came then, from outside, from high above, like a muted beehive. But occasionally it was as if the hive was shaken, and then on a down-draught of mountain air the villagers could hear a prolonged murmuration, that swelled and died away again. And, from time to time, a faint tintinnabulation, like nails sprinkled on stones.

'The deer were crossing the mountain, right enough,' said Abel the weaver. 'I never saw them in such a hurry. Birds, too.'

'Well,' said Bill from the sawmill, 'let the fools bide up there on the mountain. Let them freeze, every last one. It's got nothing to do with us.'

'Yes,' said the vintner. 'There's a third army. It belongs to the Emperor too. He's a clever soldier, that Emperor. They had blue uniforms, didn't they, Simon? I thought so. You see the way it is. The Emperor has one army twenty miles outside the city. The Prussians and the Austrians, all that mixter-maxter, are inside the city, or they soon will be. Now, unbeknown to them, the Emperor has brought a secret army to the mountain here. He'll crush the city like a nut. Ho, I tell you, that Emperor knows what he's doing. Now then, look at it from my point of view, soldiers are thirsty men. Hungry too, but thirsty above all. A few of the soldiers might come down to the village, on errands. Best be prepared. It's always sound policy to be on friendly terms with troops in the neighbourhood.'

'Do it at once,' said Simon. 'Lock women. Send your doors away under trees.'

Simon slumped down in the corner between counter and wall. 'Hawk safe,' he mumbled. 'Tens-a-thousands blue hawks.'

'There's the girl!' cried Samuel. 'Over there, among the tombstones. Look!'

By the time they had lumbered to their feet and put six faces to the webbed window, the girl was gone. (Nothing much could be seen, in any case, through that thick green whorl of glass, even on the brightest summer day.)

'A few crumbs might come our way,' said the vintner. 'Drag Simon outside. I never saw him so drunk so early. I don't want him sick all over the floor. He owes five francs for the wine. Hold on a minute, I'll take it out of his purse. That's it. That's fine. Now take him out from here.'

The vintner was right, as always. Crumbs and crusts came his way: a modest way of putting it, for his moneybox rang and rattled almost continuously for the next ten days. During that time little groups of soldiers, some in black uniforms, some in blue uniforms, drifted in and out of the village, from the mixed army that had invested the city below and from the Emperor's second army encamped openly now, but hidden, just below the snow-line.

As soon as the first little group of soldiers, five young laughing off-duty fellows, appeared in the village, a panic fell on the village men. That same evening in the first shadows they hustled all the women into the forest, carrying blankets and boxes. The babies and the old grannies too were herded into the sanctuary of the forest. 'Bide among the trees,' said Andrew, 'till the soldiers go away again. It won't be long. There's a hut here and there where you can shelter. It'll be a bit crowded, but never mind that. It's summer, you can sleep under the trees. In a week or a fortnight you'll be back in your own houses. Some of us'll come to see you every night – how you're getting on.'

So the burdened women were herded, grumbling, into the forest. They didn't see why they should miss out on all the excitement. The young unmarried women, especially, were resentful. 'Soldiers': the word, merely, put a kind of spell on them. It was a species of 'glamourie' deeply engrained in the female psyche; here were young men who diced daily with Death; so perilous was their trade, so loaded with Fate, that they drank deeply and loved marvellously, quite unlike the crude kissings and claspings of the young woodmen and shepherds. So they had heard, the young women, and they fully believed it. 'Just leave me alone, you clod,' shrilled Jeanne to Trod the tailor (her 'intended') as he thrust her with his staff among the first green forest shadows.

And the babies yelled in this strange green place smelling of rot and growth, and the old women mumbled this and that through gravestone teeth.

'The wolf'll get us,' yelled Jeanne. 'Then you'll be sorry. You turd!' Trod hit Jeanne smartly across the cheek, and then she was all sobbings and snufflings, her thick hands up at her face, her knuckles glittering.

The village men, after grave consideration, had decided to take Simon the falconer's advice (though he had been drunk when he gave it). They themselves would stay in the village, behind shuttered windows and barred doors. They intended to see well to it that there would be no casual looting in this particular village. If any soldier tried, his skull would come into close contact with a heavy oak cudgel. Old Andrew would take word at once of any misbehaviour to the quartermaster in the camp.

Of course, during the day the men went out to their various callings; before going, they made sure the doors were locked. One or two, before getting out, would give his door a thump with a thick shoulder. Hercules or Samson would have had difficulty getting in.

The only open places in the village were the church and the wine-shop.

The priest could be seen in mid-morning moving among the tombstones reading his breviary.

The vintner began, as he had foretold, to do brisk business. It was a most extraordinary thing: soldiers from two armies, enemies, came and bargained in the wine-shop. It was not at all like dealing with the thick-heads of the village. The soldiers lived dangerously and gaily, even in the ordinary business of buying things. The vintner entered into the spirit of it; he enjoyed his wrangles with the soldiers of the black army and of the blue army, quite apart from the high profits he made. How provident he had been, to buy in all those extra provisions! The village women, the day before they were thrust complaining into the forest, had brought to the inn great quantities of edibles: sacks of potatoes, salted poultry, apples and bread and great round cheeses, and much more besides, including vats of beer. The merchandise stood in mounds behind the counter. The vintner paid the women well. That was a little consolation to the women, that jingling silver, for being forced to leave their hearths by their jealous men folk. Of course, some of those same ox-heads were soon jingling that same silver in their own pockets. 'What can you do with florins in the forest?' Paul the shepherd had said to his young wife Margrete, twisting her wrist until she cried out with pain and opened her palm, and the silver made music on the stone floor.

There was enough of it for Paul to get drunk five nights in a row – and that despite the fact that the price of the vintner's wine was rising alarmingly; from night to night a new figure was chalked on the wine barrels and the ale-vats.

'It always happens in a war,' said the vintner. 'The prices of everything go up. You're too thick in the head to understand such things.'

Thick and dull it was, indeed, to have dealings with those villagers. But the soldiers! – the very fact that they had to bargain, vintner against 'black' soldiers and 'blue' soldiers, in a medley of tongues, added unwonted spice to his days.

The first soldiers were dismayed, of course, that there were no girls in the village. To march on forced roads a hundred miles, and then to come to a place without women!

Sometimes a 'black' soldier or a 'blue' soldier would swear he had seen a girl in the village – a mere glimpse, from below or above, then she was gone.

'No, sergeant,' said the vintner on the seventh morning, 'there are no girls in the village. I assure you. The villagers drove all the girls to the forest a week ago. The forest is so thick you'd not find them in a year. It's true. I solemnly assure you.'

'A saw a girl just now as we were coming up,' said the sergeant. 'She was standing over there at the end of the church.'

'You're wrong,' said the vintner. 'There's not one piece of skirt left in the village.'

'Oh well,' said the sergeant, 'I see you have plenty of wine this morning. Two flagons of red wine and a flagon of brandy.'

'Certainly,' said the vintner. 'Fifty francs.'

'It was thirty francs at the weekend,' said the sergeant.

'I can't help that,' said the vintner. 'I have extreme difficulty getting supplies out of the city. I have to deal in the black market. The city gates, they're closed. You ought to know that, being garrisoned in the city. Still, there's a hidey-hole here and there for them that know. Secret hogsheads. Very very expensive. It's this war.'

The sergeant said to one of the common soldiers, 'Put the brandy in the basket, you. Don't spill a drop. It's for the colonel.'

The sergeant laid out fifty francs on the counter. The vintner rattled the coins into his till.

The sergeant nodded. His little black-uniformed troop turned and went off down the road towards the river and the city, where all the wine-shops for a week now had been blank shuttered echoing emptinesses.

The sun shone. The regular clack of the shuttle came from Adam the weaver's house where he worked at his loom behind shutters and locks.

But why, on such a beautiful day, did not one bird sing in or around the village? The trees were bare of poems and praisings.

Ah, there was a bird! Listen. The vintner listened. No, it was not a bird, it was a few flute notes. But nobody in the village, as far as he knew, played a flute. He frowned.

Never mind that, the music his money made as he spilled it time and again through his fingers back into the till – that was the best music in the world, as far as he was concerned.

Half-an-hour later there were more soldiers in the village, 'blue' soldiers of the Emperor from the Emperor's second army encamped above, ice-high, falcon-high. Down the little troop had come, down the goat-path, gingerly, carrying sacks and baskets, to the village without women.

The corporal was a big jovial man with a fine sweep of black moustache that outreached his cheeks.

'Have you got them ready for us?' said the corporal to the vintner. He produced a scrap of paper from his breast pocket, held the writing at some distance from his eyes, and intoned, 'Four goat cheeses, three dozen eggs, five hares gutted and salted, hundredweight garlic sausage' . . .

'Ready and waiting, corporal,' said the vintner. 'Not easy, getting delicacies like that in wartime. I had to comb the mountain. I had to drive my cart twelve miles down to the valley.'

The goods were there, ready in one pile, on the counter. The corporal gestured. His men bestowed them in the sacks and baskets they had brought.

'How much?' said the corporal.

'One hundred and seventy-five francs,' said the vintner.

The corporal made an outraged gesture; he threw out his arms; he cast his merry blue eyes skywards, as if to implore heaven itself for justice. The private soldiers stood all around him, grinning. They knew what a character their corporal was. They were lucky soldiers indeed – they considered – to be in this comedian's troop. If they were fated to die, there was a faint possibility that they would meet death laughing. That corporal, he even made scrubbing the latrines a jovial matter.

Now the corporal spoke again, his appeal to the gods over. 'One hundred and seventy-five francs,' he said in an awed whisper.

'That,' said the vintner, 'is the price, indeed, of the goods.'

The corporal threw back his head and let out a huge guffaw. The five privates laughed, just to hear their corporal laughing.

The corporal smote the vintner on the shoulder. 'You're a scoundrel,' he said, 'a highwayman! I swear I haven't met the likes of you in any city in Europe. Such cleverness, Such melo-dramatic pronouncements, so quietly spoken. You are a scoundrel of the deepest dye. A hundred and seventy-five francs. Soon we will be climbing among the stars with our figures.'

He turned to one of the chuckling soldiers. 'Pay the scoundrel,' he said . . . 'Scoundrel, here's pencil and paper. Write a receipt.'

'I make my mark, corporal,' said the vintner, 'I never learnt to write.'

'Ah, how far you would go, my friend,' said the corporal, 'if your mother had packed you off to school, if you had been able to write and cipher. You might have been the prime minister. No, the chancellor who looks after the nation's money, that's what you would have been, with your skill in manipulation of numbers, which no doubt you had even in your mother's womb. Ah, what a great accountant the world has lost, what a prince among merchants! And here he rots, in this god-forsaken eyrie of a place.'

Meantime the soldier with the purse had counted out a hundred and seventy-five francs on the wine-shop counter; and the vintner, with great difficulty, with screwing of his mouth and furrowing of the brows, managed to make at last a simple cross on the receipt, which mark the corporal witnessed with a flourish of the pencil, meantime chuckling and growling by turns.

'If my mother had sent me to school to read and write,' said the vintner sweetly, 'I'd be a moth-eaten clerk in some office in the city down there.' And he sent the coins into his till with a glorious rush and a rattle.

'Scoundrel,' said the corporal, 'I think there's truth in what you say.'

Then, on the point of departure, the blue corporal said suddenly. 'Before I forget. The major would like to know about the very pretty girl who lives in this village.'

The vintner sighed. He said with great patience, 'Corporal, I told you yesterday, the women are all in the forest, hidden. The old women too and the small girls.'

On the huge palm of his left hand the corporal drew a sketch with his right forefinger. 'The major saw a girl among the grave-stones early this morning. Through a glass. Standing at the wall, over there, she was. The major called to me. "Corporal," says he, "look through this glass, say what you see . . ." I saw the girl distinctly, through the prism. Says I, "You're right, major. There's a girl."'

'There's no girl,' said the vintner. 'Not one. I live here. I know everybody. All their comings and goings. I know everything that happens.'

'You're a liar,' said the corporal. 'A scoundrel and a liar.'

The corporal and his men, laden, trudged out of the village. At the end of the village street they turned their faces to the snow and the eagles.

A score of eyes watched their departure through slits in shutters.

Now it was afternoon in the village – a sleepy time – and sleepier and quieter since the women had all been packed off to the forest.

Even Abel's loom had fallen silent.

The vintner nodded in the sun in his rocking chair, on the wooden balcony before his wine-shop.

Then this singular thing happened. Two soldiers entered the village at the same time, as casual as wayfarers, one in a blue uniform from above, and one in a black uniform from the em-battled city below.

Their shadows fell across the vintner. He started out of a dream: he was awake as quick as a bee-sting.

'Well, soldier,' he said to the one. 'Well, soldier,' he said to the other. 'It's very quiet in your camps today. What can I do for you, eh? Tobacco, is it? Tell me now, will it come to a battle down below? And when?'

The 'blue' soldier was an old scarred veteran. 'A battle,' he said. 'Well, you never know nowadays, do you? Not since the French changed all the rules. That corporal from Corsica, His Mightiness the Emperor. He's a man for the battles all right. He thrusts a battle on his enemies, and on his friends too, whether they want a battle or not. A blood-thirsty Corsican bandit. It isn't like it was in the old days, when I was a young soldier. Then there was hardly ever a battle – it was all manoeuvring, like chessmen on a chessboard. The armies would sit looking at each other for a week or a month, from their fortified positions. Oh, I know all about it, I've marched with

the regiments all over Europe: Greece, Germany, Poland,
Spain. I'm a mercenary, I fight for the general who offers me
most loot. Well, there they sit in their fortified positions, with
redoubts and stockades. It's so boring you feel like going mad.
Here's what happens. One of the generals sits down and writes
a letter to the other general. The other general replies. A lieutenant with a little flag of truce carries the letters from HQ to
HQ. Then one army marches away to a new place that the
general thinks has a more advantageous situation. The other
army ups and follows. They encamp. They sit looking at each
other across a river maybe – sometimes across a city wall. More
soldiers, reinforcements, march to join them. Meantime, they
bleed the countryside dry. Soldiers are locusts when they aren't
being heroes. Locusts and parasites. This new confrontation
goes on maybe a whole winter. Then the other general writes a
letter. Time for another move, another counter-move on the
chessboard of Europe . . . Meantime, on a loftier plane altogether, the kings and their ambassadors are in constant touch
with each other. Before you know where you are, in the middle
of a forced march, word comes through, word passes down to
such riff-raff as us common soldiers: *A treaty has been signed,
in London or in Vienna. Your contract, mercenaries, is termi-
nated. At the nearest garrison you will hand over your
armaments and uniform, and you will be paid your wages. God
Save the King* . . . And there we are, vagrants on the road again,
looking for some new army and some new war . . . That's right,
isn't it, soldier?'

The soldier in the black uniform obviously knew nothing
about war and warfare. He was a tall golden-haired handsome
young fellow. His blue eyes were crinkled a little, as if from
probing horizons. He had large capable hands, scarred here
and there from the erosions of ropes and salt. His uniform did
not sit well on him as it did on the old mercenary, who looked

as if he had worn his blue so long it had become a part of him, like his skin and beard.

The young 'black' soldier said, in a kind of sea-cadence, 'I know nothing about it. I'm not a soldier, I'm a fisherman. I'll tell you what happened to me – I was dragged from a boat at the shore. Far away, long ago. I'd go back there today, only they'd come after me and shoot me for a deserter.'

'Leastwise,' said the old 'blue' soldier, 'that's the way war used to be, in the good old days. But it's all changed now. This Bonaparte, he's changed everything. Battles here, there and everywhere – he must be gorging himself with battles all the time. It's no fun being a soldier nowadays – well, not for you young chaps anyway – I've had my day. Death can come for me any time he wants. But you see my point, in the old soldiering days before this Emperor, a mercenary like me had every chance of ending his days quietly, telling lies outside some beerhouse on a summer evening, showing his scar, honoured and respected in his home village. Not now. I'll die near the mouth of a cannon, I know it. Look at this mountain – you'd swear it was impossible to fight a battle on the side of a mountain like this, wouldn't you? The old generals would have had a fit. But it's all the same to this Napoleon – mountain or bridge or swamp, he'll fight anywhere. He usually arranges it so that his enemy has its twenty-five thousand backs to the swamp. Either that, or their good position on the side of the mountain is suddenly not so good when the morning mist rolls away and they're totally sun-blind and bewildered. Then the Emperor moves in on them, ten thousand bayonets glittering in the sun. Oh, he knows what's what, all right. Mars the god of War never had a prince-archbishop like that Bonaparte. A battle? There'll be a battle, make no mistake about that. Down there, round the city gates. But you see how clever our Emperor is – he has one army down there, and they'll give a good account of themselves, you can be sure of that. The Emperor has only to shout *Glory!* to them and they're drunk with the thought of a hero's death. But to make assurance doubly sure the Emperor has this other army, including me, up there, hidden by the forest, and waiting. So, if things start to look a bit dodgy down below, when the fighting hots up, if too many of the Emperor's heroes are getting killed, then our brave marshal gets a signal and his army sweeps down the mountain past this village, and on through the farmlands to the river and the bridge, and God help you poor 'black' soldiers then – you'll be between devil and deep sea. (Pardon: I've spoken too much. That comes from sitting round too many camp fires.) Mister wine-man, give me a bumper of your red wine and give this soldier one too. We're never likely to meet again, soldier, and if we do, it'll be other red spillings than wine between us. Keep the change, wine-man. I don't think, somehow, I'll be needing money after next week. Your health, soldier! You have fifty years in front of you, if you're lucky. I drink now to your good homecoming.'

The two soldiers, the 'blue' and the 'black', touched their pewter, till a few red drops fell between them and made little dusty ruby beads on the road.

'I drink to the girl in this village with the music,' said the press-ganged soldier; and looked around with wet lips and expectant eyes.

'Now,' said the old soldier, 'that's how we think the battle *ought* to go. That's what all the modern manuals say, that's been printed since Bonaparte. But very likely it won't go that way at all. In fact, you may be sure of it. The Emperor is always doing the thing his enemy least expects. For example: the enemy general – *your* general, young fellow (and may God see you safe through the horrors to come) – the enemy general has already had doubts sown in his mind. Fair enough, he knew all along about this army of Napoleon's marching on the city. He knew he would have to fight that army. Maybe he's a good general. Maybe he thinks he stands a fair chance of beating Bonaparte, though that's never happened up to now. But for the last week his spies have been coming in with news of this other French army on the mountain, high up between the forest and the snow. What will he do? What can he do? He knows quite well, even if he defeats Bonaparte down below, he'll be so damnably mauled he can't offer battle a second time. What would you do, wine-man, if you were that general? It's enough to put Alexander the Great in a panic. In a panic, a general is liable to do a very foolish thing, such as go for the mountain army first, leaving a skeleton army in the city . . .'

The old soldier sat on the balcony, his legs dangling. He cut tobacco from a plug, and rubbed it between his withered hands, and slowly filled his clay pipe.

'Yes, yes,' he said. 'Changed days. You never know, now, what might happen from day to day . . . Wine-man, be so good as to light a spill at your stove for my pipe.'

The young soldier who had been dragged from his fishing boat was putting his sea-blue eyes everywhere about the village. What shuttered house hid the girl? From what house, silent now, had it come, the music that, last night, had put such enchantment on his ear?

Nothing stirred in the village. The old priest moved about among the tombstones, reading his breviary. The village men were with their sheep or their trees, or indoors with sleepy eyes, beside loom or last or anvil.

'Last night was the third night,' said the young soldier. 'I heard it, sure as I hear the wine you're pouring. Yes and as sure as I hear the crackling of the tobacco-and-spit in the old soldier's pipe. Only much, much more beautiful.'

'There's no girl in this village plays music,' said the vintner. 'There's no music. No girl. I am tired of telling soldiers that. I will not say it any more. Let them find this ghost.'

The old soldier was surrounding himself with pipe smoke and silence. He passed his reeking pipe to the young enemy soldier. 'Have a puff or two, comrade,' he said. 'The pipe of peace. We'll be seeing another kind of smoke before long. We'll lose each other in that kind of smoke.'

The young soldier puffed, and coughed and sputtered, and handed the pipe back to its owner; who surrounded himself with grey hanks of smoke and silence again.

'No girl,' said the vintner. 'I said, there's no girl. Get that straight. I had a daughter and she died.'

The word 'girl' dropped into the old soldier's pool of silence. He got to his feet. 'Girl,' he said. 'A girl. Yes, that's why I'm here. The major sent me. The major will give five gold pieces for the girl to visit him. Tonight. You're to have the girl ready and waiting at eight o'clock. Don't let the major down. The major's a terrible man if he's thwarted.'

'*There's no girl*,' screamed the vintner. 'Can I make a girl out of air? The girls, old and young, are all in the forest. Ask the tailor – he lives in that house. Ask the weaver next door. There's the priest – ask him. They'll tell you. Nobody here plays a flute.'

The vintner went inside and shut his door. He had heard just about enough of this ghost-girl. Two penniless private soldiers, one old and one young: there wasn't more profit to be squeezed out of the likes of such. Come night, he would open up again; for then the peasants, shepherds, and foresters stole out of their little wooden castles for tappings of the wine barrel, broachings of the ale barrel.

Outside, the sun went down over a shoulder of the mountain, leaving a red forge-glow in the west that promised a fine tomorrow.

The old soldier knocked the wet dottle out of his pipe. 'Well, comrade,' said he, putting his hand on his enemy's shoulder, 'if we meet again, let's hope it's at a bench under an oak-tree, in some more fortunate village than this.'

The old mercenary paused, and frowned. 'Listen, lad,' he said. 'I don't see why a good love-hungry lad like you should be in any battle anywhere – least of all when you were dragged into it against your will. My advice to you is: hide in the village till the battle's over. Then find the girl and take her with you – yes, take her home to the fishing-hut.' He paused again, and shook his head. 'No,' he said, 'I'm sorry I said that. You've taken the king's shilling – you must stand and fight like the rest of us. We're soldiers – we have our duty to do. I wish that you may come sound and strong out of tomorrow's battle.'

'Farewell, soldier,' said the young conscript. 'God be with you.'

'As for the girl,' said the mercenary, 'I hope she's well hidden. I hope she isn't here at eight o'clock tonight when that corporal and his gang come looking for her. I wouldn't put a foul old hag in front of that major, far less a beautiful lass.'

'I think the girl must be very beautiful,' said the conscript. 'She'll play her music tonight – I know that. Maybe I'll see her tomorrow.'

The two soldiers took leave of each other, under the first star: with heads laid upon shoulders, and girdling arms.

Night in the village. The last villager had drunk his wine and gone in and double-locked his door. The stars came out, silently, in galaxies, and the whole great starwheel turned westwards, seeking the hidden silent Atlantic.

Soon there was nothing to be seen in the village but the silhouette of the vintner at his window, beside the lamp. He was counting, over and over again, the day's takings. He was going to die a much wealthier man than he had ever imagined. He was calculating what stocks to cart from the black market in the city, the day after tomorrow.

Presently, sated with the dream of gold, the vintner blew out his lamp and presumably went to bed.

A shadow separated itself from the black bulk of the church. It went to the well in the village square; it lingered there, a frail glimmer, star troubled.

The night frost came suddenly. Then the stars seemed to snap their fingers in their merry march westward, towards the faint lingering primrose light between the mountains.

The frost crepitated in the well, forging brittle armour, deep down.

The shadow at the well shivered. Yet still it stayed, the sole wakeful one in the village, vigilant, between the two armies.

[XI]

The Battle

Dawn came seeping between the eastern mountains. No bird preluded this dawn. Instead, above and below, there were stirrings and movements – horse-hoof, iron wheel, erratic drum-beats, a bugle-call, challenge and response, the bark of a sergeant-major, the thunder of the shifting of a great gun, horse-whinny, the hum (rising and sinking) that thousands of men make as they take up their positions.

Dawn touched the bronze weathercock on the steeple. It blazed for a minute. One by one the shadows of night left the village: except for the shadow who stood at the wall girdling the village's fount of water.

The shadow was the girl who has followed us all through this tale. (Or perhaps it is we who have been following her.) The sun came dazzling through the trees into her eyes: into the curving eye-fringes that sifted and strained the light: and the light ran like quicksilver where lid met globe, the eye's quivering horizon. She did not turn her head. Her forehead took the rose and gold of the morning.

The old priest was there, leaning over the churchyard wall. As he spoke he spilled some snuff on to the back of his hand. 'Listen, girl,' he whispered. 'Come back into the church. You'll be safe there, in the church.'

The girl said nothing. She did not even turn her head.

The priest drew the snuff into one wide-flanged nostril.

'You understand,' he said, 'I can't compel you into the sanctuary. You have your free will like everybody else. But I'm telling you, as solemnly as I can, that there's going to be a battle on this mountain today, soon. Listen – can't you hear the hellish belling and baying of the war dogs, eh? Up above and down below. They're straining at the leashes. It isn't safe for a Christian soul to be sitting where you are. Come now, I'll soon be saying Mass. You'd like that, wouldn't you? Then we could have a bite of breakfast in the kitchen. Then back with you to the sanctuary, and all the hell-hounds in the world won't touch you there.'

She could have been a carved statue, but for the faint flutter at lip and nostril, the slow lift and fall of bosom, the slatting of the eyelashes against the sun, the eyes' quicksilver.

By now another villager was up and stirring: the vintner. He had opened his door wide. (Sometimes soldiers drink round the campfires all night, and then there's nothing for it but a reviver in the morning, first thing.) The morning jangled and clopped and rumbled and brazened and neighed all round the village, as never before, above and below. It looked like being a busy day.

Doors were unlocked and opened in the village, for the shepherds and foresters to get away, breakfasted, to their flocks and trees. Then, hearing what the priest had called 'the dogs of war', the nascent growlings, they one after the other (some with hesitations) decided that it might be better to stay at home, take a little holiday; for this kind of carnival was an unknown quantity. The houses must be kept. The good angels would look after the sheep and the oaks and the hidden women.

It was then that the vintner saw the girl.

The priest was angry with her, a little. 'I *order* you to come inside,' he said.

There was, thought the vintner, many a better-clad gypsy-girl than this much-sought-after stranger, with her torn stained coat that had once been white; but had any girl so beautiful ever sat beside the old village well? No wonder, thought the vintner, the soldiers were filled with joy and longing, after briefest glimpses. This girl, thought the vintner, if she deployed her resources of beauty to the full, could end up by becoming a magistrate's lady, or even mistress to some prince or field-marshal. Yet here she was, a random wind-blown stranger, in rags, like Cinderella. What a girl like this needed was someone to manage her, to give her introductions here and there. Not that the vintner had any influence with anyone of consequence; but in his humble sphere he could do his best, whisper in this ear and that: and await his reward.

The priest was shaking his head and tapping his snuff box again.

The girl was in full sunlight now. The vintner caught his breath. It was as if the girl and the well had been made for each other; centuries since, when the first water-seeking spade was sunk, there she had been, the guardian of the source, touching the first drop of the first rising circle to her lips: pure and thrilling. Now here she was, at last, visible (and with a little pulse in her throat), the incarnate spirit of a sweet mountain spring . . . Nonsense: she was a poor gypsy girl with possibilities.

The vintner tip-toed over to the churchyard wall and the priest. He jerked his thumb at the well. 'Who is she, padre? it seems you know her.'

The priest shook his head. 'A stranger,' he said. 'She's a stranger. She came a week ago. On the very day the village women took to the forest she came. I know nothing about her. She says nothing. She smells of fire. I don't know – it's as if she had escaped from a burning house.'

'I'd like a word with her,' said the vintner. 'Something to her advantage.'

The priest muttered, 'A burnt shadow. She moves among the candles. She lingers a long time at the circle of water in the font. Her face is very old sometimes. Then, soon, she has the look of a child. No fire smell about her, not inside the church. Water drops, bright brow and fingers. She has a flute of some kind. "Be quiet," I say, "there are spies, they'll hear you." There was never such beautiful music in the church. Peace and joy, ripeness and laughter, loaves and fishes, while the music lasts. Sometimes I think the armies have followed her here to finish her off for good and all. Sometimes I think she's keeping them apart. God knows . . . Now I must go to the people in the forest. They'll be very frightened before this day's done.'

The old priest: he turned then and blessed the village, the shuttered tradesmen, the girl seated at the well, the vintner who was approaching the girl now diagonally and whispering to her as he came. The old priest walked quickly in the direction of the forest, stirring the dust of the road with his stick.

The vintner whispered, 'Girl. You there. I have a proposal to put to you. Listen—'

Suddenly, from the ploughlands below, there was a violent explosion: a whine overhead: trees splintered and crashed in that part of the forest between the village and the snow. The single explosion was followed by a cluster of explosions. Trees groaned and split. Then a different sound, a cannon ball striking rock. And again. And again. Rocks and branches were torn from one shoulder of the mountain. Then a dull thud, and faint cries of agony and anger. The artillery had found the true range at last; cannon balls thudded among a pack of men, a square or a column, amid cries and cheers and thin splinterings, just at the snowline.

The 'black' general had come to a decision: he would attack the enemy on the mountain first.

There was a brief silence. The vintner scuttled back across the square into the wine-shop and locked the door.

How shall a writer who has never seen a shot fired in anger describe what followed? Tolstoy would have done it well, with his wild brave groups of men lost in the smoke of war and not knowing what is happening all around them, whether among the slaughter and the wounds they are being caught up in a ground-swell of victory, or whether their comrades are broken and in flight behind them? – They can't tell, they stand there and prime their muskets, some laughing; some crying; some praying; some seemingly apathetic, having abandoned themselves to Fate, and careless of the outcome . . . And Shakespeare, with his little bare stage and balcony and curtain, his soldiers (maybe half-a-dozen or ten extras in each army) march and countermarch across the boards. Sometimes the armies that consist of only a handful of actors turns and confronts each other, then they clash their wooden swords together and yell, and 'a soldier' here or there falls, mortally wounded; this single fall might signify defeat, the turning of a whole wing, the comrades of the fallen one turn and flee. Then the climax of the battle, the two enemy generals, prince and rebel, meet in single combat; they dance about each other, feint, whirl, thrust: for perhaps a minute in the play's two hours. At last the upstart, or the fated one, lie dead. From afar sounds the tin-pot trump of victory. The half-dozen or ten in 'the victorious army' march back, huzza-ing, across the stage. At last a fat man appears, a rollicking comedian under whose bulk the stage creaks, and he cleanses the blood and the agony in a gale of laughter . . .

After the mighty statements of the guns, and a silence, came the throb and tremor of drums, approaching from below, and the onset of marching feet. It was suddenly there, on the road skirting the village, a column of 'black' infantry, muskets aslope on shoulders. Ten minutes or more it took for the thousands of men, four deep, to march past the village and set their rhythmic feet on the broken mountain path, going up. Once above the village, it would no longer be possible for them to march four abreast; the path was too rocky, the press of trees would break their rhythm.

The villagers, including the vintner, peered through warpings and fissures in their shutters. The bayonets made thin flashings in the sun; the villagers marked a face here and there that seemed to have no expression. The soldiers had been ordered to march in a column up the mountain, to destroy – so they had been told – a small army half-demoralised with coldness and hunger. They struck the mountain-side with their feet.

High and thrilling, above, a single bugle call! It was a summons to the big guns, they roared a black welcome to the attackers who had exchanged forest gloom for flashing whiteness-of-snow. The mountain above was a desolation of scattered cries. The bugle, again. The waiting horses and horsemen were roused. They rode against the assault on their stockade and camp. The mountain throbbed with a surge of cavalry: hooves over cold stone. Then the whole mountain seemed to ring like a mad bell, again and again.

Then this pitiful thing was seen, that the 'black' column, the thousands of men in strict order that had marched up, returned in utter rout. It was no longer a disciplined column, it was each man for himself. Wild-eyed, yelling with rage or fear or recrimination, they stumbled down to the base camp below. One soldier had been blinded; a comrade had him by the elbow, urging him down. But then the comrade could wait no longer. He abandoned the man whose face was half blown away; he joined the other defeated soldiers in their desperate downward broken surge.

In three minutes the rout was clear of the village. Last came a soldier with a red gash at his side, which he was trying to close with his hand. Downwards he flung; his fingers suddenly gorged and gloved in red stuff; and out.

A door creaked open. The vintner stuck his head out. The face was drawn, that for a week and more had been all merry roguishness. 'You, girl,' he called. 'Is that it? Is the battle over?'

The girl said nothing. The vintner withdrew.

A quarter of an hour passed. A hawk hung up beside the sun, keeper of the noon. There was a scraping and a thudding inside the tavern. The vintner was manoeuvring his heaviest barrel against the door.

A great shout from below, twin bugle calls, a stammering of drums. The village shook again with the tread of marching feet. Preceded by the colours, a second longer column, fate-marked, came into view and trod, with twenty thousand feet, the mountain down. Flashings here and there from the shoul-dered bayonets, cries from a young lieutenant, yells from a grizzled sergeant. Four deep, they surged up the mountain, but steadily, in obedience to the metronome of discipline. Twenty minutes and more it took for that ten thousand to pass the end of the village. Such splendour, such pageantry, the village had never beheld before, and was never likely to see again.

What was wrong now? As the rear rank strutted and jerked up the mountain, just skirting at right angles the village street, a soldier broke rank. He fell out, he hesitated, he took a few eager steps towards the girl at the well. Did ever a wolf howl more hideously then than the sergeant at the rear; you might have sworn that the man had gone berserk! The wayward soldier, the rim of whose shako was washed with clusters of bright hair, cast one longing piteous look at the keeper of the well; then, inured to authority, he turned and stumbled after the column, and found at last his place in the line-of-four. The metronome throbbed through him again; he trod with ten thousand comrades towards the hidden guns and the cavalry: that, they had been told an hour before, had been spiked and overturned, (not without loss).

Three drummers brought up the rear. With a roll and flourish of drums the second wave of assault was clear of the village and streaming up – broken-ranked, because of the narrowness of the goat path and the congregated trees.

What had gone on in the head of the 'black' general, at his HQ in the city, between the first broken assault and this new thrust? No doubt there had been a half hour of near panic in the general's tent: dismay, disbelief, squabbles, a quick summoning of the lees of resolution, in his staff. 'The mountain can never be taken!' 'What, call the battle off because of one repulse?' 'We have lost the best of our soldiers, the regulars.' 'But consider – we have suffered, but who knows how much more the enemy has suffered. It wants but one more overwhelming attack, a hammer-stroke, and they're broken, done for . . .' The general stood at his table before the maps. He looked coldly in front of him, but his mind was a turmoil, tossed this way and that as each colonel in turn gave his opinion, or kept a prudent silence. 'If we attack again, and are repulsed, Bonaparte will have what's left of us by the throat . . .' The general ordered that the major who had led the first assault be summoned into the tent. The major was ushered in, dazed. 'Yes, general, the enemy has a most strong defensive situation. Much stronger than our intelligence reported . . . We lost hundreds when their guns began. There was no way of getting near them. Then the cavalry, those whirling hooves, the whirling sabres!' The major wept at the awfulness of it; he had never seen, never imagined, such a concentration of fire and steel. He wept openly, in front of the raging colonels and the cautious colonels and the cold general fingering a map. 'But surely, man, the enemy was shaken. It could not be otherwise' – this from a red-faced colonel who had never been in a battle in his life: his duty had been with the commissariat, the supply of the fighting men with guns, shelter, ammunition, fuel and food. 'Those muskets are the best in Europe, the finest in the world.' The major replied that it had not seemed to him that the enemy on the mountain had been shaken at all . . . 'To storm a mountain,' said a young colonel, a man from the military college, 'impossible. Not Caesar, not Alexander, would have dared such a thing!' . . . The general seemed to nod assent to the maps on the table. Another colonel spoke, a young man too, with fine handsome fair moustaches and decorations on his uniform. 'Alexander?' he said softly. 'Caesar? In the past ten or fifteen years Alexander and Caesar have been cast down like time-eaten statues. Things have happened in our generation that were hitherto undreamed of. Bonaparte himself, out there beyond the city wall – didn't he storm a mountain at Austerlitz, and clear it of Russians and Austrians in under an hour? The thing can be done. We can pluck a famous victory out of the jaws of seeming defeat. We have the men. We have the arms. Perhaps there is, after all, a general greater than Bonaparte. This could be a glorious day.'

The shattered major was led out.

'Folly, folly,' muttered an old colonel with a fringe of silver hair.

The general turned. He looked into the faces of his staff, one after the other. He smiled. He said, 'We will go up the mountain once more.'

Such had been the scene in the general's tent below, between the first assault and the second . . . What the Emperor thought, watching from the château of the absentee baron, through a long glass, the river of black soldiers streaming upwards, twenty thousand of them, urged on by drum and flag and bugle – that has not been recorded. We can imagine the one snap of the fingers, the telescope clapped shut, the look of utter disbelief and scorn, followed at once by that charming smile, and the playful tweaking of the ear of the nearest staff-officer. 'I think,' he might have said, 'when the annals of war are finally recorded, this will be marked as a day of purest folly.'

When the first troops of the second assault broke out of the trees, what they saw, apart from the guns and the masses of men spanning the mountain from slope to slope – what they saw were hundreds of black strewn uniforms, prone and supine; those dead who had gone up an hour before to crack the enemy open. The same guns spoke again, nodding and opening their red mouths. Sergeants and corporals yelled above the din, urging their men to storm the guns! – break the cavalry! – capture the standards and the eagles.

The 'black' soldiers erupted then out of the trees; bravely they ran at the murderous mouths, and at the motionless columns of infantry behind the guns, and at the snorting prancing ranks of horses and the plumed and sabred horsemen at each side. The blue uniforms looked almost black against the snow.

The 'black' army debouched in column after column from the forest on to the open slope and ran on. The guns spoke; and spoke; and spoke.

Black heaps grew here and there, or lay singly like unstrung puppets. And still the forest teemed with new 'black' soldiers, surging out and up, and yelling.

The guns spoke again, and were silent.

A bugle sounded, clear and thrilling, from the flank of the light cavalry. Three hundred cavalrymen raised their sabres: sun flashings, snow flashings, circles of light.

The slow thunder of hooves began, and quickened and became urgent.

Five thousand disordered 'black' soldiers, dazed and terrified by the batteries, awaited the onset. But – such is the
heroism and folly of war – here and there, singly or in small
groups, 'black' soldiers ran on and knelt and fired at the great
guns. And ran at the horses, as if bravery itself would break the
stretched and whirling hooves and the high-held sabres. The
bravery was trodden down and cut to pieces.

One 'black' soldier, a corporal, got as far as the enemy
general's tent. Perhaps he ought to have hurled himself at the
general with his nails and teeth. Instead, he just stood there; he
shook his head as if he had awakened from a dream. 'A brave
soldier,' said the 'blue' general. 'See that this brave soldier has
his wound bandaged. He is to be given bread and beef and beer.
Yes, in my tent, off my plate.' The 'blue' general leant down across
his grey's neck and put a coin into the 'black' soldier's hand.

And the 'black' soldier, still shaking his head, was taken
away to the ambulance tent first.

The mountain was all broken throbbings. The light cavalry
and the heavy cavalry were engaged: the first waves of them
had gone among the trees.

Within a quarter-hour there was not one living 'black'
soldier to be seen between the forest and the snow.

The infantry had had nothing to do since the battle began.
They raised ragged cheers, since now it was likely that they
would get away at last from this place of snow and rock and
black trees: as soon as the order 'Pursuit' was sounded.

In the village, the men behind their shutters heard the distant
bugle-cry of retreat sounded, thrown down thin and clear
from the snow crags under the summit. The bugle-call was
followed at once by a cheer from thousands of young throats.
The hunter's blood was up in them; they were free, more or less,
to do what they liked with the quarry.

The hidden women in the forest heard it; some huddled close and clutched each other; the eyes of Jeanne shone, her lips parted a little with rage and wonderment. She had never heard such thrilling sounds; here she was, in the forest clearing, among dead charcoal fires, corralled with old women and little girls.

If the girl at the well heard the music of victory, her face revealed nothing: a deeper coldness perhaps. A statue she seemed in the village square, with blank sun-cancelled eyes.

The torrent of black uniforms hurried and hurtled and cascaded down the mountain, on past the end of the village, on and down to their general and the walls of the city occupied uncertainly by their accoutred untried comrades.

Packs and muskets were thrown away in the rout. Men crashed into each other and fell and trod on fallen bodies. The younger soldiers had the bolt-eyes of hares; the older ones cursed and kicked and fought their way past obstacles – trees, rocks, reeling and fallen comrades.

One soldier paused at the end of the village. He looked with wonderment at the red stump of his arm. Then he joined again the ragged downward-streaming torrent.

But, in the rout, there were wholesome scenes – one soldier helping a crippled comrade – a strong thick soldier with a broken soldier across his shoulder – a blinded soldier spoken to soothingly by a soldier that lingered beside him, whispering constantly, as if to say: 'Don't fret, man. I'll see you safe to the ambulance tent, they'll wash your eyes there. Blind? Who says so? It's just that you went too close to the smoke and the flame. Come on, now, here's my arm, hold on to me, I'll see you home and dry . . .' And down they moved, slowly, with linked arms, the eyeless face staring up at the sun . . . And here an old corporal stopped beside a boy who was screaming, out of his mind with terror – first he threw the whole weight of his hand against the distorted face, so that the boy was shocked into silence; then the veteran put his arm about the boy and poured words like oil and wine into his wounded senses; and together, smiling, they lingered at the edge of the village, as if for reassurance that such places could exist after all; then, slowly, the old soldier led the cannon-shocked boy down the mountain road.

Yet those Samaritans among the defeated army, who lingered to administer comfort, knew well that in a matter of minutes the pursuit might be on top of them, with unbated bayonets and musket-butts, given full liberty to loot and slaughter: the hounds of victory in full cry.

And now only the dregs of the defeated army were hirpling and slouching down, singly or in little groups. A soldier pointed to the shuttered houses of the village; perhaps they could hide here, till the worst was past? Despondent head-shakings – every last nook and corner would be flushed out – they must try to get across the bridge and back to the city, before the torrent of bayonets struck them from behind. Already, in the forest above, there were shouts and crashings, coming nearer. The loose remnants stumbled down as fast as wounds and utter weariness allowed.

Surely we have seen this crippled soldier before: a bright-haired blue-eyed one, he who had been seeking, on the eve of battle, an image of a girl with a flute? It was the same soldier, the one who had been dragged from his fishing-boat to fight in foreign wars. But he was woefully altered. He had been wounded in the thigh, just above the left knee. Vainly he tried with both hands to staunch the flow of blood, but his knuckles dripped redness. It was clear that the soldier was far gone, that he could go no further, that he neither knew what had happened to him nor where he was. He reached the village end. He raised his dull face and saw the cluster of houses with shutters and locked doors. If he saw the girl at the well, she was nothing, a mirage. All the soldier knew was that he could go no further. Here, in this foreign village, was journey's end. It reminded him of another village. He would lie down. He took, falteringly, his wound to the gap between two houses, and let himself down, biting on his lip to keep the pain quiet. He found a clay humped hollow with an opening. He crept into it.

From below, from the city wall, sounded a broken drumbeat; a forlorn bugle sounded superfluous 'Retreat'. In his tent, the general gazed at the map; as if it was his death-warrant. The staff officers stood here and there; from time to time they looked at him: uneasily, contemptuously, angrily.

The city gates had been thrown open to admit the remnants of the second assault: they came in groups, laughing, weeping, crying out in pain, a few cursing their officers and their general and Bonaparte and the merciless butchers above with their cannons and cavalry: cursing every battle and every war that had ever been fought. A few of those loudmouths were quickly taken in charge by the military police – a night in chains would cool them off.

The general could not take his eyes from the map with its blue and black squares and wedges, the written dispositions of corps and column. The map had become a stone mirror. He was gazing at the skull on his tombstone.

The Emperor, on his balcony three miles away, shook his head in wonderment. Such ineptitude! Tomorrow, his two armies would crack the city open like a rotten nut.

Now that the last soldier in the 'black' army had laid himself down in an empty pig-sty, the village was silent for a half-hour or so. Not even the vintner stirred in his wooden fortress. There was one faint 'clank-clank', as if he was hiding bottles in a hurry.

Then the first spindrift from the wave of victory fell into the village: seven blue soldiers, jigging a few steps, clapping their hands, waving their caps, laughing. One carried a broken wheel on his shoulder.

'Six miles to the city!' one shouted. 'Wine-shops and women. Hurry!'

'There's a wine-shop here,' said another. 'And I'm thirsty.'

'No,' yelled a third. 'The city – that's where the loot is.'

'We're soldiers,' said the one with the broken wheel. 'We've been in battle. We won! We'll take our drink where we find it.'

They stopped at the door of the wine-shop.

'Wine and women!' cried a loud-mouth. 'The soldier's bounty.'

'As for women,' said a soldier with a purple-black beard, 'there's a fine-looking one over there – see – standing beside the well. She must be – yes, she's the one they've been making songs about in the barracks.'

The others looked. They saw nothing.

'A strange thing about this wine-shop,' said another. 'It's locked. A wine-shop door should be open wide, especially on the day of a great victory.'

He gave the vintner's door a violent kick, till the timbers trembled.

'Wine should be flowing in torrents,' said a small thick soldier. 'Let me have a go.'

He hurled himself at the door, shoulder first. The door splintered, but remained fast. Slivers of wood fell on the wooden balcony.

'Some way to welcome liberators,' said the black-bearded foot-soldier. 'This wine-keeper should be taught a lesson.'

The one who had splintered the door rubbed his sore shoulder. 'It's my opinion,' he said, 'there's a heavy barrel wedged behind the door.'

'Hans,' said a corporal, 'you have the soldier's key,' tapping Hans' musket.

Hans primed his musket, put it to his shoulder, aimed, and discharged it at the lock. A black splintered star opened where the lock had been. Did they hear a whimper from inside? It was, possibly, the broken lock tinkling along the floor.

How those soldiers heaved then, to overcome the resistant wine-barrel wedged behind the door! They strove harder than they had done in the battle. There was a scraping, a lumbering, a heavy squelching crash, and the door, forced, hung upon one hinge. Out over the tavern threshold surged a flood of red wine. The barrel, falling, had dislocated one of its staves. The red wine gurgled and oozed and made rich mud of the dust under the balcony.

'Plenty more where that came from,' said the corporal. 'Hans! Jacques! Go inside, discover what delights there are.'

A soldier knelt and did his best to lap the wine flowing across the balcony from the broken barrel.

Hans and Jacques emerged from the wine-shop. Their arms brimmed and clanked with flagons. The victorious soldiers plucked two each. They kissed the flagons. They laughed and jigged and stamped their feet.

The corporal considered for a moment. He said, 'We'll drink in the gully down there. The captain said, no looting till he gives the order. He's a great stickler for discipline, Captain Fournier.'

The soldiers nodded, clasping their flagons. They wandered away to a hidden gully under a fringe of trees. The village wine first, then the brimming city cellars.

'Wait for us, sweetheart,' shouted blackbeard, 'we'll be back.' (His comrades saw no one.)

They crossed the ditch, bottles clanking, towards a hollow that was hidden from the road.

'No singing. No shouting,' came the hoarse whisper of the corporal. 'We're not supposed to be doing this. Not yet. There could be trouble.'

Where were the hordes of 'blue' soldiers, the victors? One might have thought they would be yelling and snapping at the heels of the demoralised broken army. One might have had the image of a breached dam.

A lieutenant and a sergeant and two privates entered the village from above. The sergeant said, 'Sir, a disgraceful business – one of my men panicked. A coward. He simply broke rank and ran off yelling down into the forest.' The sergeant turned to the privates. 'I want that man found. Bring him back to the camp. Is that clear?'

'But where will he be, sergeant?' said one of the soldiers.

'That's for you to find out,' said the sergeant. 'Follow the stink of fear.'

'No pursuit of the enemy,' said the lieutenant. 'The general issued an order immediately after the battle. No mopping up. He wants the city to be crammed with rumours and wounds and death. So the half-rotten fruit will fall into our hands in the morning, at the first shaking. I'm sorry to say, seven of my lads disobeyed the order. They sneaked off, a bit of private looting. Corporal Lefranc and six others. Well, it's understandable, I suppose. It's a soldier's instinct to go for a crippled enemy and strike him down. A lot of grumbling up there, I can tell you, in the ranks. They'd been led to expect loot, cartloads of it. I told them, "Look, lads, have a bit of patience. What'll you get off a few frightened broken soldiers? We'll be in the city tomorrow, or the day after. Plenty of shops to break into, in the city. Plenty of taverns. Plenty of girls. Just one more night – then you'll live like lords for a week." Still they grumbled. I hear, we lost only twenty-five men in the battle. I can't get over Lefranc, the corporal. A good soldier, that. Away he slips with half-a-dozen others.

They'll be found, of course. I'll be sorry to lose Corporal Lefranc. Still, an army is run on strict discipline, or it's nothing.'

'This village,' said the sergeant, 'doesn't look too friendly disposed. Empty as a graveyard. Barred and shuttered. They could have put out a flag or two. I wonder if our coward is lurking here somewhere? I thought I told you men to go find the coward.'

'We looked,' said one private. 'There's an enemy soldier, next door to death over there, in that pig-house. It might be an act of mercy to put a bayonet in him.'

'Leave him alone,' said the sergeant. 'I want the deserter.'

The two privates wandered away along the village street. They passed, the well, one on either side, without seeming to see the girl: as if she was made of sunlight and water reflections.

'There's been a story about this village, for the past week,' said the lieutenant. 'A very beautiful girl. Hundreds of men have seen her, either early in the morning or just at sunset.'

'I don't see her,' said the sergeant.

It was high noon. They were standing, the lieutenant and the sergeant, facing the village square. The girl sat now on the parapet of the well, her eyelashes meshed against the sun, the lids thin broken lines of quicksilver; the tremulous pulse in her throat.

They did not see her.

'There's always stories like that, sir,' said the sergeant. 'The princess in the tower. It's stories like that that keep soldiers going. That's what we're bleeding and sweating for always, to rescue innocence and beauty. When we break down the door of the tower at last, there's nothing inside but rats and bones and spiders' webs.'

'True, sergeant,' said the lieutenant. 'I wonder why the door of that place – is it a wine-shop? – is smashed in. I think my beauties have been there. Well, I hope for their sakes they get so drunk they won't know much about the firing squad till they wake up in hell with hangovers.'

'Sir,' said the sergeant, 'will I look for them now?'

'Presently,' said the lieutenant. 'Yes, you'd better. I will be very sorry to lose Lefranc. A fine soldier. What got into him? I think, sergeant, we'd best be getting back, or they'll be marking us down for deserters too.'

The lieutenant and the sergeant left the village. They trudged up the goat-path that petered out among the first forest trees. There, a green silence enclosed them. They did not hear the first drunken song from the gully beside the village; that after an hour slurped, slurred, and lapsed into grunts and syllables. The looters were having a sodden time of it. Corporal Lefranc yelled once, 'Stop that! Stop the tomfoolery, you! Do you want a court-martial, eh? Drink like monks, quietly.'

In the early afternoon silence; all that could be heard in the village was a barely-audible thread of water deep in the well, unspooling, spilling, splashing, rising, risen to be gathered into the surface web of water-music that shifted and glittered. A wail and a groan came occasionally from inside the wine-shop. What stirred under the meanest village roof? The soul of the wounded soldier, it stirred and lingered about the grievous wound. It had come to a place where two roads part. Where will he take his wound, that soldier – to the ultimate festering and clean skeleton of the graveyard? – or to old age and a silver storied scar? The soul of the soldier stirred and lingered about the wound, seeking this way and that.

And then, suddenly, the ruined vintner could hold back no longer. He broke through his broken door. He yelled to the shimmering girl and the wounded shifting soldier and the shutters and locks of the village, 'Ruined! I'm ruined! After all I've done for them! I'll speak to the brigadier in person. I will . . . You, girl, do you think any more soldiers will come?'

No answer: her silence was sunk well-deep.

From somewhere above, powder and spark met, and a musket roared. Perhaps the deserter was getting his deserts. Whatever it was, it was too much for the vintner: he leapt and staggered as if the ball had gone into his umbles. He steadied himself. He gave one last despairing look at his drink shop. He shook his fist at the mountain above, then at the river and the city below. He gathered his hair in both clenched fists. He turned and ran as fast as his short fat legs could carry him, in the direction of the forest, where the women were. He abandoned his little castle of grapes, and the village whose heart he had gladdened many a moon, many a snow, many a shearing-time.

From above, from the victorious army, an incessant wavering bronze undersong, as if a hundred hives had been shaken, and the thousands of bees sang savagely in the bee-keeper's acre: forbidden as yet to forage among the delectable gardens below.

A shutter in a village house was opened cautiously, and the cropped russet head of Abel the weaver thrust out like a gargoyle.

'You, girl,' he called to the girl at the well – 'you seem to know a thing or two. What next? What'll happen now, eh?'

Silence: the buried bell of water, deep down, barely moved. Then the girl whispered, 'You should go to the forest.'

'All right, don't speak,' said Abel. 'There'll be looting. I know it. I'm going to no forest. Did you say forest? I have a loom I wouldn't sell for a hundred crowns, and bales of good cloth. Forest, indeed! Talk sense.'

No sound from the air bell in the steeple.

No sound from the sty but a spider's spinning. The soul had gone a little way out of the wounded soldier to find a place, its peace and bourn. That journey – some say – is marked out for us from before the beginning.

Another shutter creaked open. It was Hans, an old shepherd. He squinnied across at the weaver. 'Did I hear right?' he said in a weak high voice. 'Did that slut of a strange girl tell us to go to the forest? What does she want, sitting there beside the well? Who's she, I'd like to know, to order us to go to the forest? I'm going to no forest. Forest, indeed! What do I want with forests? I'm a hill man; if I go anywhere it's up among the hills with my few sheep – yes, up among the brooks and the grass. Forest – that old Maria of mine's in the forest. I'd rather have the soldiers than Maria any day . . . You're an impudent girl – you don't belong here. Go away.'

Another creak, another half-opened shutter, another head. It was Walter, wood-chopper and drunkard. He said, in awe, 'The wine-shop's broken. What'll we do now, eh? There might be a flagon or two left. I thought that girl said – or was I wrong? – that we ought to go to the forest. I tell you this, I wouldn't feel safe, far from the wine-shop, broken or not. Is there drink in the forest? No. Walter stays here. Walter and wine-shop were made for each other.'

The bees were hived and savage still, above.

And now came, stepping solicitously down the steep path into the village, a colonel and two majors and an ensign, guiding and guarding and hedging a figure of immense splendour. It was the general and his staff.

The three heads at open shutters gawped and squinnied at them. The girl looked past them. The general glanced at the well. He did not seem to see the girl.

The general was a fine-looking man with first threads of silver in his dark curling sideburns. He carried himself erect and masterful: in contrast to his staff officers, whose neck-bones and knee-bones were slack as they hovered about him, ready for instant acquiescence or instant rebuke.

The general's coat was a thing to marvel at, festooned with braid, orders, medals, ribbons, gilt buttons. It was as immaculate, that coat, as if it had been newly tailored that morning; nor were mud splashes, blood stains, or smoke smears on it. He touched, delicately, his dark moustaches. Then he spoke: 'So this is the village. Perhaps we ought to call the battle after this village, whatever its name is. You, major – look up the name of the village on the map. Have the goodness. A pretty place. I see one of the houses has been broken into. I gave distinct orders there was to be no petty looting. There'll be abundance of loot for them once we're in the city. Is it a tavern? It smells like a kind of wine-shop. You, Ensign Fauvel, discover the names of the men who looted the wine-shop. Have the kindness. See that they are dealt with. What good does it do the reputation of a general, eh, interfering with simple people carrying on with their peaceful trades? Men such as us, soldiers, we do what we must do, we put a hedge about the lives of ordinary people, to save them from a worse evil. Our battles and blood-spillings are for this only, that the order of society may be kept in being: a concord of work and goodwill, a kind of music, flowing down from the Emperor to the simplest peasant and fisherman.'

They murmured agreement all about him. The general stood, lost for a minute in a high austere conception of the state. Every syllable he uttered was a precious polished stone to his officers.

'May we congratulate you, general, on a famous victory,' said one of the colonels, daring (once he judged the moment opportune) to break upon the general's musing.

'Indeed,' said the other colonel. 'A brave day – it has been a brave day. The mountain pass is ours. The bridge below is ours. See – the last of them are straggling across the bridge now. Tomorrow the city will be ours.'

'You have won a great victory, general,' said the major.

'No,' said the general. 'Not so. Nothing of the kind. You are not to say that again. It was the victory of the whole army.

Every man, down to the humblest cook and orderly, played his part.'

The four shuffled and nodded agreement all about him. If such was the general's considered opinion, it was theirs too, of course.

The general mused again, for a full minute, in silence. The officers stole glances at his intent face. What gems would fall next from the august mouth?

A dozen village heads were gazing now from open shutters at the general and his watchful solicitous staff. None of them had ever dreamt that such splendour of gold and scarlet could visit their village – a general, no less, a not-too-old handsome victorious general. There was to be no looting – they had heard him say that with his own oracular mouth. Only the wine-shop. Only the hard man in the wine-shop. And the ruffians who had done that were going to be brought to book.

Occasionally, from the hidden hollow half-a-mile away, a voice was lifted in drunken song. There was a broken shout of laughter, as the sun, westering, touched the rim of the mountain.

And now the philosopher in the victorious general gave way, all at once, to the good fellow, the comrade-in-arms, the laughing cavalier. The fact of victory, known soberly up to now, rose up in him like a fountain. He linked his arm happily with the old colonel (who could have been his father); he gestured, smiling, for the others to come closer.

'Listen, my friends,' he said. 'Two days ago I spoke with the Emperor in his tent. We discussed, naturally, our strategy with regard to this battle. We discussed it with great minuteness and at some length. The Emperor said, to conclude our confer-ence – for, you understand, we were alone together in the tent, the Emperor and myself. "General," he said to me, "it is my opinion they will attack the mountain army first. When you have turned them, when you have broken them and sent them in confusion back over the bridge, it would be fitting for you to send a message. Of course, in a sense, it will not be necessary, a message, for victory is certain. Besides," said the Emperor, and tweaked my ear in that familiar way of his, "I will be studying the action through my glass, from the turret of the château there. All the same," said His Majesty, "between sunset and the first star, a signal fire on the side of that mountain would make a brave sight. I would know beyond a peradventure that the day was ours. Not that the day could ever conceivably be theirs", and he nodded towards the city and the doomed army. "A fire," he said, "a big fire, I like the image even as I speak it. A fire under the first stars – those same stars that have written our destiny across the night from the first beginnings of time. Let there be such a fire, general, as will douse the light of the constellations, for an hour. Will you do that for me?"

'Those were the very words of the Emperor to me. I remember each syllable. The speech is graven on my heart . . . So, the village is a pool of shadows now, the mountain will soon be a black hulk. It is time for us, in obedience to our Emperor's wishes, to make it otherwise . . . Ensign, I will leave the pyre and the lighting of it in your so capable hands.'

'I will arrange, sir, at once, for tar and kindling,' said the ensign.'I will detail a company of pioneers . . . Sergeant,' he called to a hidden attendant soldier, one of a small company who lingered under the trees above.

The sergeant was there, quick as a sheepdog to a shepherd.

'Sergeant,' said the ensign.'A hundred or so pioneers. Get logs from the forest, branches, twigs, anything that will burn. Two barrels of tar will be required, no, three. There is a suitable rock-ledge over there. That should do for siting the pyre.'

'Sir,' said the sergeant, and barked as fiercely and inarticulately as any dog to a hidden company that was waiting still further up. There was a stirring and cracking of branches. Broad-faced low-browed pioneers clambered down out of the sylvan shadows, patient as oxen for the yoke.

The general seemed displeased. He frowned. The staff officers gave each other sidelong glances. 'Ensign,' said the general, 'you surprise me sometimes. There is a certain obtuseness about you. Ensign, has it not dawned on you that by the time sufficient kindling had been gathered for the fire – for a fire, you understand, suitable for the eyes of our Emperor – by the time the first torch was put to the pyre, it would be morning again? Between sunset and the first stars, said the Emperor. Have you no eyes in your head, man?'

The ensign mumbled and shuffled his feet. The three other officers gave him dark looks: they wished to have no part in his stupidity. (But in what the ensign's stupidity consisted, they could not as yet say.)

'I'm sorry, sir,' said the ensign, his eyes on the dust.

The general made a wide sweep with his hand. 'Here,' said he, 'is a village. It is a wooden village. This village is as dry as tinder. Three hundred years of hearths, ham-curing, pipe-smoke, baking. Ensign, you would oblige me by setting the village ablaze. The sun is almost down.'

'Sir,' said the ensign, brightening. He shouted to the sergeant. The sergeant barked at the pioneers. Two pioneers were despatched to the store above for an armful of tarred torches.

'I saw at once,' said the general, 'as soon as I set eyes on it, that the village is deserted. No doubt the villagers have taken to the forest over there. They will come back. They will build a better village than this group of hovels. For this is a time, after all, when all things are being made new. Their grandchildren and their great-grandchildren will speak with pride of the famous battle that bears the name of their village.'

'Sir,' said the major. 'There is a young woman sitting at the well over there. She ought to be warned.' He pointed. Sunset clothed the girl in red from throat to ankle.

The general glared at the well. 'There's nobody there that I can see,' he said. 'I shadow. The torches! Have we to wait till midnight for the torches?'

A hundred pioneers in single file, each with his blazing torch, came down the mountain path. Their free hands glinted. They were carrying new axes.

'Pioneers, halt!' yelled the sergeant. 'Ready. Step forward, first rank. Axes.'

Shutters were smashed on each side of the street: crashings, wood groanings, splinterings.

'Pioneers!' cried the sergeant. 'Ready second rank. Step forward. Torches.'

Torches were thrust or thrown into the wrecked shutters.

Then this singular thing happened in the uninhabited village, that there was a swift near simultaneous unbarring of doors, and a score or more shadows emerged, clutching clocks and pots and a bolt of cloth and little squealing pigs and fluttering squawking hens; and the burdened shadows ran coughing and cursing towards the black forest, under the first stars.

The first house to flower into flame was the weaver's, no doubt on account of the vast quantity of wool and cloth in it.

The general stroked his moustaches; he nodded.

Another house, old Liza's, stuttered into smoke and flame.

Another roof-tree, further on, was a tall burning column. A forester's house went roaring, earth rooted, up among the stars.

From this house and that came crackles and shy little curls of smoke: then the first of a score of tiny flames that ran together, and circled, and leapt, and chorused, and danced.

Who blundered into the village during this first of the fire's seven stages, like a bewildered moth, but the vintner? His own establishment was giving out little burbling bubbling noises; then a little keg of brandy burst open and burnt like a forge; then a hundred firebirds fluttered up in his rafters. The vintner gazed at the burning wine-shop. Something had gone wrong with the man. He was smiling. He stood there tittering. 'Oh,' said the vintner, 'little did I think! Mulled ale in the morning! Mulled ale, nothing but mulled ale. Mulled ale always, all next winter.'

A stream of burning brandy ran from his wrecked reeking door.

You should have seen Andrew the elder's house, what a brave crimson and yellow gown it wore: no doubt because, seven or eight generations since, the finest best-seasoned oak had gone to the building of it. That fire towered highest of all the hundred fires. It was still being said three generations afterwards that a lump of molten gold big as a man's head was found later under the foundations: old Andrew's hoard, against the rags and wrinkles of age.

The general and his staff and the common soldiers had now to retreat out of the village. It was too hot and bright. They stood under an oak. A red cinder bumped and sang like a bee on the general's coat, and died there, in a small smoulder and singeing.

The vintner, bent double with laughter, staggered about on his smouldering balcony. 'O the good mulled wine,' he sang, his voice small and strained with excess merriment. 'A shilling a cup to soldiers. Foresters, free.'

Under the tree where now a little cool of night air stirred, the general took his sword from its scabbard. He examined the hilt, musing. Then he raised it high. The blade flung out fire flashings. 'Emperor, the victory!' he cried. A hundred bee embers fell among the smiling staff. They all retreated to an oak slightly further back. Their faces were painted a lurid shifting red, like carnival masquers.

We will leave the fire at this point, well into the second of its seven stages. There is nothing much to say about a burning village. The same thing happened, roughly, to every house – a kind of haphazard pattern of yellow unfoldings, flames, high roaring star-quenching towers and conflagrations, sinkings, smoke, smoulderings, a few late flowerings, sighings, sinkings, glowings, a line of hot crepitating blacknesses.

The priest came back when the fire was entering its fifth stage. A blazing rafter fell before him – a window burst as he passed and a shower of hot glass fell and tinkled round his feet. He came at last and stood before the stone church. He went inside.

Once, in the burnt village, the well shone; as if a cold star flashed out of it.

In the pig-sty that was shaped rather like a boat upturned against the gales of winter, the soldier lay quiet. The soul had gone out of him. It had gone, questing, to find the place and the peace that all his life, since birth, the man had been preparing for himself, in secret even from his desiring bone and flesh and blood: its true bourne.

The Longest Journey

All night, in the stone sty where the smith's pig had once been kept, where now the soldier lay, his soul dallied at a crossroads. It was so engrossed as to which road it must take, that it did not hear the noise of the village burning; nor did it feel the wound in the thigh, nor the fire bees that fell and stung and died for an hour and more on face and hands. The coldness of the stars pierced the man; he did not feel that, either. His soul was intent on the two roads that branched before it; it lingered, tremulously, waiting for the sure urge. For one signpost said LIFE, and it would venture some steps along that way. It had been a happy time, those twenty years in the fishing village in the North Atlantic. Not that it had been easy, by any means: fortune is capricious always to the fisherfolk, and often enough the man would bring brimming baskets of fish or crabs back to the village at sunset; but sometimes he set his brown-patched sail for home with only three or four sickly haddocks to show; and worse, one of those sudden gales would get up, and then he had to forget about his lines and creels and make for the nearest land. Thrice he had escaped drowning literally by his finger-nails, clawing at a rock and dragging himself on to it, drenched, while the unguided boat went with the sea, wherever it was driven. Next morning, when it was calm again, he found his boat thrown up on the shore of a strange island.

Twice a timber had been stove in; once the mast had snapped; once his oars and gear were lost entirely. Yet they said he was a lucky fisherman: some of the other fishermen had lost everything, their boats sunk or smashed to matchwood, their livelihood threatened. Yes, in his own time a dozen fishermen had gone down with their boats, never to be seen again, or seen in such guise that men made haste to bury the huddled miscellany of rags and bones. And then, for months after, it was a piteous thing to see those widows and their children at the shore when the lucky boats came in – the sea's darlings – the star-led ones. Well behind the other women, and the mewling cats and gulls, those bereaved ones lingered. Always they were noticed last – a haddock jaw or a cod jaw was hung on the widow's crooked finger – and only the cruellest village women complained about those free offerings; most of them were well aware that one day or another, late or soon, they might be taking the same lonely stance.

But happy times had been in the village, often enough. Four years ago, a strange thing had happened. Gathering limpets for bait at the shore, the man had looked up to see Sally Bergson sitting at the rockpool and looking deep into it – the vain empty creature, she should have been at home, helping her mother to make butter or brew ale. He could not be bothered with her – he wished she would go away, she was a distraction to him at his limpet-gathering. 'Then why look, man – make the limpet-bucket ring – let the foolish creature shake her bright hair down till her face and neck are obliterated with spun gold once more. Limpets, fish, the boat – that's your concern . . .' He had frowned when that voice of commonsense spoke inside him. For the next half hour he looked at nothing but the limpet-studded rock and his stone hammer and ringing bucket. Then he had looked back over his shoulder again, for the idle slut might have slipped off on her bare feet over the

sand, meantime. But no: she was still there, entranced by her
reflection, the bright frame about her head, the lappings of gold
at her breast. There was something about her posture, the delicate poise of her head, the gesture her hand made pushing her
hair back or writing with her finger (it seemed) on the surface
of the pool, that made his breath tremble and his heart miss
beats. She, Sally, was simply the most beautiful adorable
creature he had ever seen . . . ! And that first stroke of longing
cancelled limpet-gathering for that day. The poor enchanted
youth could not summon the courage to talk to her. His
hammering heart would have broken up any words he could
utter. At last Sally became aware that the fisherman's boy was
looking at her more often than he struck limpets. She smiled,
but not to him. On him she put a cold look, and got to her feet,
and was off across rocks and sand, with not so much as one
look back. If she had spat in his face, he could not have felt such
pain . . . What was this that had come to turn his life topsy-
turvy? The image of Sally sat opposite him at the scrubbed
dinner table. His baited lines got tangled, thinking about Sally
in his directionless boat. He would stand at the barrel in the
ale-house, alone, with joyous secrets thronging his mind:
courtship, marriage, a new hearth, a new boat, a cradle in a
corner. The other young men saw the change that had come
over him; in the end they turned their backs on him and played
their dominoes or pontoon; and he was glad to be left alone, in
the great brimming shoal of his thoughts. No need to tell how
he set about trying to waylay her, as if by accident, at the stile or
at the end of the village. Sometimes Sally smiled at him, and
then the poor youth was in a very heaven of ecstasy. The next
time, she would give him a cold look, she might even look
through him as if he was a glass man, or a ghost. And then, for
the rest of that day, what dolour, what heart's withering! 'Eat
thee egg and bread, boy,' his mother would say – 'What ails

thee, thu looks like a sick dog? Eat, or thu'll go into a decline.'
That was the evening his father had said, suddenly, between a
mouthful of fish and a mouthful of ale: 'The boy's in need of
a wife – that's it.'

The secret was out – the boy, red in the face, in a torment,
took his enchantment out under the cold eyes of Fate, the stars,
that ruled love and fishing and the doors of death.

It lasted an entire winter, that enchantment. Never once did
he have the courage or the rashness to speak to Sally. The very
idea of it interfered with his breathing. And yet he laid plans,
he arranged that they should come face to face twice or thrice a
week, with dire or joyous consequences . . . Then this strange
thing happened, that one day, by pure chance, he went for
tobacco to the village shop, and there she stood, Sally, bargaining with old Silas the shop-man over the sale of two of her
mother's large white cheeses. She stood there; a foot inside the
threshold he stopped and stared at her. She was, once more, an
ordinary, rather silly, lass. All the honey was drained out of
her. Sally accepted the shopman's offer, and put the white coins
in a purse. Then she turned and gave the boy from the fishing-
boat one of her cold hurtful looks. And he said, 'Sally, is it? Oh
yes, it's Sally. If you don't mind, Sally, let me get to the counter.
I wonder, Sally, if you'll still be going down to the rockpool
when you're old and grey? It won't be that long. And if that day
ever comes, Sally, I'll be there to put a limpet or two in your old
rheumaticky hands.'

The boy had never made such a long speech to anyone in
his life.

Sally flushed, then looked at the floor of the shop with a
bitten lip. The spell was broken. She would never be able to
hurt or delight him again.

In the course of the next three years, he had fallen in love
half-a-dozen times, with girls from the village and girls from

the farms. Always, into the alternate fire and ice of his heart, this image came: a small stone cottage beside the sea, a new hearth and a tight boat, a cradle in a corner. From time to time, as I said, a thread of enchantment was shuttled into him; only for it to fade, after a few months, into the grey of common day. 'My days fly swiftly as a weaver's shuttle . . .'

Doris was the lass he had loved last: Doris, granddaughter of old Silas the shop-man. It was of Doris he was thinking when the men of the press-gang put their ropes about him suddenly down at the shore, as he worked on his boat *Sea Quest*; and the strangers had carried him off, a long, long sea way, to the wars.

On the transport ship, on the quayside, on the long hard marches, one among thousands of soldiers, Doris too had been slowly drained of her honey. He tried often to recapture the lost splendour – it was no good, she was just a lass who kept house for a skinflint old man: a grey thread that the shuttle was finished with.

They came to a mountain, loud with iron on rock; multitudinous with manes and bugles and muskets.

They marched up, among fires and hooves. A village. A girl's face, a thread of music! The great scything swing of a sabre. The blood. The pain. The stumble downward, among stricken thousands. Then the low door. Then the torpor and coldness of sleep.

Ah, but his soul yearned to get back to that village beside the Atlantic. It was not much of a life – dangers, sudden sea-bounties, lingering sea-hungers, a fading splendour in this island lass or that. Then, at last, this *must* be – the cottage and the hearth, the board and the crib; and a new boat, some day; but the old wave-trampler, *Sea Quest*, might have to do for a few years yet.

Eagerly, then, his soul set off down the road of Life. Then doubts crept in: was it worth while, after all? For a young able man, yes. But this foreign war had broken him. What kind of a creature would come limping home, never able more to handle sail and rudder, or sink a spade for potatoes or for peats: the winter fire? The soldier would be a burden on the community. Already they had half-forgotten him, surely. He would be a thing, if ever he got home with his wound, for the children to dance around, pointing and shrilling. At last a box of bones, sunk in the green wave of the kirkyard, sunk deep, loveless, unmourned by all.

Shuddering at that prospect, the soul turned away. And retraced its steps. And came again to the crossroads, and fixed its light on the sign-post that pointed and said DEATH.

That way the shining foot went, a few faltering steps at first, but then eagerly, for the way was sweet, and all of springtime was about it, with birdsong and blossom, and honey-tasting sun.

For sure, this was the way it was fated to go. Why had the soul of the man ever dreamt of venturing along that other road, with the sharp stones and clinging briars? This road, this was the one only road; in the sense that, however far one walked or danced or lingered down the road marked LIFE, at length (after maybe seventy years) the soul must retrace its steps, get back somehow to the crossroads, and travel the road marked DEATH, till it came to the sure place. And as the soul of the man went on its eager way, it saw near and far other souls, and pitiful things they were to behold, with scars and erosions of time on them. Some hirpled, some drooped. And this was the most pathetic thing of all, that those bitter time-worn souls seemed all grey and fearful, as if it was to a shambles they were bound, and not to the fire and comfort of the Inn.

This soul knew what must be at the end of the road – an Inn. What more cheers the heart of fisherman or any man whatsoever at the end of a day's darg but the Inn with its fire and lamp and barrel: and more, the stories repeated and repeated till they become a kind of chant, the end known and foreseen and expected and yet hung upon with rapt delight, that such random happenings could have such marvellous closes? And the pewter pots ebbed or had new froth-caps put to them, and now and again a square of brown heavy turf was cast on lessening flames . . . An Inn seemed the good end to every day's journey. And (for no reason that he could think of, for the Ottervoe Inn was barren of any young voice) this image of the Inn of Night was quickened – it became so lovely and sweet that the sea stone that was his heart trembled towards bud and blossom – by the sure knowledge that a child, a small girl probably, would open the door to his knock. Then, to be led by that young candle-splashed hand into a chamber where a new-laid fire was burning, and into which drifted from the kitchen the mingled good smells that whet the edge of hunger and weariness.

Yes, happy the man who can walk early the road that all men must take, while his hands are still strong from the creel-weaving, and his eyes keen from gazing at horizons; whose whole body is vibrant from the coldness and salt of the sea.

This was the road. Why had he ever doubted? He hastened, he made quick steps to pass, here and there, those withered reluctant souls. How their eyes look pleadingly, as if to say: 'Good soul, you are young, have you come to summon us back to the warmth of blood and flesh? Take us back. We will come . . .' And the soul of the soldier looked cheerily at them as it passed, and urged, 'It's a good place you're bound for, none better.'

And yet –

And yet – here the soul hesitated awhile among the bird-song and blossoming – the man lying in the burning village, wounded, never once had he known the true raptures of love. True, he had burnt for a season after this girl and that, but not one of those dewy sweet-fleshed ones had ever opened their hearts to him. A few careless kisses, laughter in the darkness, a mingling of hands in a sea cave: these things had been, truly – but never to the point of certainty, so that the image of the new house, the table, the crib in the corner, the new boat stacked well in the stern with new creels, became an urgent necessity to him, then an actuality. Not once had a girl's lips put the seal upon the image.

Young, then, but maimed and incomplete, the soul must make its way to the kindly Inn of Death.

The soldier's soul had come a long way on this road. Yet it might not be too late to retrace steps, and find, after many a league, the crossroads again: so that, when it came at last to the Inn of Death (as come it must, after however long) it would have the seal and fulfilment of earthly love upon it.

No girl had loved him truly in the time of his strength. What girl would bake bread for him, and light fires for him, and rock their child in a new crib, now that he had passed through the mangling fire and iron of war? . . . Girls do not give their lives and hearts to cripple men, with no strength left in them to unhook a fish or turn peats into the sun and wind.

On it went, the soul of the soldier, with that ache in it.

And now the way seemed harder and more wearisome. He bore on his shoulder the burden of a hot foreign sun. The road was thick with dust. On either side were fields of inert tarnished corn. The bees went here and there, heavy, like hot embers of the sun. The peregrine soul did not see how bread or honey would issue from such a rainless land.

Still it passed soul after trudging soul, and a little of their languor passed into it. The soul was weary. If the Inn of Death was at the end of the road, let that road not be too long.

The image of the child at the door of the Inn made the soul pause, and smile. Then, under the bronze-beaten nail in the zenith, that was the sun, it hastened on more eagerly for a while.

At last! – over there, in a little field, a man and a woman were toiling. The scene touched the soul with delight. Here were people in no hurry to get to the Inn of Night. No, they had obviously made pause here for a whole summer, beside a little stone hut that they had built somewhat crudely, to grow green things and have joy of each other before they went another stage of their journey to the Inn of Night. What rejoiced the soul was that those two were like so many households in the remembered islands, that gathered a living from a small field and from the sea, until such time as a new generation gently took over from the father and mother. As it got nearer on the road, the soul could see that (alas!) no children would ever issue from those withered bodies. They were old, old! And the kale heads they were bent among had been eaten skeleton-thin by worm and caterpillar. 'What joy have you in all your labour under the sun? . . . ' And yet the two shadows were bent still over their ruined crop, picking from here and there a caterpillar that had lorded it in a cabbage head for a brief ruinous season.

Leaving them, he saw a little wooden grave-cross on the edge of their glebe: a child's grave.

Now a first salting of thirst came on the traveller.

There would be a mug of cold ale at the Inn, at a table with other contented shadows, as the sun went down: under a tree in a courtyard.

It passed many whispering shadows on the road, going singly or in small groups that held no communication with each other. The soldier's soul had long since ceased to raise a hand or voice in greeting to the travellers on this road. It had passed hundreds that had paid no attention to it; either their eyes were in the dust, or stared ahead at the horizon blankly.

The soul came to a little yard of most intense industry. A thick-set man stood between a flame and an anvil, on one side of him a great mound of iron balls. Again and again the smith drew from the fire a white-hot iron sphere, and he set it on his anvil and smote again and again with his hammer. What was passing strange to the lingerer at the wall of the smithy was that the meetings of anvil, hammer, hot iron, gave out no sound whatever, but only hollow reverberations; nor did the forge give out any heat-blast but only tremors and cold quiverings. What the smith was endeavouring to shape from those endless iron spheres were shapes of peace: ploughs, harrows, horse-shoes: but only the most wretched ludicrous replicas of those implements issued from his dark hands. As he set them in a lugubrious row on the cobbles, to join the other caricatures of the glebe, the blacksmith sighed. Now our traveller could see that the man, who had had a certain dignity between forge and anvil, was in reality a sorry worn-out creature, whose days of useful craftsmanship were long since gone. The blacksmith wiped a glister from his brow. He glowered at the traveller. He said, 'I dare not take the road till I have some pledge of peace to take with me to the Inn . . . ' And again he said, bitterly: 'My wife is gone long since. It is hard here without her . . .' Then, in a kind of rage at having wasted words, the ruined smith flung himself into the dance of forge and anvil, hammer and iron; and all that issued were black-and-red sound- less shudders, as the things of war strove to become the things of peace.

The soul of the soldier went on its way. The place had made it more thirsty than ever.

As it went, it was aware of a sharpness in the air. The fruitless summer was over. The first frost of autumn was in the air. (So swiftly time passed on this road: not like the sweet minutes, hours, days that we hoard and spend so capriciously in our seventy years.)

Then, the feet in their rise and fall beating down a little surge of hill, the eye of the traveller beheld this terrible thing, that filled the whole horizon below him: a ruined stone labyrinth, a multitude of houses in which many thousands of people had lived, but all broken and empty now, like eyeless skulls. The labyrinth seemed to have six ports, or gates, and through one of them – the most distant one – trooped men and women and children, singly or in groups, driblets and dollops of humanity: and those exiles mingled and merged until they formed a rivulet of souls streaming (it seemed endlessly) along the Road of Death. That the road should hold such multitudes! – Death, as the soldier's soul remembered it, had visited his island at every season of the year, but especially winter, and had gone to this or that door, with a kind of courtesy, and had been suffered to enter; and then Death had emerged, after a seemly interval, with the soul of an old person, but occasionally with the flower-like soul of a child. Or, more violently, Death had plucked three or four men from a boat, between many waves and a rock: and that had been a grief to the whole community. But this slaughter-house of death! – this vast shoal caught in the one dark net! – That had been to him unthinkable. Yet here it was, before him, as far as his eye could see, out of the shattered city that had been home to them, a long grey river of death.

The way of the traveller lay through the city. The soul passed among wrenched and crumbling walls, a long way smelling of burnt stones and the sweet clinging odour of putrefying flesh; and the traveller discovered, to his slight surprise, that he was no longer interested in the smells and scenes on either side. No, mostly the traveller stared straight ahead, blankly following the road, or else he looked down into the dust.

He did not – having at last won clear of the sieged and burnt and looted city – hasten to catch up with the multitude of shadows that he had seen from the top of the little hill. What desolation, to be one among thousands of ants from a beast-broken anthill! – More and more, he was preoccupied with himself and his sufferings. For now his thirst was an actual ache. And this thirst of his – it seemed to consist not in any physical craving for the quenching of the fires of salt in him; no, it was more an ache caused by things ill-done and ill-spoken in the time of his youth, before those wars; a metaphysical burning, small smoulderings of remorse. Such as: once, when he had come to shore fishless from the west, he had seen old Thord's brimming basket of haddocks at the rock, untenanted, for Thord had gone up to the croft to fetch his wife and a gutting knife and a jar of salt. This for Thord had been a great bounty, a rare sea-gift; for old Thord was one of the unlucky fishermen. That day, however, Thord's lines had broken a shoal of fathoms-deep fish, while our fisherman had let down his hooks into nothingness. Now Thord had gone up with the cheerful news to his clucking old hen of a wife. 'Bring the knife, Betsy – sharpen it first! Bring salt! Yes, I'm telling you, the biggest haul I ever took . . .' There was no eye or window in sight. Our fisherman scooped a dozen fat haddocks out of Thord's basket; and made up the loose stones to the road above, and carried the stolen fish to his mother's croft . . . Why should that little theft trouble him now? He had all but forgotten it, it had been no great crime, for there were still a hundred good fish in old Thord's basket. Indeed, if he had told Thord about his ill-luck, the good old man would have pressed a score of fish on him. 'Thu're welcome, boy! I've had two or three from thee this past summer. Take what thu wants – no, another one – and one for thee mother's cat.'

A pang of thirst.

Another earlier year, a schoolmaster had come to the island: a nervous bespectacled young man who spoke in a precise

English almost unintelligible to the islanders. The old men and women, the fathers and mothers, had welcomed the dominie into their houses, and pressed generous rations of butter, eggs, cheese, milk, and fish upon him. 'The poor man, he looks that delicate!' . . . Besides, this stranger from near Edinburgh was to raise their sons and daughters out of the dung and mud and fish-slime that had been their immemorial lot; he was to bring to them the gifts of reading, writing, ciphering, that might fit them at last to sit at an office desk in Kirkwall or Hamnavoe, or serve behind a shop-counter. Their children would be free at last from the cycles of clay and salt. And the young school-master had done his best with the twenty wide-eyed pupils ranged before him in the new-built subscription school. Wonderingly, at the beginning, they had tried to enter the mysteries he unfolded before them. And some of the children took eagerly enough to letters and numbers, in their beguiling variety and combinations; but a few of the boys began bitterly to resent those summer afternoons in the droning schoolroom. They could have been in the cave, playing pirates! They could have been opening a thousand oysters, seeking a pearl. They could have been turning peats on the windy hill, among twenty laughing peat-cutters, making with wild honey sticky golden webs of their fingers.

They took to torturing the schoolmaster in the subtle ways that schoolboys have: putting a live rat in his desk, for example, or letting a hand-cupped starling loose in the class-room, that beat wildly from window to wall! They soon got to know that the schoolmaster was afraid of such small living panic-stricken things – his own panic outmatched the instinctive darts and thrusts of the creatures loosed upon him. How they sniggered then behind their hands, that little gang of half-a-dozen school- detesting boys! How at last they rushed to fling rat out of door, bird out of window. But it was the end of teaching for that day – the poor man was so worn out with terror that he told them (his voice weak) to close books and desks – school was over for the day . . .

One winter night, about the time of the first Latin instruction, the half-dozen rebels, in an access of savagery – it was winter, the first snow and stars had put some dark enchantment on them – had gathered stones and approached the window of the school-house where the lamp was. There the young teacher was sitting at his table, with a pile of copybooks in front of him, making marks in an open copy-book with a pen and red ink. And his black kitten, that he spoiled, sat singing beside the fire . . . In one wild surge and splintering the stones smashed every pane. They saw, before they scattered into the night, the startled face of the dominie, the flare of the lamp in the sudden draught, the terror- stricken leap of the kitten from rug to furthest corner . . .

Of course this evil deed was soon known from end to end of the island. The old islanders were shocked and sorrowful. The hill boys blamed the shore boys. The shore boys said it was Stoorie the tramp, who had found a bottle of Hollands gin at the shore. Everyone, at last, knew the little knot of education-wreckers who must have done the appalling deed; but there was no proof. The guilty ones sniggered among themselves, half ashamed. The young teacher – who had threatened to resign and go home – but had been overpersuaded by minister and laird and all the good folk of the island – he was treated with courtesy for the rest of the term, especially by those who had tormented him hitherto.

Forgotten – it had been soon forgotten – it had passed into laughter and legend. The traveller, passing a ruined city school, remembered, with a clarity time had dimmed, the terror-stricken face of the young teacher that winter night, and the lamp's leaping flame . . .

A hundred other dark memories shuttled across his mind, with an intensity never before experienced, even while the events were taking place. Those had been the shadows – this was truth's dark imperishable fabric.

With that web, in some mysterious way, his deepening thirst was associated.

There had been another occasion . . . The events had been painful enough, in their outcome. A friend had come to him, privately. The young fisherman, his friend who sailed with him in *Sea Quest*, was in debt, temporarily. He must have a certain sum of money, and soon, otherwise it would go ill with him, he would find himself in jail, in Perth or Peterhead, with a chain about his ankles and a stone-breaking mallet in his hands, if the money, the loan, was not in his possession, and soon too, very soon. What was the fifty pounds needed for, so urgently? The reason could not be uttered: not yet. In due course: not today or tomorrow. But he himself, the fisherman friend, had hardly fifty pence to lend. True: but he had a great-uncle, the miller who also worked such-and-such a farm – a widower with no children – it was known in all the islands round about that the old miller, the great-uncle, had hundreds of pounds, maybe as much as a thousand, in the locked wooden chest under his bed. And so? It would not be difficult for a trusted great-nephew, one in fact who was the clear and only heir of the skinflint, to force the lock either when the old man was asleep or out seeing to his pig-farrow, and take the fifty pounds – not steal, of course, borrow the half-a hundred gold sovereigns: which would be back in the chest before the next moon, never missed. There they stood, the two young fisher-men, one white-faced and pleading, the other (our death-farer) shocked at what was being suggested. *Not theft, a loan. Or else I go to jail.* The great-nephew thought about it, while they turned this way and that beside *Sea Quest*, revolving like twin planets about each other, shaking heads, frowning, looking now at the horizon, now at clouds, now at a tassel of weed on a rock? 'I will not steal the money from the old man, not even to keep you out of jail. I will ask him for the loan of fifty pounds, simple and straightforward. I will pledge my strength and honour that the money will be returned . . .' The desperate one nearly wrung his hand off, in relief and gratitude. Then alone he went, up the stony brae to the lonely mill. The old man was sitting at his meagre supper: oatcake and ale. 'You would oblige me much by the loan of fifty pounds, urgently. I can't say now why I need the fifty pounds. But there will be much suffering if the fifty pounds is not in his hand – that's to say, in my hand, rather – before the weekend . . .' The old miller said, mildly, that he had not such a small fortune to give. Oh, he knew well what was said sometimes in the ale-house and round the village well, that he had a lifetime's hoard under the bed. It was not true. He had worked hard all his life, that much was true, both before and after the death of old Thomasina, but the truth was, he hadn't been a good or a lucky farmer, no, nor miller either. 'Look, I'll show you exactly how much money I've saved – you have a supple back – bend down and pull the chest from under the bed. No, it isn't locked, every man in this island is an honest man, as far as I know. I have neither locks nor keys. Open it. There, that's the savings of a lifetime. Count it. Take it. It's nowhere near fifty pounds. Yet if I were to take the two dappled cows to the Hamnavoe mart come Wednesday, and a wicker-box of chickens, it might be that we would top the fifty pounds. I say, we, because of course you can have the money, especially now when you have an urgent need of it. What better time? Anyway, whatever I have is yours after I'm in the kirkyard with Thomasina, bedded forever at last. And may the need turn to a blessing, in the end. Take it, boy. God bless you. The mart money for the heifers and the hens will be yours, Wednesday night . . .' Bitterly ashamed – and yet thankful too, on account of his friend – he had gathered up the little hoard of gold and silver (it came, when counted, to thirty-eight pounds) and hastened to the cottage above the shore where his friend lived with his father and mother. He had summoned his friend outside, to the gable-end of the croft, and poured the money in a little ringing torrent into cupped hands. 'This isn't fifty pounds!' A blank bitter look. The explanation, then: there could be no doubt about it, the fifty pounds would be there, the residue, safe in his hand.

So it had turned out. The balance was made up – and at the end of next Wednesday the great-uncle, the miller, had exactly two pounds six shillings and threepence to show for a lifetime of hard work on grudging acres, and among fruitful thundering stones.

What happened almost immediately was that the friend began to put cold looks on his fellow-fisherman of the *Sea Quest*. He announced, curtly, at the next weekend, that he wouldn't be fishing with him any more – he had engaged to fish with so-and-so and so-and-so instead. He would rather they didn't meet so much in future.

This from his friend, who had been dearer than a brother to him! There was a seething silence between them, as they stood one on each side of *Sea Quest*, after hauling her high up the noust.

'But the fifty pounds! . . .' The fifty pounds was in fact nothing to the sudden savage sundering of a since-childhood friendship.

'What fifty pounds? – I don't know what you're talking about. I'll take my share of the catch, then I'll go my own way. Fifty pounds – I've long been getting sick and tired of your nonsense. The big lobster's mine – hand it over.'

And so it fell out. Nor did he ever get to know for what the fifty pounds had been so desperately needed. For some spend-thrift girl? To buy a partnership in the other boat? To lay a new- foundation stone, so that there might be a rooftree, and under it a hearth and table, cupboard and spinning-wheel and kirn and cradle? These things happened, in the course of the following year, to his estranged friend. He went to sea, out into the dangerous bountiful west, alone and heavy-hearted, all that summer and the winter following: and *Sea Quest* gave him a living, and enough to pay his rent of croft and boat to the factor.

As for the old great-uncle, what could he say to him? There was no need to say anything. The old man greeted him kindly whenever they met on the road or down by the shore (for now he was too ashamed to venture up to the mill). Not once were the words 'fifty pounds' mentioned between them. How could they ever be mentioned, since for the young fisherman the fifty pounds had melted in his hand like snow, and would never now be repaid? Nor would he ever betray the friend who had, for gratitude, put a knife into him. (The loan, of course, had never been drawn up in writing, and signed and witnessed.)

Next winter the old miller began to fail. Neighbours helped with the beasts and kept the great wheels thundering. When the fisherman went up at last to see how things were with him, the old man had taken to his bed, and he laboured much in his breathing. 'Boy,' he managed to say at last, 'the mill is not mine to give thee, as thu well kens. The mill and farm are the laird's. The beasts and the crop are thine, and them few sticks of furniture, such as they are, such as they are. I like thee well, boy. I love thee better, I think, than any son. Everything is in God's hands. I do not question thee ways or thee purposes. In God's hands, all in God's hands. I think I will not lie in a pauper's grave. The sale of the ox – that'll bury me. Bless thee, boy . . .' At these words the young fisherman had turned away, so that the shadowy women moving here and there in the room might not see his grief. The young man felt his way out into the sun and the cold wind.

Once more he ventured back into the death-chamber, that same evening after sunset; and how fervently, later, he wished he had stayed in the black-tarred hut with his creels. For the old dying man, between two sleeps, had opened his eyes and seen him there, at the side of the bed, and he had said, in a surprisingly strong voice, 'Come to see what more you can wring out of me, is that it? See to it. This boy that I loved and trusted, he is to be given every last ha'penny, once I'm away. He likes money, this boy. Life is sorrowful enough – a sorrowful business – let him get what he needs to comfort him, there's not that much left . . .' At that, the young man cried out with pain, and now he didn't trouble to conceal it from the hushed watching women. The old miller sank into another brief sleep. 'Let me go in peace,' said the fisherman in a low voice. It was as if the words summoned the dying one to wakefulness again. The eyes opened, he looked with glad eyes at his great-nephew, the thin-spun breath on his lips managed to whisper, 'Bless thee, boy. God bless thee . . .'

And Simon groped his way out under the stars.

These events, painful enough at the time of their enacting, came now upon our traveller in all their starkness and pity: especially this, that what we do for others' good on earth may end in bitterness and terrible heart-wounds: and yet what we see as 'an end' is not the true end; no, all is gathered into a web beyond our computing or comprehension; and while we must seek always to do good, yet that good and every earthly striving to make things well are (because of ignorance and the vain illusions of the self) but rags of the perdurable seamless garment: Truth itself.

The thirst deepened in the traveller: as if he was a soul in a desert, or in a vast waste of sea.

It was a forest that he found himself in now – a forest on the edge of winter, for the forest path was drifted deep in wet foliage, and only a few last leaves hung in the branches.

He was aware, in the gloom, of other souls about him: five shadows drifting, light as the falling leaves themselves, through the dark woodland airs. He peered at their faces as they passed dolorously on, one after the other. He saw by their vestures that they were soldiers like himself – but the uniforms were out of ancient wars – those soldiers had had no part in his late campaign. And he saw that each soldier had a noose about his neck, and the end of the ropes had been hacked and cut with a knife. Those soldiers had been hanged, for mutiny or cowardice or desertion . . . One by one they went past him, trailing their halters, and not one looked him in the eye.

He tried to say something like 'Bless you, soldiers', to ease their going; but the words were dust in his mouth.

And as the five soldiers went on, one after the other, winter fell on the forest. Their going was hidden in a first swirl of snow.

He must get to the Inn, before the deepening winter froze the springs of his heart.

The image from early in his death-faring came to him: the ruddy fire-glow in the window of the Inn, his knock at the door, and the door opening to show, there on the inner threshold, the enchanting welcoming child.

Once inside that image, he was safe. There were mysteries of lovelessness and suffering and bad faith that might, at last, be revealed to him there: there would be a time for that, after the long and dreamless sleep that was his due and his reward.

But first, the child, or some other kindly one in the service of the Inn, would bring from some well near at hand a jug of the water for which he thirsted now with an almost quenchless burning. Sulphur, and salt, and the smoke of fire; ardencies deeper than these went to the making of this thirst.

And here, in a clearing of snow, was the Inn!

But there was no fire-glow from its windows, no smoke from the chimneys. From a hidden well, somewhere, came the creak and knell of thickening ice.

The stars were shrouded.

The long-nurtured image began to wilt in him, here, as he stood at the door of the Inn, his fist raised to summon the Innkeeper and the scullions and the enchanting child.

Instead, a frightful shape would open to him: a bent hag with a shawl about her, shadowing a withered face! No, in the light of her brief candle, it would be a skull with hollow eyes and no mouth.

As he stood there, appalled, the traveller heard, from very far back along the road he had travelled, a voice of utmost sweetness and urgency, it called, through the winter air, from very far back, from a place of greenness and green shadows: 'Come back. I'm here. I'm waiting for you. I am keeping the water for you.'

There, at the door of the Inn of Death, the traveller turned back. He began, painfully, to retrace his steps: to seek that voice from the land of the living, the girl in whose cupped hands the water of youth glistened.

[XIII]

The Tryst

The girl stood there in the door of the sty. 'Water,' she was saying. 'Why should you have water? Why should I go to the trouble of bringing water to scum like you?'

'Water,' he pleaded (and in their two languages the word had a vaguely similar sound: but even if the words had been as remote as tinder from flame, there was no doubting what the gestures of soldier and girl meant, nor their tongue-minglings, with all the pauses for wonderment and anger and eagerness).

'You're a soldier. Fire, that's your trade, soldier. You should be at home in a place like this.'

Her gesture took in the blackened smouldering village: that still, in the merest stir of wind, put out a hundred quick cat tongues.

It was morning. All night the victorious army had marched down – as far as strict order could be kept on a rough mountain road – past the hot-breathing end of the village; going down for the second decisive battle tomorrow or the day after, of the outcome of which there could now be no doubt.

Here, not a bird sang.

'My leg hurts me,' said the soldier. He lay among the pig litter, moving restlessly. His face gushed once with sweat as a stang of pain went through him. 'A horseman wounded me.'

'Did he?' said the girl. 'A horseman. His sabre must have been sharp.' The wound had coagulated, as if a red seal had been stamped on it; but still there was a feeble ooze of blood.

Of all the villagers, apart from the priest, only the vintner had returned. He sat, or slept, his head in his fist, on the stone step that led up to the wine-shop balcony. The smell of the burnt wine wafted from time to time across the road from wine-shop to sty. The soldier retched.

'I have a wound,' said the soldier, after a time.

A gust of rage went through the girl. 'Die, then,' she cried. 'That's what soldiers are for. Death. Die, soldier. After wounds, death. Do your duty. Die.'

'I have to live,' said the soldier.

'Look, soldier,' said the girl. 'Look what you've done to a good village. Shepherds, foresters, falconers, weavers, their wives and mothers and children. A famous fire this, soldier. You lit it. I think it must be one of your best fires. After this, why should it be necessary for you to live?'

The soldier managed to get head and shoulders clear of the ground. He heaved up, he leant his weight on his left elbow. The movement caused a new seepage of blood from the cut.

He said, 'I'm not a soldier. Don't call me soldier. I come from a village not much different from this. Would I harm a cat or a gull of my own village? Only my village isn't a mountain village, it's a sea village.'

There was a silence. She looked full into his face for the first time, and saw the throb and smoulder of pain in the half-closed blue eyes.

Then, from (it seemed) far away, came the words of the priest at his morning Mass. *Judice me, Domine* . . . The soldier and the girl listened, he painfully on his elbow, she keeping the door; as souls in purgatory might hear, far and near, a blessed singing . . . The priest was back, as well as the vintner. No, there was a third, for a boy's voice responded. It was the charcoal burner's boy. Then three or four women, shawled, coughing from the smoke, went into the church. One, a young woman, wept bitterly: signed a cross of holy water on face and breast, genuflected.

The village whispered from end to end: last eatings of fire. The dragon was almost fully gorged.

'*Dominus vobiscum*', sang the priest. Then the altar boy's pure treble: '*Et cum spirito tuo*'.

'You come from the sea.'

'Yes, girl. A wave or two from here.'

'The sea,' she said, as if she was testing with all her senses awake a new music. 'A sea village. Boats and fish. Is this true, that the sea brims and shrinks like the moon? I've heard that. The sea is kin to the moon. I've never seen the sea.'

'Plenty of water there,' said the soldier. 'Never seen the sea? – How can that be, a person not knowing ebb and flood? The sea's everywhere. I'd take you to the place, and gladly, but it's far away and this wound is hurting me . . . That madman on the horse. He nearly took my leg off! The sea – just now I'd give the sea and all that's in it for one cup of water.'

The girl was on her knees beside the soldier. She looked deeply into the wound. She touched with her finger the purpling flesh round the hard red medal of the sabre-cut.

'It's a clean wound,' she said. 'So far, it's a clean wound. But lie for half-a-day more, it would rot, and the rot would get into your blood – it would touch your heart. I might be able to help you. Lie quiet, soldier.'

'Fisherman,' he said, and clenched his teeth, for a new thrust of pain went into his groin. 'Fisherman, not soldier.'

In the church the dialogue of priest and people went on – as if this ceremony of bread and wine was so perdurable that world-girdling fire or flood was nothing in comparison. Out of the ashes the anguish and joy of the community was offered once again. The stone church had ridden out the fire-tempest; the dove was hovering somewhere; it was about to fall.

A young forester appeared at the far end of the village. Across his shoulder he carried, slantwise, a beam of new wood from the sawmill. He stopped at a burnt-out house. He blackened his hands tearing down the door-frame, that still smoked and crepitated and let fly a few sparks. He set, carefully, the new seasoned beam against the hearthstone.

A young woman carrying a child stood behind him.

The forester yelled as the fire-pain went into the bones of his hand.

A jar of water stood near the entrance to the sty. The girl brought it in now. The shadow-glister worked on her arm, eddies and moving whorls of light, as the ellipse caught the sun.

'You need a bandage, fisherman,' she said, going on her knees beside him again, 'You need bandaging and a rest. I think you can't stay here. The village men will be back soon. They'd kill a soldier if they found one. I tell you what you must do. Wait in the forest. The women will be there till their men nail a few boards together against the wind and rain. I'll speak to the women – I think they might suffer you for a few days till you're able to walk. They *might*. Of course they may tear you to pieces. Tell them you're a peaceful fisherman, not a soldier at all. But a young man like you, in pain, that opens a well of kindness in some women. I've seen it. I've been in a few wars, man – my heart isn't that easily opened. For a fisherman I can still be doing this and that.'

He yelled in agony as she dropped handfuls of water, cold splashings and quickenings, on his mortifying leg. How shameful, to cry out like that before a strange girl! He channelled the pain into words – 'My boat! I need to get back to my boat, soon. If I don't they'll think I'm dead. Ah! – you're giving me much pain, girl. The factor – I tell you what he'll do – he'll sell my boat. I think I must lose this leg. But I have a very long way to go. I should have the water in my mouth, not on my leg.'

The girl tore off the sleeve of her smock. It was a filthy rag. 'Keep still,' she said. 'I'll be back soon. Don't cry out. The men are coming back from the forest.'

The church: now it was a few whispers – it was a small jubilant bell, twice (quickly silenced), it was the small noise of a broken wafer, it was a small wash of wine and water in a silver cup. The church was a random clacking of wood or bone or ivory, as the women prayed.

The fisherman curled silent, teeth gritted, against the probing pain of water.

The girl came back. The torn sleeve shone between her hands. 'I washed it in dew,' she said, 'There's no water purer than dew. I've wrung it out. Now lie still.'

'Why don't you set the jug to my mouth? Please.'

She wound the bandage tight over the wound, and tied it with torn ends. More pain! He cried, 'I must go now, at once. You hurt me worse than the horseman! I must leave this terrible place.'

'You'd die before the first milestone,' she said. The essence of the dew seeped into his wound deep, and the new pain was worse than fire or sabre-swing. He bit on his lip till blood came.

'I've been cut before,' he said. 'Fishermen sometimes cut themselves, flensing a whale for example, or slitting halibut. Tar and salt – that's the stuff for a sea cut.'

'Well water for sealess folk,' she said. 'Well water, and what's purer still, the dew from grass and flowers ... There now, if that doesn't help you, you're as good as dead – you won't be seeing the sea again.'

As if to assert his claim on life, he heaved up from his elbow, he looked about him and found a stone and sat down on it.

Time in a Red Coat

And sweat gushed again at brow and upper lip, and dripped from his chin.

'Is there a child in the village?' he asked, between the steel pain and the water pain.

(Bethlehem was in the church, as well as Nazareth and Galilee and Jerusalem and Golgotha – all the world's cities and deserts, hamlets and hermitages, were gathered into one small stone building: where now more than a dozen women were kneeling at the altar-rail with expectant mouths. *Corpus Christi*.)

'No child,' said the girl, 'except for that altar-boy.'

'Of course not,' said the fisherman. 'I dreamed the child. I didn't *see* her in the dream – no, but I knew the child was waiting for me. She was there, in the heart of winter, behind a closed door. She had blown up a fire for me. She had warmed ale in a pot over a fire. She was like a child I might have known somewhere, sometime. Only in the dream I never saw her face.'

'A strange thing that,' said the girl, 'not to see the person you're dreaming about. You'd known her and yet she wasn't there. Now I think you should have a drink.'

She put the jug into his hands. He tilted it. He drank with strong throat convulsions. Water splashed over his tunic.

'No,' said the soldier-fisherman at last, 'but when I got to the door of the good inn where the child was waiting for me, the dream changed. No child – it wasn't her that was standing behind the door listening for my knock. I knew – but again I didn't see her – that it was a loathsome hag that would open the door to me. No old woman either, but a skull wrapped in a gravecloth.'

'And you didn't see that hostess either,' said the girl. 'You're a strange kind of dreamer, fisherman . . . I think it's time for you to drink again.'

'Where I come from,' said the young man, 'Death is rigged out like that. (This is good water.) That ancient hag – five or six times a year she forces young fishermen to drink her bitter water, and they drown. You mustn't think the sea such a beautiful thing. She's a generous giver, but once or twice a winter, always, she renders an account. I have a small debt outstanding. I need to get back.'

'*In principio erat verbum.*' The Mass was over. The women, one by one, with glistening fingers, began to come out of the church.

The fisherman drank cold smoke-tasting water, tilting the jar steeply.

'Then the dream changed again,' said the fisherman. 'The face was there. Now it was a girl with a flute. She couldn't play it – she was crying too much.'

'You talk too much, fisherman,' said the girl.

'It must be this,' said the fisherman, 'I see in every girl the infant she has been and the old woman she will become.'

He got up from the stone, took a step, two steps; then he had to hold on to the wall, grunting with pain and, again, gushing such sweat that a drop or two fell from his chin.

And now the women from the church, and a few others newly come out of the forest, were standing in a ragged half circle about the door of the sty.

'I tell you,' said the girl, 'you must stay here for a week or ten days till you can walk. I can't wait with you. I have places to go to. It may be I'll see you again but it isn't likely. May it go well with you when you get back to the sea village.'

'Your face is good with the first sun on it,' said the fisherman, his hands up at the wall.

The girl said, 'My face is my own.'

And the village women came closer. There were now more of them. They peered in at the door of the sty. They were of all ages, children and old women and young women with rings and babies and young girls with eager lips.

'I'm going now,' said the girl to the fisherman. 'There's worse fires to put out. The Dragon gets hungrier. Century by century he gets more dangerous.'

'Thank you,' said the fisherman. 'You make a good bandage. Water from your hands tastes very good. Thank you for leaving me to the villagers. That man over there has a knife in his hand already.'

'What's the name of your sea village?' said the girl.

'Ottervoe.'

'I think Ottervoe must be a good place.'

'It's just a village. It's a safe place, except in a westerly storm. That old man over there is shaking his fist at me. That man with the red beard has just drawn his hand across his throat. Thank you for leaving me in this den of lions.'

'The women will see to you,' said the girl.

She turned to the flock of women round the door. She opened her purse, loosening the strings. She put a gold coin in the hand of Mada, the old howdie-wife, who had first held up most of those villagers into the light and the wind.

'Listen,' said the girl to the women, 'you are to look after this man until such time as he's able to walk. He has a long journey to go. Give him broths. Give him goat-cheese. I tell you, this man came crying into the world like all other men. He is not a soldier. You must understand this. *He is not a soldier.* He is a peaceful villager like yourselves. He was a fisherman. He is going home, a long way, to be a fisherman again, in his sea village.'

Did they understand her? Old Mada seemed to understand. She turned and spoke rapidly to the other women. She held up the coin till it flashed in the sun. She pointed at the bandage, that had a spreading pink star on it. She pointed into the far distance – beyond forest and river and mountain – far far away: to the cloud-breeding ocean. The women looked in wonderment at the two strangers, but mostly at the soldier-fisherman.

To make quite sure that the village should understand, the girl drew the outline of a fish in the dust and soot of the village square.

With the village men, the thing was not so clearly understood. Every man that had come out of the forest – there must have been a score of them now – carried aslant on his shoulder a beam of seasoned wood from the hidden sawmill. The village would be rebuilt, and that without delay.

They stood further back than the women. Some of them had curled their lips like dogs. Some had a gathered thunder on their brows. All looked as if they would gladly have flailed the soldier to death with their beams.

The falconer had taken two steps forward. He looked with his cold fowler's eye at the soldier, still and alert, as if seeking the place to bring the beam down: the shoulder, the skull, the suffering leg.

The priest came out of the church. He came to investigate this gathering of his folk – a strange gathering surely, divided as it was into a solicitous group of women and a snarling fist-shaking pack of men.

The soldier-fisherman stood there, supporting himself in the doorway of the meanest building in the village, which, being built of stone and clay like the church, had alone survived the red wave of war. The girl was touching his elbow, to reassure him. Shadows of delight and terror moved across his earth-turned face; then a stab of pain that made him gnaw his lip again.

The old priest said, 'You men are to go back to your houses. Take the new beams back to your houses. The foundations are sound, they're set into the granite of the mountain. You are to use the new wood for building, not for killing. Do you not see the sign in the dust, the fish? That means – are you men so mulish that you don't understand it? – that signifies that this young man is a Christian soul like yourselves. Go back to your places. You will behave like Christian men, with faith and hope and charity.'

To the women he said, 'You are to treat him like your own son. Mada, my dear, you know what to do with him, till he's better. God bless you.'

To all he said, 'We will build the village better than it was before.'

Then the old priest turned and went back among the tombstones to the church; pausing once to observe the meander of a white and blue butterfly that he had not seen in the village before.

The men went sullenly back, each one to his own ruined threshold with the beam aslant on his shoulder. Old Rupert's shoulder was too frail. He carried in his hands a cuckoo clock, the only thing he had saved from the flames.

Then the girl kissed the fisherman.

And a murmur went through the watching lingering women. This was the way a good story should have its ending: but rarely did, in their experience.

'Your mouth is real too,' said the fisherman. 'It's real, like a crab or a creel or a seapink. I think now I might get home.'

'Not with me,' said the girl. 'I have more dangerous places to go than this. Your mouth tastes of salt, in spite of the smoke and the blood.'

It was like a play, to the watching women. Sometimes a strolling group had visited the village. But there were no wigs or masks in this piece of enthralment. That there might be another kiss, three, a storm of kisses, there in their blackened, gaunt village! – so urged, wordlessly, the young women. The old women shook grey heads – it was a bit shameful. Kisses were for stars and mothflight, not now, out here in the broad sun! For it was not a play, after all. They were strangers, true, but real people. And yet the old village women were enchanted. And the little girls laughed and clapped hands.

The girl said to the fisherman, 'Listen. You have a long way to go. They will be good to you, here in the village, till you're able to walk again. I know that now. Take this flute. You'll have to go by a hundred villages and towns before you get back to the sea village. You can't play it? You'll learn to play it as you go. You'll earn pennies at street corners – yes, in inn-yards and market-places. There's not that much to it, a dance of the breath, a dance of fingers. The flute has a hundred songs in it. Follow the smell of the sea. Don't lose the flute. If you lose it, the whole world might end in fire and ashes. I warn you.'

The fisherman put the flute clumsily to his lips, and blew, and his fingers went here and there. A sound like a little wave against a rock came.

The watching women smiled. This was the way a play should end, with music. But the flute uttered sounds that were strange to them.

'That's the way,' said the girl. 'Fill the flute with sea songs. That'll take you home.'

The flute uttered a few more notes: like a gull, like an echo in a cave, like a seal splashing.

The girl kissed him. She went out with many new scorch marks and blood marks on her coat. She did not once look back. But the women and the fisherman; their eyes followed her out of sight.

The fisherman stood in a ring of smiling women. He frowned at the flute. Once more he put it to his mouth.

[XIV]

The Magus

His lordship, being greatly intrigued by a letter which he received yesterday, confided to me some of the contents thereof. The letter had been sent from an inn in the seaport of Dover; the author a woman whose script, or hand of writing, was so curious and involved that we could by no means decipher the signature, though we looked at it from all angles, and brought it over to the light of the library window that was illuminated by the full sun of early afternoon, and at the last went over it, letter by letter, hook by dot by dash, under a magnifying glass. The signature was, I repeat, impossible to decipher, but the main body of the letter, though not as pellucid as spring water, yet had a drift of some kind of meaning.

From the main body of the contents, his lordship gathered that 'the lady in the white coat' (for so she styled herself more than once) was upward of a thousand and five hundred years old. Also, that it was her task or calling to pursue 'the dragon of war' (again, her own phrase) until, like a knight of olden time, she had given the dragon his quietus, not with a sword, like St George, but with an antique musical instrument made of ivory, some kind of flute, or oboe, or pipe. In thus wise, said she of the white coat, she would in the end reconcile the dragon with certain other creatures that were, respectively, the horse, the dove, and the fish.

But this reconciliation, or 'dance' as she sometimes termed it, might take some time to effect. She dreaded (she said) that it might take another thousand years; that was unthinkable; a hundred years, even so brief a time, and the dragon might well have glutted the whole earth with his flames.

His lordship was greatly intrigued by what he had read thus far. He would read a phrase, such as 'lady in the white coat' or 'the dragon, the horse, the dove, and the fish', and he would take a mighty pinch of snuff and his head would explode with mingled merriment and the fiery powder of tobacco. 'Upward of a thousand and five hundred years' – and he would shout at me, 'Erasmus, this calls for a brandy and port', the alcohol giving thus an added relish to the reading, or rather, the slow deciphering. And 'By God,' said he at last, 'here we have such a capital madwoman as we are not like to entertain again under this roof. Erasmus, we must see to it that this ancient sibyl comes, and that without delay. You will pen a letter for me after dinner. We will enclose her fare, we will let her know the time of the first stage-coach. From Dover? She will have to pass through London. But no matter.'

(I should say that my master, in addition to other earlier maimings, such as the loss of his right hand at Blenheim, lost the sight of his right eye in the late Crimean campaign, as a consequence of which I have to write his letters as he dictates them to me, and as also the sight of his remaining eye is dim, I read to him nightly from this book or that in his library, or from *The Times* newspaper, and from some other documents that I need not detail here: though they are the most curious and enthralling manuscripts that ever eye of man beheld.)

But how had the letter-writer gotten knowledge of the museum, the famous galleries that are his lordship's whole enthralment? It is known in a fairly select circle that his lord-ship's hobby is to collect, from all over the globe, implements and accoutrements and depictions and documents of war, which are lodged in a series of galleries, and which he shows openly and willingly to all guests who profess themselves interested. Lately some of what I have seen, or guessed at, has disturbed me more than a little; but always then his lordship (back in the sanctuary of the library) half-chokes with merriment and claps me on the shoulder with his strong left hand; and, 'By God, Erasmus,' he cries, 'what's the white face for, man? Why that tremble in the hand? These are matters that our children and children's children will have to endure, come what may – and who are you, or I, that we should shrink from the terror and the beauty? There is no stopping of a river in spate, or a breeding thunderstorm.'

What, near the end of the letter, caused another storm of fiery powder and merriment, was the lady's saying that she 'knew his lordship was most poor and in most miserable estate'. And, she added, she intended to bring with her, as a gift to him, a small coin that might pay his fare 'across the great river' on the far side of which he would find peace, fire, and the comfort of a good inn at last.

A small coin – It is well known that his lordship is one of the wealthiest men in Europe, especially since the opening of the surface coal workings on his estate ten miles away, and since the navigators finished the construction of the canal some ten years later.

During the reading of this most strange letter, that was carried out by fits and starts – broken, as I say, by laughter and sips of brandy and snuff-chokings – the babble of his lordship's ward, little Jemima, came from the Italian garden, together with the chidings and shrill exhortations of Mrs Baillie her governess; to which interludes his lordship listened from time to time, inclining his head and smiling; as, during the silent perusal of one of his favourite poems, *Ode on Intimations of*

Immortality or Blake's *Songs of Innocence*, he might sip from a glass of cold spring water.

The very next day, I wrote to 'the lady in the white coat' at her inn in Dover, extending his lordship's invitation to her to stay at his country house. I stated furthermore that his lordship's third coachman, a trusty fellow called Perkin, would call with coach and horses at her inn at the week's-end, on Saturday in the late afternoon. His lordship, I added, had been in no small degree intrigued with the intelligence contained in her letter. He would be pleased to show her whatever, within reason, she might want to see of the estate and the collection.

Perkin left yesterday morning in the second-best coach. I wrote a brief note of identification, which he put into his purse. Then he touched his hat, took his perch, and whipped up the horses.

Perkin came back today, Tuesday. He was, for Perkin, in a state of some excitement. Yes, indeed, the lady was below, in the coach, safe and well. His errand had been beset by stones and thorns after he had arrived in Dover. For, first, at the inn specified, no one knew anything of a lady bearing the description he gave. White coats were not in fashion – a lady in a white coat had not been seen for a decade and more in that worthy establishment. The landlord and his goodwife had been most kind and considerate to Perkin. They opened the guestbook to Perkin: surely her name was known, surely he would recognize it in the list of houseguests. Alas, Perkin had to acknowledge with shame that he had never learnt to read.

'Well,' said the goodwife to Perkin, briskly, 'I cannot parade all my guests for your inspection. Most of them are taking the air, it being such a beautiful evening, along the cliffs.' In fact, she went on, the only guest in her room was the poor young woman who had been so horribly sick on the Channel passage, and had not yet quite recovered, indeed she was, from her accent, a foreign lady. She had hardly eaten a bite since her arrival at the inn. They had been seriously concerned about her; but she had quite stubbornly refused to see a doctor. It was nothing, she insisted, her poor face white and peaked as she spoke. She had managed to take fragments of toasted bread and a sip or two of wine, on the second morning.

On and on (said Perkin) the inn-wife would have babbled the sun under the sea, but that Perkin requested her to take the note he carried up to that particular room, for the young lady described seemed as if she might be the one. But 'White coat,' protested the old fluttering hen, 'I assure you she has but one coat, and that as black as night or ink.' Nonetheless she took the note up to the room; and presently descended, beaming and nodding to Perkin, as if betwixt them they had solved a mystery. Indeed she was the one Perkin had come for. She would be down presently. She was hardly in a strong enough state of health to travel, but now she was packing her box with all eagerness and would be down within a quarter of an hour.

Meantime, while he waited, Perkin was given a great balloon of brandy in the kitchen. The more he sipped and swallowed, the more he was intrigued with the cluster of maids and serving girls in the kitchen, and endeavoured to beguile them with winks and smiles. (Perkin rejoices to talk always about his little amorous quirks.) He had just reached the stage of pinching a pretty soup-stirrer on the cheek, when word came that his passenger and her box were safely bestowed in the coach, and both she and the horses were eager to be off.

Perkin drove north all through the night. The road was lit by only a few stars. From the shrouded figure behind came no words – perhaps (thought Perkin) she had fallen asleep. What with the brandy and the monotonous rhythm of hooves and wheels, Perkin himself nodded off once or twice: he had a fragment of a dream in which he dined at a sumptuous table with a noble figure that gleamed with silk and sewn pearls but whose face was masked. And as he leant forward to put his gross hands into her shining tumult of hair, a stern voice addressed him from behind the mask, 'How dare you? I'm the girl that stirs the soup.' Whereupon Perkin, jerking awake, was just in time to prevent himself from going in a whirl of arms and legs into the ditch! Dawn was reddening the east. Perkin urged on the horses. He turned round. 'The lady in the white coat' sat, open-eyed, inside; and Perkin caught his breath at the beauty of her face, to such an extent that he nearly went over into the ditch for the second time. 'Like a flower with the dew on it,' was Perkin's poetical description. No, but the man, who is so impudent and frivolous with girls, was obviously much moved by that one glimpse of her face. As the light grew he saw – furtively turning once more – that she had drawn a veil over her face.

They stopped at another inn, to rest the horses and for Perkin to breakfast. The lady would not leave the coach. 'But ma'am,' said Perkin, 'you must eat.' As a reward for his concern, she lifted her veil and smiled at him, and Perkin felt 'that the lump of ice that was his heart would melt like it was April'. (A pity the man can't read or write, it is possible that in Perkin we have lost a poet.) She asked 'in a voice like harps and flutes' (Perkin again) for a glass of water to be brought out to her. Perkin watched her sipping the first few drops 'as if they was dew and honey'. Then, not wishing to seem to be staring at the lady, he went inside and stuffed himself with a brutish breakfast of steak and eggs and beer.

Thus, late in the afternoon the coach's arrival was announced at the great door. I went down at once, to open the coach door to the lady, our guest. Seeing how frail and ill she seemed, I gave her at once into the keeping of Mrs Stuart the house-keeper, who took her to a prepared room in the west wing. Here I must say, that as soon as 'the lady in the white coat' set her foot on the gravel, the guard dog Brutus that is chained by day to the wall (but at night he roams the grounds freely) set up such a hellish yowling and snarling as I had never heard out of him before; so that to quiet him I was forced to put a heavy boot into his ribs, and then he whimpered and whined for a full half-hour, as if it was some thief or criminal that we had taken into the hall, and he had but tried to do his duty . . .

Then, in the stable yard, Perkin gave me the account related above. Such a lyrical coach he had never driven before, and never would again. He kept to the end the rarest jewel of all. As the coach proceeded out beyond Oxford, about noon, the passenger said suddenly, 'I see that you have an injury to your hand' . . .

Perkin endeavoured quickly to cover up the silver scars on his hand, and his ruined knuckles, by pulling down his shirt-cuff. 'Yes, my lady,' said he. 'The fact is, I was in a kind of battle at a place called Lucknow in India ten years ago or so, and didn't I come face to face with a grinning sepoy, and this Indian, he had a kind of curved dagger in his fist, bright as a new moon it was. Very nice type of weapon, if you see it in a glass case. Well, the long and the short of it is, ma'am, this dark fella tried to take first my head off and then my hand. With regard to the hand, ma'am, he succeeded to a small extent. I am sorry that the lady should have been troubled by such a horrible sight.' Then, according to Perkin, this happened. The lady leaned out, she took Perkin's war-twisted hand from the rein, and she put it to her mouth, 'gentle as if she was the kindest sweetheart or sister a man ever had since time began. Listen, Erasmus, how many girls have I not been in love with! Chaff and dust. I swear, April flooded into this ruined hand of mine.

The sun and the light are still in it. I better not wash it for a day or two.'

In the evening, before dinner, I brought word to his lordship that his guest was arrived and safely installed.

For six days after the arrival of our strange guest, nothing happened. Or rather, this recurrent and troublesome thing happened, that the child fell sick again. When little Jemima is ill, his lordship can do nothing. He will see no one, he will transact no business. His food is brought up to his room thrice in the day, by me, and taken away again two hours later scarcely tasted. (The decanter of claret, though – that is drunk to the last drop.) I swear that the child's indisposition causes him much more acute pain than the child herself suffers; for generally, after a few days, Jemima throws off her paleness and fever, and is out shouting and laughing again in the garden: which childish gaiety the old man watches, greyly, from the library window. Then too, but more slowly, his wonted cheerfulness returns, and once again he packs snuff into his nostrils, and his head explodes into his red spotted handkerchief like a musket.

But this time it was more serious with the child. The little head 'brimming over the curls' lay damp and still on the pillow. The governess never left her side, nor Beth the wise old woman from the lodge gate that styles herself 'nurse', and is most certainly indispensable within a radius of five miles at every birthbed and deathbed. What ailed the child? Was it measles, typhoid, consumption? She displayed none of the symptoms. Two doctors, one old and one young, were summoned from Oxford. Gravely they examined the child; gravely they consulted with each other over by the window. They bled her, twice a day. They prescribed tinctures of this and that. Since there was no hope of luring solid food down the child's throat, they ordered that she be fed sips of goat's milk. She must be bathed each morning in tepid water ... Nothing availed. A famous specialist, who had entry into certain royal chambers, was summoned from London. He looked closely at the child's fingernails, and teeth, and hair, and he probed her stools, meagre as they were. He opened the delicate closed eyelids and looked into the dull eyes as though they were precious stones that but wanted his polishing. At last this illustrious disciple of Galen took his lordship aside. 'It may be,' he said, 'that this child will get well again, but not for months; it will take her all summer to climb out of the pit she has fallen into. She is seriously ill, make no mistake about that. There is here some kind of masked decline, different from phthisis or consumption, whose symptoms are coughing, stanchless sweats, fevers bright as roses. This kind of decline is more subtle, much harder to come to grips with; it is like the snake that puts in a lingering death sting and then glides off unseen ...' So his lordship reported to me that same evening, with a stricken trembling mouth. Perkin drove this famous medico to the railway station in the village. For that piece of medical sapience his lordship was the poorer by fifty guineas.

Ten times a day he went into the little invalid's room, looking down at the sweet cold face with a most piteous expression on his own face; then came away again. Asked, in a whisper, by his lordship whether Jemima showed any signs of improvement, both the governess and Beth mutely shook their heads.

Then the master went back along the corridor to the library and the claret decanter. The snuff-horn lay on his desk untouched; as if that fiery powder, and the shattering noises it fired off in his head, might hasten the beloved one's end.

There was no question of his lordship seeing 'the lady in the white coat'. She had been told, of course, about the child's illness and his lordship's all-consuming concern. She did not leave her room by day. Twice or thrice, after sundown, I saw her wandering here and there in the garden, moving among the fountains and the statues, a veiled somewhat sinister figure. On one of those evenings a nightingale began to sing out of the great beech-tree, and then for a full five minutes she stood as still as one of the statues, enraptured I must believe by that peerless sequence of syllables, 'eternal passion, eternal pain'. On another evening that week I observed an extraordinary thing. On the day of her arrival, I said earlier, the bull-mastiff Brutus had evinced a most extraordinary hostility to her, tearing the day apart with his raging mouth, and foaming. Fortunately, he had been secured by a chain, as always during the day. But, as I said too, Brutus is set free at night to range about the domain for the encouragement of thieves, gypsies, tramps etc.

On the third evening that I happened to observe 'the lady in the white coat' in the garden, under the first star, I saw with a shock of horror that Brutus was padding towards her over the lawn. The creature was bristling. I knew what kind of growl would be in his throat. The stranger heard it well enough, for it was a calm darkling dewfall. She went to meet Brutus, and the dog leapt at her and laid its forepaws on her shoulders as she knelt. As near as a dog and a human being can embrace, they clasped each other. His reeking tongue and brief throbbing tail were sufficient warranty of his joy. He went with her, in a kind of dance, all the way back to the marble steps, and left her at the octagonal sundial (for Brutus is a clever dog, and knows his proper bounds).

At the end of the week, the child's condition had not changed either for the better or the worse.

His lordship rang for me on the Tuesday morning. 'Erasmus, that guest, "the lady in the white coat", is she still in the house?'

I said that she was.

His face was grey, with red patches on the cheeks, sewn there no doubt by claret and brandy and insomnia. 'Damn me, Erasmus, I can do nothing for our little invalid but pray. I have sent word to the rector to pray hard too, every matins and evensong. It can do no worse than those damned doctors have done. I sit here, I drink claret, I fret and I fume. It has struck me, perhaps this melancholy of mine, this welter of self-pity, this purely negative orientation of the mind, this full ebb and desolation, must communicate itself to the child, seemingly unconscious though she is. Well then, I chided myself this morning, be up and stirring! Be about the proper business of the day! Do what you have planned to do. So those positive strokes, though undertaken with a heavy heart, may (who knows how?) open dormant wells in the child's psyche, and the wholesome lymph may begin to well up in her again, and she will be restored to us. This is what I have been arguing with myself. So, we have a guest. We have installed her here. She has come to be shown through the galleries. Have you seen her, Erasmus? Does she appear mad to you? Mad she must be, judging from her letter, with her talk of being fifteen centuries old, and of her mission to reconcile dragon with bird and fish and horse, and – what was it? – that she might ease my abject poverty with a little silver coin. Music, I seem to remember, much this lady would accomplish with music. Erasmus, this very day – though I am sick at heart – I intend to show the lady a certain area of the museum, and you shall come with us. Will you arrange for word to be sent to her? We will see whether she proves to be a Cordelia or a crazy Cassandra.'

Knowing how wretched he was within himself, on account of the dear child's illness, this was a brave speech, as heroic as anything he had performed at Blenheim or Inkerman.

The lady and the lord came together at last, that same afternoon, outside the library door. They greeted each other with a restrained courtesy. They exchanged words; and here I saw at once that there would be difficulties of communication, for the music their mouths made bore no resemblance one to another. His English manner trod down that obstacle. He would speak to her as he spoke to everyone, in bluff forthright tones. If she understood, well. If she did not understand, well also: to him it mattered not a deuce.

'Madam,' he said, 'permit me to say, you do not look as old as you suggest in your letter. Old Beth looks very much older, and she is only seventy-six. I judge by the smoothness of your hand, for I do not see your face, or but darkly, on account of that veil you're wearing. When one writes, as you did – when one describes oneself as the wearer of a white coat, one expects a white coat, or at least a lightish grey coat. But you are dressed as if you had come for a funeral . . .' And at that my poor master's voice faltered, for it reminded him of the child who might be sick unto death in a separate cell of the great Hall: that honey doomed to fester, while he lived on, a broken Tithonus.

He put away quickly that sudden mask of woe. But from then on he did not look so kindly at 'the lady in the white coat' – no, he gave her a dark glance or two before addressing her again more quietly. 'I have said I will show you round my famous museum, and so I shall. Understand this, there are only certain galleries fit for a lady to see. Other doors I will not open to you, in consideration of your sex and the gentleness generally ascribed to it. Would you follow me, please? Erasmus has the key to the first chamber.'

We climbed, all three, a spiral stair and went in single file – the lady between – to the door of Gallery One, which I unlocked and threw open.

Inside, as all the connoisseurs of Europe and America know, the collection of artefacts and paintings is magnificent. To the works in the centre of the gallery, his lordship beckoned the lady first; from case to case he led her, making cold comments.

'Those are paintings which I have either commissioned or purchased. Some of them are thought to be very fine. They bring out, I think you will agree, all the latent heroism and endurance in men – those qualities which have established us in our present condition – imperfect, it is true, but as our laureate says, 'rising on stepping stones of our dead selves to higher things . . .' Death – yes, there is death, burning and wounding, in those great pictures, but the danger only serves to make more splendid a greatness of heart and spirit. Every man, even the basest, is heir to it. Does a man arm himself only in defence of his family and his nation? In part he does. I grant it. But there is something beyond those natural heart-impulses that lures him on – a hunger for what men used to call chivalry – an abhorrence of all that is mean and grasping and cowardly in the human condition. Yes, wars are fought for territory, trade, sovereignty. I grant that too. But the Greek poet, old blind Homer, he saw into the heart of it. There is a flawless goal beyond the trash of materialism: something etherially lovely and desirable, whose symbol was a woman – Helen of Troy.'

Along the walls hung his lordship's magnificent collection of martial engravings, drawings, and paintings from every nation and culture on earth: Persia, Japan, France, Italy, the Americas, Spain, India, England: scenes of battle by land or sea or delta or desert. Artists who had never seen a shot fired in anger had expended utmost skill to satisfy the aggressiveness that lies buried deep in the minds of the most pacific of men: horses, banners, armour, spears, missiles, soldiers: all melled together, the threatening edges, the stretched soundless mouths, in well-devised patterns of violence, so that the little cold ember that is the civilian heart might feel, momentarily, a stir of flame!

We paused, all three, before a painting that his lordship himself had commissioned from a famous living artist, the subject being the battle of Inkerman: puffs of grey smoke from the batteries, the prancing columns of cavalry, the squares of red-coats, the Highland lines manoeuvring to take up position on a ridge, the earth-works and redoubts, Lord Raglan and his staff gathered in a group about a spread map; and far in the background, like a disturbed anthill, the dense seething masses of the enemy. 'If you would be so kind as to look closer, ma'am,' said his lordship. 'Observe that soldier, cavalry-man, on the grey gelding, among his fellow-officers, so innocent, so eager to be at the Muscovites' throats – that young soldier, ma'am, is myself, a hour or so before I came by this wound.' With the stump of his wrist he indicated his black eye-patch. *'Dulce et decorum est.* It would have been great joy to me, ma'am, believe me, if the Ruskies' muskets had been more accurate, and had found a way to my brain or my heart that day. it was not to be. Alas, it is not to be, ever.'

Again, he turned in upon himself that passing look of woe, and immediately masked it, bottled it up, and went on in a brisk half-jocular vein. 'In your letter, ma'am, you gave out as your sworn mission in life to slay the dragon of war, or at least to reconcile the dragon with the peaceable creatures of the earth. That was so, was it not? That was the drift of your letter, in part, it seemed to me. Well, ma'am, I think I am right in saying this to you – your mission is near an end. The dragon is not dead – how could it be, being a seed sowed in the heart of Cain, and immortal? But the dragon – your metaphor, I take it, for war – is about to be tamed, yes indeed, a cage and a keep has been prepared for it, its flaming jaws will be muzzled, its fire-belching nostrils will be cauterised, its fangs drawn. And how shall this happen? Ma'am, there will be small wars here and there, I grant you, small skirmishes and rebellions and outbreaks till the end of time. But the great nations will never go to war again: England, France, Russia, America, Spain, Austria, China. Why not? Because increasingly they are becoming bound to each other by strong economic necessity. One nation's welfare depends on the welfare of all the others. There is coming, and that soon, a time when hunger and poverty will have no place in the human condition – no, nor sickness either, although (God have pity on us) it bears off to the grave unbetimes many a one that is winsome and innocent and lovely, and leaves untouched those who pine for death ... Well, never mind that. I was saying, ma'am – and many of the best authorities are agreed upon it – that humanity is about to enter a long age of peace and prosperity. The philosophers and the economists have said it. More important, the poets say it: for example, Lord Tennyson. Flute songs to the dragon are being uttered, make no mistake about that – I would refer you to the fine section of *In Memoriam* that begins, "Ring out, wild bells ..." But even if it were not apparent from their arguments and inspirations, to contemplate a future war is too utterly frightful for words. For the truth is, the science of physics upon which all weaponry from the beginning is based, is nowadays advancing with such astonishing rapidity that, within a century, war would mean the destruction of a great city such as London or Paris or Pekin, together with all its inhabitants, by means of a single missile. What war-mongering general, what future Genghis Khan or Alexander or Caesar or Napoleon can contemplate such a horror with equanimity? For, ma'am, it would make our fertile globe a reeking cinder, with only a few sick spectres moving here and there. It is not to be thought of. We are, in spite of all, rational creatures. If such horrors threatened us, our common sense – and by "common sense" I mean the united goodwill and self-interest of all decent men and women in every nation upon earth – would rise up to assert the rule of universal law . . .' Thus his lordship, my poor friend, plied his rhetoric, for he can rise to near Ciceronian heights when the passion is on him: even though at that very moment we were meandering and lingering, all three, under framed depictions of war such as had never been seen on this earth before. 'The lady in the white coat' was paying but little attention to his lordship's flights – indeed, while he spoke so urgently she had made little dismissive gestures with her hand – but she was looking curiously at certain paintings, one in particular that showed a sylvan landscape utterly bare of leaves and men and birds; the tree stumps broken and blackened, the roots lost in a maelstrom of indescribable churned-up mud. On another, even stranger, she mused for a long time: in this painting the fair dance of creation had become a welter of destruction, a screaming horseskull, falling houses, a lamenting woman, a dead child; all distorted and lacking proportion and perspective, and yet the pattern was true, it cohered well about a core of violence; and the whole work seemed to announce: 'The future! This is how our children's children will experience war! Behold what blessings o'erbrim from the hands of science!'

In the silence of the gallery I could hear his lordship whispering, 'It may be that a country death is after all the best thing for the child. God is good. God is wise. His will be done. Yes, let her die. I will see this, and other worse things. But let her die in her green time.'

He became aware suddenly that he was not alone, and at once resumed his stoical mask. 'These – these are nothing – fantasies, vain imaginings. We will proceed to the second gallery now. There is an hour till tea. We will have it on the lawn, I think. It is a very pleasant day outside – if that west window was open we would hear the thrushes. There is much to intrigue you, ma'am, I assure you, in the next gallery. But possibly you have seen enough? Tomorrow, perhaps. I confess to being a little tired.'

Did 'the woman in white' understand an old man's babble? From inside her coat she drew a soft worn leather pouch. She loosed the thong. She brought out a silver coin with markings on it the like of which I had not seen before. She looked at the Magus and held it up; then she made the motion of putting the coin under her tongue; and, last, she offered the coin to him.

Death: this was the sign of death. This was the ferryman's fee, for carrying a soul across a dark river. Whose soul? What soul could it be but that of a sick child in another room of the great house?

His lordship looked at the stranger with sudden terror and revulsion. He made a single violent gesture with his fist. His face darkened. Then he turned on his heel and strode out of the gallery.

An hour later, Bryce the footman brought a note from his lordship to my room. 'You are to see to it that that woman is out of this house first thing tomorrow morning. The child may then begin to recover.'

I gave Perkin orders at once about the coach and horses, and a dawn departure. I had a word with Mrs Stuart.

That moon-silvered night, from the library window, I saw the rejected guest in the garden, her drifting feet leaving silver-and-black dove-shapes in the dewy grass. And the dog Brutus came to her, and was stroked and petted, and made pacific circles about her. (I had already sent her word by the house-keeper that her presence was no longer desirable in the house, and that she was to have her box ready for sun-up.) She went among the plants, plucking a considered leaf here and there, until her glimmering ungloved fist was full of herbs and flowers. Then – strange to say – the old nurse Beth came up the steps from the servants' quarters, very furtively, and approached the lady; who engaged her for ten secret minutes or thereby, with whisperings and pointings at this leaf and that wild-blossom, and mutual noddings of the head. In the end old Beth took the nose-gay and departed the way that she had come . . . The full moon rose higher, and drenched the lingering madwoman in its crystal light.

'The lady in the white coat' left at first light this morning. Perkin was back within the hour; he must have driven her to the station in the village: no further.

The child is worse, much worse.

His lordship drifts about the great house like a stricken creature, but ever returns to the hushed chamber where but one tremulous breath is spun, thin and fretted, from the lips of the child. Were it to break . . .

And Mistress Baillie: 'The specialist doctor must be got again, at once . . .' Whereupon the master vehemently shook his head, as much as to say the man from Harley Street had, far from curing her, helped to bring her to this pass, with his leeches and nostrums.

Then old Beth, 'If your lordship permits . . .' He was not listening to her, he was intent on the lips of the child, as though the ghost of a rose lingered there. 'My granny,' said Beth, 'and some other old wives, many a one they stayed from death with herbs and roots, but I don't know their mixture nor the gathering and mixing times. Old lost things. But lately a cure was passed to me, simple natural weeds from marshes and ditches. If I might make so bold . . .'

And his lordship, in a low fierce darkling whisper, the curtains being drawn against the sun: 'Bid that old hag be silent. I cannot suffer it. Herbs and simples! We are in the age of scientific medicine. There were witches enough when I was a boy.'

I raised an admonitory finger against old Beth. And old Beth was once more a silent deathbed watcher.

Notwithstanding the drawn curtains and the latched casement, the room was full of summer scents and fragrances. Jemima lay in a thickening caul of shadows.

Then the master again, in whispers: 'A good thing – it may be a good thing, to depart so early out of the vale of tears – yes, and that her children's children will not suffer the holocausts to come, world's woe. Not the sorrows of this one and that, they are in the natural order, and so are beautiful and touching and wholesome, in a sense, in spite of the pain . . . No, she must not be taken from me – I hold it against the angels if they give me that cureless wound!'

Drink, as always, had made him more eloquent.

In the following ebb of silence, I whispered to his lordship that perhaps it was time now to summon Father Fitzherbert from the town. 'Do, do,' he said abruptly. 'I will not see him myself.'

The old woman was kneeling beside the bed. Even in that gloom I could see the glitterings of grief on her face. His lordship must have seen it too, and probably – he being a kind man – regretted his late harsh words to her. He stepped towards her round the foot of the bed. 'Do what pleases you, my dear,' said he, in quite a cheerful voice. 'It may be, the old ways are as good as any. I mind well, an old dame cured my toothache with a dock-leaf or some such thing when I was a lad. Your cure can do her no harm, she being the way she is. It is likely, poor creature, God rest her, to be her last smell or touch of flowers.'

Then, a shadow, he left the room, and I – his shadow – followed him. In the library he bade me pour port into crystal, to flush two shadows with some semblance of endurance.

And so we sat in silence for the rest of the afternoon, while the clown's piteous red patches spread on his cheeks with every glass. (I prudently took but one glass in every three.) Once he said, in a plain matter-of-fact voice, 'She may be gone now. There is a change in the house. I feel it. I trust that Perkin got the priest in time, and did not wink or whistle at too many milkmaids on the way. Erasmus, a little more port, if you please.'

I do not know how long after that, that there was a stirring outside the library door, and a knock. His lordship stiffened. 'Come in,' he said in a cold voice.

Father Fitzherbert entered, easing his long bony frame into the room. He was smiling. He held still the ebony box with the oil of extreme unction in it.

'Well,' said he, 'I understood I was being summoned to a deathbed. So Perkin said. I thought it was to prepare little Jemima for heaven. See, here's the box and the oil. I had them all ready. There she was, sitting up on her pillows, a little pale to be sure, but smiling. She greeted me well. She made signs for the curtains to be drawn back and the window to be opened. Then she said, "There's worse things in the world than a thrush and a scent of white roses" . . . And then, "Father, you're to stay to tea, please. There'll be muffins." And then again, "I wish grandpa would come" . . . So that's why I'm here. Hello, Erasmus, I'm sorry if I interrupt you. Thank you, Erasmus, I don't mind if I do have a glass of port.'

His lordship had gotten quite drunk in the course of that afternoon, he had all the extravagant gestures and slurred talk of over-indulgence. Now he stood up and said quietly, 'In that case, I'll go and see her.' And he walked as straight as a guardsman out through the door.

And Father Fitzherbert, 'Well now, that's the way it often is with children. One hour they're at death's door, the next they're as bright as a bee. I suppose it must be a good thing to go fresh and young and clean into heaven. But, then too, Jemima has it in her to shed a lot of happiness through this bad world. God will take her in his own good time. This is a very good port, Erasmus.'

There seems to be no doubt, it was the old woman's herbs that worked the cure. Mistress Baillie has said it a score of times, no sooner had his lordship and I left the sick-room, than old Beth brought out a linen bag that she had under her gown, hidden. The bag, opened, contained fresh blossoms and leaves and roots – what kind, Mistress Baillie couldn't tell on account of the gloom of the chamber. The old woman proceeded, with whispers, as if she was recalling and reciting some precise list of instructions, to press these herbs here and there on the child's face: on her closed eyelids, on her forehead, on her throat, on her cheeks, on her temples, and last she smeared juice of what seemed to be a wild rose on the feebly-fluttering mouth.

Once or twice, the governess had felt like saying, 'Enough. Have a care. It's too much, to use her mouth like that'; but she held her peace. The old woman put another rose in the child's lightly folded hands. The grave-blossom spilled petals across her fingers.

And that was all.

Mistress Baillie prayed that the priest might hurry. And after she had said, silently, a *Hail Mary*, she looked at the child and saw that her eyes were open after a week of sweet sad shuttering. And the flutter was on her lips, but stronger, so that she could whisper a few syllables – what, Mistress Baillie couldn't say. But one hand lifted then in a scatter of white petals, and she said, 'Why is it night and a blackbird singing?'

Mistress Baillie had been at more than one death-bed. She knew that sometimes this cruel thing happens, that in the hour before the end the patient is seemingly much better, he is lucid in mind and speech, so that the watchers think, 'He is past the crisis – All will be well – He is on the road to recovery.' Alas, it is only the last leap of the candle-flame before it gutters out . . . Mistress Baillie dreaded that this sudden resurgence in Jemima was but the prelude to death.

The child said, 'My neck is sore. I need another pillow, no, two pillows. Beth – what are you crying for, Beth? Beth, I have something to thank you for, I don't know what. Thank you, dear Beth. Don't kneel. Why are you kneeling? People shouldn't kneel except when they're in the chapel . . . I tell you what I'd like, an egg and a piece of toast and a cup of milk. I was never so hungry.'

At that moment Father Fitzherbert, looking very solemn, entered the room. And Jemima cried, 'Father! What are you doing here? I'm pleased to see you. Sit down' – clapping her hands, scattering the last of the petals. 'Father Fitzherbert has come to tea.'

'No,' said old Beth, 'but it was no recipe I ever learnt. What I'd learnt from my granny and the old ones I'd long forgotten. It was the foreign lady in the black coat that was here – she gave me the herbs and roots and showed me what must be done. Yes, two or three nights in a row she instructed me in the garden until I had it off perfect, what to do. Not that I understood a word of what she said, but she kind of spoke with her hands and her eyes better than most folk do with their mouths. And I said to her, "Well, I can but try, but what old Beth says carries small weight in this great house – except when it's swaddling time or shrouding time – and I doubt we're wasting our time with all this rosemary and thyme and meadow-sweet. Yes, and the grass and beech-leaves. What if I was given leave and then the poor child took harm from it? No, for I know you're a good lady and wish no harm to little Jemima nor to any living soul," said I to her – "I'll put the herbs in a clean linen bag, and keep it by me. And we'll see what happens . . ." And then she kissed me, as kind as if she was my own grand-daughter, and said she must leave in the morning. It's that kind one that must be thanked, your lordship, not me. No, I don't know where she is nor what might have become of her. God be with her, wherever she is. Five golden guineas! No – your lordship is too kind, I did little or nothing. It's enough reward to see the dear creature up and about, her that was at the very door of death and the latch lifting from inside to let her in. There she is now, sitting on the bowl of the fountain, whistling and kicking her heels. Ah God, but it does my heart good . . .'

And Perkin, questioned as to the lady's departure, and whether she had happened to mention where her destination might be, became very confused – an extraordinary state of affairs for a bold forward creature like him – and blurted out at last that the lady had not left on the train on that particu-lar morning, after all. No: instead of boarding the train the lady had gone straight to the inn in the village and had signed in there. At first Perkin had thought that she was tired and upset owing to the abruptness of her dismissal, and that, having refreshed and composed herself, she would catch a later train to London. This had not happened; thrice in the last two days he had seen her entering or leaving the inn, and looking through this shop window and that in the village square. Unless, therefore, she had resumed her journey within the last six hours, she was, as far as Perkin knew, still in the vicinity.

'The lady in the white coat' has returned. As she got out of the coach, before the great door, the child Jemima ran down the steps towards her and they flowed into each other's arms and kissed each other again and again, with such access of tenderness and delight that it pained me to behold; for those pleasant springs have long since dried up in my heart.

This beautiful greeting was the more remarkable, in that 'the lady in the white coat' and the child had never seen each other before.

Later, his lordship received her in the library. He apologised most humbly for his harshness towards her: such a breach of hospitality was unforgivable. Would she please forgive him? He was an old man, he had forgotten many ancient courtesies, he said. In view of the great blessing she had brought to his house, the which could never be repaid, namely the summoning back to life of his most dear child Jemima, she must consider herself his guest, yes and Jemima's and old Beth's and all the household's, for as long as she desired, and longer, if that were possible.

Ah, until she had seen through all the remaining galleries of war? – only so long – then she must be on her way; then she had a certain rendezvous on a sea coast. Well, alas, that would not take long. All the doors of all the galleries were open to her; his man, Erasmus, would show her round. All except one door.

'And now, my dear young lady, you have the liberty of this house. Should you desire anything – anything in my power to give – Erasmus here, my friend and brother, he will see that you get it. I see you get little peace, wherever you go, from that little imp Jemima. You must be quite firm with her – tell her when she pesters you, that you must read, or pray, at least have silence for an hour or two. No – you like to have her about? So do I, ma'am, so do I: within reason, it is an enchanting creature, in spite of all the prattlings and cavortings of her. She is doubly precious to us now, since you put flowers into her hand and led her up, like Persephone, from the underworld.'

Again, our guest took out her purse and proffered the silver coin to his lordship; as much as to say, 'The coin-of-passage was not for the child; it is for you. Take it. Be free soon.'

And my master accepted it, smiling. He kissed it. He put it in his purse.

In the course of the following week, I unlocked for 'the lady in the white coat' door after door into the intricate museum of war. We did not hurry through them, nor did we unduly linger. His lordship had previously excused himself; he had seen all the exhibits in the museum before, many times, and a staleness had come into his mind concerning them; or rather, a scab, which he by no means wished to have scratched open to the point of bleeding and suppurating again. He trusted, over and over, that the young lady his guest would take no harm from the deeper recesses of his ordered and labelled collection. He had only allowed her to penetrate so deeply into it because of her insistence. After what she had wrought for him and his house he would not deny her. There remained one door that might not be opened – could never again be opened, indeed, because (he seemed to hint) the key had either been destroyed or hidden in such a secret place that not even himself knew where it was: it was lost in the lake, like Excalibur – MacWilliam had long since melted it in his forge – something like that – no matter – that chamber was sealed for ever.

If at any time she wished to discontinue her perusal of the museum, let her do so by all means; he would be more glad than sorry. In any case, she was welcome to be his guest for as long as she pleased – longer, if possible; what would Jemima do if she were suddenly to go away? The creature might begin to pine again.

'Go then, with my blessing. Erasmus, my friend and brother, will conduct you. And may God keep you from all affrights and portents. My dear young lady, when you enter the door of the next gallery, and the next and the next after that, it is into future time as well as past time that you will be going, those

things that arc not yet but assuredly will be, as thorns grow out
of a cruel sun seed. It is a perilous journey – may your good
angel keep you safe.'

Thus my master, standing outside the door of Gallery Two
with myself and her of the white coat. I had not heard him
babble on so for months, not even when the tide of port wine
was full in his veins and o'erbrimming. I think it was to delay
as long as possible our passage through the door into this
gallery, and possibly those beyond. And still he went on, holding her lightly by the elbow with his strong left hand: 'There are
still mysteries – the matters in your original letter – like the
phrase in which you give your age as fifteen centuries or
thereby. That, of course, is impossible, for it is plain to be seen
that you are no more than a score years old, or twenty-two at
most. Therefore, I take it that you were speaking figuratively. I
think it may be that you see yourself as a symbol for all the
world's women, particularly those that have had to stand by
and witness the innumerable horrors of war like a Greek
chorus, unable to quench the fires and the torrents of blood,
except in so far as they can apply a salve here and there to a
wounded man, or a bandage, or a kiss of comfort: or what is
worse, to wait alone at the loom. War is a ravening dragon
indeed, that grows the more hideous and powerful the more it
gluts itself on grief and blood. You will kill this dragon, you say
in your letter – this is to say, if I understand you well, generation on generation of women, sickened by the diplomacy of
statesmen that has always its ultimate flowering in war, will in
the end take the reins of power into their own hands, and make
an end of the dragon and his breed. Music: with a flute the
dragon is to be slain – here again, on reflection, I think the
symbolism to be most apt. Did not Orpheus quell the wild
beasts with his lyre? There is a Greek comedy – I can't recall
the title – in which the women by various hilarious natural

sanctions bring their warmongering men to their senses; and a play, like an ode or a beautiful building, is, I take it, but an extension of the flute symbol. Yes: at the very beginning, according to the poet Dryden and others, it was music that put order and harmony upon the black original whirl of chaos. Yet I think that chaos has never entirely forgotten the wild free anarchy of its origins. Time after time, as far as human history extends into past and future, this original chaos (only in part tamed) breaks out again in crime, in isolated acts of violence, in family feuds, in piracy and organised brigandage, but principally (and with the seal of sovereignty on it) in the form of war. That is the terrible Dragon that ravens through the generations. My dear, you will need great endurance and strength, you will need to utter music of unimaginable beauty, to bind up those world-wounds. That is to say, not only you in your own person, but all the women of earth in chorus: all their pity, all their sorrow, all their rage and indignation. And our little Jemima, she—'

I think his lordship would have babbled the afternoon out; but at this point his guest, with gentleness and firmness, put his hand from her elbow, and gestured to me, smiling, that I should open the door. I put in the key. Still muttering and shaking his head, his lordship meandered along a corridor weighty with portraits of his ancestors, and with portraits of those not yet born – a half-dozen or so – who will one day be masters here.

For the next three mornings I led 'the lady in white' through the sequent galleries of the museum of war. There, in ranked glass-covered cases, were odds and ends, fragments that had fallen unnoticed between the turning millstones of war through the ages, and somehow been salvaged. His lordship had scoured the earth for this piece and that, not pausing to count the expense. All were adequately labelled, and it was apparent that she could read the inscriptions, yet on this particular day – I don't know why – I was unnerved by the silence of those rooms; and so I spoke each item of the catalogue aloud. This journal will never be read by any eye but mine. I am glad to know that no living eye will peruse it; for if any did, he would think that many of the items that are at this present moment still taking shape in the womb of time are the imaginings of a madman; or perhaps such as Perkin or MacWilliam the blacksmith would say, 'Erasmus, he drank too much port wine with the master the day he wrote them things down!' – with winks and guffaws. But other eyes had seen them, the eyes of educated and enlightened men, friends of his lordship, and they had lingered and passed on with a mere lifting of the eyebrows, or an indulgent smile, or an embarrassed cough.

We paced from case to case, the lady in white and myself. 'An antique stone with what might pass for fighting men scratched on it . . . A Grecian frieze or bas-relief, with swords and horses rampant and warriors with eroded faces . . . flint arrowheads found in Pictish heather . . . a bronze helmet from Hadrian's Wall . . . a burnt stone from a medieval Irish castle – see, there is a rune on it – the mark is as yet undeciphered . . . a battering-ram from Acre that either crusaders or infidels had used . . . a Viking axe-blade from Lindisfarne . . . a cannonball from the Low Countries, Spanish . . . a skull from the battle-field of Naseby with a streak of bright hair on it still, see – observe too how the chambers of the skull have been breached by the violent passage of a lance or a musket-ball . . . This is a full suit of armour, this is what a knight wore when he thundered into battle at Bannockburn or Crecy . . . This pathetic fragment in the silver box – it is a piece of oatcake, it was saved from the battle-field of Culloden Moor, it was intended for a Highlander's last mouthful . . . This will interest you – it is the dragon head of a Norse ship that sailed to Clontarf in Ireland . . . an early crossbow . . . an early musket . . . a set of grappling irons (a dragon jaw indeed) . . . a ram's horn, possibly Egyptian or Judaic, for sounding advance or retreat . . . a worn shred of a raven banner . . . Here one of his lordship's prize pieces, a wheel from the field of Borodino with (see) a splash of mud on the hub still . . . Now this is a placard that some old soldier with a begging can must have hung about his neck: *i am a blinded sojer charitee for Jesu's sake i thank you* . . . This manuscript – smell the paper, it has a frail scent of roses on it still, it was written by a lover to his lady before he rode out to the wars: *Tell me not, sweet, I am unkind* – very sentimental . . . Ah, and the other manuscripts of course, hundreds of them in this one case (some of them not yet written, for the poets are unborn, they are yet but dust and rain and far-off tremors of springtime): *There was a sound of revelry by night* – I should think the whole world knows that famous beginning. *Now all the youth of England are afire* – that's our Shakespeare, alas not in his own hand, even my master's wealth could not summon that manuscript out of the silence, it was very likely burnt to light a candle or a tobacco pipe in the Boar's Head tavern. *Move him into the sun:* that is a poem not yet written, it lacks the martial fire, does it not? – there is a kind of womanish pity in it. *Steadily the shining swords/In order rise, in order fall, In order on the beaten field/The faithful trumpets call.* That too is out of the future: yet it seems, does it not, like a tapestry in words to describe all the wars that have ever been or ever will be, it reduces all the triumphs and terrors to a ritualistic form . . .'

And so we bestrode together, slowly, the second gallery. Our guest appeared interested in all she saw. But yet she was impatient too, as if all those things were known to her already: I excused myself – I was tired – the remaining galleries would have to wait till the morning.

That evening, Mrs Baillie said, 'the woman in white' and Jemima sat together in the nursery and they made together a doll's house of cards and paste, cutting patiently, ordering and patterning, and applying watercolour paint, till they had constructed, with much silent absorption broken by occasional laughter, the passable semblance of an inn. There was even a well outside and a screen of trees beyond. Inside, a red fire set upon a stone. And a table and chairs and a cupboard and three beds, two broad and one narrow crib, in a back room. There was even (said Mrs Baillie) a card loaf and a joint of ham painted pink, and a pale yellow flagon on the table. How the child clapped her hands when the inn was finally replete and furnished! 'The people!' she cried then. 'There must be people. Where are the people?' Whereupon Mrs Baillie said that was enough for one night – it was past her bedtime – she was too excited, she would tire herself utterly, she would be ill again!

But already her friend was cutting bits of cloth with scissors, and stuffing the hollow rags with scraps of paper and wool, and stitching with speed and precision. In half an hour she had made little dolls that fitted perfectly into the inn: an innkeeper and his stout wife, and a child (a girl) sitting on the doorstep, waiting. There was even a little card dove-shape on the doorstep, beside the child. 'The lady in white' quickly cut out and stitched another figure, obviously a guest, and set it with its face to the open door of the inn. But one of the guest's hands was red, a red rag being all that was available; and Jemima said, drawing her brow together, 'What's wrong with his hand? Is it bleeding? Is he carrying fire? I think I don't like this newcomer.'

'Bedtime,' cried Mrs Baillie, by now quite exasperated. 'Wounds, fire! There'll be nighmares next.'

The child bent as if to take the whole inn and its people in her arms, to protect them from the wounds or the flame – and the house of card collapsed, as though it stood upon a slipping earth fissure. Then Jemima was borne, weeping bitterly, to her bed. And she did not stop her tempest of sobs until her friend came and kissed her goodnight, after assuring her that all was well with the inn and its people. She would put it together again, stronger than before, in the morning. And the guest – the doll with the red hand – he or she had come in peace, after all. The redness was a glass of wine he had been given, to welcome him, to comfort him after a hard journey.

On the day following, we did not linger long in the massive library of war books, that clad four walls from floor to ceiling, many thousand of volumes; and not only books, but scrolls and boxes of papyrus fragments from (it seemed to me) the sources of recorded time. Our guest passed through this imposing chamber with a shrug, as if to suggest that she had suffered the coldly annotated contents in her own flesh. Near the opposite door, she did bend down and select a book with illustrations in it. The book has not yet been published – it will not, I believe, be published for another century; the illustrations too, of course, lie far in the future; and they are a kind of illustration that have, at this point in time, only been falteringly and laboriously experimented with – the daguerreotype. In the volume whose pages she turned, the art had been (that is to say, will be) more fully developed, so that what we call 'becoming' or 'actuality' or 'action' is held in momentary repose. Those advanced daguerreotypes were all of course battle scenes. Does it matter where those enactments of violence were set? In one of those illustrations – cunning cagings of light and darkness and the many hues of greyness that lie between – I (looking over her shoulder) saw a flag fluttering statically among guns and a troop of lolling soldiery, standing and leaning and sitting at ease; and the flag was that of our former American colonies, which is now the Republic of the United States, 'the stars and stripes'. Against what fort were these cannons mounted? . . . And again, a smoke-breathing ship without sails, and steel-plated, like a knight of old, bestrode a nameless ocean, and from her foremast fluttered (one had to imagine the wind and the urgency of the battle-ship's errand) the flag of a nation but newly emerged from an antique barbarism: Japan.

Fallen burnt stones – silent waiting women – children with gaunt cheeks and pot bellies – men struggling in honeycombs of mud, men hung like puppets upon spiked wire between honeycomb and quagmire, endless canals or trenches that one imagined must stretch from sea to mountains – men in dung-coloured clothes running on with bayonets, men buckling: these and other images she thumbed through quickly and coldly, as if she had seen them a score of times.

(Truly, there are hideous gashes yet to be made in the deli-cate exquisitely-balanced God-ordained web of creation: in spite of the assurance his lordship had given us the week before.)

The tearings and trenchings and web-rending had hardly begun. These photographs (as they are soon to be called) showed only the clumsy beginnings of total war. Hitherto war had been fought by armies, and horrible and protracted and confused as their confrontations had been – as in the Thirty Years War and the manifold campaigns of Napoleon – there had lingered elements of honour and chivalry. Soldiers – at least before going into battle – had knelt and drunk from heroic, even pious springs; though after every battle they had made themselves bestial with blood and loot and wine.

The young woman soon had had enough of the library. I turned the key in the door of the fourth gallery.

Again case after case, ranged in ranks: containing meaningless fragments, for the exhibits had been summoned here,
into this chamber, out of the future, from the wars of three
generations as yet unborn. His lordship had appended no
placards or tickets. There were simply the objects; and if there
were sequence and order in them, only he could tell.

It is not my place to grow weary of my duties and obliga-
tions, but I have shown visitors, singly or in groups (friends
and neighbours of his lordship) so often through this fantast-
ical collection that I am weary of it myself: though I know that
such things must be, and that I may even live, unlike his lordship (who has now the silver coin of death-faring in his pocket),
to suffer them in my own flesh and spirit. The choice visitors,
the privileged ones: some of them look knowingly, and ask
ignorant questions – others go with bored masks from case to
case – others I have seen sniggering behind their scented hand-
kerchiefs. Lieutenant-General Squires, on his one visit, grew
russet in the face, and that not with rum. To them his lordship
is, at best, a harmless eccentric; at worst a heretic and a
hindrance to the resistless course of history, whose end is some
Elysium or Tir-Nan-Og or Eden: or, as our laureate has so
movingly imagined the final bourne of all chivalry and heroism, 'the island valley of Avilion, where falls not hail or rain or
any snow; nor ever wind blows loudly' . . . War, empire, indus-
trialism, anarchy: all will be rounded by such a quiet
pastoral – never in the horrors exhibited in those cases and
albums! To many of his passing guests he is unhinged, he is
more than half-mad, he ought for his own good, and especially
for the good of that dewy innocent creature, to be kept under
proper ward and watch. Besides, there is something uncanny
about the man. Not the oldest squire in the county, not the
most ancient and venerable member of his London club, can
remember his lordship other than he is, except for the

honourable eye-wound sustained in the Crimea, at Inkerman. Where had he come from? How long had he lived and reigned in the great house? No one, none of the neighbouring gentry, had even set eyes on the vault-tombs of his father, grandfather, great-grand-father. Oh, I have come on them whispering to each other, at the end of corridors, in the winter garden (reeking of their host's brandy): 'It is more than strange – it's downright uncanny – the atmosphere is entirely unwholesome – yes, there ought to be enquiries made – Mrs Radcliffe, Monk Lewis, I swear it must be from here they got their spectres and chains – a derangement of the imagination – well, but he's harmless, there is a flame at his heart, however his mind is darkened – still, there is that child to be thought of, I don't wonder she's so delicate, poor Jemima, breathing such dank dangerous airs . . .'

Yet they come, again and again, to partake of his lordship's bounty. But, two or three years now, not one of them has asked to be shown through the many-chambered museum of war; other than the picture gallery, and even there but seldom. They and their ladies eat and drink, they 'squeak and gibber', they go their ways.

The Magus and his symbols endure.

My pen hastens and stumbles to make an end. But the young woman in those few days was in no hurry. She looked at most of the exhibits with awe or dread or acceptance; so, in a Greek theatre, one might have watched for the tenth time Oedipus entering with bleeding eyes; or, in the Globe, mad Lear receiving, with heart woundings and wonderment, the gibes of his Fool.

She looked at a wooden cross with a number on it; a poster with a cold eye and finger aimed out of it: YOUR COUNTRY NEEDS YOU; a rag tangled in a length of barbed wire; a lampshade made of the tattooed skin of a man; a stone that had a shadow burnt on it by such pure close intensity of heat that the sun, in comparison, is a feeble candle; a gas mask; seven rats' skeletons, with teeth marks, and even an incision to show that in some cellar a human being had feasted on them; an armband with a swastika; drawing-board sketches of such future weaponry as the submarine, the tank, the aeroplane, the entire rocket family from the V-1 on to the air-to-air missile; a skull that had a shell and drifted crystals of salt in its chambers – a sailor's; seven tin helmets, of different designs, one dented, one with a bullet-hole clean through it; a cluster of incendiary bomb-fins that must have made a merry little fire in some vennel; a crust of grey bread from some place called Stalingrad.

One case in this gallery seemed out of place, in that there was nothing there apparently with any war connotation. There was a crystal vial, or flagon, filled almost to the neck with a grey liquor. She murmured, 'Women's tears to water a little field' . . . There was such a Grecian jar as the poet Keats celebrated, painted with symbols of peace, sacrifice, springtime, love, joy, the idea of timelessness marvellously suggested by the Attic shape; within the hollow of this marvel of rotundity, this extension of the circle both finite and boundless, this tranquil storm of curves and ellipses, lay a handful of fragrant dust. She murmured, 'Men that took their ploughs to the red fire' . . . Between the crystal and the clay lay a gold medallion, of ancient Chinese minting, and it made the girl pause and cry out; it depicted round the circumference a dragon, a dove, a fish, and a horse, all circling in a kind of dance (except that the head of the dragon was turned somewhat against the stream of stillness), and in the middle of this ballet was minted a shrouded figure playing on a kind of primitive harp . . . From this priceless coin she could not be moved for fully ten minutes; and my own mind was meantime troubled by something I had recently heard or read. (Her own original letter as it turned out.)

In the last case lay a lump of uranium ore.

Each evening, precisely at eight, we dined together; never in the huge cold dininghall but in a small comfortable room between the library and the child's bedroom. Nothing could have been more cheerful, the leaping coal-fire, the prints of hunting and angling and fowling and grouse-shooting on the walls, the ancient oak panelling that seemed to hold, worked into its very graining, the happiness and good fellowship of hundreds of such small social feasts and communings over many generations; and, as the evening wore on, the panelling released among us ghost-whispers that sometimes startled the guests. 'To be sure,' said his lordship, laughing, 'it is only the wood expanding as the hearth sends out wider and wider its circles of warmth.'

Generally, at those evening meals, besides his lordship and 'the lady in white' (who gave her name, always, with such muted music that I never got to know it precisely), Mrs Baillie and myself, might be some neighbouring squire and his lady; occasionally an invited guest, such as an officer his lordship had known in the Crimea, or a Member of Parliament whose father he claimed to have been to school with, or one of those modern 'captains of industry' who could conceivably – so it was rumoured – have bought up his lordship lock, stock, and barrel, but who was manifestly uneasy on account of his regional accent and his clumsiness in matters of etiquette. No matter: his lordship, as the dinner progressed, soon had everyone at his or her ease, even those who had at a first introduction set cold looks on each other. The single eye put benignity like the sun on the broad table, as course followed upon course; the single hand was ever a generous inviter and offerer.

To be sure, his lordship drank too much; in this continuing the traditions of a more libertine age than our good Queen Victoria's. Often towards the end of the meal, over the cheese or the peach brandy pudding, his speech came slurred and slovenly, his head drooped, his cheeks flushed almost as dark as the wine. Then, if I judged it necessary, I made a point of breaking the rather banal music of the conversation; I gathered him to his feet, and supported him to the door; where, as if some instinct had prompted him, William was waiting with a flaming candle. And so, all three, we made a solemn and somewhat ungainly procession along the corridor to his lordship's bedroom.

This happened so frequently that no guest, to my knowledge, ever commented on this intimation that the dinner was nearing a close. A cotton manufacturer from Lancashire, how his jaw dropped and his eyes bulged on the one and only occasion of his dining here! (Such rakes and topers had withered and died, surely, with King George and King William – 'and him so old,' said this ignorant evangelistic Croesus in an awed voice, as William held the candle high at the door.) It was on that same evening, just before I eased him out of his chair, that 'the lady in white' took his powerful useless hand in hers and kissed it with the utmost gentleness and gravity.

Soon after that the Lancashire millionaire called for his carriage. 'I hope he'll take none harm from this,' were his last anxious words to me, as he stepped into his vehicle.

His lordship was of course down for his breakfast at eight o'clock sharp, his single eye roving between the salvers of smoked haddock and grilled kidney: hungry for both, his nostrils flaring.

There was one evening, a fortnight later, when he raised suddenly a large glass of cognac and said, 'I want all here to drink a special toast – no need to rise.' Then, when we all gestured with many-faceted flashing goblets, he said smiling, 'I have lately had good news – I have been assured of my early release from this wearisome round – I am about to enter into my rest – In fact, friends, I am to die fairly soon, perhaps, if I'm lucky, next winter. That would be a good time, eh, when the fields are drifted under with snow, when the branches are bare and no birds sing? The knight-at-arms has been promised release by the lady in the meads, full beautiful, with the light step and the wild hair . . . But no, I think high summer, June say, would be the best time for my going, when the bees are foraging in the rose-bushes and the hives are waiting on the honey-hoards. Let me not hear of wars or war-rumours when I lie on my last bed, waiting – that's all I ask. Ladies and gentlemen, I pray you, drink to my death . . .'

A Scottish lady who was there with her husband that evening was so astonished that the goblet fell from her hands and smashed into glittering splinters between the jar of tulips and the laden fruit-bowl. And many burning drops spilled involuntarily out of other pledged glasses. (The lady, Mrs Nimmo, whose husband was the immensely wealthy owner of a whaling fleet out of Dundee, looked increasingly, as the evening wore on, as if she had been invited by mistake to a mental asylum.) 'The lady in white' pledged and sipped, unsmiling, from a glass of pure water.

The host who had proclaimed with such exuberance his early death, proceeded thenceforward to get very drunk. The joyous mood did not last long with him that evening. He began to ramble disjointedly and with a vehemence sometimes savage and sometimes dismissive, on this and that fragment from the past. No one dared interrupt. In his incoherence he was complete master of his own table. None of the eight guests that evening could make any sense of his mutterings and thunderings; all they guessed, if they had that much wit, was that it was not contemporary or recent matters he was recalling; no, it was events out of dead centuries, what might have happened in the days of their great-great-great-great-grandfathers: and very violent unpleasant events they seemed to have been. 'You,' he said angrily, pointing to a fairly well-known Member of Parliament for a neighbouring constituency, assistant under-secretary at the War Office, 'You watch your step . . . You are here as my guest – I welcome you – but mind how you handle those papers. The Dutch farmers in Africa, are they doing us any harm, eh? No, they work hard, they earn their bread by the sweat of their faces, and soon – well, maybe in a quarter of a century or so, you're going to turn your guns on them. Watch it. Not that the Dutch farmers are innocent them-selves. Everybody is guilty. Dead, alive, unborn, everybody's hands are stained with blood, red-clotted and curdled . . . Look at this vacancy I have for a right hand. Look at the scar that was my good eye once. Nothing, the scratch and the bruise a boy gets, playing . . . I tell you, my friends, I came into this world crying against a cannonball that had breached my father's wall. And you' (here he pointed again at the man from the War Office) 'your ancestor was at the cannonade. Yes, he was standing behind the great gun, he wore one of Cromwell's hellish helmets on his ignorant self-satisfied head. When that assault on the Hall was at its height, my mother gave me birth, out of terror – it was two months before my time. And down below, among the copper pots and the wash-tubs, there was another child brought forth that day. There he sits, Erasmus my friend and my brother, we are children of war. We are doomed to linger on and suffer and sweat until the last peace-treaty is signed – yes, until that age comes that was spoken of by the prophet, when the lion shall lie down with the lamb . . . And furthermore, we shall acknowledge our blood guilt before the beasts and the birds and fish that we have been stuffing our bellies with all evening...' At this point Mrs Nimmo excused herself; she murmured that she was feeling unwell; she rose from her chair with a tiny clash of diamonds at neck and bosom, and her coarse whisky-faced husband, disconcerted and angry, led her from the room without a thanks or a farewell. 'Whale-killers,' said his lordship, decanting more wine, 'let them go, a good riddance.'

Then for a moment it seemed that the grossness of his inhospitality broke in upon him. He spread his left hand and his invisible right hand to embrace the whole company. 'No, you are welcome... You are most welcome... Fill your cups full, I mean us to have a merry evening. I ask you to drink to my birth, this very day two hundred and twenty-two years ago, among the powder, the cries, the broken masonry and the cannonballs. And Erasmus too, my brother and friend, I bid you drink to him. No upstanding. It is Erasmus' birthday too. Erasmus and I, we came crying into this murderous world together, long, long ago, when you were grains of dust and rain-drops and stirs of wind, and better so, better so. I greet you all, you are welcome.'

Long before those poor wayward revelations were out, I should have been bearing him to the door where William the candle-bearer stood; but on this night William was not there, his subtle instinctual intelligence had for once failed him; and as for me, I knew that, this anniversary or that, my master would have perforce to empty himself of what so grievously was sealed in his heart and memory, inwardly festering and suppurating: so that only rarely could he unburden himself to me; as now and then happened, on our common birthday. But never before had he lanced his boil before guests.

The truth was out. But who would believe it, in this polite and embarrassed company of dinner guests? ('He was more drunk, my dear, than I have ever seen him, and that is saying a lot' . . . 'It was a bit of a bore, really – I won't be accepting any more of his invitations.')

'That we may live to see the fall and furl of the dove with the branch' – These were his last words that night. With a crash that shook the porcelain, the parquet, the china, the Venetian glass, his old sightless head fell on the table. A sliver of crystal gashed his brow; the cut ran six or seven drops of blood on to the immaculate linen.

'Really,' said the parliamentarian, 'don't you think you ought to—'

But I was beyond speech or action. The old man's ramblings had put a kind of spell on me. The inertia of seven generations was a burden beyond bearing. Or it may be simpler and more honest to say that that night I did not care about the old man or what happened to him, because I was almost as drunk as himself.

The guests were bestirring themselves to be gone as quickly as possible.

William was there, at last, with the wavering light of the candle about his head and shoulder. The woman so ancient that she had made the full circle, almost, back to the first springs of time, had him by the elbow that I usually supported.

Like Oedipus on the arm of his daughter, the old man allowed himself to be led to that place which is the narrow place of rehearsal for our dying, our death, and our shrouding.

Next morning, at eight o'clock, he was as merry as I had seen him for many a day. 'That was a most successful little dinner party,' he said. 'I think our guests enjoyed themselves. We must have another dinner very soon. I shall have two kippers, and soda bread, and tea. Erasmus, see to it – there's a good chap.'

He crammed snuff into his nostrils like priming a musket.

*   *   *

Great strides it would make, the art of the daguerreotype, in five or six decades, since the time of the Crimean War and the American Civil War: those marmoreally-disposed uniformed figures, indistinctly washed with gleams and shadows – half ghosts, half statues.

In the time beyond our present time, the 'camera obscura' will evolve, so that the images it captures will be clearer and more defined, and creatures appear in the subtle poses of life itself, laughing, walking, mourning, even caught in the spasm of heroic death: the rendezvous of bullet and man. The science of photography will advance so spectacularly as to play tricks with time: one can see a drop of water falling back into a bowl of water, the very point of impact when it begins to become a lucent coronet.

This trick with time and with techniques is to have another consequence: what is at first to be called 'the kinema', whereby a sequence of images is photographed so rapidly that, to begin with, a semblance of the motions of life are shown before the astonished eyes – the intricate web of movement on a city street, with tram-cars, horse omnibuses, pedestrians rushing silently hither and thither – or the stealthy life in a swamp, with predatory crocodiles disguising their murderous jaws as logs of wood – or men climbing over glaciers and outcrops of rock, perilously roped together. Exotic scenes from every corner of the globe, 'shot' with those cine-cameras, will in the space of two or three generations be shown in darkened theatres to hushed audiences, projected from a secret chamber of light at the rear upon a square white screen about the size of a billiard table.

Amazing gift of science, that can bring all of life into any little provincial theatre! – Javanese dances, an elephant hunt in Kenya, naked Indians floating on logs on the Amazon.

The first films were jerky and fast, ludicrously so: men moved like automata in a hurry; in a rage, it seemed, to put time behind them. 'Real time' and 'cinematograph time' were quickly synchronised, so that creatures on the screen moved to the rhythms of their own hearts, not like puppets. But still tricks with time became ever more sophisticated, so that not only the moment of the water-drop falling back into the bowl of water was caught and held in its corona; the entire individual existence of the drop from its formation to its merging back – that might in actual time last for half-a-second – that blink of time could be lengthened to the space of twenty or thirty seconds, or more, so that the whole 'biography' of the drop could be studied at leisure: the gathering half-reluctant globule at the lip of the inverted jar, its pure glistering descent through six inches of space, its ending, death, glorification in the source from which it had originally been drawn to slake an idle thirst . . . Conversely, kinema time could be so speeded that one could see, within the space of a few seconds, the whole biography of a rose from the broken bud to its glorious outbursting in petals, veil after silken voluptuous veil; but the actual time was a long English summer day.

That cold eye! – The life of a man from birth to death, will it ever be able to look upon that most private and precious and vain thing, and sum it up in a few minutes? No: the mystery of the inner life will always be beyond it, or so we hope: what only the gods see and estimate in their scales. Meantime, one holds one's breath at the audacity of science: that has so extended and deepened the human eye, until soon we shall be able to look at marvels of minuteness and immensity never seen before, and hardly imagined: molecules, the immense black stellar whirls so dense that even light, that leaping angel, is a prisoner at the heart of it.

I remember one dinner when there was present a fairly well-known historian – a pedant if ever there was one – who boomed sententiously, on and on, about 'the great smithy of history' – and how out of the din and flame of centuries of conflict a super-race was to evolve, compared to which nineteenth-century men would be but jabbering jungle apes.

'Speak for yourself,' said his lordship, and put on the wretched scribbler his one stone eye.

'No,' said he, stumbling on, 'but there is to be another anvil-stroke soon – I know it – Prussia and France . . . I am a historian. I have read and pondered a thousand books, from Thucydides to Carlyle, and I know whereof I speak – I have looked deep into the roots of such things.'

'Pooh,' said the host as if he was blowing away some bubble or piece of thistledown. (Indeed he looked like an airy nothing, that historian, for the rest of the meal) . . . After a decent interval, his lordship delivered himself of some remarks that had the guests all glancing covertly at one another. 'It is the claret . . . Tonight he seems on the verge of his second childhood . . .'

'Behind the events of history (his lordship was mumbling) which we accept only because we have been taught them in school and college, or read them in books or in documents, behind the wars and machinations of statesmen and the venturing of merchants; yes, and the earlier minglings of peoples, either peacefully and pastorally, their history united perhaps by a boy and a girl of different kin with a kiss, or by the savage weldings of war; behind all these happenings lie a few images and episodes and characters that have been uttered or listened to by innumerable generations of "illiterate" folk: the knight, the virgin, and the dragon – the queen, the mirror, the drop of blood, the glass coffin, a random princely wayfarer – the girl sweeping ashes on a hearth while all around ugliness swathes itself in silk – the lazy boy whose clever adventurings rescued a kingdom from a sea monster – two children lost in a dark forest, dropping bread and stones – the girl with the fish-tail who yearned to dance and suffer and die – the snow princess – the girl who became a tree to escape her unwanted suitor . . . These round out our days and our destinies – the legend will remain when all your tomes and documents are dust.'

Five minutes later we carted him off to bed.

Our next two galleries were well stored with war documentaries, together with 'projectors' and 'screens'.

How – it will be asked – was it possible for such things to be, in the seventh decade of the nineteenth century: when only the crude daguerreotype was known?

Not for nothing do I call him the Magus. Was he not, while still a young man, a founder member of the Royal Society, and a friend of the war-branded war-hating King Charles himself? No longer to China or India or America he voyages, in pursuit of his whims and fancies, his growing collection of artefacts. He is content, within the little microcosm of hall and garden and village, to see that all is well there, as far as in him lies. His forays now are into the past and into the future; from which he comes back suddenly and secretly, generally at dead of night, under the stars; and his flung pebble wakes me out of sleep; and there and then I help Perkin unload into the galleries this or that new treasure, purchased (who knows how?) from brokers buried or unborn.

I need not go into details – I have ventured into enough by-ways to get to this place in my narrative, I have over-extended myself. I think, in part at least, I have lingered out the account in order to delay the last episodes, to spare both myself and my master.

Let this suffice – in one darkened gallery, upon what will be called some day 'the silver screen', I projected motion films of actual events in the future, chiefly the great wars of the twentieth century, in which perhaps little Jemima's grand-children – God help them! – may be enmeshed.

Scenes from Verdun, the Somme, Ypres; the one naval engagement in the North Sea; the 'eastern front'; combat in the skies with early aeroplanes, the airmen jousting among the clouds like knights-of-old. Then the grey peace; the comings and goings of ageing statesmen and ambassadors; the little silent wide-moustached proletarian dictator in the Kremlin, the rise of that other proletarian leader in Germany, with the little clipped moustache, he that could whip enormous open-air crowds into frenzies of adoration, hatred, battle-lust.

The first mutterings then of the Second World War, truly so called, because hardly an individual on the globe wasn't influenced by those horrendous festivals of fire and blood.

Italian armies overran Abyssinia, so that the bull-frog dictator of Italy could add the empty title 'Emperor of Ethiopia' to the impotent royal house in Rome, and distract an impoverished badly-ruled people with a poor dream of glory. Reactionary professional armies in Spain destroyed protractedly over three years amateur armies of socialists, anarchists, idealists and 'progressives'. First bombs were dropped on an open city: Guernica. These dreadful scenes were but a prologue.

I need but name places: names will suffice. Warsaw, Sedan, Dunkirk, Narvik – Minsk, Smolensk, Kiev, Leningrad, Moscow, Stalingrad – Pearl Harbour, Singapore – the North Atlantic convoys and the iron sharks that preyed on them – London, Coventry, Hamburg, Dresden – the long battle for the Pacific islands – Berlin, Hiroshima, Nagasaki.

These were the terrible scenes that, over three or four afternoons, 'the woman in white' and I looked at and listened to on the flickering silver square.

I had no means of observing her reactions, because the gallery was dark and she sat with her back to me, right in front of the screen.

When finally the day's session was at an end, and the projector whirred on into silence, and I put on the lights, she had left: his lordship's secret cinema was empty.

But the next afternoon, she was there again waiting for me to unlock the door.

On the last morning what she saw had, in a sense, nothing to do with actual fighting, soldier against soldier, fighter-plane against bomber, submarine against battle cruiser. It was a by-product of war. It was the deliberate attempt to uproot a race of people from one continent of the earth – and a race moreover that had enriched the earth's culture and enormously expanded its spiritual horizons: the Jews. Six million of them – civilians – were done to death in the space of three years, in conditions of utmost cruelty: by mass shootings beside open graves, by herding into gas chambers and then shovelling the poor naked gold-rifled corpses into incinerators, the smoke and stench of which burnings spread over neighbouring European villages a ghastly miasma.

Only fools and madmen could have conceived such a plan in the first place. How can an entire race be destroyed, when its roots reach out to every nation on earth? Even if all the Jews in Europe and Western Russia had been killed, there were millions that could not be touched, in America, for example. Indeed, it is quite possible that the planners and executants of genocide had themselves, far or near, some drops of that sad ancient wise blood in them.

All the dogs of Europe became rabid in the first half of the twentieth century.

Again, I have let my pen run away with me. I will mention names: Dachau, Auschwitz, Treblinka, Babi Yar.

A writer called Huxley, who is not yet born (though his grandfather holds the stage in matters of progressive science), imagined in a book called *Brave New World* a time beyond the 'movies', when cinema-goers would have tactile and olfactory connections with the screen: 'the feelies'.

In those films of the last day, 'the lady in white' and I were able to smell and to touch the recorded events.

For the solitary watcher it must have been very different from the touch and smell of the rose-leaves in the garden, or little Jemima's lips on her cheek. Through those unspeakable tumults she held on; she let the circle of hell wheel and flame through her.

It was intolerable. It was the young good-looking blond faces, the herders of the dead, that made the evil so palpable: the sweet smells of toothpaste, hair cream, shaving-lotion, coffee and new-baked bread.

It was intolerable. I groped for the light-switch with reeking fingers. The young woman was not there.

But the soundtrack went on for a while that afternoon, for some reason; rats' teeth, burning bones, snarling mountain dogs, voices pedantic rather than cruel, a child's lost wondering voice, fate-filled voices, whisper of gas . . .

What music could wash away such evil?

She had given her flute, she said, to a fisherman in the mountains. She had said that last night, over supper, to the Magus.

It came, last words of an old rabbi – then silence.

There is one gallery into which no one except the Magus himself has penetrated; and that happened on a day, it must be two hundred years ago or more, which I will remember to my dying day with a pang of dread and pity.

His lordship kept once the key to this chamber. I must presume, it contains exhibits from wars of the far future, the twenty-first century perhaps, but perhaps earlier.

Imagine three people standing in a group at the door of this ultimate gallery. The time is a few days later than the last of the 'film-shows'. One of the group is old and scarred; he is very agitated; he gestures, urges, reasons, denies, over and over. The second is a young woman; today she has put off her black habit and is dressed in a white coat, like a vestal. She seems to hear none of the old man's pleadings and urgings, no more than if she was a statue indeed. The third of the group is myself, Erasmus; and who has ever been able to describe himself? (I will not make the attempt.)

This 'statue' has her right hand outstretched, palm upwards, in a gesture that she knows will not be denied.

I will let the old man babble and stammer on: nothing more need be said or indicated.

'I promised you – I know it – the full freedom of this place. Yet I beg you, dear girl, from the bottom of my heart, not to press me. You shall not go in there. I forbid it. What you will see in there is too hideous and horrible for words. I assure you I would not answer for your health, no, for your sanity, were I to give you the key to it. Here indeed is the door. You must not press me. What the wife of Bluebeard saw beyond the forbidden door – that is a rosegarden to what waits you on the other side of this door. Could a young woman walk among the flames of hell, and come back, and be sound again in her flesh and mind? It is unthinkable. Look: I have opened that door once – oh many years ago, a long time, you will not believe this if I say, almost two hundred years ago, but it is true, I am so deep in time – older – far older – but I am here, in this most wretched adamantine prison of a body for only a short winter yet – thanks to you, I have the fare, the piece of silver in the top right-hand pocket of my waistcoat. Now I know, since you came, since (so to speak) you put the silver under my tongue, that there will be soon a fair release for me, I will sleep with the old gardeners and blacksmiths and coachmen . . . My dear lady, I am I assure you unutterably glad that you have come to be my guest here in Howthton Hall, you have spared a most dear and delicate and precious creature, my child, that heaven had sent to be a comfort to me in my wretchedness. I beg you, therefore, 'lady in the white coat' who until yesterday was black-clad from brow to ankle, that you come with me back to the supper table. Jemima, she will be there; that will delight her, there will be candles and flames and music and wine and laughter. I have a gift for you, a parting gift; I have chosen it with my own hands; it is a dove carved from ivory, very beautiful and precious, Chinese beyond a doubt and very ancient, a symbol of peace. I have had an oak casket made for it, specially; Stevens the carpenter made the box yesterday in his workshop. Come now – I have ordered a treat for you, cold lobster and a sallet of greens.'

So he babbled on, pleading, a tear standing bright at last in his one eye, his mouth trembling.

The 'lady in the white coat' held out her hand, palm up.

He put the key (two centuries hidden) into it. Then he turned, his face working, and as swiftly as an old man might, he made for the door at the far end of the corridor: as if to put a great distance between the once-and-never-again-to-be-seen room and his health and sanity.

The lady unlocked the door. She went in. She closed the door behind her.

What should I care for the foolhardiness, or the heroism, or the madness, of a strange woman? What should I expect to hear from the far side of the door?

I listened, my ear not too far from the keyhole.

It began to be wearisome; for nothing happened, not even a lingering footfall, far less outcries of anguish. (These I had heard, on one memorable occasion, from my dear master, in the days of his youth: so that I thought no frame could endure such torment and live: I loved him even then deeply; I went so far that far-distant day as to batter with my fists on the panels, and weep, and plead with him to come out; which at length he did, with the first cold flame-mark of Tithonus on him; and he fell with most bitter weeping into my arms.)

I listened. What I heard after – it may be – an hour, after a bird and flower and bee pause, was the sound of the laughter of many children . . . And then I found I had fallen into a drowse, on my knees, stooped there outside the door, and the thread of a pleasant pastoral dream had passed through me.

I knocked. There was no answer. The door was locked from inside. Presently I went away.

Ottervoe

In the sea village, in an island in the North Atlantic, some kind of an open-air meeting was taking place.

There was in the group one man of authority – that much was plain. He was much better rigged out than the villagers, being clad in a grey worsted jacket belted at the waist, and in grey worsted knickerbockers, grey stockings, and brown well-polished brogue shoes. He was a man of middle years, with a black-bearded face that was both kind and stern. (They were obdurate people that he had to deal with – no point in being soft with them – that would be bad for the whole island, especially for the revenues and well-being of the master of all of them: the laird. On the other hand, treat them too roughly and they could be, those islanders, as stubborn as oxen, that turn their heads from the sun to the rooted stone in the glebe, and will not move. A judicious mingling of sternness and kindness, that was what was called for, dealing with the crofters and the fisher folk.)

This man was, in fact, the laird's officer in the island, the factor, charged with the gathering-in of rents, both for crofts and boats, and for the agricultural and fishing policy in general – if the laird in fact had a policy, other than replenishing his none-too-deep coffers. Also the factor had to see to it that the islanders did their stint of labour in the laird's big farm at hay-time and oat-harvest. He saw to it that the fields and boats were supplied with gear, at a fair price, that could be exacted in laird-work if there was no cash in their little stone jars in the wall-niche. (Often enough there was none.) Occasionally, this factor had the stern duty of putting a bad crofter out of a croft-house and steading – one who was lazy, for example, or drunken, or grossly overdue with his rent, or a bad worker with plough or scythe. Out that crofter must go, with his lamenting wife and a few children clinging, grey-faced, to her skirts. Where could they go, since every available acre was taken – and anyway, a bad glebe-man in one croft would undoubtedly do no better among other fields? It was no concern of his – the factor's – where the unfortunates went: so long as they were out of the croft on such-and-such a date with their few sticks of furniture, and a flutter of hens. There were always men needed for the wars – let the man join a regiment at Fort George; there any skills and endurance he had would be properly channelled by a harsher discipline than was ever put upon him in the island; and his wife and children would be given more comfortable quarters than the ruckle of stones they had called 'home' . . . That was what happened to bad tenants, in theory. Or there were ample opportunities for them, quite outwith the home cycles of agriculture and fishing, in the vast unexploited territories of Canada, South Africa, Australia, New Zealand. But it happened not infrequently that an islander and his family clung with such ox-like stubbornness to the island that was the only place they knew, that they would rather beg or starve than have a passage booked for them on one or other of the emigrant ships. Yes, if necessary they would live on limpets and roots, in a cave or a ruined unwanted hovel somewhere. Was it love that bound them so cruelly to the island, or brutish stupidity? It rarely came to an exchange of croft for cave or hovel; for the other islanders would gather round, half in secret, and see to it that the stricken ones had food and shelter, until their fortunes changed. (None of the islanders knew for sure that the same fate might not happen to him and his family, by reason of sickness, for example; or if there should be a new young spendthrift of a laird who wrung their purses and thews beyond endurance. They knew, deep down, that they were only as prosperous as the poorest family among them. Therefore the haddock, the bannock, the bundle of old clothes, the shelter were never, or rarely, withheld from the evicted family.)

And this factor, who was both strict and mild, was not such a stony-hearted man that he exacted the law to the utmost letter. He would take the evicted crofter into his office. He would say, 'Andrew, man, look here – you're out of that croft of Bigging for ever – let there be no mistake about that. Three years' rent unpaid – your oatfield a wilderness of thistles – that won't do, that's unthinkable, now or any time. Listen, man, listen carefully to me. You're still young and strong, and I know well that Katie's going to have her seventh bairn in the winter. With all that noise and nagging and commotion in Bigging, it's no wonder you take a dram too much, often, in the ale-house. That must stop, and your bone-idleness. (Well, no one'll grudge you a drink at Hogmanay or the Lammas Fair.) Andrew, I'm going to give you another chance – one last chance. I'll make a breach in the boundary wall that divides the corn-fields from the heather and moor, the turf-wall that keeps the beasts outside all summer. Beyond that breach, the moor is well dunged, well broken with hooves and the rooting snouts of swine. I'll see that a plough is put in your hands. Go up there, to the quoy, this very day. Take your plough through the breach, break open a new piece of moor. Yes, it will have to be drained. I'll ask the other crofters to patch a hut for you and Katie and your infants to winter in. Afterwards, you can build a better house and steading around it. It will be a poor twelve-month for you, Andrew: but it's your last chance. You'll have to sow and harrow and reap at the proper season (not like before, when you paid small regard to the sun and wind and rain). Work the new quoy well, Andrew, and I'll not be exorbitant in the matter of rent. Make a mess of it again, man, and it's out of this island with you for good and all. You can go to Fort George and the army, or to Canada or Australia – but on this island, be sure of it, you will not set foot again. Here's a crown piece, man – it will see you and yours through the next month or so . . .'

This was the factor who stood, one fine day in summer, in the sea village called Ottervoe. The road through the village was steep; the factor had been careful (he being a man of smaller stature than the villagers) to take his stance higher up the slope, on an outcrop of rock, so that he could in a sense dominate the proceedings, and at the same time not have his smallness noticed, by comparison.

In his right hand the factor carried a sheaf of papers that fluttered in every gust like a caught hen. Those documents gave him an added authority.

At last they were all there, the women standing a little back from the men-folk, around the well in the centre of the village; that being a familiar place to the women in any case. The children had no interest in what was to happen. They had all trooped down to the shore. They played, bright-limbed and shrill-tongued, among the rock-pools and the dunes and the seabirds. One small boy, though, had decided to stay among his elders. He stood, a little to the side, one forefinger plucking the inside of his cheek, and he gazed with wide eyes at this factor who held all their fates in his hands.

'Now then,' the factor was saying, 'are all the men here?' (The women at the well did not count.) 'They *should* be here – I knocked on every door at the weekend. Well, listen. There are one or two things to discuss, things you ought to know about. First, there's one house in the village here that hasn't been lived in for five years.'

'Simon Thorfinnson's house,' said a fisherman.

'Simon Thorfinnson's,' said the factor. 'The house, for want of fire and airing, is in poor shape. The stones inside are dripping. It's going to pieces, in fact. The laird hasn't had a penny in rent – not for five years. It's a good house – stone built, oak rafters from a wrecked ship. If none of you want it, it will be demolished. The rent is two guineas.'

'What do we want with two houses?' said another fisherman.

'There'll be more empty houses soon,' said an old fisherman. 'Canada, Australia – the young ones have to go there, to make a living. Tell the laird that . . .' This old fisherman was smoking a clay pipe. He spat.

'Simon might come back,' said a young fisherman.

'Five years Simon's been away,' said the factor. 'Not a whisper, not a scratch of the pen. We won't be seeing Simon again.'

'Simon was press-ganged,' said another fisherman. 'He didn't want to go.'

What commotion was this, among the women at the well? It was the kind of commotion that breaks out among sea birds on a cliff ledge, when an intruder hovers near. It *was* an intruder, a young woman none of them had ever seen before. She had appeared at the end of the village while the factor was speaking. Now she joined the village women. None of them seemed over-pleased. They stirred; they shifted away from her.

Only the boy gave her any kind of greeting. He edged towards her; the beginnings of a smile lit his mouth and eyes; he went so far as to touch her hand with his.

Indeed she was an extraordinary-looking person, this stranger. In the first place, she was filthier than any vagrant the villagers had ever seen. The wonder was that the soiled and torn coat she wore held together at all. One sleeve had been torn out of it. Originally it must have been a grey colour, perhaps even white; but dust and grime had worked their way into every stitch and seam. There were scorch-marks on the coat, and what was very frightening to the village women, daubs and splashes of what seemed to be dried blood. Where had she come from, this sinister creature? The more they looked at her, the more the village women ebbed from her, until at last they were all standing at the shadowed side of the well, and she alone at the other, the bright side.

It was not likely such a fearsome-like vagrant would be taken in through any of their doors! She had nothing to sell, that much was sure; no pack on her back, no cluster of tin mugs at her shoulder, making low keen clangings. All she carried, thonged to her waist, was a leather bag: perhaps it contained herbs for the cure of asthma, or for putting a spell on reluctant lovers. Such women had been to the village.

In her dress she was foul, but her black hair fell fresh about her shoulders, and her skin shone, as if she never passed a burn without dabbling her hands and face and feet in that freshness.

Now the boy went so far as to put his hand into the stranger's hand. And the girl smiled, briefly, as if she had been waiting for such a greeting.

The men had noticed nothing amiss. They were too taken up with the fate of Simon Thorfinnson's house in which no fire had been lit for five years. Once it had been a hive of comings and goings, fragrant with new-baked bread, noisy with children, smoky with peat fires, silver and grey with the dried fish and the smoke-curing fish; and at every day's end, a chanted prayer. Such had been the Thorfinnson house once. The oldest fisherman remembered it well.

'Two guineas,' said the factor tartly, 'or it's left to rot.'

'I'll give three guineas a year for Simon Thorfinnson's cottage.'

Who had spoken? And in such a strange voice, it sounded more like some kind of musical instrument than human utterance. All the faces turned to the stranger. The eyes of the men opened; as if they had seen a mermaid on a rock once the sea mist had silently split like the valves of an oyster. And, 'Tut-tut-tut-tut-tut' went the women in muted hostility.

The factor was as astonished as the others. No one set foot on the island without his knowing. Only a dozen at most came and went in the course of a year – Dutch sailors, tinkers, the sherriff's officer from Kirkwall, high-tongued guests of the laird.

'What's this?' he said. 'Who are you?'

'Does it matter who I am? I'm looking for a place to live. I've been looking for a place like this for a long time. I have the money.'

Had she spoken, or was it mime and mouth-music only? She had pointed at Simon Thorfinnson's cottage. Now she unthonged the leather poke from her waist. She held it up and rang it like a bell. Soon three gold coins shone between her fingers.

Here was a quandary for the factor. The laird would be only too pleased with the extra guineas, for these days he had growing expenses: the Hall needed re-roofing, his youngest daughter must be sent to Edinburgh at summer's end to study decorum and refinement, lest peasants' ways coarsen her entirely . . . Yet, the peasants and fishermen – he had to think of them also. They had an ox-like obstinacy about them, especially with regard to anything new in their settled routine. Their lives were hard, true – they accepted that – but they had come to terms with it over twenty generations and more. They knew where they stood. Any change, as far as they were concerned,

would be a change for the worse. The factor was having a hard
enough time of it, trying to instil new methods of agriculture
into them, such as the squaring of the old ruinous runrigs into
fenced fields, and the introduction of new stock, so that their
cattle and horses and sheep and pigs might yield them far
greater returns, in wool and milk and meat. So, everyone
would be the richer: the laird and the peasants. Whenever such
beneficent change was mooted, they turned their ox-heads
from the sun and glowered into the stony glebe . . . For his first
five years among them the crofters had treated him, the factor,
with suspicion and a slow dark smouldering anger. Now they
were getting more used to him; they might even invite him
into their crofts for a mug of ale in passing. But no change!
They knew where they stood. New stock – the breaking up of
immemorial ancestral acres – that would be to take the solid
foundations from under them . . . Or, at least, no change yet.
Perhaps in their sons' day, when the new ideas would have had
time to take root. But now – they would rather live as their
fathers had lived, those good pious old folk gathered in the
anonymous kirkyard.

Such was the quiet cautious war that was going on between
laird and factor on the one hand, and the small tenant-farmers
on the other.

With the fishermen matters were different. For one thing,
little could be done to improve their conditions. They fished
with boats and gear of immemorial design, according to immemorial custom. It was a dangerous element they worked in, not
the safe green surge of the hills where the ploughs went.
Fishermen read the skies and seas for portent or promise. Their
blood told them, in the fairest of weathers, that a storm was
brewing westward. Their nostrils widened to the wind: over
there, ten miles north of the Ness, the great shoals must be
swimming. Seabirds and men cooperated in the endless quest

for fish. Gannets plummeted, charting the extent and drift of the shoal. The fishermen rowed home singing, at sunset, and thousands of wavering gulls followed the wake of the boats, screaming, as the torn fish-guts were thrown to them. At the rock, women and cats, and more gulls, and a lantern.

The sea was the great provider. It was a vast incalculable environing presence, whose moods of gentleness and rage were, however keen their instincts, ultimately beyond the fishermen's ken. Arbitrarily, three or four or five times a year, the great sea-spirit took a boat and the boat's crew to itself. The waves covered them – they were no more – maybe an oar or a rudder might be found a week later on the shore of another island. The fishermen and their wives expected that. The possibility of drowning was engrained. The sea gave, the sea took; if a boy drowned, it was the sea's due. Indeed, it was at that time extremely unlucky to pluck a drowning man out of the waves; thereby you were taking what belonged to the sea, and the sea would not forget. If the unfortunate one struggled ashore on his own, good: then they could set about pumping life back into him – the sea did not want him, not yet; maybe never; maybe the half-drowned fisherman was destined, after all, to lie with ploughmen under the green surge of the hill, one with roots and springs.

Did the sea feel a sympathy with those seekers and hunters, the horizon-breakers? It was impossible to say. Certainly, over fifty generations and more there had come to be a great intimacy between sea and fishermen. They understood each other's ways, to such an extent that the sea seemed to have some knowledge of the language of men, and certain words that could be safely used on the solid ground were abhorrent to it, words like 'church', 'rabbit', 'pig' and maybe a hundred others. Men uttered those taboo words in a fishing-boat at their peril. It was a great mystery. They spent their lives beseeching the sea. The sea, in turn, gave them answers as if she grudged them home and hearth and fire, where they must spend most of their time. Was not the sea cleaner and greater than a pigsty? Wasn't the mystery of the sea greater than all their communings with the earth powers, root and bone and trow and stone and worm?

Yes, their ears brimmed all their lives with sea sounds, the gentle murmuring among beach-stones, the great thunders and organ-peals in the caves and against the cliff bases. Their own voices were attuned to that mysterious and beautiful and terrifying music. Their eyes were level and blue as horizons.

There was more to the sea than ebb and flow, skua and whale and lobster. The sea opened magic casements to them: mermaids, seal men and seal women, a foreign seaman on the shore who passed rum and tobacco out of his boat into theirs, in exchange for a sheep or a basket of eggs, a Russian child beached in its cradle from a wreck. No marvel is utterly strange to a fisherman. His days, though hard, are shot through with the enchantment and mystery of poetry – whereas the land workers keep rather to the sturdy predictable rhythms of prose.

All this went through the factor's mind, more as a swift impression than a worked-out argument, as he stood on the steep road with his neat shrewd little head out-topping somewhat the heads of the fishermen, and eyed the stranger speculatively.

She was not a castaway from beyond the horizon, a sea-girl – that much was sure. She seemed rather to be some kind of a refugee from the sudden out-blaze of a volcano at the far side of the world, and she carried with her the mined and forged and minted ore of mountains in her purse.

Money: that was the important thing. The fire-marked stranger girl had money. Those crofters and fisher-folk were only slowly, and with reluctance, coming to accept money as a medium of exchange. They paid their rents, still, in butter and fish and bacon and in free labour: the real earth and salt equivalents of 'two guineas'. They would have to be made to learn that, in a few years' time, the laird would accept his rents from them in silver and gold coin of the realm: in that only.

There was a cottage vacant, and dripping with dampness inside. Here stood a stranger with a bag of money: sufficient, as far as he could judge from the coins she held up now into the sun, to pay five years' rent at least. How the stranger proposed to live was not his concern. She might spin – she might weave – she might get by on limpets and seaweed. Certainly, in May, she ought to be a good worker at the peat banks with all the fire marks on her!

The boy was no longer there. No one had noticed his going.

'Simon Thorfinnson's cottage is yours for three guineas rent a year,' said the factor.

A fisherman turned on the stranger. 'If you pay three guineas, we'll all be charged three guineas come Martinmas. *Two* guineas is the rent.'

'I offer two guineas,' said the girl.

'You said three guineas,' said the factor.

'I offer two,' said the girl.

'Very well,' said the factor. 'I'll speak to the laird. There will be one or two details to settle. Two guineas then. I welcome you to Ottervoe.'

'Thank you,' said the girl.

Over the shoulder of the hill, on the mild air, came a few notes of music. They had never heard such sounds before. The women turned their faces from the sea to the hill. On a morning that had begun like this, anything seemed possible; even a messenger from the far side of earth, a phoenix, a fire-bird . . . But they shifted even further away from the new islander, their neighbour from now on.

The factor cleared his throat and consulted a paper in his hand. 'Now,' said he, 'the question of Thorfinnson's boat *Sea Quest. Sea Quest* isn't exactly improving with time. Badly warped – I had a look at her this morning. She used to be the best fishing-boat in the island. She isn't beyond repair – of course not. A nail here and there, a lick of tar. I say this for Simon, he kept that boat in perfect shape . . . If nobody wants to take on *Sea Quest*, the laird says, "Break her up . . ."'

'That'd be a shame,' said the youngest fisherman. 'She's a good boat, *Sea Quest*.'

The boy came running back to the village, right into the middle of the serious discussion about the fishing boat *Sea Quest* and what was to happen to her. 'Mr Baillie,' he cried to the factor, 'guess what I saw. I saw a tramp, a cripple man! He played a song on a pipe. He's sitting on the milestone beside the bridge. He's pinched a turnip out of a field. He's eating it.'

'Run away home, you brat!' cried one of the women, an old fierce one. 'How dare you interrupt the factor? . . .' And 'Tut-tut-tut-tut-tut,' clucked the other women in annoyance. One took a swipe at the boy with her open hand.

'I offer two guineas for *Sea Quest*,' said the stranger.

'One guinea!' cried the oldest fisherman. 'That's the rent for a boat.'

'One guinea,' said the girl-in-rags.

The factor didn't know what to make of it. He gave the girl a long scrutiny. Was she some kind of play-actor? Were the coins in her poke bits of lead and tin? Was she making fools of the islanders – even of the laird and himself – and their simple forthright way of life? And now this tramp music, coming closer. An unseen thief had eaten a turnip. Perhaps a troop of play-actors was converging on the village, and she the first-comer.

'Lady, excuse me,' said the factor. 'You're not proposing to fish out of here, are you?'

'I might,' said the girl

'*Sea Quest* is yours, then,' said the factor, rather uncertainly. 'One guinea a year. Ten-and-sixpence payable on signing.'

The boy cried out, 'The tramp – look! He's coming on a stick.'

And there, passing the kirk a quarter of a mile away, came the second stranger of the day, hirpling, making heavy weather of it.

'He's like a gull with a broken wing,' said a fisherman, and shook his head. They all knew what happens to a gull with one wing.

They waited in silence. Why should a crippled tramp interrupt their business? The tramp fairly stirred the dust with his stick as he hobbled on his urgent way to the village. (Most tramps linger, they're never in any hurry, they look at a cloud or a dandelion for a long time, then they drift on again.) This was a tramp with a purpose. On he came, crookedly, as if one leg was a broken wheel. Yet he seemed to know every stone on the road.

'His face is a bunch of thistles,' said a young woman.

Then the tramp was there, in the village. He stopped right beside them, in the gap between the men and the women: out of breath for the moment. Most tramps would go cautiously about such a crowd. This one put his hand on the boy's bright head and ruffled his curls. He looked eagerly from face to face.

The factor cleared his throat. Occasionally one gets an impudent vagrant like this; best to be firm, to stand no nonsense from them. 'Move on, my man,' he said. 'There's nothing for you here. This is a poor village. No paupers, no vagrants, no musicians or beggarmen. I hear you stole a turnip. I intend to do nothing about that. But you'll be out of this island before sunset. See to it.'

The tramp with the flute in his breast pocket was paying no attention to authority. He had turned his back on the village and the villagers. He was looking at a rock on the shore, and the beautiful cluster of wooden curves leaning against it.

'She's still there,' he whispered. '*Sea Quest* is in one piece. Thank God.'

'He talks the way we do,' said the boy.

There was something in what the boy said. This creature from the far curve of time and space had in his mouth their own rhythms and intonations.

'He's a tramp,' said the factor, quite fiercely for such a mild man.

'Tom,' said the tramp to a young fisherman, 'you might have given *Sea Quest* a coat of tar! She's half rotten.'

'Simon Thorfinnson,' said another fisherman. (The name shone like a star in his mouth.)

The women were all round him, like gulls round a man with a basket of fish. 'Simon! Simon! . . .' 'Where have you been all this time, Simon? . . .' 'Simon, what's that bandage? . . .' 'Simon, what's wrong with your leg? . . .' 'You're dark as a tinker, Simon . . .' 'No wonder we didn't know you.'

'I have plenty of stories,' said Simon the tramp-fisherman. 'Wait till winter. They'll take all winter to tell . . .' One by one he recognised the village women: five years had flowered some and withered others. The youngest girls he knew only by a fleeting resemblance to elders.

'Kate, you're bonnier than ever! . . . Ruth, is it? . . . Anna, have you got ale in that kirn of yours? – I'm thirsty, I tell you – I've walked a thousand miles, snow, fire, mountains, rivers . . . Sigrid, we used to go to the hill for blackberries . . . Hild. You sat beside me in the school . . .' For each of them an embrace, a gentle laying of cheek upon cheek. (In northern villages and islands, one does not kiss in public; even this cheek-upon-cheek caused some of the women to blush like roses, though it was plain to see they were delighted, one and all.)

The girl who had rented house and boat took no part in this storm of greetings. She had turned away; she seemed to be utterly absorbed in the small summer curling waves on the beach, and the gull's broken circles, and the trembling isle-and-reef broken arc of the west horizon.

And the boy, he was off again, quick as a bird!

'Welcome home, Simon Thorfinnson,' said the factor gravely, and extended his hand for Simon to grasp. (Not many tenants had that honour paid them, before or since.)

'My house!' cried Simon, and threw the factor's hand from him. 'The roof's half off. The door's on one hinge.'

'You were away a long time,' said the oldest fisherman.

'We didn't know what to think, boy,' said the woman called Ruth, and put her hand on his shoulder, to placate him.

'So that's it,' said Simon bitterly. 'You all thought, Simon's dead. Let the house die too. Let his boat go to pieces.'

The boy was back again, hopping bird-like among them. 'I've seen to the water, Simon,' he cried. 'I've seen to the fire.'

'That boy'll feel the weight of my hand,' cried old Ruth.

It was then that Simon noticed the stranger who had her back turned on them. Simon nodded in her direction. 'Who's that girl? Over there, her with the torn sleeve? I seem to know her but I can't put a name to her.'

The women looked at her resentfully. 'She's a stranger.'

There was silence in the village, but for the gulls and the small breaking waves and the factor's embarrassed cough and shuffling of papers.

The impudent boy broke the spell. 'The patch and the tear match each other,' he said wonderingly. He pointed first to the bandage on Simon's leg, above the knee, then to the rent in the girl's sleeve.

Still the girl did not turn. Simon said, turning back to the women, 'I'll tell you this much. They dragged me from the beach that morning. They rowed me out in a longboat to a ship. They gave me a shilling – the King's shilling – and a uniform to put on. They sailed me far beyond the fishing grounds. We docked in a foreign port. I was a soldier among thousands of soldiers. It might have been Spain or America or the Low Countries. We were marched into the mountains. We were marched up among guns and horses. It was terrible! The army was blown to pieces. I woke up in a village. I was wounded, a horseman had trampled me and scored me. I woke up and I was dreaming. The village was on fire from end to end. A girl came out of the flames. She gave me a cup of water from the well. Never was heather-and-honey ale like that cold drench. She tore her dress, she tied up the wound in my leg. And she – she kissed me! Then she went away. She faded like music. She was a part of the dream, of course . . . Well, we can't live on dreams, can we? I got this old flute from a pawnshop somewhere and I learnt to play the flute and I begged my way through this country and that till I came to the sea and a Leith-bound ship. And here I am.'

It was a long speech for an islander. Towards the end of it Simon was no longer addressing the ragged circle of women about him. His words were spoken to the girl, the sea-searching stranger.

'That slut,' cried old Ruth. 'Pay no attention to her. Why are you looking at her? Simon, you're not to worry. We'll look after you.'

'I was telling you,' said Simon, 'about the burning village and the girl and the cup of water. It's a pity dreams have to be better than the things that do happen . . .'

It was then that the girl turned. 'Fisherman,' she said. 'You promised me the sea for that cup of water. Far away, long ago.'

'I have nothing left to give,' said Simon. 'No house. No boat, I'm sorry. And I'm very very glad.'

The factor cleared his throat, and shuffled his papers. 'Simon,' he said, 'this lady has just paid the rent for your house and also for *Sea Quest*. You'll have to sort things out between you.'

The girl said, 'They're yours, fisherman.'

One of the women cried, 'Look, smoke from Simon's chimney.'

The boy was back again. 'I lit a fire,' he said. 'Of course there's smoke. A few pieces of driftwood – I broke a peat. I put two plates and two spoons on the table, too. I set a bucket of water on the doorstep.'

'You're a very clever boy,' said Kate.

Simon touched the bandage on his leg. 'I'd be pleased,' he said, 'if the lady of the house up there would let me go in and sit down for half-an-hour. My leg's tired.'

'You're welcome, fisherman,' said the girl.

'Maybe,' said Simon, 'the lady would be so kind as to give an old soldier a piece of bread and a cup of milk.'

'I'm sorry, fisherman,' said the girl, 'I haven't had time to plough or buy a beast yet.'

Then the village women were all outcry and kindness. 'Never mind that . . . We have fish and a few bottles of ale . . . Yes, and new bread . . . You can have a bag of peats, Simon . . . I made a cheese yesterday . . .'

'Will the lady let me stay the night?' said Simon.

'You're welcome, fisherman. The house is yours. The house is mine. We'll stay as long as we can pay the rent.'

At that, some of the younger women began to look sullen again, but that soon passed; they were still borne up on the tide of generosity.

'It's a peaceful village, this,' said the girl. 'Is it the end of the road? Maybe I'm home at last.'

'Of course you are,' cried the women. 'You'll get used to our ways . . .' 'Simon needs somebody to look after him . . .' 'Yes, for a month or two, till he's better . . .' 'Do you know the way we light fires here? . . .' 'She looks as if she has good hands for a fish knife . . .' 'Yes, and for keeping a doorstep and windows clean . . .'

Thus the fisherwives of Ottervoe led Simon and the girl to the door of their cottage.

The hithering-thithering boy had found a means to open the door.

'My name is Maurya,' said the girl.

Hand in hand, Simon and Maurya went inside.

A grey pigeon fluttered down and stood on the doorstep.

The fisherfolk lingered about the threshold. Old Ruth clapped her hands. Then they were all clapping their hands – an extravagant manifestation of satisfaction in the stoical village of Ottervoe; as if they had just heard a good story. Then they stopped, they looked at each other, half amused and half ashamed; and they went their ways.

The factor, alone on the village street, smiled. 'It turned out well, after all,' he said, nodding. 'I suppose the minister will have to be told. It looks like a wedding.'

A small wind fluttered the papers in his hand. The men and women of Ottervoe were going into their cottages, one after another. The boy was up in the big barley field: he seemed to be shouting, or chanting, to the scarecrow.

The wind blew the clouds apart. The sun came out; it glittered on the sea, a swift dazzle.

'A wasted morning,' said old Amos. 'We could have been setting creels. All that palaver for nothing.'

'I forgot to tell them,' said Mr Baillie the factor when he was alone. 'There are men coming at the weekend to make probes into the hill. High up, among the corn rigs. The laird has given permission. What the samples are for, I don't know. Nothing, I expect. But the village and the island ought to be told . . . They've sweated on that hill a thousand years to raise a few heads of corn. What if they've been toiling above a great treasure of silver and diamonds? What if they'd lived and died and never known about it? It'll be nothing like that, of course. Nothing like that . . .'

Someone in the cottage was trying to make music – a breath, a whisper, lucent lingering notes. The faltering flute-song went out to mingle with the long rush of Atlantic breakers among the reefs, and with the wind-surges in the high corn, and with the shouts of the boy on the far side of the hill, fading now.

It was a pastoral, a country blessing, a song of peace without end.

It drew strength from all the island noises – it put a fleeting beauty upon them – and then returned to itself, completing the pure lyric circle.

[XVI]

Old and Grey and Full of Sleep

An old woman sat alone in a chair beside a fire. Her bowed head was silhouetted against the single window.

She stirred. The fire sifted soft ash, with a new red leap; licks of flame, lessening.

She spoke. In and out of sleep she spelt and spoke.

'Dead. Am I dead? I think I may be dead. I am a stone mouth in the kirkyard. I am speaking. Listen. Where has it gone, all my treasure? Who took it? This is what we come with at last, fare for a far-faring, two last pennies. A shroud has no pockets.

'Simon, is that you? You there, on the far side of the fire. Are you long in from the sea? That's only his bonnet on the nail. No. Kind and cripple he went, a many a wave ago, to the kirkyard. I poured whisky for the mourners. The women all sniffles and sobs, the fools. I was glad, that afternoon, Simon was come to a fire in an inn at the far side of time. "Fisherman, sit down. Welcome. Stretch out your hands to the fire."

'If I had the strength in me to walk out of this place, what I'd see is this. Now, listen. You won't believe this that I'm going to tell you but it's true. I'd see a row of ruins, roofs fallen, black dead hearths, no sea village. A skull on every doorstep. "A fine morning, Anna . . . Could you lend me such a thing as a cup of sugar, Kate? . . . Good fishing weather this, Ruth," I say to skull and skull. I say, "Their boats are rotten, a pity . . . Simon, he went out before light," I say. The skulls grin. They grin and they whisper, "Bert, Ned, James, Willie, they're up at the mine. Good money there, up at the mine. It was always a poor living, that, from the sea. Poor they lived and they died, the old ones."

'Simon and I, we don't speak to each other – nothing to say, year in year out – nothing to say, not one word. Silence is a good thing. A hundred thousand words, then silence. Simon, he always had plenty to say: lies about his brave days in the war. O, what a hero was Simon! There's worse things than silence.

'What old red coat is that – over there – hanging from a nail? Leave it.

'I won't light the fire. The peat-stack's worn down whatever, black crumbs. There's no more fire in the world. Fire's all used up. All the volcanoes dead. No lamps. Not so much as the stump of a candle. A poor time for moths. The little box on the mantelpiece, it's full of dead matches. That's good. But it's cold – so cold! A person feels the cold at my age.

'Listen. Was it the school bell ringing? It's *Sea Quest*. Simon and a basket of fish. The oars are putting salt drops back into the sea. I used to be able to hear that. Shells too, their song – far-away-long-ago singing – surging singing sighing – in the spirallings, deep in the secret glimmering whorls, the cells.

'Stone. My ears are two stones. What way would I hear kirk bell or sea bell?

'Maurya. Foolish old woman.

'Once I could hear a leaf unfolding, a snowflake falling. I could. Far away, long ago. If ever such things were, at all.

'Then I came at last to the end of the road, the sea. I made a cup of my hands, I drooped head, dipped mouth. Such bitterness! – The tears of all the seashore widows and orphans and sweethearts that have ever been.

'No fire, no lamp. I think maybe I'm sitting here, dead. Who'll find me, who'll lift the feather to my lips? I will soon be a skull and a stone like the rest of them. I hope nobody leaves rotting roses on top. Worse still, wax flowers. Let them lay me under and leave me alone.

'The roof fell in, oh long ago. And the spiders' houses, all down too. I saw a spider in that old flute – long life to the spider in his ivory house. There it is, the flute, between the red coat and Simon's cap, on the wall, on a nail. No songs more. The child has never once put it to her mouth. (Her tapes and her discs.)

'The bad village boys threw stones at the window. "Maurya, Maurya, old witch, you old foreign slut!" Stones flew round me like birds.

'The skulls of the little boys, black with fire, all over the hill and the shore.

'Listen. A cry at the door, "Grandma, didn't you hear the school bell? What a nice fire. Bakehouse bread, butter and rhubarb jam, just what I like. Is he not in from the sea yet? Now then, the story – you promised. I'll cut the jammy piece, you tell the story. I'm ready. Begin."

'That sweet skull, where is it? I have seen a little fish in the chambers of bone. Yesterday it might have been, in a rock-pool.

'"Story. What story, child? What have I got to do with stories? Look, my fingers are crooked and cut. Sea knives. Silver scars. That's the only story in this place, a poor monotonous babble, waves' ruin, idle chatter at rockpools and the well, cave echoes.

'"No, you must do your lessons first. History, is it? Battles and kings and dates. (That rigmarole! Sweetly they sugar it.) There's a crumb at the corner of your mouth. It's stuck with jam. A mouse'll come and lick it when you're sleeping. You must be clever. You must study hard and pass your exams. You must get away from this place soon. A poor life here for a lass.

'"A story? Oh, well. Listen.

'"Far away, long ago. There was once a sea witch; she was old and poor and crooked. One day she looked in a rockpool, and a princess looked back at her. A girl. And the princess in the mirror cried, 'Come. Come quickly. Soldiers are burning the gates. Come with water. Come with your arms full of the sea. I am a princess. They have a red coat to put on me'.

So the old witch put down her sea knife and she took two fish and she left that village. She set out to find the princess whose coat was made of red flames.

And the witch went through all places of heroism and glory and cruelty in this world with her two fish. O, a hard road – the stones hurt her feet. Her ears throbbed with iron! Her mouth tasted of cinders. 'Follow the smell of fire.'

On one battlefield a soldier lay, broken with hooves. She kissed the soldier into breath and forth-faring. She put a red horseshoe in her bag. The witch and the soldier went their ways.

As the witch went she grew younger and younger. The stones shining with rain told her that. Yes, and her grey sea-coat had patches of white on it here and there, sweet-smelling patches white as snowdrops.

She planted an apple-tree beside a hut and a cabbage patch.

Far back, she came to a burning city. There were vultures above and rats in the cellars.

She came to a forest with lawless hunters in it. There she was changed to a green tree among many green trees. A grey bird flew down to a branch of her. 'April!' cried the bird.

And near an inn were soldiers with red torches. She was a snow-girl then lost in snow. Nothing but ice and a dead blackbird. Snow choked the flames and the soldiers.

On she went, across rivers and mountains and a desert. The cornlands streamed with horses and swords, mile after mile.

She came at last to the castle of the lost and the starved.

The burnt-out ruin – she knew it was filled with the pitiful ghosts of the children of war – thousands, thousands.

The witch laid her two fish on fallen crossed smouldering beams, the last guttering fire in the castle. 'Here's the sea,' she sang. 'Fish enough for all . . . I think maybe I've come too late'.

Somewhere inside the castle a voice answered her:

In the garden four creatures

Dwelling together.
AIR, a dove. EARTH, a horse.
    WATER, a fish. FIRE, a dragon.
A harp and a flute.
The four creatures dancing together.

Iron fingers
Tore the strings from the harp.
Then the four creatures
Fought.
The dragon was king at last in the
    flame-ruined garden.
The fish the bird and the horse
Outside, in the wilderness, wandering, wounded.

Come back, follow the song.
Here is the door of the lost garden.
Come, fish.
The dragon is sick of his lonely flames.
Come fish, speak to the dragon.
Come fish, first,
The horse and the bird will follow.

It must have been the princess in the long red coat. She sang on and on between a gutted harp and a blackened mirror, deep in the inmost cell of the castle.

The little fire was out at last. When the witch looked – listen well, child – when she looked into the last black embers, where the two fish had been were a flute and a sack of silver!

The coat she wore was white as snow or salt. But it smelt like a white rose . . ."'

'And that's my story, take it or leave it, like it or lump it. It's a lie, like all stories. For even the sea was burnt at last. All broken, the harps and the mirrors. An island strewn with skulls. I am a stone mouth that speaks. There's no need for you or anyone to listen any more. Go away. Let me rest in silence at last. If you want to know more, read the stone.'

The old woman who had been the girl stirred in her chair. There was a little breath in her still. She sighed. Another dream! A few steps to go toilsome before the stone, still.

And over the island a wind blew, bringing sea sounds.

'Grandma, the boats are in! *Sea Quest* has the biggest catch again. Oh, you've nearly let the fire go out! – I'll poke it. Young Simon, he's coming up now. Yes, we got history again, of course. The kettle'll soon be singing.'